SINS
OF THE FATHERS

Other short story collections edited by Mark Bryant:

CAT TALES FOR CHRISTMAS
COUNTRY TALES FOR CHRISTMAS
CHILDHOOD TALES FOR CHRISTMAS

SINS
OF THE FATHERS

An Anthology of Clerical Crime

Edited by

MARK BRYANT

VICTOR GOLLANCZ
LONDON

First published in Great Britain 1996
by Victor Gollancz
An imprint of the Cassell Group
Wellington House, 125 Strand, London WC2R 0BB

Introduction and anthology copyright © Mark Bryant 1996

The right of Mark Bryant to be identified as editor of
this work has been asserted by him in accordance with
the Copyright, Designs and Patents Act, 1988.

A catalogue record for this book is
available from the British Library.

ISBN 0 575 06384 X

Typeset by Falcon Oast Graphic Art, Wallington, Surrey
Printed in Great Britain by
St Edmundsbury Press Ltd, Bury St Edmunds, Suffolk

96 97 98 99   10 9 8 7 6 5 4 3 2 1

For Max

Contents

Acknowledgements

Anton Chekhov, 'The Black Monk' from *The Lady with the Dog and Other Stories* (translated by Constance Garnett), reprinted by permission of Chatto & Windus Ltd and the Estate of Constance Garnett.

Agatha Christie, 'Sanctuary' from *Miss Marple's Final Cases* © Agatha Christie Ltd 1979, reprinted by permission of Hughes Massie Ltd and Agatha Christie Ltd

Guy de Maupassant, 'The Olive Tree' from *Short Stories* (translated by Marjorie Laurie), reprinted by permission of Everyman's Library Ltd and David Campbell Publishers Ltd

Sherwood Anderson, 'The Strength of God' from *Winesburg, Ohio*, reprinted by permission of Jonathan Cape Ltd and the Estate of Sherwood Anderson

E. F. Benson, 'The Hanging of Alfred Wadham' from *More Spook Stories*, reprinted by permission of A. P. Watt Ltd and the Estate of E. F. Benson

G. K. Chesterton, 'The Hammer of God' from *The Innocence of Father Brown* reprinted with permission of A. P. Watt Ltd and the Estate of G. K. Chesterton

Sir Arthur Conan Doyle, 'The Adventures of the Devil's Foot' from *His Last Bow*, © Northolme Ltd 1917, reprinted by permission of Jonathan Clowes Ltd and Northolme Ltd

M. R. James, 'The Treasure of Abbot Thomas' from *The Ghost Stories of M. R. James*, reprinted with permission of N. J. R. James and the Estate of M. R. James

Introduction

'The Lord moves in mysterious ways', the saying goes and by definition the Church and its sacred ministers deal with the supernatural. But sometimes the shepherds of God's humble flock lose their path ... and instead of being loving and compassionate curators of tortured souls become themselves victims of unholy passions and are found to practise the opposite of what they preach.

Sometimes, too, the very House of God can be transformed from a divine place of worship, a sanctuary and a shrine, into a hall of horror, the backdrop to unspeakable crimes and unpardonable sins, giving succour to the wicked and profane instead of the blessed and pure of heart. And whether cathedral, monastery or humble chapel, its proximity to the serried ranks of the dead in adjoining graveyard, mausoleum or crypt may induce it to play unwilling host to a satanic congregation of restless spirits.

This book is an anthology of the very best tales of clerical crime, mystery and vice from some of the most distinguished short-story writers of all time. The subject matter includes not only every one of the Seven Deadly Sins, but also many more heinous evils committed by or against the clergy. The stories feature murder, suicide, exorcism, hidden treasure, ghosts, sex, visions and much more, in locations as varied as Britain, France, Germany, Russia and America, both in cities and in the countryside.

All the tales presented here are complete. Though I have tried to make the book as balanced as the limitations of length and copyright availability have allowed, I have generally avoided stories written exclusively in regional dialect. *Sins of the Fathers* contains contributions from both women and men (including a canon of St Paul's), from the nineteenth century to the present day. It covers every imaginable subject, from comedy to the macabre and from romance to melodrama, but always with that edge of mystery and detection.

So, whether you are bishop or curate, abbé or metropolitan, unbutton your dog-collar, put your surplice aside and settle back in the vestry at the end of the day as the organist plays the final bars of evensong. And then, as the chimes ring out and the sunlight fades, and you begin to drift into a world of literary fantasy, spare a thought for all those people beyond the churchyard walls – both believers and unbelievers – who have also picked up this little volume and started to turn the pages. Perhaps they too are now beginning to wonder, as the bats flit from the belfry and the owls hoot eerily, just what might happen in 'God's little acre' tonight ...

MARK BRYANT

The Hammer of God

G. K. Chesterton

The little village of Bohun Beacon was perched on a hill so steep that the tall spire of its church seemed only like the peak of a small mountain. At the foot of the church stood a smithy, generally red with fires and always littered with hammers and scraps of iron; opposite to this, over a rude cross of cobbled paths, was the Blue Boar, the only inn of the place. It was upon this crossway, in the lifting of a leaden and silver daybreak, that two brothers met in the street and spoke; though one was beginning the day and the other finishing it. The Reverend and Hon. Wilfred Bohun was very devout, and was making his way to some austere exercises of prayer or contemplation at dawn. Colonel the Hon. Norman Bohun, his elder brother, was by no means devout, and was sitting in evening-dress on the bench outside the Blue Boar, drinking what the philosophic observer was free to regard either as his last glass on Tuesday or his first on Wednesday. The colonel was not particular.

The Bohuns were one of the very few aristocratic families really dating from the Middle Ages, and their pennon had actually seen Palestine. But it is a great mistake to suppose that such houses stand high in chivalric traditions. Few except the poor preserve traditions. Aristocrats live not in traditions but in fashions. The Bohuns had been Mohocks under Queen Anne and Mashers under Queen Victoria. But, like more than one of the really ancient houses, they had rotted in the last two centuries into mere drunkards and dandy degenerates, till there had even come a whisper of insanity. Certainly there was something hardly human about the colonel's wolfish pursuit of pleasure, and his chronic resolution not to go home till morning had a touch of the hideous charity of insomnia. He was a tall, fine animal, elderly, but with hair startlingly yellow. He would have looked merely blond and leonine, but his blue eyes were sunk so deep in his face that they looked black. They were a little too close together. He had very long yellow moustaches: on each side of them a fold or furrow from nostril to jaw, so that a sneer seemed to cut into his face. Over his evening clothes he wore a curiously pale yellow coat that looked more like a very light dressing-gown than an overcoat, and on the back of his head was stuck an extraordinary broad-brimmed hat of a bright green colour, evidently some oriental curiosity caught up at random. He was proud of appearing in such incongruous attires – proud of the fact that he always made them look congruous.

His brother the curate had also the yellow hair and the elegance, but he was buttoned up to the chin in black, and his face was clean-shaven, cultivated and a little nervous. He seemed to live for nothing but his religion; but there were some who said (notably the blacksmith, who was a Presbyterian) that it was a love of Gothic architecture rather than of God, and that his haunting of the church like a ghost was only another and purer turn of the almost morbid thirst for beauty which sent his brother raging after women and wine. This charge was doubtful, while the man's practical piety was indubitable. Indeed, the charge was mostly an ignorant misunderstanding of the love of solitude and secret prayer, and was founded on his being often found kneeling, not before the altar, but in peculiar places, in the crypts or gallery, or even in the belfry. He was at the moment about to enter the church through the yard of the smithy, but stopped and frowned a little as he saw his brother's cavernous eyes staring in the same direction. On the hypothesis that the colonel was interested in the church he did not waste any speculations. There only remained the blacksmith's shop, and though the blacksmith was a Puritan and none of his people, Wilfred Bohun had heard some scandals about a beautiful and rather celebrated wife. He flung a suspicious look across the shed, and the colonel stood up laughing to speak to him.

'Good morning, Wilfred,' he said. 'Like a good landlord I am watching sleeplessly over my people. I am going to call on the blacksmith.'

Wilfred looked at the ground and said: 'The blacksmith is out. He is over at Greenford.'

'I know,' answered the other with silent laughter; 'that is why I am calling on him.'

'Norman,' said the cleric, with his eye on a pebble in the road, 'are you ever afraid of thunderbolts?'

'What do you mean?' asked the colonel. 'Is your hobby meteorology?'

'I mean,' said Wilfred, without looking up, 'Do you ever think that God might strike you in the street?'

'I beg your pardon,' said the colonel; 'I see your hobby is folklore.'

'I know your hobby is blasphemy,' retorted the religious man, stung in the one live place of his nature. 'But if you do not fear God, you have good reason to fear man.'

The elder raised his eyebrows politely. 'Fear man?' he said.

'Barnes the blacksmith is the biggest and strongest man for forty miles around,' said the clergyman sternly. 'I know you are no coward or weakling, but he could throw you over the wall.'

This struck home, being true, and the lowering line by mouth and nostril darkened and deepened. For a moment he stood with the heavy sneer on his face. But in an instant Colonel Bohun had recovered his own cruel good humour and laughed, showing two dog-like front teeth under his yellow moustache. 'In that case, my dear Wilfred,' he said quite carelessly, 'It was wise for the last of the Bohuns to come out partially in armour.'

And he took off the queer round hat covered with green, showing that it was lined within with steel. Wilfred recognized it indeed as a light Japanese or Chinese helmet torn down from a trophy that hung in the old family hall.

'It was the first to hand,' explained his brother airily; 'always the nearest hat – and the nearest woman.'

'The blacksmith is away at Greenford,' said Wilfred quietly; 'the time of his return is unsettled.'

And with that he turned and went into the church with bowed head, crossing himself like one who wishes to be quit of an unclean spirit. He was anxious to forget such grossness in the cool twilight of his tall Gothic cloisters; but on that morning it was fated that his still round of religious exercises should be everywhere arrested by small shocks. As he entered the church, hitherto always empty at that hour, a kneeling figure rose hastily to its feet and came towards the full daylight of the doorway. When the curate saw it he stood still with surprise. For the early worshipper was none other than the village idiot, a nephew of the blacksmith, one who neither would nor could care for the church or for anything else. He was always called 'Mad Joe', and seemed to have no other name; he was a dark, strong, slouching lad, with a heavy white face, dark straight hair and a mouth always open. As he passed the priest, his moon-calf countenance gave no hint of what he had been doing or thinking of. He had never been known to pray before. What sort of prayers was he saying now? Extraordinary prayers surely.

Wilfred Bohun stood rooted to the spot long enough to see the idiot go out into the sunshine, and even to see his dissolute brother hail him with a sort of avuncular jocularity. The last thing he saw was the colonel throwing pennies at the open mouth of Joe, with the serious appearance of trying to hit it.

This ugly sunlight picture of the stupidity and cruelty of the earth sent the ascetic finally to his prayers for purification and new thoughts. He went up to a pew in the gallery, which brought him under a coloured window which he loved and which always quieted his spirit; a blue window with an angel carrying lilies. There he began to think less about the half-wit, with his livid face and mouth like a fish. He began to think less of his evil brother, pacing like a lean lion in his horrible hunger. He sank deeper and deeper into those cold and sweet colours of silver blossoms and sapphire sky.

In this place half an hour afterwards he was found by Gibbs, the village cobbler, who had been sent for him in some haste. He got to his feet with promptitude for he knew that no small matter would have brought Gibbs into such a place at all. The cobbler was, as in many villages, an atheist, and his appearance in church was a shade more extraordinary than Mad Joe's. It was a morning of theological enigmas.

'What is it?' asked Wilfred Bohun rather stiffly, but putting out a trembling hand for his hat.

The atheist spoke in a tone that, coming from him, was quite startlingly respectful, and even, as it were, huskily sympathetic.

'You must excuse me, sir,' he said in a hoarse whisper, 'but we didn't think it right not to let you know at once. I'm afraid a rather dreadful thing has happened, sir. I'm afraid your brother –'

Wilfred clenched his frail hands. 'What devilry has he done now?' he cried in involuntary passion.

'Why, sir,' said the cobbler, coughing, 'I'm afraid he's done nothing, and won't do anything. I'm afraid he's done for. You had really better come down, sir.'

The curate followed the cobbler down a short winding stair which brought them out at an entrance rather higher than the street. Bohun saw the tragedy in one glance, flat underneath him like a plan. In the yard of the smithy were standing five or six men, mostly in black, one in an inspector's uniform. They included the doctor, the Presbyterian minister, and the priest from the Roman Catholic chapel to which the blacksmith's wife belonged. The latter was speaking to her, indeed, very rapidly, in an undertone, as she, a magnificent woman with red-gold hair, was sobbing blindly on a bench. Between these two groups, and just clear of the main heap of hammers, lay a man in evening dress, spread-eagled and flat on his face. From the height above Wilfred could have sworn to every item of his costume and appearance, down to the Bohun rings upon his fingers; but the skull was only a hideous splash, like a star of blackness and blood.

Wilfred Bohun gave but one glance, and ran down the steps into the yard. The doctor, who was the family physician, saluted him, but he scarcely took any notice. He could only stammer out: 'My brother is dead. What does it mean? What is this horrible mystery?' There was an unhappy silence; and then the cobbler, the most outspoken man present, answered: 'Plenty of horror, sir,' he said, 'but not much mystery.'

'What do you mean?' asked Wilfred, with a white face.

'It's plain enough,' answered Gibbs. 'There is only one man for forty miles round that could have struck such a blow as that, and he's the man that had most reason to.'

'We must not prejudge anything,' put in the doctor, a tall, black-bearded man, rather nervously; 'but it is competent for me to corroborate what Mr Gibbs says about the nature of the blow, sir; it is an incredible blow. Mr Gibbs says that only one man in this district could have done it. I should have said myself that nobody could have done it.'

A shudder of superstition went through the slight figure of the curate. 'I can hardly understand,' he said.

'Mr Bohun,' said the doctor in a low voice, 'metaphors literally fail me. It is inadequate to say that the skull was smashed to bits like an egg-shell. Fragments of bone were driven into the body and the ground like bullets into a mud wall. It was the hand of a giant.'

He was silent a moment, looking grimly through his glasses; then he added: 'The thing has one advantage – that it clears most people of suspicion at one stroke. If you or I or any normally made man in the country were accused of this crime, we should be acquitted as an infant would be acquitted of stealing the Nelson Column.'

'That's what I say,' repeated the cobbler obstinately, 'there's only one man that could have done it, and he's the man that would have done it. Where's Simeon Barnes, the blacksmith?'

'He's over at Greenford,' faltered the curate.

'More likely over in France,' muttered the cobbler.

'No; he is in neither of those places,' said a small and colourless voice, which came from the little Roman priest who had joined the group. 'As a matter of fact, he is coming up the road at this moment.'

The little priest was not an interesting man to look at, having stubbly brown hair and a round and stolid face. But if he had been as splendid as Apollo no one would have looked at him at that moment. Everyone turned round and peered at the pathway which wound across the plain below, along which was indeed walking, at his own huge stride and with a hammer on his shoulder, Simeon the smith. He was a bony and gigantic man, with deep, dark, sinister eyes and a dark chin beard. He was walking and talking quietly with two other men; and though he was never specially cheerful, he seemed quite at his ease.

'My God!' cried the atheistic cobbler; 'and there's the hammer he did it with.'

'No,' said the inspector, a sensible-looking man with a sandy moustache, speaking for the first time. 'There's the hammer he did it with, over there by the church wall. We have left it and the body exactly as they are.'

All glanced round, and the short priest went across and looked down in silence at the tool where it lay. It was one of the smallest and the lightest of the hammers, and would not have caught the eye among the rest; but on the iron edge of it were blood and yellow hair.

After a silence the short priest spoke without looking up, and there was a new note in his dull voice. 'Mr Gibbs was hardly right', he said, 'in saying that there is no mystery. There is at least the mystery of why so big a man should attempt so big a blow with so little a hammer.'

'Oh, never mind that,' cried Gibbs, in a fever. 'What are we to do with Simeon Barnes?'

'Leave him alone,' said the priest quietly. 'He is coming here of himself. I know these two men with him. They are very good fellows from Greenford, and they have come over about the Presbyterian chapel.'

Even as he spoke the tall smith swung round the corner of the church and strode into his own yard. Then he stood there quite still, and the hammer fell from his hand. The inspector, who had preserved impenetrable propriety, immediately went up to him.

'I won't ask you, Mr Barnes,' he said, 'whether you know anything about what has happened here. You are not bound to say. I hope you don't know, and that you will be able to prove it. But I must go through the form of arresting you in the King's name for the murder of Colonel Norman Bohun.'

'You are not bound to say anything,' said the cobbler in officious excitement. 'They've got to prove everything. They haven't proved yet that it is Colonel Bohun, with the head all smashed up like that.'

'That won't wash,' said the doctor aside to the priest. 'That's out of detective stories. I was the colonel's medical man, and I knew his body better than he did. He had very fine hands, but quite peculiar ones. The second and third fingers were the same length. Oh, that's the colonel right enough.'

As he glanced at the brained corpse upon the ground the iron eyes of the motionless blacksmith followed them and rested there also.

'Is Colonel Bohun dead?' said the smith quite calmly. 'Then he's damned.'

'Don't say anything! Oh, don't say anything,' cried the atheist cobbler, dancing about in an ecstasy of admiration of the English legal system. For no man is such a legalist as the good Secularist.

The blacksmith turned on him over his shoulder the august face of a fanatic.

'It is well for you infidels to dodge like foxes because the world's law favours you,' he said; 'but God guards His own in His pocket, as you shall see this day.'

Then he pointed to the colonel and said: 'When did this dog die in his sins?'

'Moderate your language,' said the doctor.

'Moderate the Bible's language, and I'll moderate mine. When did he die?'

'I saw him alive at six o'clock this morning,' stammered Wilfred Bohun.

'God is good,' said the smith. 'Mr Inspector, I have not the slightest objection to being arrested. It is you who may object to arresting me. I don't mind leaving the court without a stain on my character. You do mind, perhaps, leaving the court with a bad set-back in your career.'

The solid inspector for the first time looked at the blacksmith with a lively eye – as did everybody else, except the short, strange priest, who was still looking down at the little hammer that had dealt the dreadful blow.

'There are two men standing outside this shop,' went on the blacksmith with ponderous lucidity, 'good tradesmen in Greenford whom you all know, who will swear that they saw me from before midnight till daybreak and long after in the committee-room of our Revival Mission, which sits all night, we save souls so fast. In Greenford itself twenty people could swear to me for all that time. If I were a heathen, Mr Inspector, I would let you walk on to your downfall; but, as a Christian man, I feel bound to give you your chance and ask you whether you will hear my alibi now or in court.'

The inspector seemed for the first time disturbed and said, 'Of course I should be glad to clear you altogether now.'

The smith walked out of his yard with the same long and easy stride, and returned to his two friends from Greenford, who were indeed friends of nearly everyone present. Each of them said a few words which no one ever thought of disbelieving. When they had spoken the innocence of Simeon stood up as solid as the great church above them.

One of those silences struck the group which are more strange and insufferable than any speech. Madly, in order to make conversation, the curate said to the Catholic priest:

'You seem very much interested in that hammer, Father Brown.'

'Yes, I am,' said Father Brown; 'why is it such a small hammer?'

The doctor swung round on him.

'By George, that's true,' he cried; 'who could use a little hammer with ten larger hammers lying about?'

Then he lowered his voice in the curate's ear and said: 'Only the kind of person that can't lift a large hammer. It is not a question of force or courage between the sexes. It's a question of lifting power in the shoulders. A bold woman could commit ten murders with a light hammer and never turn a hair. She could not kill a beetle with a heavy one.'

Wilfred Bohun was staring at him with a sort of hypnotized horror, while Father Brown listened with his head a little on one side, really interested and attentive. The doctor went on with more hissing emphasis:

'Why do those idiots always assume that the only person who hates the wife's lover is the wife's husband? Nine times out of ten the person who most hates the wife's lover is the wife. Who knows what insolence or treachery he had shown her – look there?'

He made a momentary gesture towards the red-haired woman on the bench. She had lifted her head at last and the tears were drying on her splendid face. But the eyes were fixed on the corpse with an electric glare that had in it something of idiocy.

The Reverend Wilfred Bohun made a limp gesture as if waving away all desire to know; but Father Brown, dusting off his sleeve some ashes blown from the furnace, spoke in his indifferent way.

'You are like so many doctors,' he said; 'your mental science is really suggestive. It is your physical science that is utterly impossible. I agree that the woman wants to kill the co-respondent much more than the petitioner does. And I agree that a woman will always pick up a small hammer instead of a big one. But the difficulty is one of physical impossibility. No woman ever born could have smashed a man's skull out flat like that.' Then he added reflectively, after a pause: 'These people haven't grasped the whole of it. The man was actually wearing an iron helmet, and the blow scattered it like broken glass. Look at that woman. Look at her arms.'

Silence held them all up again, and then the doctor said rather sulkily: 'Well, I may be wrong; there are objections to everything. But I stick to the main point. No man but an idiot would pick up that little hammer if he could use a big hammer.'

With that the lean and quivering hands of Wilfred Bohun went up to his head and seemed to clutch his scanty yellow hair. After an instant they dropped, and he cried: 'That was the word I wanted; you have said the word.'

Then he continued, mastering his discomposure: 'The words you said were, "No man but an idiot would pick up the small hammer".'

'Yes,' said the doctor. 'Well?'

'Well,' said the curate, 'no man but an idiot did.' The rest stared at him with eyes arrested and riveted, and he went on in a febrile and feminine agitation.

'I am a priest,' he cried unsteadily, 'and a priest should be no shedder of blood. I – I mean that he should bring no one to the gallows. And I thank God that I see the criminal clearly now – because he is a criminal who cannot be brought to the gallows.'

'You will not denounce him?' enquired the doctor.

'He would not be hanged if I did denounce him,' answered Wilfrid, with a wild but curiously happy smile. 'When I went into the church this morning I found a madman praying there – that poor Joe, who has been wrong all his life. God knows what he prayed; but with such strange folk it is not incredible to suppose that their prayers are all upside down. Very likely a lunatic would pray before killing a man. When I last saw poor Joe he was with my brother. My brother was mocking him.'

'By Jove!' cried the doctor, 'this is talking at last. But how do you explain –'

The Reverend Wilfred was almost trembling with the excitement of his own glimpse of the truth. 'Don't you see; don't you see,' he cried feverishly, 'that is the only theory that covers both the queer things, that answers both the riddles. The two riddles are the little hammer and the big blow. The smith might have struck the big blow, but he would not have chosen the little hammer. His wife would have chosen the little hammer, but she could not have struck the big blow. But the madman might have done both. As for the little hammer – why, he was mad and might have picked up anything. And for the big blow, have you never heard, doctor, that a maniac in his paroxysm may have the strength of ten men?'

The doctor drew a deep breath and then said: 'By golly, I believe you've got it.'

Father Brown had fixed his eyes on the speaker so long and steadily as to prove that his large grey, ox-like eyes were not quite so insignificant as the rest of his face. When silence had fallen he said with marked respect: 'Mr Bohun, yours is the only theory yet propounded which holds water every way and is essentially unassailable. I think, therefore, that you deserve to be told, on my positive knowledge, that it is not the true one.' And with that the odd little man walked away and stared again at the hammer.

'That fellow seems to know more than he ought to,' whispered the doctor peevishly to Wilfred. 'Those popish priests are deucedly sly.'

'No, no,' said Bohun, with a sort of wild fatigue. 'It was the lunatic. It was the lunatic.'

The group of the two clerics and the doctor had fallen away from the more official group containing the inspector and the man he had arrested. Now, however, that their own party had broken up, they heard voices from the others. The priest looked up quietly and then looked down again as he heard the blacksmith say in a loud voice:

'I hope I've convinced you, Mr Inspector. I'm a strong man, as you say, but I couldn't have flung my hammer bang here from Greenford. My hammer hasn't any wings that it should come flying half a mile over hedges and fields.'

The inspector laughed amicably and said: 'No; I think you can be considered out of it, though it's one of the rummiest coincidences I ever saw. I can only ask you to give us all the assistance you can in finding a man as big and strong as yourself. By George! you might be useful, if only to hold him! I suppose you yourself have no guess at the man?'

'I may have a guess,' said the pale smith, 'but it is not at a man.' Then, seeing the scared eyes turn towards his wife on the bench, he put his huge hand on her shoulder and said: 'Nor a woman either.'

'What do you mean?' asked the inspector jocularly. 'You don't think cows use hammers, do you?'

'I think no thing of flesh held that hammer,' said the blacksmith in a stifled voice; 'mortally speaking, I think the man died alone.'

Wilfred made a sudden forward movement and peered at him with burning eyes.

'Do you mean to say, Barnes,' came the sharp voice of the cobbler, 'that the hammer jumped up of itself and knocked the man down?'

'Oh, you gentlemen may stare and snigger,' cried Simeon; 'you clergymen who tell us on Sunday in what a stillness the Lord smote Sennacherib. I believe that One who walks invisible in every house defended the honour of mine, and laid the defiler dead before the door of it. I believe the force in that blow was just the force there is in earthquakes, and no force less.'

Wilfred said, with a voice utterly indescribable: 'I told Norman myself to beware of the thunderbolt.'

'That agent is outside my jurisdiction,' said the inspector with a slight smile.

'You are not outside His,' answered the smith; 'see you to it.' And, turning is broad back, he went into the house.

The shaken Wilfred was led away by Father Brown, who had an easy and friendly way with him. 'Let us get out of this horrid place, Mr Bohun,' he said. 'May I look inside your church? I hear it's one of the oldest in England. We take some interest, you know,' he added with a comical grimace, 'in old English churches.'

Wilfred Bohun did not smile, for humour was never his strong point. But he nodded rather eagerly, being only too ready to explain the Gothic splendours to someone more likely to be sympathetic than the Presbyterian blacksmith or the atheist cobbler.

'By all means,' he said; 'let us go in at this side.' And he led the way into the high side entrance at the top of the flight of steps. Father Brown was mounting the first step to follow him when he felt a hand on his shoulder, and turned to behold the dark, thin figure of the doctor, his face darker yet with suspicion.

'Sir,' said the physician harshly, 'you appear to know some secrets in this black business. May I ask if you are going to keep them to yourself?'

'Why, doctor,' answered the priest, smiling quite pleasantly, 'there is one very good reason why a man of my trade would keep things to himself when he is not sure of them, and that is that it is so constantly his duty to keep them to himself when he is sure of them. But if you think I have been discourteously reticent with you or anyone, I will go to the extreme limit of my custom. I will give you two very large hints.'

'Well, sir?' said the doctor gloomily.

'First,' said Father Brown quietly, 'the thing is quite in your own province. It is a matter of physical science. The blacksmith is mistaken, not perhaps in saying that the blow was divine, but certainly in saying that it came by a miracle. It was no miracle, doctor, except in so far as man is himself a miracle, with his strange and wicked and yet half-heroic heart. The force that smashed that skull was a force well known to scientists – one of the most frequently debated of the laws of nature.'

The doctor, who was looking at him with frowning intentness, only said: 'And the other hint?'

'The other hint is this,' said the priest: 'Do you remember the blacksmith, though he believes in miracles, talking scornfully of the impossible fairy-tale that his hammer had wings and flew half a mile across country?'

'Yes,' said the doctor, 'I remember that.'

'Well,' added Father Brown, with a broad smile, 'that fairy-tale was the nearest thing to the real truth that has been said today.' And with that he turned his back and stumped up the steps after the curate.

The Reverend Wilfred, who had been waiting for him, pale and impatient, as if this little delay were the last straw for his nerves, led him immediately to his favourite corner of the church, that part of the gallery closest to the carved roof and lit by the wonderful window with the angel. The little Latin priest explored and admired everything exhaustively, talking cheerfully but in a low voice all the time. When in the course of his investigation he found the side exit and the winding stair down which Wilfred had rushed to find his brother dead, Father Brown ran not down but up, with the agility of a monkey, and his clear voice came from an outer platform above.

'Come up here, Mr Bohun,' he called. 'The air will do you good.'

Bohun followed him, and came out on a kind of stone gallery or balcony outside the building, from which one could see the illimitable plain in which their small hill stood, wooded away to the purple horizon and dotted with villages and farms. Clear and square, but quite small beneath them, was the blacksmith's yard, where the inspector still stood taking notes and the corpse still lay like a smashed fly.

'Might be the map of the world, mightn't it?' said Father Brown.

'Yes,' said Bohun very gravely, and nodded his head.

Immediately beneath and about them the lines of the Gothic building plunged outwards into the void with a sickening swiftness akin to suicide. There is that element of Titan energy in the architecture of the Middle Ages that, from whatever aspect it be seen, it always seems to be rushing away, like the strong back of some maddened horse. This church was hewn out of ancient and silent stone, bearded with old fungoids and stained with the nests of birds. And yet, when they saw it from below, it sprang like a fountain at the stars; and when they saw it, as now, from above, it poured like a cataract into a voiceless pit. For these two men on the tower were left alone with the most terrible aspect of the Gothic: the monstrous foreshortening and disproportion, the dizzy perspectives, the glimpses of great things small and small things great; a topsy-turvydom of stone in the mid-air. Details of stone, enormous by their proximity, were relieved against a pattern of fields and farms, pygmy in their distance. A carved bird or beast at a corner seemed like some vast walking or flying dragon wasting the pastures and villages below. The whole atmosphere was dizzy and dangerous, as if men were upheld in air amid the gyrating wings of colossal genii; and the whole of that old church, as tall and rich as a cathedral, seemed to sit upon the sunlit country like a cloudburst.

'I think there is something rather dangerous about standing on these high places even to pray', said Father Brown. 'Heights were made to be looked at, not to be looked from.'

'Do you mean that one may fall over?' asked Wilfred.

'I mean that one's soul may fall if one's body doesn't,' said the other priest.

'I scarcely understand you,' remarked Bohun indistinctly.

'Look at that blacksmith, for instance', went on Father Brown calmly; 'a good man, but not a Christian – hard, imperious, unforgiving. Well, his Scotch religion was made up by men who prayed on hills and high crags, and learnt to look down on the world more than to look up at heaven. Humility is the mother of giants. One sees great things from the valley; only small things from the peak.'

'But he – he didn't do it,' said Bohun tremulously.

'No,' said the other in an odd voice; 'we know he didn't do it.'

After a moment he resumed, looking tranquilly out over the plain with his pale grey eyes. 'I knew a man,' he said, 'who began by worshipping with others before the altar, but who grew fond of high and lonely places to pray from, corners or niches in the belfry or the spire. And once in one of those dizzy places, where the whole world seemed to turn under him like a wheel, his brain turned also, and he fancied he was God. So that though he was a good man, he committed a great crime.'

Wilfred's face was turned away, but his bony hands turned blue and white as they tightened on the parapet of stone.

'He thought it was given to *him* to judge the world and strike down the sinner. He would never have had such a thought if he had been kneeling with other men upon a floor. But he saw all men walking about like insects. He saw one especially strutting just below him, insolent and evident by a bright green hat – a poisonous insect.'

Rooks cawed round the corners of the belfry; but there was no other sound till Father Brown went on.

'This also tempted him, that he had in his hand one of the most awful engines of nature; I mean gravitation, that mad and quickening rush by which all earth's creatures fly back to her heart when released. See, the inspector is strutting just below us in the smithy. If I were to toss a pebble over this parapet it would be something like a bullet by the time it struck him. If I were to drop a hammer – even a small hammer –'

Wilfred Bohun threw one leg over the parapet, and Father Brown had him in a minute by the collar.

'Not by that door,' he said quite gently; 'that door leads to hell.'

Bohun staggered back against the wall, and stared at him with frightful eyes.

'How do you know all this?' he cried. 'Are you a devil?'

'I am a man,' answered Father Brown gravely; 'and therefore have all devils in my heart. Listen to me,' he said after a short pause. 'I know what you did – at least, I can guess the great part of it. When you left your brother you were racked with no unrighteous rage to the extent even that you snatched up the small hammer, half inclined to kill him with his foulness on his mouth. Recoiling, you thrust it under your buttoned coat instead, and rushed into the church. You prayed wildly in many places, under the angel window, upon the platform above, and on a higher platform still, from which you could see the colonel's Eastern hat like the back of a green beetle crawling about. Then something snapped in your soul, and you let God's thunderbolt fall.'

Wilfred put a weak hand to his head, and asked in a low voice: 'How did you know that his hat looked like a green beetle?'

'Oh, that,' said the other with the shadow of a smile, 'that was common sense. But hear me further. I say I know all this; but no one else shall know it. The next step is for you; I shall take no more steps; I will seal this with the seal of confession. If you ask me why, there are many reasons, and only one that concerns you. I leave things to you because you have not yet gone very far wrong, as assassins go. You did not help to fix the crime on the smith when it was easy; or on his wife, when that was easy. You tried to fix it on the imbecile, because you knew that he could not suffer. That was one of the gleams that it is my business to find in assassins. And now come down into the village, and go your own way as free as the wind; for I have said my last word.'

They went down the winding stairs in utter silence, and came out into the sunlight by the smithy. Wilfred Bohun carefully unlatched the wooden gate of the yard, and going up to the inspector, said: 'I wish to give myself up; I have killed my brother.'

Sanctuary

Agatha Christie

The vicar's wife came round the corner of the Vicarage with her arms full of chrysanthemums. A good deal of rich garden soil was attached to her strong brogue shoes and a few fragments of earth were adhering to her nose, but of that fact she was perfectly unconscious.

She had a slight struggle in opening the Vicarage gate which hung, rustily, half off its hinges. A puff of wind caught at her battered felt hat, causing it to sit even more rakishly than it had done before. 'Bother!' said Bunch.

Christened by her optimistic parents Diana, Mrs Harmon had become Bunch at an early age for somewhat obvious reasons and the name had stuck to her ever since. Clutching the chrysanthemums, she made her way through the gate to the churchyard, and so to the church door.

The November air was mild and damp. Clouds scudded across the sky with patches of blue here and there. Inside, the church was dark and cold; it was unheated except at service times.

'Brrrrrh!' said Bunch expressively. 'I'd better get on with this quickly. I don't want to die of cold.'

With the quickness born of practice she collected the necessary para-phernalia: vases, water, flower-holders. 'I wish we had lilies,' thought Bunch to herself. 'I get so tired of these scraggy chrysanthemums.' Her nimble fingers arranged the blooms in their holders.

There was nothing particularly original or artistic about the decora-tions, for Bunch Harmon herself was neither original nor artistic, but it was a homely and pleasant arrangement. Carrying the vases carefully, Bunch stepped up the aisle and made her way towards the altar. As she did so the sun came out.

It shone through the East window of somewhat crude coloured glass, mostly blue and red – the gift of a wealthy Victorian churchgoer. The effect was almost startling in its sudden opulence. 'Like jewels,' thought Bunch. Suddenly she stopped, staring ahead of her. On the chancel steps was a huddled dark form.

Putting down the flowers carefully, Bunch went up to it and bent over it. It was a man lying there, huddled over on himself. Bunch knelt down by him and slowly, carefully, she turned him over. Her fingers went to his pulse – a pulse so feeble and fluttering that it told its own story, as did the almost greenish pallor of his face. There was no doubt, Bunch thought, that the man was dying.

He was a man of about forty-five, dressed in a dark, shabby suit. She laid down the limp hand she had picked up and looked at his other hand. This seemed clenched like a fist on his breast. Looking more closely she saw that the fingers were closed over what seemed to be a large wad or handkerchief which he was holding tightly to his chest. All round the clenched hand there were splashes of a dry brown fluid which, Bunch guessed, was dry blood. Bunch sat back on her heels, frowning.

Up till now the man's eyes had been closed but at this point they suddenly opened and fixed themselves on Bunch's face. They were neither dazed nor wandering. They seemed fully alive and intelligent. His lips moved, and Bunch bent forward to catch the words, or rather the word. It was only one word that he said:

'*Sanctuary*.'

There was, she thought, just a very faint smile as he breathed out this word. There was no mistaking it, for after a moment, he said it again, 'Sanctuary . . .'

Then, with a faint, long-drawn-out sigh, his eyes closed again. Once more Bunch's fingers went to his pulse. It was still there, but fainter now and more intermittent. She got up with decision.

'Don't move,' she said, 'or try to move. I'm going for help.'

The man's eyes opened again but he seemed now to be fixing his attention on the coloured light that came through the East window. He murmured something that Bunch could not quite catch. She thought, startled, that it might have been her husband's name.

'Julian?' she said. 'Did you come here to find Julian?' But there was no answer. The man lay with eyes closed; his breathing coming in slow, shallow fashion.

Bunch turned and left the church rapidly. She glanced at her watch and nodded with some satisfaction. Dr Griffiths would still be in his surgery. It was only a couple of minutes' walk from the church. She went in, without waiting to knock or ring, passing through the waiting-room and into the doctor's surgery.

'You must come at once,' said Bunch. 'There's a man dying in the church.'

Some minutes later Dr Griffiths rose from his knee after a brief examination.

'Can we move him from here into the Vicarage? I can attend to him better there – not that it's any use.'

'Of course,' said Bunch. 'I'll go along and get things ready. I'll get Harper and Jones, shall I? To help you carry him.'

'Thanks. I can telephone from the Vicarage for an ambulance, but I'm afraid – by the time it comes . . .' He left the remark unfinished.

Bunch said, 'Internal bleeding?'

Dr Griffiths nodded. He said, 'How on earth did he come here?'

'I think he must have been here all night,' said Bunch, considering. 'Harper unlocks the church in the morning as he goes to work, but he doesn't usually come in.'

It was about five minutes later when Dr Griffiths put down the telephone receiver and came back into the morning-room where the injured man was lying on quickly arranged blankets on the sofa. Bunch was moving a basin of water and clearing up after the doctor's examination.

'Well, that's that,' said Griffiths. 'I've sent for an ambulance and I've notified the police.' He stood, frowning, looking down on the patient who lay with closed eyes. His left hand was plucking in a nervous, spasmodic way at his side.

'He was shot,' said Griffiths. 'Shot at fairly close quarters. He rolled his handkerchief up into a ball and plugged the wound with it so as to stop the bleeding.'

'Could he have gone far after that happened?' Bunch asked.

'Oh, yes, it's quite possible. A mortally wounded man has been known to pick himself up and walk along a street as though nothing had happened, and then suddenly collapse five or ten minutes later. So he needn't have been shot in the church. Oh, no. He may have been shot some distance away. Of course, he may have shot himself and then dropped the revolver and staggered blindly towards the church. I don't quite know why he made for the church and not for the Vicarage.'

'Oh, I know *that*,' said Bunch. 'He said it: "Sanctuary." '

The doctor stared at her. 'Sanctuary?'

'Here's Julian,' said Bunch, turning her head as she heard her husband's steps in the hall. 'Julian! Come here.'

The Reverend Julian Harmon entered the room. His vague, scholarly manner always made him appear much older than he really was. 'Dear me!' said Julian Harmon, staring in a mild, puzzled manner at the surgical appliances and the prone figure on the sofa.

Bunch explained with her usual economy of words. 'He was in the church, dying. He'd been shot. Do you know him, Julian? I thought he said your name.'

The Vicar came up to the sofa and looked down at the dying man. 'Poor fellow,' he said, and shook his head. 'No, I don't know him. I'm almost sure I've never seen him before.'

At that moment the dying man's eyes opened once more. They went from the doctor to Julian Harmon and from him to his wife. The eyes stayed there, staring into Bunch's face. Griffiths stepped forward.

'If you could tell us,' he said urgently.

But with his eyes fixed on Bunch, the man said in a weak voice, 'Please – *please* –' And then, with a slight tremor, he died . . .

Sergeant Hayes licked his pencil and turned the page of his notebook. 'So that's all you can tell me, Mrs Harmon?'

'That's all,' said Bunch. 'These are the things out of his coat pockets.'

On a table at Sergeant Hayes's elbow was a wallet, a rather battered old watch with the initials W.S. and the return half of a ticket to London. Nothing more.

'You've found out who he is?' asked Bunch.

'A Mr and Mrs Eccles phoned up the station. He's her brother, it seems. Name of Sandbourne. Been in a low state of health and nerves for some time. He's been getting worse lately. The day before yesterday he walked out and didn't come back. He took a revolver with him.'

'And he came out here and shot himself with it?' said Bunch. 'Why?'

'Well, you see, he'd been depressed . . .'

Bunch interrupted him. 'I don't mean *that*. I mean, why here?'

Since Sergeant Hayes obviously did not know the answer to that one he replied in an oblique fashion, 'Come out here, he did, on the 5:10 bus.'

'Yes,' said Bunch again. 'But *why*?'

'I don't know, Mrs Harmon,' said Sergeant Hayes. 'There's no accounting. If the balance of the mind is disturbed –'

Bunch finished for him. 'They may do it anywhere. But it still seems to me unnecessary to take a bus out to a small country place like this. He didn't know anyone here, did he?'

'Not so far as can be ascertained,' said Sergeant Hayes. He coughed in an apologetic manner and said, as he rose to his feet, 'It may be as Mr and Mrs Eccles will come out and see you, Ma'am – if you don't mind, that is.'

'Of course I don't mind,' said Bunch. 'It's very natural, I only wish I had something to tell them.'

'I'll be getting along,' said Sergeant Hayes.

'I'm only so thankful,' said Bunch, going with him to the front door, 'that it wasn't murder.'

A car had drawn up at the Vicarage gate. Sergeant Hayes, glancing at it, remarked: 'Looks as though that's Mr and Mrs Eccles come here now, Ma'am, to talk with you.'

Bunch braced herself to endure what, she felt, might be rather a difficult ordeal. 'However,' she thought, 'I can always call Julian in to help me. A clergyman's a great help when people are bereaved.'

Exactly what she had expected Mr and Mrs Eccles to be like, Bunch could not have said, but she was conscious, as she greeted them, of a feeling of surprise. Mr Eccles was a stout florid man whose natural manner would have been cheerful and facetious. Mrs Eccles had a vaguely flashy look about her. She had a small, mean, pursed-up mouth. Her voice was thin and reedy.

'It's been a terrible shock, Mrs Harmon, as you can imagine,' she said.

'Oh, I know,' said Bunch. 'It must have been. Do sit down. Can I offer you – well, perhaps it's a little early for tea –'

Mr Eccles waved a pudgy hand. 'No, no, nothing for us,' he said. 'It's very kind of you, I'm sure. Just wanted to . . . well . . . what poor William said and all that, you know?'

'He's been abroad a long time,' said Mrs Eccles, 'and I think he must have had some very nasty experiences. Very quiet and depressed he's been, ever since he came home. Said the world wasn't fit to live in and there was nothing to look forward to. Poor Bill, he was always moody.'

Bunch stared at them both for a moment or two without speaking.

'Pinched my husband's revolver, he did,' went on Mrs Eccles. 'Without our knowing. Then it seems he come out here by bus. I suppose that was nice feeling on his part. He wouldn't have liked to do it in our house.'

'Poor fellow, poor fellow,' said Mr Eccles, with a sigh. 'It doesn't do to judge.'

There was another short pause, and Mr Eccles said, 'Did he leave a message? Any last words, nothing like that?'

His bright, rather piglike eyes watched Bunch closely. Mrs Eccles, too, leaned forward as though anxious for the reply.

'No,' said Bunch quietly. 'He came into the church when he was dying, for sanctuary.'

Mrs Eccles said in a puzzled voice, 'Sanctuary? I don't think I quite . . .'

Mr Eccles interrupted. 'Holy place, my dear,' he said impatiently. 'That's what the Vicar's wife means. It's a sin – suicide, you know. I expect he wanted to make amends.'

'He tried to say something just before he died,' said Bunch. 'He began, "Please," but that's as far as he got.' Mrs Eccles put her handkerchief to her eyes and sniffed.

'Oh, dear,' she said. 'It's terribly upsetting, isn't it?'

'There, there, Pam,' said her husband. 'Don't take on. These things can't be helped. Poor Willie. Still, he's at peace now. Well, thank you very much, Mrs Harmon. I hope we haven't interrupted you. A vicar's wife is a busy lady, we know that.'

They shook hands with her. Then Eccles turned back suddenly to say, 'Oh, yes, there's just one other thing. I think you've got his coat here, haven't you?'

'His coat?' Bunch frowned.

Mrs Eccles said, 'We'd like all his things, you know. Sentimental-like.'

'He had a watch and a wallet and a railway ticket in the pockets,' said Bunch. 'I gave them to Sergeant Hayes.'

'That's all right, then,' said Mr Eccles. 'He'll hand them over to us, I expect. His private papers would be in the wallet.'

'There was a pound note in the wallet,' said Bunch. 'Nothing else.'

'No letters? Nothing like that?'

Bunch shook her head.

'Well, thank you again, Mrs Harmon. The coat he was wearing – perhaps the Sergeant's got that too, has he?'

Bunch frowned in an effort of remembrance.

'No,' she said. 'I don't think ... let me see. The doctor and I took his coat off to examine his wound.' She looked round the room, vaguely. 'I must have taken it upstairs with the towels and basin.'

'I wonder now, Mrs Harmon, if you don't mind ... We'd like his coat, you know, the last thing he wore. Well, the wife feels rather sentimental about it.'

'Of course,' said Bunch. 'Would you like me to have it cleaned first? I'm afraid it's rather – well – stained.'

'Oh, no, no, no, that doesn't matter.'

Bunch frowned. 'Now I wonder where ... excuse me a moment.' She went upstairs and it was some few minutes before she returned.

'I'm so sorry,' she said breathlessly, 'my daily woman must have put it aside with other clothes that were going to the cleaners. It's taken me quite a long time to find it. Here it is. I'll do it up for you in brown paper.'

Disclaiming their protests she did so; then once more effusively bidding her farewell the Eccles departed.

Bunch went slowly back across the hall and entered the study. The Reverend Julian Harmon looked up and his brow cleared. He was composing a sermon and was fearing that he'd been led astray by the interest of the political relations between Judaea and Persia, in the reign of Cyrus.

'Yes, dear?' he said, hopefully.

'Julian,' said Bunch. 'What's *sanctuary* exactly?'

Julian Harmon gratefully put aside his sermon paper.

'Well,' he said. 'Sanctuary in Roman and Greek temples applied to the *cella* in which stood the statue of a god. The Latin word for altar *"ara"* also means protection.' He continued learnedly: 'In A.D. 399 the right of sanctuary in Christian churches was finally and definitely recognized. The earliest mention of the right of sanctuary in England is in the Code of Laws issued by Ethelbert in A.D. 600 ...'

He continued for some time with his exposition but was, as often, disconcerted by his wife's reception of his erudite pronouncement.

'Darling,' she said. 'You *are* sweet.'

Bending over, she kissed him on the tip of his nose. Julian felt rather like a dog who has been congratulated on performing a clever trick.

'The Eccles have been here,' said Bunch.

The Vicar frowned. 'The Eccles? I don't seem to remember ...'

'You don't know them. They're the sister and her husband of the man in the church.'

'My dear, you ought to have called me.'

'There wasn't any need,' said Bunch. 'They were not in need of consolation. I wonder now.' She frowned. 'If I put a casserole in the oven tomorrow, can you manage, Julian? I think I shall go up to London for the sales.'

'The sails?' Her husband looked at her blankly. 'Do you mean a yacht or a boat or something?'

Bunch laughed.

'No, darling. There's a special white sale at Burrows and Portman's. You know, sheets, table-cloths and towels and glass-cloths. I don't know what we do with our glass-cloths, the way they wear through. Besides,' she added thoughtfully, 'I think I ought to go and see Aunt Jane.'

That sweet old lady, Miss Jane Marple, was enjoying the delights of the metropolis for a fortnight, comfortably installed in her nephew's studio flat.

'So kind of dear Raymond,' she murmured. 'He and Joan have gone to America for a fortnight and they insisted I should come up here and enjoy myself. And now, dear Bunch, do tell me what it is that's worrying you.'

Bunch was Miss Marple's favourite godchild, and the old lady looked at her with great affection as Bunch, thrusting her best felt hat further on the back of her head, started on her story.

Bunch's recital was concise and clear. Miss Marple nodded her head as Bunch finished. 'I see,' she said. 'Yes, I see.'

'That's why I felt I had to see you,' said Bunch. 'You see, not being clever –'

'But you *are* clever, my dear.'

'No, I'm not. Not clever like Julian.'

'Julian, of course, has a very solid intellect,' said Miss Marple.

'That's it,' said Bunch. 'Julian's got the intellect, but on the other hand, I've got the *sense*.'

'You have a lot of common sense, Bunch, and you're very intelligent.'

'You see, I don't really know what I ought to do. I can't ask Julian because – well, I mean, Julian's so full of rectitude . . .'

This statement appeared to be perfectly understood by Miss Marple, who said, 'I know what you mean, dear. We women – well, it's different.'

She went on, 'You told me what happened, Bunch, but I'd like to know first exactly what you think.'

'It's all wrong,' said Bunch. 'The man who was there in the church, dying, knew all about sanctuary. He said it just the way Julian would have said it. I mean he was a well-read, educated man. And if he'd shot himself, he wouldn't drag himself into a church afterwards and say "sanctuary." Sanctuary means that you're pursued, and when you get into a church you're safe. Your pursuers can't touch you. At one time even the law couldn't get at you.'

She looked questioningly at Miss Marple. The latter nodded. Bunch went on, 'Those people, the Eccles, were quite different. Ignorant and coarse. And there's another thing. That watch – the dead man's watch. It had the initials W.S. on the back of it. But inside – I opened it – in very small lettering there was "To Walter from his father" and a date. *Walter*. But the Eccles kept talking of him as William or Bill.'

Miss Marple seemed about to speak but Bunch rushed on, 'Oh, I know you're not always called the name you're baptized by. I mean, I can understand that you might be christened William and called "Porky" or "Carrots" or something. But your sister wouldn't call you William or Bill if your name was Walter.'

'You mean that she wasn't his sister?'

'I'm quite sure she wasn't his sister. They were horrid – both of them. They came to the Vicarage to get his things and to find out if he'd said anything before he died. When I said he hadn't I saw it in their faces – relief. I think, myself,' finished Bunch, 'it was Eccles who shot him.'

'Murder?' said Miss Marple.

'Yes,' said Bunch. 'Murder. That's why I came to you, darling.'

Bunch's remark might have seemed incongruous to an ignorant listener, but in certain spheres Miss Marple had a reputation for dealing with murder.

'He said "please" to me before he died,' said Bunch. 'He wanted me to do something for him. The awful thing is I've no idea what.'

Miss Marple considered for a moment or two, and then pounced on the point that had already occurred to Bunch. 'But why was he there at all?' she asked.

'You mean,' said Bunch, 'if you wanted sanctuary you might pop into a church anywhere. There's no need to take a bus that only goes four times a day and come out to a lonely spot like ours for it.'

'He must have come there for a purpose,' Miss Marple thought. 'He must have come to see someone. Chipping Cleghorn's not a big place, Bunch. Surely you must have some idea of who it was he came to see?'

Bunch reviewed the inhabitants of her village in her mind before rather doubtfully shaking her head. 'In a way,' she said, 'it could be anybody.'

'He never mentioned a name?'

'He said Julian, or I thought he said Julian. It might have been Julia, I suppose. As far as I know, there isn't any Julia living in Chipping Cleghorn.'

She screwed up her eyes as she thought back to the scene. The man lying there on the chancel steps, the light coming through the window with its jewels of red and blue light.

'Jewels,' said Bunch suddenly. 'Perhaps that's what he said. The light coming through the East window looked like jewels.'

'Jewels,' said Miss Marple, thoughtfully.

'I'm coming now,' said Bunch, 'to the most important thing of all. The reason why I've really come here today. You see, the Eccles made a great fuss about having his coat. We took it off when the doctor was seeing to him. It was an old, shabby sort of coat – there was no reason they should have wanted it. They pretended it was sentimental, but that was nonsense.

'Anyway, I went up to find it, and as I was going up the stairs I remembered how he'd made a kind of picking gesture with his hand, as though he was fumbling with the coat. So when I got hold of the coat I looked at it very carefully and I saw that in one place the lining had been sewn up again with a different thread. So I unpicked it and I found a little piece of paper inside. I took it out and I sewed it up again properly with thread that matched. I was careful and I don't really think that the Eccles would know I've done it. I don't *think* so, but I can't be sure. And I took the coat down to them and made some excuse for the delay.'

'The piece of paper?' asked Miss Marple.

Bunch opened her handbag. 'I didn't show it to Julian,' she said, 'because he would have said that I ought to have given it to the Eccles. But I thought I'd rather bring it to you instead.'

'A cloakroom ticket,' said Miss Marple, looking at it. 'Paddington Station.'

'He had a return ticket to Paddington in his pocket,' said Bunch.

The eyes of the two women met.

'This calls for action,' said Miss Marple briskly. 'But it would be advisable, I think, to be careful. Would you have noticed at all, Bunch dear, whether you were followed when you came to London today?'

'Followed!' exclaimed Bunch. 'You don't think –'

'Well, I think it's *possible*,' said Miss Marple. 'When anything is possible, I think we ought to take precautions.' She rose with a brisk movement. 'You came up here ostensibly, my dear, to go to the sales. I think the right thing to do, therefore, would be for us to *go* to the sales. But before we set out, we might put one or two little arrangements in hand. I don't suppose,' Miss Marple added obscurely, 'that I shall need the old speckled tweed with the beaver collar just at present.'

It was about an hour and a half later that the two ladies, rather the worse for wear and battered in appearance, and both clasping parcels of hardly-won household linen, sat down at a small and sequestered hostelry called the Apple Bough to restore their forces with steak-and-kidney pudding followed by apple tart and custard.

'Really a prewar quality face towel,' gasped Miss Marple, slightly out of breath. 'With a J on it, too. So fortunate that Raymond's wife's name is Joan. I shall put them aside until I really need them and then they will do for her if I pass on sooner than I expect.'

'I really did need the glass-cloths,' said Bunch. 'And they were very cheap, though not as cheap as the ones that woman with the ginger hair managed to snatch from me.'

A smart young woman with a lavish application of rouge and lipstick entered the Apple Bough at that moment. After looking round vaguely for a moment or two, she hurried to their table. She laid down an envelope by Miss Marple's elbow.

'There you are, Miss,' she said briskly.

'Oh, thank you, Gladys,' said Miss Marple. 'Thank you very much. So kind of you.'

'Always pleased to oblige, I'm sure,' said Gladys. 'Ernie always says to me "Everything what's good you learned from that Miss Marple of yours that you were in service with," and I'm sure I'm always glad to oblige you, Miss.'

'Such a dear girl,' said Miss Marple as Gladys departed again. 'Always so willing and so kind.'

She looked inside the envelope and then passed it on to Bunch. 'Now be very careful, dear,' she said. 'By the way, is there still that nice young Inspector at Melchester that I remember?'

'I don't know,' said Bunch. 'I expect so.'

'Well, if not,' said Miss Marple, thoughtfully, 'I can always ring up the Chief Constable. I *think* he would remember me.'

'Of course he'd remember you,' said Bunch. 'Everybody would remember *you*. You're quite unique.' She rose.

Arrived at Paddington, Bunch went to the Luggage Office and produced the cloakroom ticket. A moment or two later a rather shabby old suitcase was passed across to her, and carrying this she made her way to the platform.

The journey home was uneventful. Bunch rose as the train approached Chipping Cleghorn and picked up the old suitcase. She had just left her carriage when a man, sprinting along the platform, suddenly seized the suitcase from her hand and rushed off with it.

'Stop!' Bunch yelled. 'Stop him, stop him. He's taken my suitcase.'

The ticket collector who, at this rural station, was a man of somewhat slow processes, had just begun to say, 'Now, look here, you can't do that –' when a smart blow in the chest pushed him aside, and the man with the suitcase rushed out from the station. He made his way towards a waiting car. Tossing the suitcase in, he was about to climb after it but before he could move a hand fell on his shoulder, and the voice of Police Constable Abel said, 'Now then, what's all this?'

Bunch arrived, panting, from the station. 'He snatched my suitcase,' she said.

'Nonsense,' said the man. 'I don't know what this lady means. It's my suitcase. I just got out of the train with it.'

'Now, let's get this clear,' said Police Constable Abel.

He looked at Bunch with a bovine and impartial stare. Nobody would have guessed that Police Constable Abel and Mrs Harmon spent long half hours in Police Constable Abel's off-time discussing the respective merits of manure and bone meal for rose bushes.

'You say, Madam, that this is your suitcase?' said Police Constable Abel.

'Yes,' said Bunch. 'Definitely.'

'And you, sir?'

'I say this suitcase is mine.'

The man was tall, dark and well dressed, with a drawling voice and a superior manner. A feminine voice from inside the car, said, 'Of course it's your suitcase, Edwin. I don't know what this woman means.'

'We'll have to get this clear,' said Police Constable Abel. 'If it's your suitcase, Madam, what do you say is inside it?'

'Clothes,' said Bunch. 'A long speckled coat with a beaver collar, two wool jumpers and a pair of shoes.'

'Well, that's clear enough,' said Police Constable Abel. He turned to the other.

'I am a theatrical costumier,' said the dark man importantly. 'This suitcase contains theatrical properties which I brought down here for an amateur performance.'

'Right, sir,' said Police Constable Abel. 'Well, we'll just look inside, shall we, and see? We can go along to the police station, or if you're in a hurry we'll take the suitcase back to the station and open it there.'

'It'll suit me,' said the dark man. 'My name is Moss, by the way. Edwin Moss.'

The Police Constable, holding the suitcase, went back into the station. 'Just taking this into the Parcels Office, George,' he said to the ticket collector.

Police Constable Abel laid the suitcase on the counter of the Parcels Office and pushed back the clasp. The case was not locked. Bunch and Mr Edwin Moss stood on either side of him, their eyes regarding each other vengefully.

'Ah!' said Police Constable Abel, as he pushed up the lid.

Inside, neatly folded, was a long rather shabby tweed coat with a beaver fur collar. There were also two wool jumpers and a pair of country shoes.

'Exactly as you say, Madam,' said Police Constable Abel, turning to Bunch.

Nobody could have said that Mr Edwin Moss underdid things. His dismay and compunction were magnificent.

'I do apologize,' he said. 'I really *do* apologize. Please believe me, dear lady, when I tell you how very, very sorry I am. Unpardonable – quite unpardonable – my behaviour has been.' He looked at his watch. 'I must rush now. Probably my suitcase has gone on the train.' Raising his hat once more, he said meltingly to Bunch, 'Do, *do* forgive me,' and rushed hurriedly out of the Parcels Office.

'Are you going to let him get away?' asked Bunch in a conspiratorial whisper of Police Constable Abel.

The latter slowly closed a bovine eye in a wink.

'He won't get too far, Ma'am,' he said. 'That's to say, he won't get far unobserved, if you take my meaning.'

'Oh,' said Bunch, relieved.

'That old lady's been on the phone,' said Police Constable Abel, 'the one as was down here a few years ago. Bright she is, isn't she? But there's been a lot cooking up all today. Shouldn't wonder if the Inspector or Sergeant was out to see you about it tomorrow morning.'

It was the Inspector who came, the Inspector Craddock whom Miss Marple remembered. He greeted Bunch with a smile as an old friend.

'Crime in Chipping Cleghorn again,' he said cheerfully. 'You don't lack for sensation here, do you, Mrs Harmon?'

'I could do with rather less,' said Bunch. 'Have you come to ask me questions or are you going to tell me things for a change?'

'I'll tell you some things first,' said the Inspector. 'To begin with, Mr and Mrs Eccles have been having an eye kept on them for some time. There's reason to believe they've been connected with several robberies in this part of the world. For another thing, although Mrs Eccles *has* a brother called Sandbourne who has recently come back from abroad, the man you found dying in the church yesterday was definitely not Sandbourne.'

'I knew that he wasn't,' said Bunch. 'His name was Walter, to begin with, not William.'

The Inspector nodded. 'His name was Walter St John, and he escaped forty-eight hours ago from Charrington Prison.'

'Of course,' said Bunch softly to herself, 'he was being hunted down by the law, and he took sanctuary.' Then she asked, 'What had he done?'

'I'll have to go back rather a long way. It's a complicated story. Several years ago there was a certain dancer doing turns at the music halls. I don't expect you'll have ever heard of her, but she specialized in an Arabian Nights turn, "Aladdin in the Cave of Jewels" it was called. She wore bits of rhinestone and not much else.

'She wasn't much of a dancer, I believe, but she was – well – attractive. Anyway, a certain Asiatic royalty fell for her in a big way. Amongst other things he gave her a very magnificent emerald necklace.'

'The historic jewels of a Rajah?' murmured Bunch ecstatically.

Inspector Craddock coughed. 'Well, a rather more modern version, Mrs Harmon. The affair didn't last very long, broke up when our potentate's attention was captured by a certain film star whose demands were not quite so modest.

'Zobeida, to give the dancer her stage name, hung on to the necklace, and in due course it was stolen. It disappeared from her dressing-room at the theatre, and there was a lingering suspicion in the minds of the authorities that she herself might have engineered its disappearance. Such things have been known as a publicity stunt, or indeed from more dishonest motives.

'The necklace was never recovered, but during the course of the investigation the attention of the police was drawn to this man, Walter St John. He was a man of education and breeding who had come down in the world, and who was employed as a working jeweller with a rather obscure firm which was suspected of acting as a fence for jewel robberies.

'There was evidence that this necklace had passed through his hands. It was, however, in connection with the theft of some other jewellery that he was finally brought to trial and convicted and sent to prison. He had not very much longer to serve, so his escape was rather a surprise.'

'But why did he come here?' asked Bunch.

'We'd like to know that very much, Mrs Harmon. Following up his trail, it seems that he went first to London. He didn't visit any of his old associates but he visited an elderly woman, a Mrs Jacobs who had formerly been a theatrical dresser. She won't say a word of what he came for, but according to other lodgers in the house he left carrying a suitcase.'

'I see,' said Bunch. 'He left it in the cloakroom at Paddington and then he came down here.'

'By that time,' said Inspector Craddock, 'Eccles and the man who calls himself Edwin Moss were on his trail. They wanted that suitcase. They saw him get on the bus. They must have driven out in a car ahead of him and been waiting for him when he left the bus.'

'And he was murdered?' said Bunch.

'Yes,' said Craddock. 'He was shot. It was Eccles' revolver, but I rather fancy it was Moss who did the shooting. Now, Mrs Harmon, what we want to know is where is the suitcase that Walter St John actually deposited at Paddington Station?'

Bunch grinned. 'I expect Aunt Jane's got it by now,' she said. 'Miss Marple, I mean. That was her plan. She sent a former maid of hers with a suitcase packed with her things to the cloakroom at Paddington and we exchanged tickets. I collected her suitcase and brought it down by train. She seemed to expect that an attempt would be made to get it from me.'

It was Inspector Craddock's turn to grin. 'So she said when she rang up. I'm driving up to London to see her. Do you want to come, too, Mrs Harmon?'

'Wel-l,' said Bunch, considering. 'Wel-l, as a matter of fact, it's very fortunate. I had a toothache last night so I really ought to go to London to see the dentist, oughtn't I?'

'Definitely,' said Inspector Craddock . . .

Miss Marple looked from Inspector Craddock's face to the eager face of Bunch Harmon. The suitcase lay on the table. 'Of course, I haven't opened it,' the old lady said. 'I wouldn't dream of doing such a thing till somebody official arrived. Besides,' she added, with a demurely mischievous Victorian smile, 'it's locked.'

'Like to make a guess at what's inside, Miss Marple?' asked the Inspector.

'I should imagine, you know,' said Miss Marple, 'that it would be Zobeida's theatrical costumes. Would you like a chisel, Inspector?'

The chisel soon did its work. Both women gave a slight gasp as the lid flew up. The sunlight coming through the window lit up what seemed like an inexhaustible treasure of sparkling jewels, red, blue, green, orange.

'Aladdin's Cave,' said Miss Marple. 'The flashing jewels the girl wore to dance.'

'Ah,' said Inspector Craddock. 'Now, what's so precious about it, do you think, that a man was murdered to get hold of it?'

'She was a shrewd girl, I expect,' said Miss Marple thoughtfully. 'She's dead, isn't she, Inspector?'

'Yes, died three years ago.'

'She had this valuable emerald necklace,' said Miss Marple, musingly. 'Had the stones taken out of their setting and fastened here and there on her theatrical costume, where everyone would take them for merely coloured rhinestones. Then she had a replica made of the real necklace, and that, of course, was what was stolen. No wonder it never came on the market. The thief soon discovered the stones were false.'

'Here is an envelope,' said Bunch, pulling aside some of the glittering stones.

Inspector Craddock took it from her and extracted two official-looking papers from it. He read aloud, ' "Marriage certificate between Walter Edmund St John and Mary Moss." That was Zobeida's real name.'

'So they were married,' said Miss Marple. 'I see.'

'What's the other?' asked Bunch.

'A birth certificate of a daughter, Jewel.'

'Jewel?' cried Bunch. 'Why, of course. Jewel! *Jill!* That's it. I see now why he came to Chipping Cleghorn. *That*'s what he was trying to say to me. Jewel. The Mundys, you know. Laburnam Cottage. They look after a little girl for someone. They're devoted to her. She's been like their own granddaughter. Yes, I remember now, her name *was* Jewel, only, of course, they call her Jill.

'Mrs Mundy had a stroke about a week ago, and the old man's been very ill with pneumonia. They were both going to go to the Infirmary. I've been trying hard to find a good home for Jill somewhere. I didn't want her taken away to an institution.

'I suppose her father heard about it in prison and he managed to break away and get hold of this suitcase from the old dresser he or his wife left it with. I suppose if the jewels really belonged to her mother, they can be used for the child now.'

'I should imagine so, Mrs Harmon. *If* they're here.'

'Oh, they'll be here all right,' said Miss Marple cheerfully . . .

'Thank goodness you're back, dear,' said the Reverend Julian Harmon, greeting his wife with affection and a sigh of content. 'Mrs Burt always tries to do her best when you're away, but she really gave me some *very* peculiar fishcakes for lunch. I didn't want to hurt her feelings so I gave them to Tiglash Pileser, but even *he* wouldn't eat them so I had to throw them out of the window.'

'Tiglash Pileser,' said Bunch stroking the Vicarage cat, who was purring against her knee, 'is *very* particular about what fish he eats. I often tell him he's got a proud stomach!'

'And your tooth, dear? Did you have it seen to?'

'Yes,' said Bunch. 'It didn't hurt much, and I went to see Aunt Jane again, too . . .'

'Dear old thing,' said Julian. 'I hope she's not failing at all.'

'Not in the least,' said Bunch with a grin.

The following morning Bunch took a fresh supply of chrysanthemums to the church. The sun was once more pouring through the East window, and Bunch stood in the jewelled light on the chancel steps. She said very softly under her breath, 'Your little girl will be all right. *I'll* see that she is. I promise.'

Then she tidied up the church, slipped into a pew and knelt for a few moments to say her prayers before returning to the Vicarage to attack the piled-up chores of two neglected days.

The Treasure of Abbot Thomas

M. R. James

*Verum usque in præsentem diem multa garriunt inter se Canonici
de abscondito quodam istius Abbatis Thomæ thesauro, quem sæpe,
quanquam adhuc incassum, quæsiverunt Steinfeldenses. Ipsum enim
Thomam adhuc florida in ætate existentem ingentem auri massam cir-
ca monasterium defodisse perhibent; de quo multoties interrogatus ubi
esset, cum risu respondere solitus erat: 'Job, Johannes, et Zacharias vel
vobis vel posteris indicabunt'; idemque aliquando adiicere se inventuris
minime invisurum. Inter alia huius Abbatis opera, hoc memoria præ-
cipue dignum iudico quod fenestram magnam in orientali parte alæ
australis in ecclesia sua imaginibus optime in vitro depictis impleverit:
id quod et ipsius effigies et insignia ibidem posita demonstrant. Domum
quoque Abbatialem fere totam restauravit: puteo in atrio ipsius effosso
et lapidibus marmoreis pulchre cælatis exornato. Decessit autem, morte
aliquantulum subitanea perculsus, ætatis suæ anno lxxiido, incarna-
tionis veto Dominicæ mdxxixo.*

'I suppose I shall have to translate this,' said the antiquary to himself, as he finished copying the above lines from that rather rare and exceedingly diffuse book, the *Sertum Steinfeldense Norbertinum.* 'Well, it may as well be done first as last,' and accordingly the following rendering was very quickly produced:

Up to the present day there is much gossip among the Canons about a certain hidden treasure of this Abbot Thomas, for which those of Steinfeld have often made search, though hitherto in vain. The story is that Thomas, while yet in the vigour of life, concealed a very large quantity of gold somewhere in the monastery. He was often asked where it was, and always answered, with a laugh: 'Job, John, and Zechariah will tell either you or your successors.' He sometimes added that he should feel no grudge against those who might find it. Among other works carried out by this Abbot I may specially mention his filling the great window at the east end of the south aisle of the church with figures admirably painted on glass, as his effigy and arms in the window attest. He also restored almost the whole of the Abbot's lodging, and dug a well in the court of it, which he adorned with beautiful carvings in marble. He died rather suddenly in the seventy-second year of his age, A.D. 1529.

The object which the antiquary had before him at the moment was that of tracing the whereabouts of the painted windows of the Abbey Church of Steinfeld. Shortly after the Revolution, a very large quantity of painted glass made its way from the dissolved abbeys of Germany and Belgium to this country, and may now be seen adorning various of our parish churches, cathedrals, and private chapels. Steinfeld Abbey was among the most considerable of these involuntary contributors to our artistic possessions (I am quoting the somewhat ponderous preamble of the book which the antiquary wrote), and the greater part of the glass from that institution can be identified without much difficulty by the help, either of the numerous inscriptions in which the place is mentioned, or of the subjects of the windows, in which several well-defined cycles or narratives were represented.

The passage with which I began my story had set the antiquary on the track of another identification. In a private chapel – no matter where – he had seen three large figures, each occupying a whole light in a window, and evidently the work of one artist. Their style made it plain that that artist had been a German of the sixteenth century; but hitherto

the more exact localizing of them had been a puzzle. They represented –
will you be surprised to hear it? – Job Patriarcha, Johannes Evangelista,
Zacharias Propheta, and each of them held a book or scroll, inscribed with
a sentence from his writings. These, as a matter of course, the antiquary
had noted, and had been struck by the curious way in which they differed
from any text of the Vulgate that he had been able to examine. Thus the
scroll in Job's hand was inscribed: *'Auro est locus in quo absconditur'**
(for *'conflatur'*); on the book of John was: *'Habent in vestimentis suis
scripturam quam nemo novit'*† (for *'in vestimento scriptum'*, the following words being taken from another verse); and Zacharias had: *'Super
lapidem unum septem oculi sunt'*‡ (which alone of the three presents an
unaltered text).

A sad perplexity it had been to our investigator to think why these three
personages should have been placed together in one window. There was
no bond of connection between them, either historic, symbolic, or doctri-
nal, and he could only suppose that they must have formed part of a very
large series of Prophets and Apostles, which might have filled, say, all the
clerestory windows of some capacious church. But the passage from the
Sertum had altered the situation by showing that the names of the actual
personages represented in the glass now in Lord D—'s chapel had been
constantly on the lips of Abbot Thomas von Eschenhausen of Steinfeld,
and that this Abbot had put up a painted window, probably about the year
1520, in the south aisle of his abbey church. It was no very wild conjecture
that the three figures might have formed part of Abbot Thomas's offering;
it was one which, moreover, could probably be confirmed or set aside by
another careful examination of the glass. And, as Mr Somerton was a man
of leisure, he set out on pilgrimage to the private chapel with very little
delay. His conjecture was confirmed to the full. Not only did the style and
technique of the glass suit perfectly with the date and place required, but
in another window of the chapel he found some glass, known to have
been bought along with the figures, which contained the arms of Abbot
Thomas von Eschenhausen.

At intervals during his researches Mr Somerton had been haunted
by the recollection of the gossip about the hidden treasure, and, as he
thought the matter over, it became more and more obvious to him that

---

*There is a place for the gold where it is hidden.
†They have on their raiment a writing which no man knoweth.
‡Upon one stone are seven eyes.

if the Abbot meant anything by the enigmatical answer which he gave
to his questioners, he must have meant that the secret was to be found
somewhere in the window he had placed in the abbey church. It was
undeniable, furthermore, that the first of the curiously-selected texts on
the scrolls in the window might be taken to have a reference to hidden
treasure.

Every feature, therefore, or mark which could possibly assist in eluci-
dating the riddle which, he felt sure, the Abbot had set to posterity he
noted with scrupulous care, and, returning to his Berkshire manor-house,
consumed many a pint of the mid-night oil over his tracings and sketches.
After two or three weeks, a day came when Mr Somerton announced to
his man that he must pack his own and his master's things for a short
journey abroad, whither for the moment we will not follow him.

II

Mr Gregory, the Rector of Parsbury, had strolled out before breakfast,
it being a fine autumn morning, as far as the gate of his carriage-drive,
with intent to meet the postman and sniff the cool air. Nor was he disappointed of either purpose. Before he had had time to answer more than
ten or eleven of the miscellaneous questions propounded to him in the
lightness of their hearts by his young offspring, who had accompanied
him, the postman was seen approaching; and among the morning's
budget was one letter bearing a foreign postmark and stamp (which
became at once the objects of an eager competition among the youthful
Gregorys), and was addressed in an uneducated, but plainly an English
hand.

When the Rector opened it, and turned to the signature, he realized
that it came from the confidential valet of his friend and squire, Mr
Somerton. Thus it ran:

HONOURD SIR, –

Has I am in a great anxeity about Master I write at is Wish to
Beg you Sir if you could be so good as Step over. Master Has add a
Nastey Shock and keeps His Bedd. I never Have known Him like this
but No wonder and Nothing will serve but you Sir. Master says would
I mintion the Short Way Here is Drive to Cobblince and take a Trap.

Hopeing I Have maid all Plain, but am much Confused in Myself what with Anxiatey and Weakfulness at Night. If I might be so Bold Sir it will be a Pleasure to see a Honnest Brish Face among all These Forig ones.

I am Sir

Your obed[t] Serv[t]

WILLIAM BROWN.'

P.S. – The Village for Town I will not Turm It is name Steenfeld.'

The reader must be left to picture to himself in detail the surprise, confusion, and hurry of preparation into which the receipt of such a letter would be likely to plunge a quiet Berkshire parsonage in the year of grace 1859. It is enough for me to say that a train to town was caught in the course of the day, and that Mr Gregory was able to secure a cabin in the Antwerp boat and a place in the Coblentz train. Nor was it difficult to manage the transit from that centre to Steinfeld.

I labour under a grave disadvantage as narrator of this story in that I have never visited Steinfeld myself, and that neither of the principal actors in the episode (from whom I derive my information) was able to give me anything but a vague and rather dismal idea of its appearance. I gather that it is a small place, with a large church despoiled of its ancient fittings; a number of rather ruinous great buildings, mostly of the seventeenth century, surround this church; for the abbey, in common with most of those on the Continent, was rebuilt in a luxurious fashion by its inhabitants at that period. It has not seemed to me worth while to lavish money on a visit to the place, for though it is probably far more attractive than either Mr Somerton or Mr Gregory thought it, there is evidently little, if anything, of first-rate interest to be seen – except, perhaps, one thing, which I should not care to see.

The inn where the English gentleman and his servant were lodged is, or was, the only 'possible' one in the village. Mr Gregory was taken to it at once by his driver, and found Mr Brown waiting at the door. Mr Brown, a model when in his Berkshire home of the impassive whiskered race who are known as confidential valets, was now egregiously out of his element, in a light tweed suit, anxious, almost irritable, and plainly anything but master of the situation. His relief at the sight of the 'honest British face' of his Rector was unmeasured, but words to describe it were denied him. He could only say:

'Well, I ham pleased, I'm sure, sir, to see you. And so I'm sure, sir, will master.'

'How *is* your master, Brown?' Mr Gregory eagerly put in.

'I think he's better, sir, thank you; but he's had a dreadful time of it. I 'ope he's gettin' some sleep now, but –'

'What has been the matter – I couldn't make out from your letter? Was it an accident of any kind?'

'Well, sir, I 'ardly know whether I'd better speak about it. Master was very partickler he should be the one to tell you. But there's no bones broke – that's one thing I'm sure we ought to be thankful –'

'What does the doctor say?' asked Mr Gregory.

They were by this time outside Mr Somerton's bedroom door, and speaking in low tones. Mr Gregory, who happened to be in front, was feeling for the handle, and chanced to run his fingers over the panels. Before Brown could answer, there was a terrible cry from within the room.

'In God's name, who is that?' were the first words they heard. 'Brown, is it?'

'Yes, sir – me, sir, and Mr Gregory,' Brown hastened to answer, and there was an audible groan of relief in reply.

They entered the room, which was darkened against the afternoon sun, and Mr Gregory saw, with a shock of pity, how drawn, how damp with drops of fear, was the usually calm face of his friend, who, sitting up in the curtained bed, stretched out a shaking hand to welcome him.

'Better for seeing you, my dear Gregory,' was the reply to the Rector's first question, and it was palpably true.

After five minutes of conversation Mr Somerton was more his own man, Brown afterwards reported, than he had been for days. He was able to eat a more than respectable dinner, and talked confidently of being fit to stand a journey to Coblentz within twenty-four hours.

'But there's one thing,' he said, with a return of agitation which Mr Gregory did not like to see, 'which I must beg you to do for me, my dear Gregory. Don't,' he went on, laying his hand on Gregory's to forestall any interruption – 'don't ask me what it is, or why I want it done. I'm not up to explaining it yet; it would throw me back – undo all the good you have done me by coming. The only word I will say about it is that you run no risk whatever by doing it, and that Brown can and will show you tomorrow what it is. It's merely to put back – to keep – something... No; I can't speak of it yet. Do you mind calling Brown?'

'Well, Somerton,' said Mr Gregory, as he crossed the room to the door, 'I won't ask for any explanations till you see fit to give them. And if this bit of business is as easy as you represent it to be, I will very gladly undertake it for you the first thing in the morning.'

'Ah, I was sure you would, my dear Gregory; I was certain I could rely on you. I shall owe you more thanks than I can tell. Now, here is Brown. Brown, one word with you.'

'Shall I go?' interjected Mr Gregory.

'Not at all. Dear me, no. Brown, the first thing tomorrow morning – (you don't mind early hours, I know, Gregory) – you must take the Rector to – *there*, you know' (a nod from Brown, who looked grave and anxious), 'and he and you will put that back. You needn't be in the least alarmed; it's *perfectly* safe in the daytime. You know what I mean. It lies on the step, you know, where – where we put it.' (Brown swallowed dryly once or twice, and, failing to speak, bowed.) 'And – yes, that's all. Only this one other word, my dear Gregory. If you *can* manage to keep from questioning Brown about this matter, I shall be still more bound to you. Tomorrow evening, at latest, if all goes well, I shall be able, I believe, to tell you the whole story from start to finish. And now I'll wish you good night. Brown will be with me – he sleeps here – and if I were you, I should lock my door. Yes, be particular to do that. They – they like it, the people here, and it's better. Good night, good night.'

They parted upon this, and if Mr Gregory woke once or twice in the small hours and fancied he heard a fumbling about the lower part of his locked door, it was, perhaps, no more than what a quiet man, suddenly plunged into a strange bed and the heart of a mystery, might reasonably expect. Certainly he thought, to the end of his days, that he had heard such a sound twice or three times between midnight and dawn.

He was up with the sun, and out in company with Brown soon after. Perplexing as was the service he had been asked to perform for Mr Somerton, it was not a difficult or an alarming one, and within half an hour from his leaving the inn it was over. What it was I shall not as yet divulge.

Later in the morning Mr Somerton, now almost himself again, was able to make a start from Steinfeld; and that same evening, whether at Coblentz or at some intermediate stage on the journey I am not certain, he settled down to the promised explanation. Brown was present, but how much of the matter was ever really made plain to his comprehension he would never say, and I am unable to conjecture.

III

This was Mr Somerton's story:

'You know roughly, both of you, that this expedition of mine was undertaken with the object of tracing something in connection with some old painted glass in Lord D—'s private chapel. Well, the starting-point of the whole matter lies in this passage from an old printed book, to which I will ask your attention.'

And at this point Mr Somerton went carefully over some ground with which we are already familiar.

'On my second visit to the chapel,' he went on, 'my purpose was to take every note I could of figures, lettering, diamond-scratchings on the glass, and even apparently accidental markings. The first point which I tackled was that of the inscribed scrolls. I could not doubt that the first of these, that of Job – "There is a place for the gold where it is hidden" – with its intentional alteration, must refer to the treasure; so I applied myself with some confidence to the next, that of St John – "They have on their raiment a writing which no man knoweth." The natural question will have occurred to you: Was there an inscription on the robes of the figures? I could see none; each of the three had a broad black border to his mantle, which made a conspicuous and rather ugly feature in the window. I was nonplussed, I will own, and but for a curious bit of luck I think I should have left the search where the Canons of Steinfeld had left it before me. But it so happened that there was a good deal of dust on the surface of the glass, and Lord D—, happening to come in, noticed my blackened hands, and kindly insisted on sending for a Turk's head broom to clean down the window. There must, I suppose, have been a rough piece in the broom; anyhow, as it passed over the border of one of the mantles, I noticed that it left a long scratch, and that some yellow stain instantly showed up. I asked the man to stop his work for a moment, and ran up the ladder to examine the place. The yellow stain was there, sure enough, and what had come away was a thick black pigment, which had evidently been laid on with the brush after the glass had been burnt, and could therefore be easily scraped off without doing any harm. I scraped, accordingly, and you will hardly believe – no, I do you an injustice; you will have guessed already – that I found under this black pigment two or three clearly-formed capital letters in yellow stain on a clear ground. Of course, I could hardly contain my delight.

'I told Lord D— that I had detected an inscription which I thought might be very interesting, and begged to be allowed to uncover the whole of it. He made no difficulty about it whatever, told me to do exactly as I pleased, and then, having an engagement, was obliged – rather to my relief, I must say – to leave me. I set to work at once, and found the task a fairly easy one. The pigment, disintegrated, of course, by time, came off almost at a touch, and I don't think that it took me a couple of hours, all told, to clean the whole of the black borders in all three lights. Each of the figures had, as the inscription said, "a writing on their raiment which no man knoweth".

'This discovery, of course, made it absolutely certain to my mind that I was on the right track. And, now, what was the inscription? While I was cleaning the glass I almost took pains not to read the lettering, saving up the treat until I had got the whole thing clear. And when that *was* done, my dear Gregory, I assure you I could almost have cried from sheer disappointment. What I read was only the most hopeless jumble of letters that was ever shaken up in a hat. Here it is:

Job.   **DREVICIOPEDMOOMSMVIVLISLCAVIBASBATAOVT**

St John.   **RDIIEAMRLESIPVSPODSEEIRSETTAAESGIAVNNR**

Zechariah.   **FTEEAILNQDPVAIVMTLEEATTOHIOONVMCAAT.H.Q.E.**

'Blank as I felt and must have looked for the first few minutes, my disappointment didn't last long. I realized almost at once that I was dealing with a cipher or cryptogram; and I reflected that it was likely to be of a pretty simple kind, considering its early date. So I copied the letters with the most anxious care. Another little point, I may tell you, turned up in the process which confirmed my belief in the cipher. After copying the letters on Job's robe I counted them, to make sure that I had them right. There were thirty-eight; and, just as I finished going through them, my eye fell on a scratching made with a sharp point on the edge of the border. It was simply the number *xxxviii* in Roman numerals. To cut the matter short, there was a similar note, as I may call it, in each of the other lights; and that made it plain to me that the glass-painter had

had very strict orders from Abbot Thomas about the inscription, and had taken pains to get it correct.

'Well, after that discovery you may imagine how minutely I went over the whole surface of the glass in search of further light. Of course, I did not neglect the inscription on the scroll of Zechariah – "Upon one stone are seven eyes", but I very quickly concluded that this must refer to some mark on a stone which could only be found *in situ*, where the treasure was concealed. To be short, I made all possible notes and sketches and tracings, and then came back to Parsbury to work out the cipher at leisure. Oh, the agonies I went through! I thought myself very clever at first, for I made sure that the key would be found in some of the old books on secret writing. The *Steganographia* of Joachim Trithemius, who was an earlier contemporary of Abbot Thomas, seemed particularly promising; so I got that, and Selenius's *Cryptographia* and Bacon's *de Augmentis Scientiarum*, and some more. But I could hit upon nothing. Then I tried the principle of the "most frequent letter", taking first Latin and then German as a basis. That didn't help, either; whether it ought to have done so, I am not clear. And then I came back to the window itself, and read over my notes, hoping almost against hope that the Abbot might himself have somewhere supplied the key I wanted. I could make nothing out of the colour or pattern of the robes. There were no landscape backgrounds with subsidiary objects; there was nothing in the canopies. The only resource possible seemed to be in the attitudes of the figures. "Job," I read: "scroll in left hand, forefinger of right hand extended upwards. John: holds inscribed book in left hand; with right hand blesses, with two fingers. Zechariah: scroll in left hand; right hand extended upwards, as Job, but with three fingers pointing up." In other words, I reflected, Job has *one* finger extended, John has *two*, Zechariah has *three*. May not there be a numeral key concealed in that?' 'My dear Gregory,' said Mr Somerton, laying his hand on his friend's knee, 'that *was* the key. I didn't get it to fit at first, but after two or three trials I saw what was meant. After the first letter of the inscription you skip *one* letter, after the next you skip *two*, and after that skip *three*. Now look at the result I got. I've underlined the letters which form words:

DREVICIOPEDMOOMSMVIVLISLCAVIBASBATAOVT

RDIIEAMRLESIPVSPODSEEIRSETTAAESGIAVNNR

FTEEAILNQDPVAIVMTLEEATTOHIOONVMCAAT.H.Q.E.

'Do you see it? *"Decem millia auri reposita sunt in puteo in at ..."* (Ten thousand [pieces] of gold are laid up in a well in ...), followed by an incomplete word beginning *at*. So far so good. I tried the same plan with the remaining letters; but it wouldn't work, and I fancied that perhaps the placing of dots after the three last letters might indicate some difference of procedure. Then I thought to myself, "Wasn't there some allusion to a well in the account of Abbot Thomas in that book the *Sertum*?" Yes, there was: he built a *puteus in atrio* (a well in the court). There, of course, was my word *atrio*. The next step was to copy out the remaining letters of the inscription, omitting those I had already used. That gave what you will see on this slip:

RVIIOPDOOSMVVISCAVBSBTAOTDIEAMLSIVSPDEERSET
AEGIANRFEEALQDVAIMLEATTHOOVMCA.H.Q.E.

'Now, I knew what the three first letters I wanted were – namely, *rio* – to complete the word *atrio*; and, as you will see, these are all to be found in the first five letters. I was a little confused at first by the occurrence of two Is, but very soon I saw that every alternate letter must be taken in the remainder of the inscription. You can work it out for yourself; the result, continuing where the first "round" left off, is this:

rio domus abbatialis de Steinfeld a me, Thoma, qui posui custodem super ea. Gare à qui la touche.

'So the whole secret was out:

Ten thousand pieces of gold are laid up in the well in the court of the Abbot's house of Steinfeld by me, Thomas, who has set a guardian over them. *Gare à qui la touche.*

'The last words, I ought to say, are a device which Abbot Thomas had adopted. I found it with his arms in another piece of glass at Lord D—'s, and he drafted it bodily into his cipher, though it doesn't quite fit in point of grammar.

'Well, what would any human being have been tempted to do, my dear Gregory, in my place? Could he have helped setting off, as I did, to Steinfeld, and tracing the secret literally to the fountain-head? I don't believe he could. Anyhow, I couldn't, and as I needn't tell you, I found myself at Steinfeld as soon as the resources of civilization could put me there, and installed myself in the inn you saw. I must tell you that I was not altogether free from forebodings – on one hand of disappointment, on the other of danger. There was always the possibility that Abbot Thomas's well might have been wholly obliterated, or else that someone, ignorant of cryptograms, and guided only by luck, might have stumbled on the treasure before me. And then' – there was a very perceptible shaking of the voice here – 'I was not entirely easy, I need not mind confessing, as to the meaning of the words about the guardian of the treasure. But, if you don't mind, I'll say no more about that until – until it becomes necessary.

'At the first possible opportunity Brown and I began exploring the place. I had naturally represented myself as being interested in the remains of the abbey, and we could not avoid paying a visit to the church, impatient as I was to be elsewhere. Still, it did interest me to see the windows where the glass had been, and especially that at the east end of the south aisle. In the tracery lights of that I was startled to see some fragments and coats-of-arms remaining – Abbot Thomas's shield was there, and a small figure with a scroll inscribed *"Oculos habent, et non videbunt"* (They have eyes, and shall not see), which, I take it, was a hit of the Abbot at his Canons.

'But, of course, the principal object was to find the Abbot's house. There is no prescribed place for this, so far as I know, in the plan of a monastery; you can't predict of it, as you can of the chapter-house, that it will be on the eastern side of the cloister, or, as of the dormitory, that it will communicate with a transept of the church. I felt that if I asked many questions I might awaken lingering memories of the treasure, and I thought it best to try first to discover it for myself. It was not a very long or difficult search. That three-sided court south-east of the church, with deserted piles of building round it, and grass-grown pavement, which you saw this morning, was the place. And glad enough I was to see that it was put to no use, and was neither very far from our inn nor overlooked by any inhabited building; there were only orchards and paddocks on the slopes east of the church. I can tell you that fine stone glowed wonderfully in the rather watery yellow sunset that we had on the Tuesday afternoon.

'Next, what about the well? There was not much doubt about that, as you can testify. It is really a very remarkable thing. That curb is, I think, of Italian marble, and the carving I thought must be Italian also. There were reliefs, you will perhaps remember, of Eliezer and Rebekah, and of Jacob opening the well for Rachel, and similar subjects; but, by way of disarming suspicion, I suppose, the Abbot had carefully abstained from any of his cynical and allusive inscriptions.

'I examined the whole structure with the keenest interest, of course – a square well-head with an opening in one side; an arch over it, with a wheel for the rope to pass over, evidently in very good condition still, for it had been used within sixty years, or perhaps even later, though not quite recently. Then there was the question of depth and access to the interior. I suppose the depth was about sixty to seventy feet; and as to the other point, it really seemed as if the Abbot had wished to lead searchers up to the very door of his treasure-house, for, as you tested for yourself, there were big blocks of stone bonded into the masonry, and leading down in a regular staircase round and round the inside of the well.

'It seemed almost too good to be true. I wondered if there was a trap – if the stones were so contrived as to tip over when a weight was placed on them; but I tried a good many with my own weight and with my stick, and all seemed, and actually were, perfectly firm. Of course, I resolved that Brown and I would make an experiment that very night.

'I was well prepared. Knowing the sort of place I should have to explore, I had brought a sufficiency of good rope and bands of webbing to surround my body, and crossbars to hold to, as well as lanterns and candles and crowbars, all of which would go into a single carpet-bag and excite no suspicion. I satisfied myself that my rope would be long enough, and that the wheel for the bucket was in good working order, and then we went home to dinner.

'I had a little cautious conversation with the landlord, and made out that he would not be over-much surprised if I went out for a stroll with my man about nine o'clock, to make (Heaven forgive me!) a sketch of the abbey by moonlight. I asked no questions about the well, and am not likely to do so now. I fancy I know as much about it as anyone in Steinfeld: at least' – with a strong shudder – 'I don't want to know any more.

'Now we come to the crisis, and, though I hate to think of it, I feel sure, Gregory, that it will be better for me in all ways to recall it just as it happened. We started, Brown and I, at about nine with our bag, and attracted no attention; for we managed to slip out at the hinder end of the inn-yard into an alley which brought us quite to the edge of the village. In five minutes we were at the well, and for some little time we sat on the edge of the well-head to make sure that no one was stirring or spying on us. All we heard was some horses cropping grass out of sight farther down the eastern slope. We were perfectly unobserved, and had plenty of light from the gorgeous full moon to allow us to get the rope properly fitted over the wheel. Then I secured the band round my body beneath the arms. We attached the end of the rope very securely to a ring in the stonework. Brown took the lighted lantern and followed me; I had a crowbar. And so we began to descend cautiously, feeling every step before we set foot on it, and scanning the walls in search of any marked stone.

'Half aloud I counted the steps as we went down, and we got as far as the thirty-eighth before I noted anything at all irregular in the surface of the masonry. Even here there was no mark, and I began to feel very blank, and to wonder if the Abbot's cryptogram could possibly be an elaborate hoax. At the forty-ninth step the staircase ceased. It was with a very sinking heart that I began retracing my steps, and when I was back on the thirty-eighth – Brown, with the lantern, being a step or two above me – I scrutinized the little bit of irregularity in the stonework with all my might; but there was no vestige of a mark.

'Then it struck me that the texture of the surface looked just a little smoother than the rest, or, at least, in some way different. It might possibly be cement and not stone. I gave it a good blow with my iron bar. There was a decidedly hollow sound, though that might be the result of our being in a well. But there was more. A great flake of cement dropped on to my feet, and I saw marks on the stone underneath. I had tracked the Abbot down, my dear Gregory; even now I think of it with a certain pride. It took but a very few more taps to clear the whole of the cement away, and I saw a slab of stone about two feet square, upon which was engraven a cross. Disappointment again, but only for a moment. It was you, Brown, who reassured me by a casual remark. You said, if I remember right:

' "It's a funny cross; looks like a lot of eyes."

'I snatched the lantern out of your hand, and saw with inexpressible pleasure that the cross *was* composed of seven eyes, four in a vertical line, three horizontal. The last of the scrolls in the window was explained in the way I had anticipated. Here was my "stone with the seven eyes". So far the Abbot's data had been exact, and, as I thought of this, the anxiety about the "guardian" returned upon me with increased force. Still, I wasn't going to retreat now.

'Without giving myself time to think, I knocked away the cement all round the marked stone, and then gave it a prise on the right side with my crowbar. It moved at once, and I saw that it was but a thin light slab, such as I could easily lift out myself, and that it stopped the entrance to a cavity. I did lift it out unbroken, and set it on the step, for it might be very important to us to be able to replace it. Then I waited for several minutes on the step just above. I don't know why, but I think to see if any dreadful thing would rush out. Nothing happened. Next I lit a candle, and very cautiously I placed it inside the cavity, with some idea of seeing whether there were foul air, and of getting a glimpse of what was inside. There *was* some foulness of air which nearly extinguished the flame, but in no long time it burned quite steadily. The hole went some little way back, and also on the right and left of the entrance, and I could see some rounded light-coloured objects within which might be bags. There was no use in waiting. I faced the cavity, and looked in. There was nothing immediately in the front of the hole. I put my arm in and felt to the right, very gingerly . . .

'Just give me a glass of cognac, Brown. I'll go on in a moment, Gregory . . .

'Well, I felt to the right and my fingers touched something curved, that felt – yes – more or less like leather; dampish it was, and evidently part of a heavy, full thing. There was nothing, I must say, to alarm one. I grew bolder, and putting both hands in as well as I could, I pulled it to me, and it came. It was heavy, but moved more easily than I had expected. As I pulled it towards the entrance, my left elbow knocked over and extinguished the candle. I got the thing fairly in front of the mouth and began drawing it out. Just then Brown gave a sharp ejaculation and ran quickly up the steps with the lantern. He will tell you why in a moment. Startled as I was, I looked round after him, and saw him stand for a minute at the top and then walk away a few yards. Then I heard him call softly, "All right, sir," and went on pulling out the great bag, in complete darkness. It hung for an instant on the edge of the hole, then slipped forward on to my chest, and *put its arms round my neck*.

'My dear Gregory, I am telling you the exact truth. I believe I am now acquainted with the extremity of terror and repulsion which a man can endure without losing his mind. I can only just manage to tell you now the bare outline of the experience. I was conscious of a most horrible smell of mould, and of a cold kind of face pressed against my own, and moving slowly over it, and of several – I don't know how many – legs or arms or tentacles or something clinging to my body. I screamed out, Brown says, like a beast, and fell away backward from the step on which I stood, and the creature slipped downwards, I suppose, on to that same step. Providentially the band round me held firm. Brown did not lose his head, and was strong enough to pull me up to the top and get me over the edge quite promptly. How he managed it exactly I don't know, and I think he would find it hard to tell you. I believe he contrived to hide our implements in the deserted building near by, and with very great difficulty he got me back to the inn. I was in no state to make explanations, and Brown knows no German; but next morning I told the people some tale of having had a bad fall in the abbey ruins, which, I suppose, they believed. And now, before I go further, I should just like you to hear what Brown's experiences during those few minutes were. Tell the Rector, Brown, what you told me.'

'Well, sir,' said Brown, speaking low and nervously, 'it was just this way. Master was busy down in front of the 'ole, and I was 'olding the lantern and looking on, when I 'eard somethink drop in the water from the top, as I thought. So I looked up, and I see someone's 'ead lookin' over at us. I s'pose I must ha' said somethink, and I 'eld the light up and run up the steps, and my light shone right on the face. That was a bad un, sir, if ever I see one! A holdish man, and the face very much fell in, and larfin, as I thought. And I got up the steps as quick pretty nigh as I'm tellin' you, and when I was out on the ground there warn't a sign of any person. There 'adn't been the time for anyone to get away, let alone a hold chap, and I made sure he warn't crouching down by the well, nor nothink. Next thing I hear master cry out somethink 'orrible, and hall I see was him hanging out by the rope, and, as master says, 'owever I got him up I couldn't tell you.'

'You hear that, Gregory?' said Mr Somerton. 'Now, does any explanation of that incident strike you?'

The whole thing is so ghastly and abnormal that I must own it puts me quite off my balance; but the thought did occur to me that possibly the – well, the person who set the trap might have come to see the success of his plan.'

'Just so, Gregory, just so. I can think of nothing else so – *likely*, I should say, if such a word had a place anywhere in my story. I think it must have been the Abbot ... Well, I haven't much more to tell you.

I spent a miserable night, Brown sitting up with me. Next day I was no better; unable to get up; no doctor to be had; and, if one had been available, I doubt if he could have done much for me. I made Brown write off to you, and spent a second terrible night. And, Gregory, of this I am sure, and I think it affected me more than the first shock, for it lasted longer: there was someone or something on the watch outside my door the whole night. I almost fancy there were two. It wasn't only the faint noises I heard from time to time all through the dark hours, but there was the smell – the hideous smell of mould. Every rag I had had on me on that first evening I had stripped off and made Brown take it away. I believe he stuffed the things into the stove in his room; and yet the smell was there, as intense as it had been in the well; and, what is more, it came from outside the door. But with the first glimmer of dawn it faded out, and the sounds ceased, too; and that convinced me that the thing or things were creatures of darkness, and could not stand the daylight; and so I was sure that if anyone could put back the stone, it or they would be powerless until someone else took it away again. I had to wait until you came to get that done. Of course, I couldn't send Brown to do it by himself, and still less could I tell anyone who belonged to the place.

'Well, there is my story; and if you don't believe it, I can't help it. But I think you do.'

'Indeed,' said Mr Gregory, 'I can find no alternative. I *must* believe it! I saw the well and the stone myself, and had a glimpse, I thought, of the bags or something else in the hole. And, to be plain with you, Somerton, I believe my door was watched last night, too.'

'I dare say it was, Gregory; but, thank goodness, that is over. Have you, by the way, anything to tell about your visit to that dreadful place?'

'Very little,' was the answer. 'Brown and I managed easily enough to get the slab into its place, and he fixed it very firmly with the irons and wedges you had desired him to get, and we contrived to smear the surface with mud so that it looks just like the rest of the wall. One thing I did notice in the carving on the well-head, which I think must have escaped you. It was a horrid, grotesque shape – perhaps more like a toad than anything else, and there was a label by it inscribed with the two words, *"Depositum custodi"*.'*

---

*Keep that which is committed to thee.

The Convict and the Clerics

J. S. Fletcher

To a man who had just succeeded in escaping from prison, Brychester, in the still hours of an autumn morning, presented possibilities and opportunities which Medhurst, who had been a shrewd citizen of the world before he became a criminal, was quick to perceive and to take advantage of. Brychester itself was unique in its arrangements. One of the smallest of English cathedral cities, it was packed into very little room; you could walk round its enclosing walls within half an hour . . . It only possessed two streets; one ran from north to south, the other from east to west; they met at the Cross in the middle of the city, and there split it up into four quarters. There were little lanes and alleys in those four quarters; there were, also, at the backs of the old houses and mansions, large, roomy, leafy gardens. It was in one of these, a veritable wilderness, that Medhurst hid himself about three o'clock in the morning, after breaking out of the city gaol, which stood a mile away beyond the walls.

There had been very little of actual breaking out to be done. Medhurst, recently sentenced to a considerable term of penal servitude, consigned to Brychester Gaol to await eventual delivery to Dartmoor or Portland, had kept his observant eyes wide open from the moment he exchanged his own smart apparel for the dingy, arrow-ornamented garb of the convict. He was naturally a man of resource and ingenuity, and he meant to escape the unpleasant consequences of his misdeeds. Brychester Gaol was old-fashioned; its warders were a little slack in attending to their duties. And Medhurst watched his opportunity, and, by means of a little interference with the lock of his cell, and a watchful observation of the movements of men on night duty, and a carefully acquired knowledge of the outer works of his prison-house, managed to get free with little difficulty. And here he was, in the earliest hours of an October day, shivering a little, but eager and ready, in the summerhouse of a shady garden – wondering what to do next.

Medhurst's great immediate difficulty was that which confronts all convicts who break prison – his clothes. There was another in the lack of money, but the clothes problem was nearest and most important. If he only had clothes he could get away – he had no doubt he could get away even in a penniless condition. Of course, if he had money, he could get away all the more easily. But clothes were the prime necessity – and he reflected that they must be good. He was a man of exceptionally good presence – a tall, well set-up, rather distinguished-looking man, as many people had observed when he stood in the dock. He felt that he would be less conspicuous in really good attire – the use of which would be natural to him – than in, say, the garb of a navvy or of a labourer. One fact was certain, before daybreak he must find garments wherein to get out of Brychester. For reasons into which it is not necessary to enter, Medhurst believed that his escape would not be noticed until six o'clock in the morning. He had, therefore, three hours in which to do something. And, believing that if one has something to do, one should do it at once, he moved stealthily out of his hiding-place and began to examine his surroundings. He was able to make out that the old-fashioned garden in which he stood was one of several lying at the rear of a number of quaint-roofed houses, situated between the high walls of Brychester Cathedral – houses, in fact, tenanted by the principal ecclesiastical dignitaries. Surely, he thought, there must be some means of penetrating into one of these quiet residences, of obtaining sober and befitting raiment? At any rate, seeing that much depended on the matter, he would have a try for it.

It was very quiet, almost painfully quiet, in these cloistered shades. Once or twice Medhurst heard an owl hoot from its retreat in some ruinous building on the outskirts of the city; now and then he caught the screech of a railway whistle far off across the land; every quarter of an hour the silvery chime of the cathedral clock rang above his head. But he heard nothing of the heavy tread of the patrolling policeman; in these quiet gardens there seemed to be small fear of interference. He climbed a wall or two, made his way through a paling or two, looked round the rearward premises of one or two houses, always careful, always watching. And suddenly, in one of the largest houses, he found an open window. It was not much open – only an inch or two – but it gave Medhurst the very chance he wanted. In another minute he had raised the sash, squeezed himself through the aperture, and dropped quietly into what appeared to be a softly carpeted passage.

Medhurst had lately spent so much time in the dark that he had learnt how to see in it. This is an accomplishment which may certainly be acquired by anyone who cares to acquire it; all you have got to do is to wait with patience until you perceive that darkness is not quite so impenetrable as you believed it to be. Objects begin to reveal themselves – especially against windows – besides, there are gradations of darkness. Medhurst, bringing his skill to work, quickly found that he was in a side passage which led into a hall; in the hall he had come to a broad staircase. The carpeting of passage, hall and staircase was particularly thick and soft; nevertheless, Medhurst sat down on the bottom steps of the staircase and took off his prison footgear. For he was going upstairs – which is where raiment is usually to be found.

Big man though he was, Medhurst went up the stairs with less noise than a cat would have made. He blessed the builder of the house; here was no inferior wood to creak at the slightest pressure. He blessed the taste of the owner of the house, who evidently loved velvet-pile carpets. And he was beginning to wish that he had a light when he saw one.

It was certainly not much of a light – a mere crack that shone from a slightly opened door. Medhurst tip-toed to it through a silence as deep as that which no doubt reigned in the aisles of the adjacent cathedral. Here, again, was matter for hearty self-congratulation; the people of the house were evidently all sound sleepers. He arrived at the door, and listened. He peered through the slight opening, and saw that the light came from an oil-stove, partially turned on. He had an idea that this might be a nursery, and he listened more carefully than before, trying to catch the sound of a child's faint breathing. But, as he heard no sound at all, he gently pushed open the door until he could introduce his head and shoulders. And he saw that this was a dressing-room. He hesitated, listened intently, and glided across the threshold.

Always an adept at sizing up a situation, Medhurst saw the splendid possibilities of this as soon as he had given it one quick, all-comprehending glance. He was in the palace of the Lord Bishop of Brychester! There, duly laid out on a dressing-bench, all ready against the morning's toilet duties, were the episcopal garments – the breeches, the apron, the gaiters, the straight-cut coat. There was spotless linen, the round collar, the episcopal stock – there was everything. It was evident that the bishop, having taken his tub of a morning, had nothing to do but walk into this comfortably warmed dressing-room and array himself in his clothes.

'Bishops, however,' soliloquized Medhurst, 'have doubtless several changes of raiment. At any rate, his Lordship of Brychester won't find these togs here when he next wants them.'

For Medhurst saw his opportunity, his magnificent chance. He would go out of Brychester in episcopal attire; he would masquerade as the lawful bishop. He knew the bishop by sight – his lordship had visited the gaol during Medhurst's time. In build and appearance the convict and the ecclesiastic were not unlike. Both were tall, well-made, and athletic-looking men. This would do excellently – excellently! In the darkness of the autumn morning nobody would be able to tell the false from the true during the few minutes at the railway station which would be necessary. It was a veritable interposition of Providence.

Always keeping his ears cocked, Medhurst swiftly stripped off his convict garb, and got into the episcopal paraphernalia. He had a little trouble with the apron, and with the gaiters, and with the stock, but he was a handy man, quick of ideas and possessed of supple fingers, and in a very few minutes he found himself properly arrayed. There was a full-length mirror on one side of the room. He caught a glimpse of himself in the half light, and smiled complacently. But he smiled a great deal more when, turning to a dressing-table, he saw, lying upon its spotless cover, a sovereign, a half-sovereign, and a little silver. He gathered the coins together noiselessly, and deposited them in the episcopal breeches, feeling heartily thankful that their owner had emptied his pockets when he went to bed. Here, again, Providence certainly seemed to be favouring him.

Medhurst now wanted nothing but these very essential things: a muffler, an overcoat, and the Doctor of Divinity's hat which bishops always wear. These, he concluded, he would find in the hall, and he was about to set off in search of them when suddenly he caught sight of his convict's dress. It would never do to leave that about. Certainly it would come out in time – in a few hours really – that a convict had broken out of his gaol and into the palace, and had exchanged his clothes for the bishop's. But Medhurst desired that the knowledge should be restricted as long as possible. Here, again, he was favoured by an inspiration, and an opportunity. He saw a black handbag, inconspicuous and much worn, on the side of which was painted in faded white letters the words, 'The Bishop of Brychester'. He lifted this on to a chair, and opened it. Inside it he found a complete Norfolk jacket-suit of dark grey cloth, together with a cap of the same material, and certain accompaniments in the way of shirts, stockings, and ties. This, in fact, was the outfit which the bishop kept in readiness for golfing expeditions. Whenever he took such jaunts there was nothing to do but pick it up, and march off with it. Medhurst saw splendid possibilities in this. Without further delay he crammed his convict garb into an empty space, closed the bag, and carried it quietly down to the hall.

Here Medhurst took a risk. After remaining for some time at the foot of the stairs he ventured on striking a match. One tiny gleam of its light showed him the coat, the hat, the muffler. He put all these things on in the darkness. No sound came from above, or from around; the house was as quiet as ever. And so, fully equipped for his journey, Medhurst sat down on a chair close to the hall door – to wait.

Medhurst knew Brychester. In his pre-criminal days he had often visited the city; in fact, he had spent a week there just before his arrest. And he knew that an express train to London left Brychester station at ten minutes past four every morning, arriving at Victoria a few minutes before six. By that train he proposed to travel – in the character of the Lord Bishop of the Diocese. According to his reckonings, nobody would stir in the palace until six o'clock; it would be some time after that before the theft of the bishop's garments was discovered. Before any hue and cry could be roused he, Medhurst, would be safe in town. All that was necessary now was to wait until the cathedral clock chimed four; then he would let himself out, walk quietly through the Close into the little station, take his ticket, and be whirled away.

Medhurst found no difficulty in putting this theory into practice. On the first stroke of four he quietly opened the front door, picked up the handbag, and stole quietly away across the Close and through the deserted streets to the station. And there everything turned out even better than he had dared to hope. He had pulled down the beribboned brim of his episcopal hat; he had swathed his face up to the tip of his nose in the episcopal muffler; he had turned the collar of the episcopal overcoat up to his ears. There were few people about in the half-lighted station, and the clerk in the booking office, and the obsequious porter who possessed himself of the handbag, and opened the door of a first-class compartment, had not a doubt that the gentleman whom they sped on his journey was the Bishop of Brychester.

'And indeed I might almost begin to believe that I am he!' laughed Medhurst, when the train was sliding rapidly away over the dark country. 'I am he, at any rate, for two hours. But what's going to happen then?'

As a preliminary to further operations, he searched the pockets of the appropriated garments. He found nothing in them, however, but a few cards in a well-worn case. He was not sorry to find these cards; he foresaw that they might come in useful later on. Then he searched the bag again. There was nothing in it but what he had already seen – and his own broad-arrowed attire. He thought once of throwing that out of the window, then of hiding it under the cushions of the carriage; on second considerations, he closed the bag on it and the bishop's mufti.

The possession of that mufti gave Medhurst a new idea. He wanted to reach the house of an old friend in Kent, a friend whom he could fully trust, and who would certainly manage to get him secretly away to the Continent. This friend lived in a small village near Sevenoaks, a village so small that its inhabitants would certainly be excited if a bishop's apron and gaiters were seen in it. But they would not take undue notice of a gentleman in an inconspicuous Norfolk jacket and knickerbockers. Obviously, then, the thing to do was to make yet another change of attire.

When the express ran into Victoria, Medhurst seized his bag and made for a taxicab which stood almost opposite the point where his compartment had come to a halt. The light was of the early morning order; the chauffeur was half asleep. He saw what he considered to be an ecclesiastical gent in leggings and a queer hat, and sprang down and opened the door.

'Go round to the hotel,' said the supposed dignitary in muffled tones. The chauffeur drove round to the Grosvenor Hotel; his fare got out, took his bag, and spoke one word: 'Wait!'

The chauffeur touched his cap, and Medhurst walked into the hall, to be welcomed by an obsequious official who knew a bishop when he saw one.

'I wish,' said Medhurst, 'for a room in which I can change my clothes. And perhaps you can send me some coffee up to it? I – the fact is, I am going into the country this morning to play golf, and I wish to put on more suitable attire. I shall leave my bag here, and call for it – and to change my garments again – towards evening. You will, of course, charge the room to me for the day.'

Half an hour later Medhurst, much more comfortable in layman's garb, walked down to the hall, intending to re-enter his cab. But with his hand on the latch, he suddenly came to a dead halt. Through the glass panel of the door, he saw the taxicab moving off. And in it, just settling himself comfortably against the padded cushions, was – a bishop.

Medhurst glanced cautiously around him. There was nobody about in the hall beyond a servant or two engaged in domestic occupations. On its stand near the window of the office reposed the register wherein guests signed their names. Medhurst went over to it, swung its heavy covers open, and found the recent entries. There, under the date of the previous day, he read one line which, to him, stood out conspicuous from the rest.

'The Lord Bishop of Tuscaloosa and Mrs Sharpe-Benham.'

Medhurst closed the heavy book, and turned away chuckling quietly. He understood the situation now. And he began to thank his stars that an unusually gloomy morning, a sleepy chauffeur, and the presence at the hotel of a Colonial prelate who, no doubt, wished to get to some very early service, had made his own circumstances much easier. It was with a feeling of immense satisfaction that he walked out of the hotel, and strolled off into the unwonted liberty of the streets.

The chauffeur whom Medhurst had bidden to wait outside the hotel, had given no particular attention to his fare. He was not very well acquainted with the pecularities of clerical attire; certainly he could not tell a dean from an archdeacon, nor an archdeacon from a bishop. All he knew was that there were clergymen who wore what he called leggings, and had the brims of their hats tied to the crowns with bits of ribbon, and that these were big pots in their walk of life.

He saw his fare go into the hotel, and he believed it was his fare who came hurriedly out of the hotel twenty minutes later, who jumped quickly into the cab, and who bade him make all haste to St Paul's Cathedral. He had not the ghost of a notion that this was not his original fare at all, but was in reality the Bishop of Tuscaloosa, a Colonial prelate, just then in England, who was due at St Paul's at five minutes to seven o'clock, who had slightly overslept himself, and who, rushing out of his hotel, had leapt into the first vehicle he saw.

And when he set this genuine prelate down at St Paul's, and had a better opportunity of looking at him, he still believed him to be the man he had taken up just an hour before, when the Brychester express steamed into Victoria. The Bishop of Tuscaloosa glanced up at the clock of St Paul's, and turned to the chauffeur.

'I think you had better wait for me,' he said. 'I shall not be here very long, and then I want to be driven elsewhere.'

Even then nothing struck the chauffeur as being different. He merely glanced at the tall and athletic figure careering up the steps (Sharpe-Benham had been a noted man in the playing-fields in his ante-Colonial days), lighted his pipe, purchased a halfpenny morning paper from a passing itinerant, and settled himself down in his seat until the bishop had finished his business or his devotions. He was still reading the latest racing news when, forty minutes later, the bishop emerged from the cathedral in company with another clergyman. The other clergyman, as they came up to the cab, made some facetious remark about the wickedness of keeping taxicabs waiting while the meters ran on unchecked.

'I know – I know,' said the bishop. 'But the fact is, I am obliged to drive some distance into the East End, and this cab is so good and comfortable that I decided to keep it.'

The other clergyman laughed, shook hands, and went off in the direction of the deanery, and the bishop turned to the chauffeur.

'I want you,' he said, 'to drive me to St Hedwige's Church at East Ham. That's a long way, isn't it?'

The chauffeur folded up his newspaper, and crammed it into his pocket.

'Pretty tidy way that, sir,' he answered. 'Whereabout is this church, sir?'

'That we must find out when we get to East Ham,' said the bishop. 'But – I think I must have some breakfast before I go so far.' He paused, gazing wistfully around him at the tall buildings. 'I suppose there is no restaurant or anything of that sort about here?' he asked.

'Cannon Street Station Hotel just round the corner, sir,' suggested the chauffeur. 'Get breakfast there, sir.'

'That,' replied the bishop, getting into the cab, 'will do excellently. We will go there first, then.'

The chauffeur drove along to Cannon Street Station, pointed out the hotel entrance to his fare, and prepared to do more waiting. The bishop, who was a man of kindly nature, looked at his driver thoughtfully.

'Perhaps you, too, would like to breakfast?' he said. 'If so, pray do. I suppose I shall be three-quarters of an hour, at any rate.'

'Thank you, sir,' said the chauffeur. He glanced at the clock and saw that eight was about to strike. 'I'll be back here at twenty-to-nine, sir,' he went on. 'Ain't had no breakfast meself yet!' he added, with a grin.

The bishop smiled, nodded, and walked into the hotel. He was shown into the coffee-room with the politeness due to his dignity. He ordered his food, he asked for *The Times*, he settled himself quietly and comfortably to his breakfast, he took his time over it. The waiter who attended to him had given him a seat near the fire; the bishop, satisfied with his own immediate affairs, did not pay any attention to the other people in the room. And he certainly did not observe a rather large, official-faced sort of person who came quietly in, and, under cover of a general look round, contrived to eye him, the bishop, with a searching inspection.

At a quarter to nine o'clock the bishop laid aside *The Times* on one hand, and his napkin on the other, and inserted his fingers in the pocket wherein he usually carried his ready cash. To his horror, he found that there was no cash there. He hastily felt for his pocket-book, in which he kept a banknote or two in readiness for possible emergencies. But his pocket was empty – all his pockets were empty. Then he suddenly remembered that, in the hurry incident upon his belated arising that morning, he had left his loose cash, his purse, his pocket-book, all his trifles, on his dressing-table. It was awkward, but it was no great matter after all. He summoned the head waiter, who came forward with a respectful presentation of the bill.

'I am sorry, but I have left my purse and all my belongings at the Grosvenor Hotel where I am staying,' said the bishop. 'I left there very hastily this morning to keep an appointment at St Paul's. But I have a taxicab waiting for me downstairs, and I will send the driver at once to fetch my purse.'

The head waiter replied that that would be quite all right, and the bishop walked out of the room, a little vexed with himself for having slept ten minutes over his time. He went downstairs, and was about to step into the station, where he saw the taxicab awaiting him, when the official-faced person who had eyed him from the door of the coffee-room, and who had exchanged a word or two with the head waiter when the bishop walked out, came up from behind, and stopped him with a polite but frigid bow.

'May I have a word with you, sir?' he asked.

The bishop turned in surprise. There was a note of firmness in the man's voice which converted the request into something very like a command. The bishop, a man of spirit, felt his face flush a little.

'You wish to speak to me?' he said.

'If you please,' replied the man. He indicated the door of a side room, and bowed the bishop within. 'I am sorry,' he continued, in the same firm and frigid tone; 'I understand your bill is not paid?'

The bishop's first flush changed to something more vivid.

'Really!' he exclaimed. 'This is –' But there he pulled himself up; after all, the fault was his own. 'I have just explained to your head waiter that I am sending for my purse,' he continued. 'I left it on my dressing-table, being in a hurry this morning. I have a taxicab outside – the driver will fetch what I want.'

The official-faced person still seemed very firm. He glanced at the episcopal apron.

'You are the Bishop of –' he began.

'I am the Bishop of Tuscaloosa,' answered the captive, with some asperity.

'Where is that?' demanded the inquisitor, more firmly than ever.

'Really, really!' exclaimed the bishop. 'This is – my good man, do you really suggest that –'

'I suggest nothing,' replied the other. 'I am merely asking for information. You come here, run up a bill, leave without paying it, and – to be plain – I may as well tell you that I am a police officer. The fact of the case is,' he went on, as another formidable-looking person entered the room, 'the fact of the case is, the palace of the Bishop of Brychester was broken into early this morning by an escaped convict, who is believed to have got away by the four o'clock train from Brychester in the bishop's clothes. Now you answer the description of that convict.'

The bishop felt as if he were suddenly deprived of speech. Just as suddenly he laughed.

'My good sir!' he exclaimed. 'This is ridiculous! Utterly ridiculous! I am the Bishop of Tuscaloosa, which is in Canada. I am at present staying at the Grosvenor Hotel; I have just come up from St Paul's Cathedral, where I am well known to many members of the Chapter. The chauffeur who is without will tell you that he has just driven me from the Grosvenor Hotel, and –'

The first man made a sign to the second, who left the room, and instantly returned with the driver of the taxicab. The first man directed the driver's attention to the bishop.

'Where did you drive this gentleman from?' he asked peremptorily.

The driver glanced at all three with signs of rising suspicion.

'Well, from St Paul's last,' he answered, 'and before that from the Grosvenor Hotel, and before that from Victoria Station!'

The bishop started.

'From Victoria Station!' he exclaimed. 'My good fellow, you did not drive me from Victoria Station! You drove me –'

The driver became actively suspicious; so far he had not seen the colour of the bishop's money. Besides, he had waited twenty minutes outside the Grosvenor.

'Ho, didn't I!' he exclaimed. 'I suppose I didn't drive you round from Victoria 'rival platform to the Grosvenor, did I, where I waited twenty minutes for yer? Oh, no!' He made a derisive face, seeing how things were going, and turned to the two men.

'He come into Victoria by the Brychester express,' he continued. 'That what gets in just afore six – course he did!'

The detectives closed in upon the unhappy bishop. There was no doubt in their minds that they had effected a smart, if lucky, capture. And it was only in accordance with the nature of things that they conveyed their captive there and then to the nearest police station.

Medhurst strolled away from the hotel towards Victoria Street, thinking. His next move, he reflected, ought to be towards definite liberty. Already the discovery of his nocturnal doings at Brychester Palace would have been made. Well – it would take some little time for the local police to communicate with London. It would be found out – nothing more easy – that he had left Brychester by the four o'clock train; very good, but even then he reckoned that he still had an hour or two's start of everything. The first thing to do was to get to his trusty friend. And he suddenly remembered that the trusty friend had an office in London, close to the Mansion House. Why not go there instead of running the risk of a railway journey into Kent? The principal stations would be watched; he had better keep away from them until he had effected yet another change of clothes.

Medhurst accordingly made for the City. He turned into the Underground Railway, and took a ticket for the Mansion House. Amongst the early crowd of men going to shops and offices he would feel himself safe; however anxious to recapture him the police might be, they could not set patrols in every street of London. He would stroll about the City until nine o'clock or so, when his friend would be likely to put in an appearance – Medhurst remembered that the friend was an early bird, who came up by one of the first trains. He felt no fear now – it seemed to him that all was going very well indeed.

In the Underground train Medhurst made an interesting discovery. In the breast-pocket of the Norfolk jacket he found a cigar-case. There were four uncommonly fine cigars in it – he at once lighted one, with the keen zest and enjoyment of a man who had not tasted tobacco for long, weary weeks. But as he was examining the case, before restoring it to his pocket, he found something else. In a slip-pocket, obviously designed to carry stamps or similar small articles, he found a couple of blank cheques of the Brychester and County Bank. Their lawful owner, the bishop, was evidently a careful man, who provided for unforeseen contingencies; he carried a blank cheque in case he should want cash; anybody, of course, will cash a cheque for a bishop.

Medhurst laughed over this discovery. It was, however, of no particular interest to him just then, and he put the cheques back in their place, and the cigar-case in his pocket, and smoked in great contentment until he came to the Mansion House Station. There he got out and went up into the streets, which were already beginning to be busy.

It was immaterial to him where he went for the next hour or so; accordingly he loafed around anywhere, but took good care always to be moving, as if with a purpose. He went along by the Bank, and round by the Guildhall, and into Aldersgate, and through various small streets into Smithfield; there he turned south, and made his way into Ludgate Hill. And loafing about there he paused to gaze into the window of a bookseller's shop, and before he was aware of it he found himself staring at a book which stood with title-page and frontispiece exposed, on a shelf immediately in front of him. The title-page conveyed the information that this was a work on Athletics and Christianity, by the Lord Bishop of Brychester; the frontispiece was a photogravure of the right reverend author. And underneath it was a facsimile of the bishop's signature.

Medhurst was a man of rapid thought, and he was temperamentally quick at seizing opportunities. He saw a fine opportunity immediately before him. In his pocket reposed two of the Bishop of Brychester's blank cheques, there before him was a very good reproduction of the bishop's autograph. A rare opportunity, indeed; for Medhurst was an expert imitator of other people's handwriting. That, indeed, was why he had come into contact with the law. Those who had administered the law in his case had been so struck by his expertness, in fact, that they had judged it well to consign him for a good many years to regions where his ability would be stultified. And the judge who had announced his fate to him had been unkind enough to remark, in dry and laconic fashion, that within the memory of man forgers had made the acquaintance of the scaffold and the hangman.

Medhurst walked into the shop, fingering his loose change. His keen sense of humour made him smile as he bought the bishop's book with the bishop's own money. It was a small, thin, genteel book – merely a reprint of two or three lectures given to young men – and he slipped it into his outer pocket and went away. Pursuing his previous plan, he continued to stroll about the streets, up one, down another, always keeping within easy reach of the block of buildings near the Mansion House, in which his trusted friend had his office. But Medhurst had a task to perform, an adventure to undertake, before he went to his friend – he was going to make use of his criminal facility of imitating penmanship.

He turned into a teashop at last, and ordered a light breakfast. While it was being brought to him he carefully studied the facsimile of the Bishop of Brychester's signature. It was an easy signature to imitate, there were no marked peculiarities in it; it was not the writing of a literary man, nor of a scholar, but rather of a business-like, straightforward sort, without twirls, flourishes, or elongated downstrokes. By the time Medhurst had finished his simple breakfast he knew that handwriting so well, had so photographed it on his brain, that he had no fear of being able to write out a cheque in such accurate imitation of it that the bishop himself would be puzzled in detecting the forgery.

Medhurst went straight to business. He had already thought of a well-known jeweller's shop in Cheapside where he could do what he wanted; it had the great advantage of being practically next door to the block of buildings into which he meant to disappear as soon as his proposed transaction was safely over. He entered the jeweller's shop with all the assurance in the world, and was politely greeted by a manager who, seeing a soberly attired gentleman in a clerical collar, set his customer down as a country parson who had come to town in his rustic garb. But Medhurst quickly disabused the manager of that impression. Drawing out the well-worn card-case, he laid one of the Bishop of Brychester's cards on the glass-topped counter. The manager bowed again, more politely than before, and gave his episcopal visitor a seat.

'I have frequently seen your watches advertised,' said the supposed bishop, 'and, as I have a little time to spare before going into the country to play golf, I thought I would call and inspect them. The fact is, I want to make a present to my domestic chaplain, who has just been preferred to a living, and I think a good watch – gold, of course – would be the best thing I could give him. As I say, I have noticed your advertisements in the newspapers. I believe you have a very good keyless hunter-watch at about – something under forty pounds?'

The manager hastened to lay before his customer a variety of gold watches of many prices. Medhurst examined them with interest and with care, talking pleasantly all the time. Eventually he selected an elegant and useful article which was priced at thirty-three guineas. And upon that he produced one of the blank cheques. 'I will make out this cheque for fifty pounds,' he remarked as the manager handed him writing materials. 'Perhaps you can give me change?'

'With pleasure, my lord,' responded the manager. He had no doubt of his visitor's identity. Had he not received the bishop's card? Was there not lying there beside the bishop's gloves a copy of a book, *Athletics and Christianity*, with the bishop's name upon it? He handed over fifteen pounds and seven shillings, and thanked his supposed lordship for his custom.

Medhurst made his most dignified bow, and put on his blandest smile. He glanced at a timepiece hanging behind the counter, and began to hurry.

'Dear me!' he exclaimed. 'I have left myself little time to catch my train at Cannon Street. I must hasten.'

The manager swept round the counter, and opened the door with a deep reverence.

'Just round the corner, my lord,' he said. 'Your lordship will do it in two minutes.'

Medhurst smiled and nodded, and passed swiftly out. He certainly went round the corner which the manager indicated. Then he went round another corner, and round another. And then he plunged into a block of buildings contrived on the principle of a rabbit-warren. Within five minutes of leaving the jeweller's shop he was in the private office of the trusty friend, who had just admitted himself, and now made great haste to lock the door on both of them.

Meanwhile the jeweller's manager, having watched the supposed bishop round the corner, went back into the shop, rubbing his hands with satisfaction at having started the day so well.

Suddenly he caught sight of the book and the gloves – entirely for-gotten by Medhurst – which still lay on the counter. He snatched them up, shouted a word to his assistants, and ran after the customer. He careered down Bucklersbury, he shot across Queen Victoria Street, he raced along Walbrook, he made a perilous dash over Cannon Street and into the station. He was almost breathless when he ran up to the barrier of the departure platform, staring about him.

'Have you seen a bishop pass in?' he panted as he approached the ticket-puncher. 'Tall gentleman – Bishop of Brychester!'

The ticket-puncher gave the jeweller's manager a glance.

'There was a party what called himself Bishop of Brychester arrested here this morning!' he growled. 'Bilked the 'otel, he did. Stuffed himself, and had nothing to pay with – that's what 'e done! D'yer want 'im? 'Cause you'll find him round at the p'leece station.'

The jeweller's manager suddenly felt very ill. His head swam. He walked away. Then he recovered just as suddenly. The bilker could not be the same man who had just visited him – impossible! Still, it would not be out of his way to visit the police station. He knew some of the officials there, and he went off to them and told his story. What he wanted to know was – how did this extraordinary coincidence come about?

The police official to whom the manager told his story listened in silence – in silence he remained for some minutes.

'Happened just now?' he suddenly asked.

'Within half an hour,' answered the manager. He smiled bravely. 'Of course,' he said, 'mine was the real bishop. But – who's your man – who's the impostor?'

The official crooked his finger.

'Come this way!' he said.

He led the manager to a certain stronghold, wherein the unhappy Bishop of Tuscaloosa was still expostulating with his incredulous guardians. But even as they entered it by one door, there was ushered in at another a very great ecclesiastical dignitary, as familiar in the City as St Paul's itself, at sight of whom everybody in the room became profoundly respectful.

He advanced upon the Colonial prelate with outstretched hands.

'My dear bishop!' he exclaimed. 'What a lamentable – what a ridiculous mistake! What an unfortunate –'

The police official who had conducted the jeweller's manager into the room suddenly swept him out of it.

'Quick – quick!' he said. 'Come and describe that fellow you've told me about! That's the real man! We must be on to him sharp! Come on! Where did you say he was off to? But, of course, he hasn't gone there – not he!'

In that the police official was quite right. At that moment Medhurst, who had already effected another change of clothes, was being quietly carried away to a reasonable prospect of ultimate liberty.

The Hanging of Alfred Wadham

E. F. Benson

I had been telling Father Denys Hanbury about a very extraordinary séance which I had attended a few days before. The medium in trance had said a whole series of things which were unknown to anybody but myself and a friend of mine who had lately died, and who, so she said, was present and was speaking to me through her. Naturally, from the strictly scientific point of view in which alone we ought to approach such phenomena, such information was not really evidence that the spirit of my friend was in touch with her, for it was already known to me, and might by some process of telepathy have been communicated to the medium from my brain and not through the agency of the dead. She spoke, too, not in her own ordinary voice, but in a voice which certainly was very like his. But his voice was also known to me; it was in my memory even as were the things she had been saying. All this, therefore, as I was remarking to Father Denys, must be ruled out as positive evidence that communications had been coming from the other side of death.

'A telepathic explanation was possible,' I said, 'and we have to accept any known explanation which covers the facts before we conclude that the dead have come back into touch with the material world.'

The room was quite warm, but I saw that he shivered slightly and, hitching his chair a little nearer the fire, he spread out his hands to the blaze. Such hands they were: beautiful and expressive of him, and so like the praying hands of Albert Dürer: the blaze shone through them as through rose-red alabaster. He shook his head.

'It's a terribly dangerous thing to attempt to get into communication with the dead,' he said. 'If you seem to get into touch with them you run the risk of establishing connection not with them but with awful and perilous intelligences. Study telepathy by all means, for that is one of the marvels of the mind which we are meant to investigate like any other of the wonderful secrets of Nature. But I interrupt you: you said something else occurred. Tell me about it.'

Now I knew Father Denys's creed about such things and deplored it. He holds, as his Church commands him, that intercourse with the spirits of the dead is impossible, and that when it appears to occur, as it undoubtedly does, the enquirer is really in touch with some species of dramatic demon, who is impersonating the spirit of the dead. Such a thing has always seemed to me as monstrous as it is without foundation, and there is nothing I can discover in the recognized sources of Christian doctrine which justifies such a view.

'Yes: now comes the queer part,' I said. 'For, still speaking in the voice of my friend the medium told me something which instantly I believed to be untrue. It could not therefore have been drawn telepathically from me. After that the séance came to an end, and in order to convince myself that this could not have come from him, I looked up the diary of my friend which had been left me at his death, and which had just been sent me by his executors, and was still unpacked. There I found an entry which proved that what the medium had said was absolutely correct. A certain thing – I needn't go into it – had occurred precisely as she had stated, though I should have been willing to swear to the contrary. That cannot have come into her mind from mine, and there is no source that I can see from which she could have obtained it except from my friend. What do you say to that?'

He shook his head.

'I don't alter my position at all,' he said. 'That information, given it did not come from your mind, which certainly seems to be impossible, came from some discarnate agency. But it didn't come from the spirit of your friend: it came from some evil and awful intelligence.'

'But isn't that pure assumption?' I asked. 'It is surely much simpler to say that the dead can, under certain conditions, communicate with us. Why drag in the devil?'

He glanced at the clock.

'It's not very late,' he said. 'Unless you want to go to bed, give me your attention for half-an-hour, and I will try to show you.'

The rest of my story is what Father Denys told me, and what happened immediately afterwards.

'Though you are not a Catholic,' he said, 'I think you would agree with me about an institution which plays a very large part in our ministry, namely Confession, as regards the sacredness and the inviolability of it. A soul laden with sin comes to his Confessor knowing that he is speaking to one who has the power to pronounce or withhold forgiveness, but who will never, for any conceivable reason, repeat or hint at what has been told him. If there was the slightest chance of the penitent's confession being made known to anyone, unless he himself, for purposes of expiation or of righting some wrong, chooses to repeat it, no one would ever come to Confession at all. The Church would lose the greatest hold it possesses over the souls of men, and the souls of men would lose that inestimable comfort of knowing (not hoping merely, but knowing) that their sins are forgiven them. Of course the priest may withhold absolution, if he is not convinced that he is dealing with a true penitent, and before he gives it, he will insist that the penitent makes such reparation as is in his power for the wrong he has done. If he has profited by his dishonesty he must make good: whatever crime he has committed he must give warrant that his penitence is sincere. But I think you would agree that in any case the priest cannot, whatever the result of his silence may be, repeat what has been told him. By doing so he might right or avert some hideous wrong, but it is impossible for him to do so. What he has heard, he has heard under the seal of confession, concerning the sacredness of which no argument is conceivable.'

'It is possible to imagine awful consequences resulting from it,' I said. 'But I agree.'

'Before now awful consequences have come of it,' he said, 'but they don't touch the principle. And now I am going to tell you of a certain confession that was once made to me.'

'But how can you?' I said. 'That's impossible, surely.'

'For a certain reason, which we shall come to later,' he said, 'you will see that secrecy is no longer incumbent on me. But the point of my story is not that: it is to warn you about attempting to establish communication with the dead. Signs and tokens, voices and apparitions appear to come through to us from them, but who sends them? You will see what I mean.'

I settled myself down to listen.

'You will probably not remember with any distinctness, if at all, a murder committed a year ago, when a man called Gerald Selfe met his death. There was no enticing mystery about it, no romantic accessories, and it aroused no public interest. Selfe was a man of loose life, but he held a respectable position, and it would have been disastrous for him if his private irregularities had come to light. For some time before his death he had been receiving blackmailing letters regarding his relations with a certain married woman, and, very properly, he had put the matter into the hands of the police. They had been pursuing certain clues, and on the afternoon before Selfe's death one of the officers of the Criminal Investigation Department had written to him that everything pointed to his manservant, who certainly knew of his intrigue, being the culprit. This was a young man named Alfred Wadham: he had only lately entered Selfe's service, and his past history was of the most unsavoury sort. They had baited a trap for him, of which details were given, and suggested that Selfe should display it, which, within an hour or two, he successfully did. This information and these instructions were conveyed in a letter which after Selfe's death was found in a drawer of his writing-table, of which the lock had been tampered with. Only Wadham and his master slept in his flat; a woman came in every morning to cook breakfast and do the housework, and Selfe lunched and dined at his club, or in the restaurant on the ground floor of this house of flats, and here he dined that night. When the woman came in next morning she found the outer door of the flat open, and Selfe lying dead on the floor of his sitting-room with his throat cut. Wadham had disappeared, but in the slop-pail of his bedroom was water which was stained with human blood. He was caught two days afterwards and at his trial elected to give evidence. His story was that he suspected he had fallen into a trap, and that while Mr Selfe was at dinner he searched his drawers and found the letter sent by the police, which proved that this was the case. He therefore decided to bolt, and he left the flat that evening before his master came back to it after dinner. Being in the witness-box, he was of course subjected to a searching cross-examination, and contradicted himself in several particulars. Then there was that incriminating evidence in his room, and the motive for the crime was clear enough. After a very long deliberation the jury found him guilty, and he was sentenced to death. His appeal which followed was dismissed.'

'Wadham was a Catholic, and since it is my office to minister to Catholic prisoners at the gaol where he was lying under sentence of death, I had many talks with him, and entreated him for the sake of his immortal soul to confess his guilt. But though he was even eager to confess other misdeeds of his, some of which it was ugly to speak of, he maintained his innocence on this charge of murder. Nothing shook him, and though as far as I could judge he was sincerely penitent for other misdeeds, he swore to me that the story he told in court was, in spite of the contradictions in which he had involved himself, essentially true, and that if he was hanged he died unjustly. Up till the last afternoon of his life, when I sat with him for two hours, praying and pleading with him, he stuck to that. Why he should do that, unless indeed he was innocent, when he was eager to search his heart for the confession of other gross wickednesses, was curious; the more I pondered it, the more inexplicable I found it, and during that afternoon doubt as to his guilt began to grow in me. A terrible thought it was, for he had lived in sin and error, and tomorrow his life was to be broken like a snapped stick. I was to be at the prison again before six in the morning, and I still had to determine whether I should give him the Sacrament. If he went to his death guilty of murder, but refusing to confess, I had no right to give it him, but if he was innocent, my withholding of it was as terrible as any miscarriage of justice. Then on my way out I had a word with one of the warders, which brought my doubt closer to me.

' "What do you make of Wadham?" I asked.

'He drew aside to let a man pass, who nodded to him: somehow I knew that he was the hangman.

' "I don't like to think of it, sir," he said. "I know he was found guilty, and that his appeal failed. But if you ask me whether I believe him to be a murderer, why no, I don't."

'I spent the evening alone: about ten o'clock as I was on the point of going to bed, I was told that a man called Horace Kennion was below, and wanted to see me. He was a Catholic, and though I had been friends with him at one time, certain things had come to my knowledge which made it impossible for me to have anything more to do with him, and I had told him so. He was wicked – oh, don't misunderstand me; we all do wicked things constantly; the life of us all is a tissue of misdeeds but he alone of all men I had ever met seemed to me to love wickedness for its own sake. I said I could not see him, but the message came back that his need was urgent, and up he came. He wanted, he told me, to make his confession, not tomorrow, but now, and his confessor was away. I could not, as a priest, resist that appeal. And his confession was that he had killed Gerald Selfe.

'For a moment I thought this was some impious joke, but he swore he was speaking the truth, and still under the seal of Confession gave me a detailed account. He had dined with Selfe that night, and had gone up afterwards to his flat for a game of piquet. Selfe told him with a grin that he was going to lay his servant by the heels tomorrow for blackmail. "A smart spry young man today," he said. "Perhaps a bit off colour tomorrow at this time." He rang the bell for him to put out the card-table: then saw it was ready, and he forgot that his summons remained unanswered. They played high points and both had drunk a good deal. Selfe lost partie after partie and eventually accused Kennion of cheating. Words ran high and boiled over into blows, and Kennion, in some rough and tumble of wrestling and hitting, picked up a knife from the table and stabbed Selfe in the throat, through jugular vein and carotid artery. In a few minutes he had bled to death . . . Then Kennion remembered that unanswered bell, and went on tiptoe to Wadham's room. He found it empty; empty, too, were the other rooms in the flat. Had there been anyone there, his idea was to say he had come up at Selfe's invitation, and found him dead. But this was better yet: there was no more than a few spots of blood on him, and he washed them in Wadham's room, emptying the water into his slop-pail. Then leaving the door of the flat open he went downstairs and out.

'He told me this in quite a few sentences, even as I have told it you, and looked up at me with a smiling face.

' "So what's to be done next, Venerable Father?" he said gaily.

' "Ah, thank God you've confessed!" I said. "We're in time yet to save an innocent man. You must give yourself up to the police at once." But even as I spoke my heart misgave me.

'He rose, dusting the knees of his trousers.

' "What a quaint notion," he said. "There's nothing further from my thoughts."

'I jumped up.

' "I shall go myself then," I said.

'He laughed outright at that.

' "Oh, no, indeed you won't," he said. "What about the seal of Confession? Indeed, I rather fancy it's a deadly sin for a priest ever to think of violating it. Really I'm ashamed of you, my dear Denys. Naughty fellow! But perhaps it was only a joke; you didn't mean it."

' "I do mean it," I said. "You shall see if I mean it." But even as I spoke, I knew I did not. "Anything is allowable to save an innocent man from death."

'He laughed again.

' "Pardon me: you know perfectly well, that it isn't," he said. "There's one thing in our creed far worse than death, and that is the damnation of the soul. You've got no intention of damning yours. I took no risk at all when I confessed to you."

' "But it will be murder if you don't save this man," I said.

' "Oh, certainly, but I've got murder on my conscience already," he said. "One gets used to it very quickly. And having got used to it, another murder doesn't seem to matter an atom. Poor young Wadham: tomorrow isn't it? I'm not sure it won't be a sort of rough justice. Blackmail is a disgusting offence."

'I went to the telephone, and took off the receiver.

' "Really this is most interesting," he said. "Walton Street is the nearest police-station. You don't need the number: just say Walton Street Police. But you can't. You can't say 'I have a man with me now, Horace Kennion, who has confessed to me that he murdered Selfe.' So why bluff? Besides, if you could do any such thing, I should merely say that I had done nothing of the kind. Your word, the word of a priest who has broken the most sacred vow, against mine. Childish!"

' "Kennion," I said, "for the love of God, and for the fear of hell, give yourself up! What does it matter whether you or I live a few years less, if at the end we pass into the vast infinite with our sins confessed and forgiven. Day and night I will pray for you."

' "Charming of you," said he. "But I've no doubt that now you will give Wadham full absolution. So what does it matter if he goes into – into the vast infinite at eight o'clock tomorrow morning?"

' "Why did you confess to me then," I asked, "if you had no intention of saving him, and making atonement?"

' "Well, not long ago you were very nasty to me," he said. "You told me no decent man would consort with me. So it struck me, quite suddenly, only today, that it would be pleasant to see you in the most awful hole. I daresay I've got Sadic tastes, too, and they are being wonderfully indulged. You're in torment, you know: you would choose any physical agony rather than to be in such a torture-chamber of the soul. It's entrancing: I adore it. Thank you very much, Denys."

'He got up.

' "I kept my taxi waiting," he said. "No doubt you'll be busy tonight. Can I give you a lift anywhere? Pentonville?"

'There are no words to describe certain darknesses and ecstasies that come to the soul, and I can only tell you that I can imagine no hell of remorse that could equal the hell that I was in. For in the bitterness of remorse we can see that our suffering is a needful and salutary experience: only through it can our sin be burned away. But here was a torture blank and meaningless ... And then my brain stirred a little, and I began to wonder whether, without breaking the seal of Confession, I might not be able to effect something. I saw from my window that the light was burning in the clock-tower at Westminster: the House therefore was sitting, and it seemed possible that without violation I might tell the Home Secretary that a confession had been made me, whereby I knew that Wadham was innocent. He would ask me for any details I could give him, and I could tell him – And then I saw that I could tell him nothing: I could not say that the murderer had gone up with Selfe to his room, for through that information it might be found that Kennion had dined with him. But before I did anything, I must have guidance, and I went to the Cardinal's house by our Cathedral. He had gone to bed, for it was now after midnight, but in answer to the urgency of my request he came down to see me. I told him without giving any clue, what had happened, and his verdict was what in my heart I knew it would be. Certainly I might see the Home Secretary and tell him that such a confession had been made me, but no word or hint must escape me which could lead to identification. Personally, he did not see how the execution could be postponed on such information as I could give.

' "And whatever you suffer, my son," he said, "be sure that you are suffering not from having done wrong, but from having done right. Placed as you are, your temptation to save an innocent man comes from the devil, and whatever you may be called upon to endure for not yielding to it, is of that origin also."

'I saw the Home Secretary in his room at the House within the hour. But unless I told him more, and he realized that I could not, he was powerless to move.

' "He was found guilty at his trial," he said, "and his appeal was dismissed. Without further evidence I can do nothing."

'He sat thinking a moment: then jumped up.

' "Good God, it's ghastly," he said. "I entirely believe, I needn't tell you, that you've heard this confession, but that doesn't prove it's true. Can't you see the man again? Can't you put the fear of God into him? If you can do anything at all, which gives me any justification for acting, up till the moment the drop falls, I will give a reprieve at once. There's my telephone number: ring me up here or at my house at any hour."

'I was back at the prison before six in the morning. I told Wadham that I believed in his innocence, and I gave him absolution for all else. He received the Holy and Blessed Sacrament with me, and went without flinching to his death.'

Father Denys paused.

'I have been a long time coming to that point in my story,' he said, 'which concerns that séance you spoke of, but it was necessary for your understanding of what I am going to tell you now, that you should know all this. I said that these messages and communications from the dead come not from them but from some evil and awful power impersonating them. You answered, I remember, "Why drag in the Devil?" I will tell you.

'When it was over, when the drop on which he stood yawned open, and the rope creaked and jumped, I went home. It was a dark winter's morning, still barely light, and in spite of the tragic scene I had just witnessed I felt serene and peaceful. I did not think of Kennion at all, only of the boy – he was little more – who had suffered unjustly, and that seemed a pitiful mistake, but no more. It did not touch him, his essential living soul, it was as if he had suffered the sacred expiation of martyrdom. And I was humbly thankful that I had been enabled to act rightly, and had Kennion now, through my agency, been in the hands of the police and Wadham alive, I should have been branded with the most terrible crime a priest can commit.

'I had been up all night, and after I had said my office I lay down on my sofa to get a little sleep. And I dreamed that I was in the cell with Wadham and that he knew I had proof of his innocence. It was within a few minutes of the hour of his death, and I heard along the stone-flagged corridor outside the steps of those who were coming for him. He heard them too, and stood up, pointing at me.

' "You're letting an innocent man die, when you could save him," he said. "You can't do it, Father Denys. Father Denys!" he shrieked, and the shriek broke off in a gulp and a gasp as the door opened.

'I woke, knowing that what had roused me was my own name, screamed out from somewhere close at hand, and I knew whose voice it was. But there I was alone in my quiet, empty room, with the dim day peering in. I had been asleep, I saw, for only a few minutes, but now all thought or power of sleep had fled, for somewhere by me, invisible but awfully present, was the spirit of the man whom I had allowed to perish. And he called me.

'But presently I convinced myself that this voice coming to me in sleep was no more than a dream, natural enough in the circumstances, and some days passed tranquilly enough. And then one day when I was walking down a sunny crowded street, I felt some definite and dreadful change in what I may call the psychic atmosphere which surrounds us all, and my soul grew black with fear and with evil imaginings. And there was Wadham coming towards me along the pavement gay and debonair. He looked at me, and his face became a mask of hate. "We shall meet often I hope, Father Denys," he said, as he passed. Another day I returned home in the twilight, and suddenly, as I entered my room, I heard the creak and strain of a rope, and his body, with head covered by the deathcap, swung in the window against the sunset. And sometimes when I was at my books the door opened quietly and closed again, and I knew he was there. The apparition or the token of it did not come often or perhaps my resistance would have been quickened, for I knew it was devilish in origin. But it came when I was off my guard at long intervals, so that I thought I had vanquished it, and then sometimes I felt my faith to reel. But always it was preceded by this sense of evil power bearing down on me, and I made haste to seek the shelter of the House of Defence which is set very high. And this last Sunday only –'

He broke off, covering his eyes with his hand, as if shutting out some appalling spectacle.

'I had been preaching,' he resumed, 'for one of our missions. The church was full, and I do not think there were another thought or desire in my soul but to further the holy cause for which I was speaking. It was a morning service, and the sun poured in through the stained-glass windows in a glow of coloured light. But in the middle of my sermon some bank of cloud drove up, and with it this horrible forewarning of the approach of a tempest of evil. So dark it got that, as I was drawing near the end of my sermon, the lights in the church were switched on, and it leaped into brightness. There was a lamp on the desk in the pulpit, where I had placed my notes, and now when it was kindled it shone full on the pew just below. And there with his head turned upwards towards me, with his face purple and eyes protruding and with the strangling noose round his neck, sat Wadham.

'My voice faltered a second, and I clutched at the pulpit-rail as he stared at me and I at him. A horror of the spirit, black as the eternal night of the lost closed round me, for I had let him go innocent to his death, and my punishment was just... And then like a star shining out through some merciful rent in this soul-storm came again that ray of conviction that as a priest I could not have done otherwise, and with it the sure knowledge that this apparition could not be of God, but of the devil, to be resisted and defied even as we defy with contempt some sweet and insidious temptation. It could not therefore be the spirit of the man at which I gazed, but some diabolical counterfeit.

'And I looked back from him to my notes, and went on with my sermon, for that alone was my business. That pause had seemed to me eternal: it had the quality of timelessness, but I learned afterwards that it had been barely perceptible. And from my own heart I learned that it was no punishment that I was undergoing, but the strengthening of a faith that had faltered.'

Suddenly he broke off. There came into his eyes as he fixed them on the door a look not of fear at all but of savage relentless antagonism.

'It's coming,' he said to me, 'and now if you hear or see anything, despise it, for it is evil.'

The door swung open and closed again, and though nothing visible entered, I knew that there was now in the room a living intelligence other than Father Denys's and mine, and it affected my being, my self, just as some horrible odour of putrefaction affects one physically: my soul sickened in it. Then, still seeing nothing, I perceived that the room, warm and comfortable just now, with a fire of coal prospering in the grate, was growing cold, and that some strange eclipse was veiling the light. Close to me on the table stood an electric lamp: the shade of it fluttered in the icy draught that stirred in the air, and the illuminant wire was no longer incandescent, but red and dull like the embers in the grate. I scrutinized the dimness, but as yet no material form manifested itself.

Father Denys was sitting very upright in his chair, his eyes fixed and focused on something invisible to me. His lips were moving and muttering, his hands grasped the crucifix he was wearing. And then I saw what I knew he was seeing, too: a face was outlining itself on the air in front of him, a face swollen and purple, with tongue lolling from the mouth, and as it hung there it oscillated to and fro. Clearer and clearer it grew, suspended there by the rope that now became visible to me, and though the apparition was of a man hanged by the neck, it was not dead but active and alive, and the spirit that awfully animated it was no human one, but something diabolical.

Suddenly Father Denys rose to his feet, and his face was within an inch or two of that suspended horror. He raised his hands which held the sacred emblem.

'Begone to your torment,' he cried, 'until the days of it are over, and the mercy of God grants you eternal death.'

There rose a wailing in the air: some blast shook the room so that the corners of it quaked, and then the light and the warmth were restored to it, and there was no one there but our two selves. Father Denys's face was haggard and dripping with the struggle he had been through, but there shone on it such radiance as I have never seen on human countenance.

'It's over,' he said. 'I saw it shrivel and wither before the power of His presence ... And your eyes tell me you saw it too and you know now that what wore the semblance of humanity was pure evil.'

We talked a little longer and he rose to go.

'Ah, I forgot,' he said. 'You wanted to know how I could reveal to you what was told me in Confession. Horace Kennion died this morning by his own hand. He left with his lawyer a packet to be opened on his death, with instructions that it should be published in the daily press. I saw it in an evening paper, and it was a detailed account of how he killed Gerald Selfe. He wished it to have all possible publicity.'

'But why?' I asked.

Father Denys paused.

'He gloried in his wickedness, I think,' he said. 'He loved it, as I told you, for its own sake, and he wanted everyone to know of it, as soon as he was safely away.'

The Secret Sin of Septimus Brope

Saki

'Who and what is Mr Brope?' demanded the aunt of Clovis suddenly.

Mrs Riversedge, who had been snipping off the heads of defunct roses, and thinking of nothing in particular, sprang hurriedly to mental attention. She was one of those old-fashioned hostesses who consider that one ought to know something about one's guests, and that the something ought to be to their credit.

'I believe he comes from Leighton Buzzard,' she observed by way of preliminary explanation.

'In these days of rapid and convenient travel,' said Clovis, who was dispersing a colony of green-fly with visitations of cigarette smoke, 'to come from Leighton Buzzard does not necessary denote any great strength of character. It might only mean mere restlessness. Now if he had left it under a cloud, or as a protest against the incurable and heartless frivolity of its inhabitants, that would tell us something about the man and his mission in life.'

'What does he do?' pursued Mrs Troyle magisterially.

'He edits the *Cathedral Monthly*,' said her hostess, 'and he's enormously learned about memorial brasses and transepts and the influence of Byzantine worship on modern liturgy, and all those sort of things. Perhaps he is just a little bit heavy and immersed in one range of subjects, but it takes all sorts to make a good house-party, you know. You don't find him *too* dull, do you?'

'Dullness I could overlook,' said the aunt of Clovis: 'what I cannot forgive is his making love to my maid.'

'My dear Mrs Troyle,' gasped the hostess, 'what an extraordinary idea! I assure you Mr Brope would not dream of doing such a thing.'

'His dreams are a matter of indifference to me; for all I care his slumbers may be one long indiscretion of unsuitable erotic advances, in which the entire servants' hall may be involved. But in his waking hours he shall not make love to my maid. It's no use arguing about it, I'm firm on the point.'

'But you must be mistaken,' persisted Mrs Riversedge; 'Mr Brope would be the last person to do such a thing.'

'He is the first person to do such a thing, as far as my information goes, and if I have any voice in the matter he certainly shall be the last. Of course, I am not referring to respectably intentioned lovers.'

'I simply cannot think that a man who writes so charmingly and informingly about transepts and Byzantine influences would behave in such an unprincipled manner,' said Mrs Riversedge; 'what evidence have you that he's doing anything of the sort? I don't want to doubt your word, of course, but we mustn't be too ready to condemn him unheard, must we?'

'Whether we condemn him or not, he has certainly not been unheard. He has the room next to my dressing-room, and on two occasions, when I daresay he thought I was absent, I have plainly heard him announcing through the wall, "I love you, Florrie". Those partition walls upstairs are very thin; one can almost hear a watch ticking in the next room.'

'Is your maid called Florence?'

'Her name is Florinda.'

'What an extraordinary name to give a maid!'

'I did not give it to her; she arrived in my service already christened.'

'What I mean is,' said Mrs Riversedge, 'that when I get maids with unsuitable names I call them Jane; they soon get used to it.'

'An excellent plan,' said the aunt of Clovis coldly, 'unfortunately I have got used to being called Jane myself. It happens to be my name.'

She cut short Mrs Riversedge's flood of apologies by abruptly remarking:

'The question is not whether I'm to call my maid Florinda, but whether Mr Brope is to be permitted to call her Florrie. I am strongly of opinion that he shall not.'

'He may have been repeating the words of some song,' said Mrs

Riversedge hopefully; 'there are lots of those sorts of silly refrains with girls' names,' she continued, turning to Clovis as a possible authority on the subject. ' "You mustn't call me Mary —" '

'I shouldn't think of doing so,' Clovis assured her; 'in the first place, I've always understood that your name was Henrietta; and then I hardly know you well enough to take such a liberty.'

'I mean there's a *song* with that refrain,' hurriedly explained Mrs Riversedge, 'and there's "Rhoda, Rhoda kept a pagoda", and "Maisie is a daisy", and heaps of others. Certainly it doesn't sound like Mr Brope to be singing such songs, but I think we ought to give him the benefit of the doubt.'

'I had already done so,' said Mrs Troyle, 'until further evidence came my way.'

She shut her eyes with the resolute finality of one who enjoys the blessed certainty of being implored to open them again.

'Further evidence!' exclaimed her hostess; 'do tell me!'

'As I was coming upstairs after breakfast Mr Brope was just passing my room. In the most natural way in the world a piece of paper dropped out of a packet that he held in his hand and fluttered to the ground just at my door. I was going to call out to him "You've dropped something", and then for some reason I held back and didn't show myself till he was safely in his room. You see it occurred to me that I was very seldom in my room just at that hour, and that Florinda was almost always there tidying up things about that time. So I picked up that innocent-looking piece of paper.'

Mrs Troyle paused again, with the self-applauding air of one who has detected an asp lurking in an apple-charlotte.

Mrs Riversedge snipped vigorously at the nearest rose bush, incidentally decapitating a Viscountess Folkestone that was just coming into bloom.

'What was on the paper?' she asked.

'Just the words in pencil, "I love you, Florrie", and then underneath, crossed out with a faint line, but perfectly plain to read, "Meet me in the garden by the yew." '

'There *is* a yew tree at the bottom of the garden,' admitted Mrs Riversedge.

'At any rate he appears to be truthful,' commented Clovis.

'To think that a scandal of this sort should be going on under my roof!' said Mrs Riversedge indignantly.

'I wonder why it is that scandal seems so much worse under a roof,' observed Clovis; 'I've always regarded it as a proof of the superior delicacy of the cat tribe that it conducts most of its scandals above the slates.'

'Now I come to think of it,' resumed Mrs Riversedge, 'there are things about Mr Brope that I've never been able to account for. His income, for instance: he only gets two hundred a year as editor of the *Cathedral Monthly*, and I know that his people are quite poor, and he hasn't any private means. Yet he manages to afford a flat somewhere in Westminster, and he goes abroad to Bruges and those sorts of places every year, and always dresses well, and gives quite nice luncheon-parties in the season. You can't do all that on two hundred a year, can you?'

'Does he write for any other papers?' queried Mrs Troyle.

'No, you see he specializes so entirely on liturgy and ecclesiastical architecture that his field is rather restricted. He once tried the *Sporting and Dramatic* with an article on church edifices in famous fox-hunting centres, but it wasn't considered of sufficient general interest to be accepted. No, I don't see how he can support himself in his present style merely by what he writes.'

'Perhaps he sells spurious transepts to American enthusiasts,' suggested Clovis.

'How could you sell a transept?' said Mrs Riversedge; 'such a thing would be impossible.'

'Whatever he may do to eke out his income,' interrupted Mrs Troyle, 'he is certainly not going to fill in his leisure moments by making love to my maid.'

'Of course not,' agreed her hostess; 'that must be put a stop to at once. But I don't quite know what we ought to do.'

'You might put a barbed-wire entanglement round the yew tree as a precautionary measure,' said Clovis.

'I don't think that the disagreeable situation that has arisen is improved by flippancy,' said Mrs Riversedge; 'a good maid is a treasure –'

'I am sure I don't know what I should do without Florinda,' admitted Mrs Troyle; 'she understands my hair. I've long ago given up trying to do anything with it myself. I regard one's hair as I regard husbands: as long as one is seen together in public one's private divergences don't matter. Surely that was the luncheon gong.'

Septimus Brope and Clovis had the smoking-room to themselves after lunch. The former seemed restless and preoccupied, the latter quietly observant.

'What is a lorry?' asked Septimus suddenly; 'I don't mean the thing on wheels, of course I know what that is, but isn't there a bird with a name like that, the larger form of a lorikeet?'

'I fancy it's a lory, with one "r",' said Clovis lazily, 'in which case it's no good to you.'

Septimus Brope stared in some astonishment.

'How do you mean, no good to me?' he asked, with more than a trace of uneasiness in his voice.

'Won't rhyme with Florrie,' exclaimed Clovis briefly.

Septimus sat upright in his chair, with unmistakable alarm on his face.

'How did you find out? I mean, how did you know I was trying to get a rhyme to Florrie?' he asked sharply.

'I didn't know,' said Clovis, 'I only guessed. When you wanted to turn the prosaic lorry of commerce into a feathered poem flitting through the verdure of a tropical forest, I knew you must be working up a sonnet, and Florrie was the only female name that suggested itself as rhyming with lorry.'

Septimus still looked uneasy.

'I believe you know more,' he said.

Clovis laughed quietly, but said nothing.

'How much do you know?' Septimus asked desperately.

'The yew tree in the garden,' said Clovis.

'There! I felt certain I'd dropped it somewhere. But you must have guessed something before. Look here, you have surprised my secret. You won't give me away, will you? It is nothing to be ashamed of, but it wouldn't do for the editor of the *Cathedral Monthly* to go in openly for that sort of thing, would it?'

'Well, I suppose not,' admitted Clovis.

'You see,' continued Septimus, 'I get quite a decent lot of money out of it. I could never live in the style I do on what I get as editor of the *Cathedral Monthly*.'

Clovis was even more startled than Septimus had been earlier in the conversation, but he was better skilled in repressing surprise.

'Do you mean to say you get money out of – Florrie?' he asked.

'Not out of Florrie, as yet,' said Septimus; 'in fact, I don't mind saying that I'm having a good deal of trouble over Florrie. But there are a lot of others.'

Clovis's cigarette went out.

'This is *very* interesting,' he said slowly. And then, with Septimus Brope's next words, illumination dawned on him.

'There are heaps of others: for instance:

> "Cora with the lips of coral,
> You and I will never quarrel."

That was one of my earliest successes, and it still brings me in royalties. And then there is – "Esmeralda, when I first beheld her", and "Fair Teresa, how I love to please her", both of those have been fairly popular. And there is one rather dreadful one,' continued Septimus, flushing deep carmine, 'which has brought me in more money than any of the others:

> "Lively little Lucie
> With her naughty nez retroussé."

Of course, I loathe the whole lot of them; in fact, I'm rapidly becoming something of a woman-hater under their influence, but I can't afford to disregard the financial aspect of the matter. And at the same time you can understand that my position as an authority on ecclesiastical architecture and liturgical subjects would be weakened, if not altogether ruined, if it once got about that I was the author of "Cora with the lips of coral" and all the rest of them.'

Clovis had recovered sufficiently to ask in a sympathetic, if rather unsteady, voice what was the special trouble with 'Florrie'.

'I can't get her into lyric shape, try as I will,' said Septimus mournfully. 'You see, one has to work in a lot of sentimental, sugary compliment with a catchy rhyme, and a certain amount of personal biography or prophecy. They've all of them got to have a long string of past successes recorded about them, or else you've got to foretell blissful things about them and yourself in the future. For instance, there is:

> "Dainty little girlie Mavis,
> She is such a rara avis.
> All the money I can save is
> All to be for Mavis mine."

It goes to a sickening namby-pamby waltz tune, and for months nothing else was sung and hummed in Blackpool and other popular centres.'

This time Clovis's self-control broke down badly.

'Please excuse me,' he gurgled, 'but I can't help it when I remember the awful solemnity of that article of yours that you so kindly read us last night, on the Coptic Church in its relation to early Christian worship.'

Septimus groaned.

'You see how it would be,' he said; 'as soon as people knew me to be the author of that miserable sentimental twaddle, all respect for the serious labours of my life would be gone. I daresay I know more about memorial brasses than anyone living, in fact I hope one day to publish a monograph on the subject, but I should be pointed out everywhere as the man whose ditties were in the mouths of minstrels along the entire coast-line of our Island home. Can you wonder that I positively hate Florrie all the time that I'm trying to grind out sugar-coated rhapsodies about her?'

'Why not give free play to your emotions and be brutally abusive? An uncomplimentary refrain would have an instant success as a novelty if you were sufficiently outspoken.'

'I've never thought of that,' said Septimus, 'and I'm afraid I couldn't break away from the habit of fulsome adulation and suddenly change my style.'

'You needn't change your style in the least,' said Clovis; 'merely reverse the sentiment and keep to the inane phraseology of the thing. If you'll do the body of the song I'll knock off the refrain, which is the thing that principally matters, I believe. I shall charge half-shares in the royalties, and throw in my silence as to your guilty secret. In the eyes of the world you shall still be the man who has devoted his life to the study of transepts and Byzantine ritual; only sometimes, in the long winter evenings, when the wind howls drearily down the chimney and the rain beats against the windows, I shall think of you as the author of "Cora with the lips of coral." Of course, if in sheer gratitude at my silence you like to take me for a much-needed holiday to the Adriatic or somewhere equally interesting, paying all expenses, I shouldn't dream of refusing.'

Later in the afternoon Clovis found his aunt and Mrs Riversedge indulging in gentle exercise in the Jacobean garden.

'I've spoken to Mr Brope about F.,' he announced.

'How splendid of you! What did he say?' came in a quick chorus from the two ladies.

'He was quite frank and straightforward with me when he saw that I knew his secret,' said Clovis, 'and it seems that his intentions were quite serious, if slightly unsuitable. I tried to show him the impracticability of the course that he was following. He said he wanted to be understood, and he seemed to think that Florinda would excel in that requirement, but I pointed out that there were probably dozens of delicately nurtured, pure-hearted young English girls who would be capable of understanding him, while Florinda was the only person in the world who understood my aunt's hair. That rather weighed with him, for he's not really a selfish animal, if you take him in the right way, and when I appealed to the memory of his happy childish days, spent amid the daisied fields of Leighton Buzzard (I suppose daisies do grow there), he was obviously affected. Anyhow, he gave me his word that he would put Florinda absolutely out of his mind, and he has agreed to go for a short trip abroad as the best distraction for his thoughts. I am going with him as far as Ragusa. If my aunt should wish to give me a really nice scarf-pin (to be chosen by myself), as a small recognition of the very considerable service I have done her, I shouldn't dream of refusing. I'm not one of those who think that because one is abroad one can go about dressed anyhow.'

A few weeks later in Blackpool and places where they sing, the following refrain held undisputed sway:

> "How you bore me, Florrie,
> With those eyes of vacant blue;
> You'll be very sorry, Florrie,
> If I marry you.
> Though I'm easy-goin', Florrie,
> This I swear is true,
> I'll throw you down a quarry, Florrie,
> If I marry you."

The Devil's Foot

Arthur Conan Doyle

In recording from time to time some of the curious experiences and interesting recollections which I associate with my long and intimate friendship with Mr Sherlock Holmes, I have continually been faced by difficulties caused by his own aversion to publicity. To his sombre and cynical spirit all popular applause was always abhorrent, and nothing amused him more at the end of a successful case than to hand over the actual exposure to some orthodox official, and to listen with a mocking smile to the general chorus of misplaced congratulation. It was, indeed, this attitude upon the part of my friend, and certainly not any lack of interesting material which has caused me of late years to lay very few of my records before the public. My participation in some of his adventures was always a privilege which entailed discretion and reticence upon me.

It was, then, with considerable surprise that I received a telegram from Holmes last Tuesday – he has never been known to write where a telegram would serve – in the following terms: 'Why not tell them of the Cornish horror – strangest case I have handled.' I have no idea what backward sweep of memory had brought the matter fresh to his mind, or what freak had caused him to desire that I should recount it; but I hasten, before another cancelling telegram may arrive, to hunt out the notes which give me the exact details of the case, and to lay the narrative before my readers.

It was, then, in the spring of the year 1897 that Holmes's iron constitution showed some symptoms of giving way in the face of constant hard work of a most exacting kind, aggravated, perhaps, by occasional indiscretions of his own. In March of that year Dr Moore Agar, of Harley Street, whose dramatic introduction to Holmes I may some day recount, gave positive injunctions that the famous private agent would lay aside all his cases and surrender himself to complete rest if he wished to avert an absolute breakdown. The state of his health was not a matter in which he himself took the faintest interest, for his mental detachment was absolute, but he was induced at last, on the threat of being permanently disqualified from work, to give himself a complete change of scene and air. Thus it was that in the early spring of that year we found ourselves together in a small cottage near Poldhu Bay, at the further extremity of the Cornish peninsula.

It was a singular spot, and one peculiarly well suited to the grim humour of my patient. From the windows of our little whitewashed house, which stood high upon a grassy headland, we looked down upon the whole sinister semicircle of Mounts Bay, that old death-trap of sailing vessels, with its fringe of black cliffs and surge-swept reefs on which innumerable seamen have met their end. With a northerly breeze it lies placid and sheltered, inviting the storm-tossed craft to tack into it for rest and protection.

Then comes the sudden swirl round of the wind, the blustering gale from the south-west, the dragging anchor, the lee shore, and the last battle in the creaming breakers. The wise mariner stands far out from that evil place.

On the land side our surroundings were as sombre as on the sea. It was a country of rolling moors, lonely and dun-coloured, with an occasional church tower to mark the site of some old-world village. In every direction upon these moors there were traces of some vanished race which had passed utterly away, and left as its sole record strange monuments of stone, irregular mounds which contained the burned ashes of the dead, and curious earthworks which hinted at prehistoric strife. The glamour and mystery of the place, with its sinister atmosphere of forgotten nations, appealed to the imagination of my friend, and he spent much of his time in long walks and solitary meditations upon the moor. The ancient Cornish language had also arrested his attention, and he had, I remember, conceived the idea that it was akin to the Chaldean, and had been largely derived from the Phoenician traders in tin. He had received a consignment of books upon philology and was settling down to develop this thesis, when suddenly, to my sorrow and to his unfeigned delight, we found ourselves, even in that land of dreams, plunged into a problem at our very doors which was more intense, more engrossing, and infinitely more mysterious than any of those which had driven us from London. Our simple life and peaceful, healthy routine were violently interrupted, and we were precipitated into the midst of a series of events which caused the utmost excitement not only in Cornwall, but throughout the whole West of England. Many of my readers may retain some recollection of what was called at the time 'The Cornish Horror', though a most imperfect account of the matter reached the London Press. Now, after thirteen years, I will give the true details of this inconceivable affair to the public.

I have said that scattered towers marked the villages which dotted this part of Cornwall. The nearest of these was the hamlet of Tredannick Wollas, where the cottages of a couple of hundred inhabitants clustered round an ancient, moss-grown church. The vicar of the parish, Mr Roundhay, was something of an archæologist, and as such Holmes had made his acquaintance. He was a middle-aged man, portly and affable, with a considerable fund of local lore. At his invitation we had taken tea at the vicarage, and had come to know, also, Mr Mortimer Tregennis, an independent gentleman, who increased the clergyman's scanty resources by taking rooms in his large straggling house. The vicar, being a bachelor, was glad to come to such an arrangement, though he had little in common with his lodger, who was a thin, dark, spectacled man, with a stoop which gave the impression of actual physical deformity. I remember that during our short visit we found the vicar garrulous, but his lodger strangely reticent, a sad-faced, introspective man, sitting with averted eyes, brooding apparently upon his own affairs.

These were the two men who entered abruptly into our little sitting-room on Tuesday, March the 16th, shortly after our breakfast hour, as we were smoking together, preparatory to our daily excursion upon the moors.

'Mr Holmes,' said the vicar, in an agitated voice, 'the most extraordinary and tragic affair has occurred during the night. It is the most unheard-of business. We can only regard it as a special Providence that you should chance to be here at the time, for in all England you are the one man we need.'

I glared at the intrusive vicar with no very friendly eyes; but Holmes took his pipe from his lips and sat up in his chair like an old hound who hears the view-holloa. He waved his hand to the sofa, and our palpitating visitor with his agitated companion sat side by side upon it. Mr Mortimer Tregennis was more self-contained than the clergyman, but the twitching of his thin hands and the brightness of his dark eyes showed that they shared a common emotion.

'Shall I speak or you?' he asked of the vicar.

'Well, as you seem to have made the discovery, whatever it may be, and the vicar to have had it second-hand, perhaps you had better do the speaking,' said Holmes.

I glanced at the hastily-clad clergyman, with the formally dressed lodger seated beside him, and was amused at the surprise which Holmes' simple deduction had brought to their faces.

'Perhaps I had best say a few words first,' said the vicar, 'and then you can judge if you will listen to the details from Mr Tregennis, or whether we should not hasten at once to the scene of this mysterious affair. I may explain, then, that our friend here spent last evening in the company of his two brothers, Owen and George, and of his sister Brenda, at their house of Tredannick Wartha, which is near the old stone cross upon the moor. He left them shortly after ten o'clock, playing cards round the dining-room table, in excellent health and spirits. This morning, being an early riser, he walked in that direction before breakfast, and was overtaken by the carriage of Dr Richards, who explained that he had just been sent for on a most urgent call to Tredannick Wartha. Mr Mortimer Tregennis naturally went with him. When he arrived at Tredannick Wartha he found an extraordinary state of things. His two brothers and his sister were seated round the table exactly as he had left them, the cards still spread in front of them and the candles burned down to their sockets. The sister lay back stone-dead in her chair, while the two brothers sat on each side of her laughing, shouting, and singing, the senses stricken clean out of them. All three of them, the dead woman and the two demented men, retained upon their faces an expression of the utmost horror – a convulsion of terror which was dreadful to look upon. There was no sign of the presence of anyone in the house, except Mrs Porter, the old cook and housekeeper, who declared that she had slept deeply and heard no sound during the night. Nothing had been stolen or disarranged, and there is absolutely no explanation of what the horror can be which had frightened a woman to death and two strong men out of their senses. There is the situation, Mr Holmes, in a nutshell and if you can help us to clear it up you will have done a great work.'

I had hoped that in some way I could coax my companion back

into the quiet which had been the object of our journey; but one glance at his intense face and contracted eyebrows told me how vain was now the expectation. He sat for some little time in silence, absorbed in the strange drama which had broken in upon our peace.

'I will look into this matter,' he said at last. 'On the face of it, it would appear to be a case of a very exceptional nature. Have you been there yourself, Mr Roundhay?'

'No, Mr Holmes. Mr Tregennis brought back the account to the vicarage, and I at once hurried over with him to consult you.'

'How far is it to the house where this singular tragedy occurred?'

'About a mile inland.'

'Then we shall walk over together. But, before we start, I must ask you a few questions, Mr Mortimer Tregennis.'

The other had been silent all this time, but I had observed that his more controlled excitement was even greater than the obtrusive emotion of the clergyman. He sat with a pale, drawn face, his anxious gaze fixed upon Holmes, and his thin hands clasped convulsively together. His pale lips quivered as he listened to the dreadful experience which had befallen his family, and his dark eyes seemed to reflect something of the horror of the scene.

'Ask what you like, Mr Holmes,' said he eagerly. 'It is a bad thing to speak of, but I will answer you the truth.'

'Tell me about last night.'

'Well, Mr Holmes, I supped there, as the vicar has said, and my elder brother George proposed a game of whist afterwards. We sat down about nine o'clock. It was a quarter-past ten when I moved to go. I left them all round the table, as merry as could be.'

'Who let you out?'

'Mrs Porter had gone to bed, so I let myself out. I shut the hall door behind me. The window of the room in which they sat was closed, but the blind was not drawn down. There was no change in door or window this morning, nor any reason to think that any stranger had been to the house. Yet there they sat, driven clean mad with terror, and Brenda lying dead of fright, with her head hanging over the arm of the chair. I'll never get the sight of that room out of my mind so long as I live.'

'The facts, as you state them, are certainly most remarkable,' said Holmes. 'I take it that you have no theory yourself which can in any way account for them?'

'It's devilish, Mr Holmes, devilish!' cried Mortimer Tregennis. 'It is not of this world. Something has come into that room which has dashed the light of reason from their minds. What human contrivance could do that?'

'I fear,' said Holmes, 'that if the matter is beyond humanity it is certainly beyond me. Yet we must exhaust all natural explanations before we fall back upon such a theory as this. As to yourself, Mr Tregennis, I take it you were divided in some way from your family, since they lived together and you had rooms apart?'

'That is so, Mr Holmes, though the matter is past and done with. We were a family of tin-miners at Redruth, but we sold out our venture to a company, and so retired with enough to keep us. I won't deny that there was some feeling about the division of the money and it stood between us for a time, but it was all forgiven and forgotten, and we were the best of friends together.'

'Looking back at the evening which you spent together, does anything stand out in your memory as throwing any possible light upon the tragedy? Think carefully, Mr Tregennis, for any clue which can help me.'

'There is nothing at all, sir.'

'Your people were in their usual spirits?'

'Never better.'

'Were they nervous people? Did they ever show any apprehension of coming danger?'

'Nothing of the kind.'

'You have nothing to add then, which could assist me?'

Mortimer Tregennis considered earnestly for a moment.

'There is one thing occurs to me,' said he at last. 'As we sat at the table my back was to the window, and my brother George, he being my partner at cards, was facing it. I saw him once look hard over my shoulder, so I turned round and looked also. The blind was up and the window shut, but I could just make out the bushes on the lawn, and it seemed to me for a moment that I saw something moving among them. I couldn't even say if it were man or animal, but I just thought there was something there. When I asked him what he was looking at, he told me that he had the same feeling. That is all that I can say.'

'Did you not investigate?'

'No; the matter passed as unimportant.'

'You left them, then, without any premonition of evil?'

'None at all.'

'I am not clear how you came to hear the news so early this morning.'

'I am an early riser, and generally take a walk before breakfast. This morning I had hardly started when the doctor in his carriage overtook me. He told me that old Mrs Porter had sent a boy down with an urgent message. I sprang in beside him and we drove on. When we got there we looked into that dreadful room. The candles and the fire must have burned out hours before, and they had been sitting there in the dark until dawn had broken. The doctor said Brenda must have been dead at least six hours. There were no signs of violence. She just lay across the arm of the chair with that look on her face. George and Owen were singing snatches of songs and gibbering like two great apes. Oh, it was awful to see! I couldn't stand it, and the doctor was as white as a sheet. Indeed, he fell into a chair in a sort of faint, and we nearly had him on our hands as well.'

'Remarkable – most remarkable!' said Holmes, rising and taking his hat. 'I think, perhaps, we had better go down to Tredannick Wartha without further delay. I confess that I have seldom known a case which at first sight presented a more singular problem.'

Our proceedings of that first morning did little to advance the investigation. It was marked, however, at the outset by an incident which left the most sinister impression upon my mind. The approach to the spot at which the tragedy occurred is down a narrow winding country lane. While we made our way along it we heard the rattle of a carriage coming towards us, and stood aside to let it pass. As it drove by us I caught a glimpse through the closed window of a horribly contorted, grinning face glaring out at us. Those staring eyes and gnashing teeth flashed past us like a dreadful vision.

'My brothers!' cried Mortimer Tregennis, white to his lips. 'They are taking them to Helston.'

We looked with horror after the black carriage, lumbering upon its way. Then we turned our steps towards this ill-omened house in which they had met their strange fate.

It was a large and bright dwelling, rather a villa than a cottage, with a considerable garden which was already, in that Cornish air, well filled with spring flowers. Towards this garden the window of the sitting-room fronted, and from it, according to Mortimer Tregennis, must have come that thing of evil which had by sheer horror in a single instant blasted their minds. Holmes walked slowly and thoughtfully among the flower-pots and along the path before we entered the porch. So absorbed was he in his thoughts, I remember, that he stumbled over the watering-pot, upset its contents, and deluged both our feet and the garden path. Inside the house we were met by the elderly Cornish housekeeper, Mrs Porter, who, with the aid of a young girl, looked after the wants of the family. She readily answered all Holmes' questions. She had heard nothing in the night. Her employers had all been in excellent spirits lately, and she had never known them more cheerful and prosperous. She had fainted with horror upon entering the room in the morning and seeing that dreadful company round the table. She had, when she recovered, thrown open the window to let the morning air in, and had run down to the lane, whence she sent a farm-lad for the doctor. The lady was on her bed upstairs, if we cared to see her. It took four strong men to get the brothers into the asylum carriage. She would not herself stay in the house another day, and was starting that very afternoon to rejoin her family at St Ives.

We ascended the stairs and viewed the body. Miss Brenda Tregennis had been a very beautiful girl, though now verging upon middle age. Her dark, clear-cut face was handsome, even in death, but there still lingered upon it something of that convulsion of horror which had been her last human emotion. From her bedroom we descended to the sitting-room where this strange tragedy had actually occurred. The charred ashes of the overnight fire lay in the grate. On the table were the four guttered and burned-out candles, with the cards scattered over its surface. The chairs had been moved back against the walls, but all else was as it had been the night before. Holmes paced with light, swift steps about the room; he sat in the various chairs, drawing them up and reconstructing their positions. He tested how much of the garden was visible; he examined the floor, the ceiling, and the fireplace; but never once did I see that sudden brightening of his eyes and tightening of his lips which would have told me that he saw some gleam of light in this utter darkness.

'Why a fire?' he asked once. 'Had they always a fire in this small room on a spring evening?'

Mortimer Tregennis explained that the night was cold and damp. For that reason, after his arrival, the fire was lit. 'What are you going to do now, Mr Holmes?' he asked.

My friend smiled and laid his hand upon my arm. 'I think, Watson, that I shall resume that course of tobacco-poisoning which you have so often and so justly condemned,' said he. 'With your permission, gentlemen, we will now return to our cottage, for I am not aware that any new factor is likely to come to our notice here. I will turn the facts over in my mind, Mr Tregennis, and should anything occur to me I will certainly communicate with you and the vicar. In the meantime I wish you both good morning.'

It was not until long after we were back in Poldhu Cottage that Holmes broke his complete and absorbed silence. He sat coiled in his arm-chair, his haggard and ascetic face hardly visible amid the blue swirl of his tobacco smoke, his black brows drawn down, his forehead contracted, his eyes vacant and far away. Finally, he laid down his pipe and sprang to his feet.

'It won't do, Watson!' said he, with a laugh. 'Let us walk along the cliffs together and search for flint arrows. We are more likely to find them than clues to this problem. To let the brain work without sufficient material is like racing an engine. It racks itself to pieces. The sea air, sunshine, and patience, Watson – all else will come.

'Now, let us calmly define our position, Watson,' he continued, as we skirted the cliffs together. 'Let us get a firm grip of the very little which we *do* know, so that when fresh facts arise we may be ready to fit them into their places. I take it, in the first place, that neither of us is prepared to admit diabolical intrusions into the affairs of men. Let us begin by ruling that entirely out of our minds. Very good. There remain three persons who have been grievously stricken by some conscious or unconscious human agency. That is firm ground. Now, when did this occur? Evidently, assuming his narrative to be true, it was immediately after Mr Mortimer Tregennis had left the room. That is a very important point. The presumption is that it was within a few minutes afterwards. The cards still lay upon the table. It was already past their usual hour for bed. Yet they had not changed their positions or pushed back their chairs. I repeat, then, that the occurrence was immediately after his departure, and not later than eleven o'clock last night.

'Our next obvious step is to check, so far as we can, the movements of Mortimer Tregennis after he left the room. In this there is no difficulty, and they seem to be above suspicion. Knowing my methods as you do, you were, of course, conscious of the somewhat clumsy water-pot expedient by which I obtained a clearer impress of his foot than might otherwise have been possible. The wet sandy path took it admirably. Last night was also wet, you will remember, and it was not difficult – having obtained a sample print – to pick out his track among others and to follow his movements. He appears to have walked away swiftly in the direction of the vicarage.

'If, then, Mortimer Tregennis disappeared from the scene, and yet some outside person affected the card-players, how can we reconstruct that person, and how was such an impression of horror conveyed? Mrs Porter may be eliminated. She is evidently harmless. Is there any evidence that someone crept up to the garden window and in some manner produced so terrific an effect that he drove those who saw it out of their senses? The only suggestion in this direction comes from Mortimer Tregennis himself, who says that his brother spoke about some movements in the garden. That is certainly remarkable, as the night was rainy, cloudy, and dark. Anyone who had the design to alarm these people would be compelled to place his very face against the glass before he could be seen. There is a three-foot flower-border outside this window, but no indication of a footmark. It is difficult to imagine, then, how an outsider could have made so terrible an impression upon the company, nor have we found any possible motive for so strange and elaborate an attempt. You perceive our difficulties, Watson?'

'They are only too clear,' I answered, with conviction.

'And yet, with a little more material, we may prove that they are not insurmountable,' said Holmes. 'I fancy that among your extensive archives, Watson, you may find some which were nearly as obscure. Meanwhile, we shall put the case aside until more accurate data are available, and devote the rest of our morning to the pursuit of neolithic man.'

I may have commented upon my friend's power of mental detachment, but never have I wondered at it more than upon that spring morning in Cornwall when for two hours he discoursed upon celts, arrowheads, and shards, as lightly as if no sinister mystery was waiting for his solution. It was not until we had returned in the afternoon to our cottage that we found a visitor awaiting us, who soon brought our minds back to the matter in hand. Neither of us needed to be told who that visitor was. The huge body, the craggy and deeply-seamed face with the fierce eyes and hawk-like nose, the grizzled hair which nearly brushed our cottage ceiling, the beard – golden at the fringes and white near the lips, save for the nicotine stain from his perpetual cigar – all these were as well known in London as in Africa, and could only be associated with the tremendous personality of Dr Leon Sterndale, the great lion-hunter and explorer.

We had heard of his presence in the district, and had once or twice caught sight of his tall figure upon the moorland paths. He made no advances to us, however, nor would we have dreamed of doing so to him, as it was well known that it was his love of seclusion which caused him to spend the greater part of the intervals between his journeys in a small bungalow buried in the lonely wood of Beauchamp Arriance. Here, amid his books and his maps, he lived an absolutely lonely life, attending to his own simple wants, and paying little apparent heed to the affairs of his neighbours. It was a surprise to me, therefore, to hear him asking Holmes in an eager voice, whether he had made any advance in his reconstruction of this mysterious episode. 'The county police are utterly at fault,' said he; 'but perhaps your wider experience has suggested some conceivable explanation. My only claim to being taken into your confidence is that during my many residences here I have come to know this family of Tregennis very well – indeed, upon my Cornish mother's side I could call them cousins – and their strange fate has naturally been a great shock to me. I may tell you that I had got as far as Plymouth upon my way to Africa, but the news reached me this morning, and I came straight back again to help in the inquiry.'

Holmes raised his eyebrows.

'Did you lose your boat through it?'

'I will take the next.'

'Dear me! that is friendship indeed.'

'I tell you they were relatives.'

'Quite so – cousins of your mother. Was your baggage aboard the ship?'

'Some of it, but the main part at the hotel.'

'I see. But surely this event could not have found its way into the Plymouth morning papers?'

'No, sir; I had a telegram.'

'Might I ask from whom?'

A shadow passed over the gaunt face of the explorer.

'You are very inquisitive, Mr Holmes.'

'It is my business.'

With an effort, Dr Sterndale recovered his ruffled composure.

'I have no objection to telling you,' he said. 'It was Mr Roundhay, the vicar, who sent me the telegram which recalled me.'

'Thank you,' said Holmes. 'I may say in answer to your original question, that I have not cleared my mind entirely on the subject of this case, but that I have every hope of reaching some conclusion. It would be premature to say more.'

'Perhaps you would not mind telling me if your suspicions point in any particular direction?'

'No, I can hardly answer that.'

'Then I have wasted my time, and need not prolong my visit.' The famous doctor strode out of our cottage in considerable ill-humour, and within five minutes Holmes had followed him. I saw him no more until the evening, when he returned with a slow step and haggard face which assured me that he had made no great progress with his investigation. He glanced at a telegram which awaited him, and threw it into the grate.

'From the Plymouth hotel, Watson,' he said. 'I learned the name of it from the vicar, and I wired to make certain that Dr Leon Sterndale's account was true. It appears that he did indeed spend last night there, and that he has actually allowed some of his baggage to go on to Africa, while he returned to be present at this investigation. What do you make of that, Watson?'

'He is deeply interested.'

'Deeply interested – yes. There is a thread here which we have not yet grasped, and which might lead us through the tangle. Cheer up, Watson, for I am very sure that our material has not yet all come to hand. When it does, we may soon leave our difficulties behind us.'

Little did I think how soon the words of Holmes would be realized, or how strange and sinister would be that new development which opened up an entirely fresh line of investigation. I was shaving at my window in the morning when I heard the rattle of hoofs, and looking up, saw a dog-cart coming at a gallop down the road. It pulled up at our door, and our friend the vicar sprang from it and rushed up our garden path. Holmes was already dressed, and we hastened down to meet him.

Our visitor was so excited that he could hardly articulate, but at last in gasps and bursts his tragic story came out of him.

'We are devil-ridden, Mr Holmes! My poor parish is devil-ridden!' he cried. 'Satan himself is loose in it! We are given over into his hands!' He danced about in his agitation, a ludicrous object if it were not for his ashy face and startled eyes. Finally he shot out his terrible news.

'Mr Mortimer Tregennis died during the night, and with exactly the same symptoms as the rest of his family.'

Holmes sprang to his feet, all energy in an instant.

'Can you fit us both into your dog-cart?'

'Yes, I can.'

'Then, Watson, we will postpone our breakfast. Mr Roundhay, we are entirely at your disposal. Hurry – hurry, before things get disarranged.'

The lodger occupied two rooms at the vicarage, which were in an angle by themselves, the one above the other. Below was a large sitting-room; above, his bedroom. They looked out upon a croquet lawn which came up to the windows. We had arrived before the doctor or the police, so that everything was absolutely undisturbed. Let me describe exactly the scene as we saw it upon that misty March morning. It has left an impression which can never be effaced from my mind.

The atmosphere of the room was of a horrible and depressing stuffiness. The servant who had first entered had thrown up the window, or it would have been even more intolerable. This might partly be due to the fact that a lamp stood flaring and smoking on the centre table. Beside it sat the dead man, leaning back in his chair, his thin beard projecting, his spectacles pushed up on to his forehead, and his lean, dark face turned towards the window and twisted into the same distortion of terror which had marked the features of his dead sister. His limbs were convulsed and his fingers contorted as though he had died in a very paroxysm of fear. He was fully clothed, though there were signs that his dressing had been done in a hurry. We had already learned that his bed had been slept in, and that the tragic end had come to him in the early morning.

One realized the red-hot energy which underlay Holmes's phlegmatic exterior when one saw the sudden change which came over him from the moment that he entered the fatal apartment. In an instant he was tense and alert, his eyes shining, his face set, his limbs quivering with eager activity. He was out on the lawn, in through the window, round the room, and up into the bedroom, for all the world like a dashing foxhound drawing a cover. In the bedroom he made a rapid cast around, and ended by throwing open the window, which appeared to give him some fresh cause for excitement, for he leaned out of it with loud ejaculations of interest and delight. Then he rushed down the stair, out through the open window, threw himself upon his face on the lawn, sprang up and into the room once more, all with the energy of the hunter who is at the very heels of his quarry. The lamp, which was an ordinary standard, he examined with minute care, making certain measurements upon its bowl. He carefully scrutinized with his lens the talc shield which covered the top of the chimney, and scraped off some ashes which adhered to its upper surface, putting some of them into an envelope, which he placed in his pocket-book. Finally, just as the doctor and the official police put in an appearance, he beckoned to the vicar and we all three went out upon the lawn.

'I am glad to say that my investigation has not been entirely barren,' he remarked. 'I cannot remain to discuss the matter with the police, but I should be exceedingly obliged, Mr Roundhay, if you would give the inspector my compliments and direct his attention to the bedroom windows and to the sitting-room lamp. Each is suggestive, and together they are almost conclusive. If the police would desire further information I shall be happy to see any of them at the cottage. And now, Watson, I think that, perhaps, we shall be better employed elsewhere.'

It may be that the police resented the intrusion of an amateur, or that they imagined themselves to be upon some hopeful line of investigation; but it is certain that we heard nothing from them for the next two days. During this time Holmes spent some of his time smoking and dreaming in the cottage; but a greater portion in country walks which he undertook alone, returning after many hours without remark as to where he had been. One experiment served to show me the line of his investigation. He had bought a lamp which was the duplicate of the one which had burned in the room of Mortimer Tregennis on the morning of the tragedy. This he filled with the same oil as that used at the vicarage, and he carefully timed the period which it would take to be exhausted. Another experiment which he made was of a more unpleasant nature, and one which I am not likely ever to forget.

'You will remember, Watson,' he remarked one afternoon, 'that there is a single common point of resemblance in the varying reports which have reached us. This concerns the effect of the atmosphere of the room in each case upon those who had first entered it. You will recollect that Mortimer Tregennis, in describing the episode of his last visit to his brothers' house, remarked that the doctor on entering the room fell into a chair? You had forgotten? Well, I can answer for it that it was so. Now, you will remember also that Mrs Porter, the housekeeper, told us that she herself fainted upon entering the room and had afterwards opened the window. In the second case – that of Mortimer Tregennis himself – you cannot have forgotten the horrible stuffiness of the room when we arrived, though the servant had thrown open the window. That servant, I found upon enquiry, was so ill that she had gone to her bed. You will admit, Watson, that these facts are very suggestive. In each case there is evidence of a poisonous atmosphere. In each case, also, there is combustion going on in the room – in the one case a fire, in the other a lamp. The fire was needed, but the lamp was lit – as a comparison of the oil consumed will show – long after it was broad daylight. Why? Surely because there is some connection between three things – the burning, the stuffy atmosphere, and, finally, the madness or death of those unfortunate people. That is clear, is it not?'

'It would appear so.'

'At least we may accept it as a working hypothesis. We will suppose, then, that something was burned in each case which produced an atmosphere causing strange toxic effects. Very good. In the first instance – that of the Tregennis family – this substance was placed in the fire. Now the window was shut, but the fire would naturally carry fumes to some extent up the chimney. Hence one would expect the effects of the poison to be less than in the second case, where there was less escape for the vapour. The result seems to indicate that it was so, since in the first case only the woman, who had presumably the more sensitive organism, was killed, the others exhibiting that temporary or permanent lunacy which is evidently the first effect of the drug. In the second case the result was complete. The facts, therefore, seem to bear out the theory of a poison which worked by combustion.

'With this train of reasoning in my head I naturally looked about in Mortimer Tregennis's room to find some remains of this substance. The obvious place to look was the talc shield or smoke-guard of the lamp. There, sure enough, I perceived a number of flaky ashes, and round the edges a fringe of brownish powder, which had not yet been consumed. Half of this I took, as you saw, and I placed it in an envelope.'

'Why half, Holmes?'

'It is not for me, my dear Watson, to stand in the way of the official police force. I leave them all the evidence which I found. The poison still remained upon the talc, had they the wit to find it. Now, Watson, we will light our lamp; we will, however, take the precaution to open our window to avoid the premature decease of two deserving members of society, and you will seat yourself near that open window in an arm-chair, unless, like a sensible man, you determine to have nothing to do with the affair. Oh, you will see it out, will you? I thought I knew my Watson. This chair I will place opposite yours, so that we may be the same distance from the poison, and face to face. The door we will leave ajar. Each is now in a position to watch the other and to bring the experiment to an end should the symptoms seem alarming. Is that all clear? Well, then, I take our powder – or what remains of it – from the envelope, and I lay it above the burning lamp. So! Now, Watson, let us sit down and await developments.'

They were not long in coming. I had hardly settled in my chair before I was conscious of a thick, musky odour, subtle and nauseous. At the very first whiff of it my brain and my imagination were beyond all control. A thick, black cloud swirled before my eyes, and my mind told me that in this cloud, unseen as yet, but about to spring out upon my appalled senses, lurked all that was vaguely horrible, all that was monstrous and inconceivably wicked in the universe. Vague shapes swirled and swam amid the dark cloud-bank, each a menace and a warning of something coming, the advent of some unspeakable dweller upon the threshold, whose very shadow would blast my soul. A freezing horror took possession of me. I felt that my hair was rising, that my eyes were protruding, that my mouth was opened, and my tongue like leather. The turmoil within my brain was such that something must surely snap. I tried to scream, and was vaguely aware of some hoarse croak which was my own voice, but distant and detached from myself. At the same moment, in some effort of escape, I broke through that cloud of despair, and had a glimpse of Holmes's face, white, rigid, and drawn with horror – the very look which I had seen upon the features of the dead. It was that vision which gave me an instant of sanity and of strength. I dashed from my chair, threw my arms round Holmes, and together we lurched through the door, and an instant afterwards had thrown ourselves down upon the grass plot and were lying side by side, conscious only of the glorious sunshine which was bursting its way through the hellish cloud of terror which had girt us in. Slowly it rose from our souls like the mists from a landscape, until peace and reason had returned, and we were sitting upon the grass, wiping our clammy foreheads, and looking with apprehension at each other to mark the last traces of that terrific experience which we had undergone.

'Upon my word, Watson!' said Holmes at last, with an unsteady voice; 'I owe you both my thanks and an apology. It was an unjustifiable experiment even for oneself, and doubly so for a friend. I am really very sorry.'

'You know,' I answered, with some emotion, for I had never seen so much of Holmes's heart before, 'that it is my greatest joy and privilege to help you.'

He relapsed at once into the half-humorous, half-cynical vein which was his habitual attitude to those about him. 'It would be superfluous to drive us mad, my dear Watson,' said he. 'A candid observer would certainly declare that we were so already before we embarked upon so wild an experiment. I confess that I never imagined that the effect could be so sudden and so severe.' He dashed into the cottage, and reappearing with the burning lamp held at full arm's length, he threw it among a bank of brambles. 'We must give the room a little time to clear. I take it, Watson, that you have no longer a shadow of a doubt as to how these tragedies were produced?'

'None whatever.'

'But the cause remains as obscure as before. Come into the arbour here, and let us discuss it together. That villainous stuff seems still to linger round my throat. I think we must admit that all the evidence points to this man, Mortimer Tregennis, having been the criminal in the first tragedy, though he was the victim in the second one. We must remember, in the first place, that there is some story of a family quarrel, followed by a reconciliation. How bitter that quarrel may have been, or how hollow the reconciliation we cannot tell. When I think of Mortimer Tregennis, with the foxy face and the small shrewd, beady eyes behind the spectacles, he is not a man whom I should judge to be of a particularly forgiving disposition. Well, in the next place, you will remember that this idea of someone moving in the garden, which took our attention for a moment from the real cause of the tragedy, emanated from him. He had a motive in misleading us. Finally, if he did not throw this substance into the fire at the moment of leaving the room, who did do so? The affair happened immediately after his departure. Had anyone else come in, the family would certainly have risen from the table. Besides, in peaceful Cornwall, visitors do not arrive after ten o'clock at night. We may take it, then, that all the evidence points to Mortimer Tregennis as the culprit.'

'Then his own death was suicide!'

'Well, Watson, it is on the face of it a not impossible supposition. The man who had the guilt upon his soul of having brought such a fate upon his own family might well be driven by remorse to inflict it upon himself. There are, however, some cogent reasons against it. Fortunately, there is one man in England who knows all about it, and I have made arrangements by which we shall hear the facts this afternoon from his own lips. Ah! he is a little before his time. Perhaps you would kindly step this way, Dr Leon Sterndale. We have been conducting a chemical experiment indoors which has left our little room hardly fit for the reception of so distinguished a visitor.'

I had heard the click of the garden gate, and now the majestic figure of the great African explorer appeared upon the path. He turned in some surprise towards the rustic arbour in which we sat.

'You sent for me, Mr Holmes. I had your note about an hour ago, and I have come, though I really do not know why I should obey your summons.'

'Perhaps we can clear the point up before we separate,' said Holmes, 'Meanwhile, I am much obliged to you for your courteous acquiescence. You will excuse this informal reception in the open air, but my friend Watson and I have nearly furnished an additional chapter to what the papers call the "Cornish Horror", and we prefer a clear atmosphere for the present. Perhaps, since the matters which we have to discuss will affect you personally in a very intimate fashion, it is as well that we should talk where there can be no eavesdropping.'

The explorer took his cigar from his lips and gazed sternly at my companion.

'I am at a loss to know, sir,' he said, 'what you can have to speak about which affects me personally in a very intimate fashion.'

'The killing of Mortimer Tregennis,' said Holmes.

For a moment I wished that I were armed. Sterndale's fierce face turned to a dusky red, his eyes glared, and the knotted, passionate veins started out in his forehead, while he sprang forward with clenched hands towards my companion. Then he stopped, and with a violent effort he resumed a cold, rigid calmness which was, perhaps, more suggestive of danger than his hot-headed outburst.

'I have lived so long among savages and beyond the law,' said he, 'that I have got into the way of being a law to myself. You would do well, Mr Holmes, not to forget it, for I have no desire to do you an injury.'

'Nor have I any desire to do you an injury, Dr Sterndale. Surely the clearest proof of it is that, knowing what I know, I have sent for you and not for the police.'

Sterndale sat down with a gasp, overawed for, perhaps, the first time in his adventurous life. There was a calm assurance of power in Holmes's manner which could not be withstood. Our visitor stammered for a moment, his great hands opening and shutting in his agitation.

'What do you mean?' he asked, at last. 'If this is bluff upon your part, Mr Holmes, you have chosen a bad man for your experiment.

Let us have no more beating about the bush. What *do* you mean?'

'I will tell you,' said Holmes, 'and the reason why I tell you is that I hope frankness may beget frankness. What my next step may be will depend entirely upon the nature of your own defence.'

'My defence?'

'Yes, sir.'

'My defence against what?'

'Against the charge of killing Mortimer Tregennis.'

Sterndale mopped his forehead with his handkerchief. 'Upon my word, you are getting on,' said he. 'Do all your successes depend upon this prodigious power of bluff?'

'The bluff,' said Holmes, sternly, 'is upon your side, Dr Leon Sterndale, and not upon mine. As a proof I will tell you some of the facts upon which my conclusions are based. Of your return from Plymouth, allowing much of your property to go on to Africa, I will say nothing save that it first informed me that you were one of the factors which had to be taken into account in reconstructing this drama –'

'I came back –'

'I have heard your reasons and regard them as unconvincing and inadequate. We will pass that. You came down here to ask me whom I suspected. I refused to answer you. You then went to the vicarage, waited outside it for some time, and finally returned to your cottage.'

'How do you know that?'

'I followed you.'

'I saw no one.'

'That is what you may expect to see when I follow you. You spent a restless night at your cottage, and you formed certain plans, which in the early morning you proceeded to put into execution. Leaving your door just as day was breaking, you filled your pocket with some reddish gravel that was lying heaped beside your gate.'

Sterndale gave a violent start and looked at Holmes in amazement.

'You then walked swiftly for the mile which separated you from the vicarage. You were wearing, I may remark, the same pair of ribbed tennis shoes which are at the present moment upon your feet. At the vicarage you passed through the orchard and the side hedge, coming out under the window of the lodger Tregennis. It was now daylight, but the household was not yet stirring. You drew some of the gravel from your pocket, and you threw it up at the window above you.'

Sterndale sprang to his feet.

'I believe that you are the devil himself!' he cried.

Holmes smiled at the compliment. 'It took two, or possibly three, handfuls before the lodger came to the window. You beckoned him to come down. He dressed hurriedly and descended to his sitting-room. You entered by the window. There was an interview – a short one – during which you walked up and down the room. Then you passed out and closed the window, standing on the lawn outside smoking a cigar and watching what occurred. Finally, after the death of Tregennis, you withdrew as you had come. Now, Dr Sterndale, how do you justify such conduct, and what were the motives for your actions? If you prevaricate or trifle with me, I give you my assurance that the matter will pass out of my hands for ever.'

Our visitor's face had turned ashen grey as he listened to the words of his accuser. Now he sat for some time in thought with his face sunk in his hands. Then with a sudden impulsive gesture he plucked a photograph from his breast-pocket and threw it on the rustic table before us.

'That is why I have done it,' said he.

It showed the bust and face of a very beautiful woman. Holmes stooped over it.

'Brenda Tregennis,' said he.

'Yes, Brenda Tregennis,' repeated our visitor. 'For years I have loved her. For years she has loved me. There is the secret of that Cornish seclusion which people have marvelled at. It has brought me close to the one thing on earth that was dear to me. I could not marry her, for I have a wife who has left me for years and yet whom, by the deplorable laws of England, I could not divorce. For years Brenda waited. For years I waited. And this is what we have waited for.' A terrible sob shook his great frame, and he clutched his throat under his brindled beard. Then with an effort he mastered himself and spoke on.

'The vicar knew. He was in our confidence. He would tell you that she was an angel upon earth. That was why he telegraphed to me and I returned. What was my baggage or Africa to me when I learned that such a fate had come upon my darling? There you have the missing clue to my action, Mr Holmes.'

'Proceed,' said my friend.

Dr Sterndale drew from his pocket a paper packet and laid it upon the table. On the outside was written, '*Radix pedis diaboli*' with a red poison label beneath it. He pushed it towards me. 'I understand that you are a doctor, sir. Have you ever heard of this preparation?'

'Devil's-foot root! No, I have never heard of it.'

'It is no reflection upon your professional knowledge,' said he, 'for I believe that, save for one sample in a laboratory at Buda, there is no other specimen in Europe. It has not yet found its way either into the pharmacopœia or into the literature of toxicology. The root is shaped like a foot, half human, half goat-like; hence the fanciful name, given by a botanical missionary. It is used as an ordeal poison by the medicine-men in certain districts of West Africa, and is kept as a secret among them. This particular specimen I obtained under very extraordinary circumstances in the Ubanghi country.' He opened the paper as he spoke, and disclosed a heap of reddish-brown, snuff-like powder.

'Well, sir?' asked Holmes sternly.

'I am about to tell you, Mr Holmes, all that actually occurred, for you already know so much that it is clearly to my interest that you should know all. I have already explained the relationship in which I stood to the Tregennis family. For the sake of the sister I was friendly with the brothers. There was a family quarrel about money which estranged this man Mortimer, but it was supposed to be made up, and I afterwards met him as I did the others. He was a sly, subtle, scheming man, and several things arose which gave me a suspicion of him, but I had no cause for any positive quarrel.

'One day, only a couple of weeks ago, he came down to my cottage and I showed him some of my African curiosities. Among other things I exhibited this powder, and I told him of its strange properties, how it stimulates those brain centres which control the emotion of fear, and how either madness or death is the fate of the unhappy native who is subjected to the ordeal by the priest of his tribe. I told him also how powerless European science would be to detect it. How he took it I cannot say, for I never left the room, but there is no doubt that it was then, while I was opening cabinets and stooping to boxes, that he managed to abstract some of the devil's-foot root. I well remember how he plied me with questions as to the amount and the time that was needed for its effect, but I little dreamed that he could have a personal reason for asking.

'I thought no more of the matter until the vicar's telegram reached me at Plymouth. This villain had thought that I would be at sea before the news could reach me, and that I should be lost for years in Africa. But I returned at once. Of course, I could not listen to the details without feeling assured that my poison had been used. I came round to see you on the chance that some other explanation had suggested itself to you. But there could be none. I was convinced that Mortimer Tregennis was the murderer; that for the sake of money, and with the idea, perhaps, that if the other members of his family were all insane he would be the sole guardian of their joint property, he had used the devil's-foot powder upon them, driven two of them out of their senses, and killed his sister Brenda, the one human being whom I have ever loved or who has ever loved me. There was his crime; what was to be his punishment?

'Should I appeal to the law? Where were my proofs? I knew that the facts were true, but could I help to make a jury of countrymen believe so fantastic a story? I might or I might not. But I could not afford to fail. My soul cried out for revenge. I have said to you once before, Mr Holmes, that I have spent much of my life outside the law, and that I have come at last to be a law to myself. So it was now. I determined that the fate which he had given to others should be shared by himself. Either that or I would do justice upon him with my own hand. In all England there can be no man who sets less value upon his own life than I do at the present moment.

'Now I have told you all. You have yourself supplied the rest. I did, as you say, after a restless night, set off early from my cottage. I foresaw the difficulty of arousing him, so I gathered some gravel from the pile which you have mentioned, and I used it to throw up to his window. He came down and admitted me through the window of the sitting-room. I laid his offence before him. I told him that I had come both as judge and executioner. The wretch sank into a chair paralysed at the sight of my revolver. I lit the lamp, put the powder above it, and stood outside the window, ready to carry out my threat to shoot him should he try to leave the room. In five minutes he died. My God! how he died! But my heart was flint, for he endured nothing which my innocent darling had not felt before him. There is my story, Mr Holmes. Perhaps, if you loved a woman, you would have done as much yourself. At any rate, I am in your hands. You can take what steps you like. As I have already said, there is no man living who can fear death less than I do.'

Holmes sat for some little time in silence.

'What were your plans?' he asked, at last.

'I had intended to bury myself in Central Africa. My work there is but half finished.'

'Go and do the other half,' said Holmes. 'I, at least, am not prepared to prevent you.'

Dr Sterndale raised his giant figure, bowed gravely, and walked from the arbour. Holmes lit his pipe and handed me his pouch.

'Some fumes which are not poisonous would be a welcome change,' said he. 'I think you must agree, Watson, that it is not a case in which we are called upon to interfere. Our investigation has been independent, and our action shall be so also. You would not denounce the man?'

'Certainly not,' I answered.

'I have never loved, Watson, but if I did and if the woman I loved had met such an end, I might act even as our lawless lion-hunter has done. Who knows? Well, Watson, I will not offend your intelligence by explaining what is obvious. The gravel upon the window-sill was, of course, the starting-point of my research. It was unlike anything in the vicarage garden. Only when my attention had been drawn to Dr Sterndale and his cottage did I find its counterpart. The lamp shining in broad daylight and the remains of powder upon the shield were successive links in a fairly obvious chain. And now, my dear Watson, I think we may dismiss the matter from our mind, and go back with a clear conscience to the study of those Chaldean roots which are surely to be traced in the Cornish branch of the great Celtic speech.'

The Strength of God

Sherwood Anderson

The Reverend Curtis Hartman was pastor of the Presbyterian Church of Winesburg, and had been in that position ten years. He was forty years old, and by his nature very silent and reticent. To preach, standing in the pulpit before the people, was always a hardship for him and from Wednesday morning until Saturday evening he thought of nothing but the two sermons that must be preached on Sunday. Early on Sunday morning he went into a little room called a study in the bell tower of the church and prayed. In his prayers there was one note that always predominated. 'Give me strength and courage for Thy work, O Lord!' he pleaded, kneeling on the bare floor and bowing his head in the presence of the task that lay before him.

The Reverend Hartman was a tall man with a brown beard. His wife, a stout, nervous woman, was the daughter of a manufacturer of underwear at Cleveland, Ohio. The minister himself was rather a favorite in the town. The elders of the church liked him because he was quiet and unpretentious and Mrs White, the banker's wife, thought him scholarly and refined.

The Presbyterian Church held itself somewhat aloof from the other churches of Winesburg. It was larger and more imposing and its minister was better paid. He even had a carriage of his own and on summer evenings sometimes drove about town with his wife. Through Main Street and up and down Buckeye Street he went, bowing gravely to the people, while his wife, afire with secret pride, looked at him out of the corners of her eyes and worried lest the horse become frightened and run away.

For a good many years after he came to Winesburg things went well with Curtis Hartman. He was not one to arouse keen enthusiasm among the worshippers in his church but on the other hand he made no enemies. In reality he was much in earnest and sometimes suffered prolonged periods of remorse because he could not go crying the word of God in the highways and byways of the town. He wondered if the flame of the spirit really burned in him and dreamed of a day when a strong sweet new current of power would come like a great wind into his voice and his soul and the people would tremble before the spirit of God made manifest in him. 'I am a poor stick and that will never really happen to me,' he mused dejectedly, and then a patient smile lit up his features. 'Oh well, I suppose I'm doing well enough,' he added philosophically.

The room in the bell tower of the church, where on Sunday mornings the minister prayed for an increase in him of the power of God, had but one window. It was long and narrow and swung outward on a hinge like a door. On the window, made of little leaded panes, was a design showing the Christ laying his hand upon the head of a child. One Sunday morning in the summer as he sat by his desk in the room with a large Bible opened before him, and the sheets of his sermon scattered about, the minister was shocked to see, in the upper room of the house next door, a woman lying in her bed and smoking a cigarette while she read a book. Curtis Hartman went on tiptoe to the window and closed it softly. He was horror stricken at the thought of a woman smoking and trembled also to think that his eyes, just raised from the pages of the book of God, had looked upon the bare shoulders and white throat of a woman. With his brain in a whirl he went down into the pulpit and preached a long sermon without once thinking of his gestures or his voice. The sermon attracted unusual attention because of its power and clearness. 'I wonder if she is listening, if my voice is carrying a message into her soul,' he thought and began to hope that on future Sunday mornings he might be able to say words that would touch and awaken the woman apparently far gone in secret sin.

The house next door to the Presbyterian Church, through the windows of which the minister had seen the sight that had so upset him, was occupied by two women. Aunt Elizabeth Swift, a grey competent-looking widow with money in the Winesburg National Bank, lived there with her daughter Kate Swift, a schoolteacher. The schoolteacher was thirty years old and had a neat trim-looking figure. She had few friends and bore a reputation of having a sharp tongue. When he began to think about her, Curtis Hartman remembered that she had been to Europe and had lived for two years in New York City. 'Perhaps after all her smoking means nothing,' he thought. He began to remember that when he was a student in college and occasionally read novels, good although somewhat worldly women, had smoked through the pages of a book that had once fallen into his hands. With a rush of new determination he worked on his sermons all through the week and forgot, in his zeal to reach the ears and the soul of this new listener, both his embarrassment in the pulpit and the necessity of prayer in the study on Sunday mornings.

Reverend Hartman's experience with women had been somewhat limited. He was the son of a wagon-maker from Muncie, Indiana, and had worked his way through college. The daughter of the underwear manufacturer had boarded in a house where he lived during his school days and he had married her after a formal and prolonged courtship, carried on for the most part by the girl herself. On his marriage day the underwear manufacturer had given his daughter five thousand dollars and he promised to leave her at least twice that amount in his will. The minister had thought himself fortunate in marriage and had never permitted himself to think of other women. He did not want to think of other women. What he wanted was to do the work of God quietly and earnestly.

In the soul of the minister a struggle awoke. From wanting to reach the ears of Kate Swift, and through his sermons to delve into her soul, he began to want also to look again at the figure lying white and quiet in the bed. On a Sunday morning when he could not sleep because of his thoughts he arose and went to walk in the streets. When he had gone along Main Street almost to the old Richmond place he stopped and, picking up a stone, rushed off to the room in the bell tower. With the stone he broke out a corner of the window and then locked the door and sat down at the desk before the open Bible to wait. When the shade of the window to Kate Swift's room was raised he could see, through the hole, directly into her bed, but she was not there. She also had arisen and had gone for a walk and the hand that raised the shade was the hand of Aunt Elizabeth Swift.

The minister almost wept with joy at this deliverance from the carnal desire to 'peep' and went back to his own house praising God. In an ill moment he forgot, however, to stop the hole in the window. The piece of glass broken out at the corner of the window just nipped off the bare heel of the boy standing motionless and looking with rapt eyes into the face of the Christ.

Curtis Hartman forgot his sermon on that Sunday morning. He talked to his congregation and in his talk said that it was a mistake for people to think of their minister as a man set aside and intended by nature to lead a blameless life. 'Out of my own experience I know that we, who are the ministers of God's word, are beset by the same temptations that assail you,' he declared. 'I have been tempted and have surrendered to temptation. It is only the hand of God, placed beneath my head, that has raised me up. As he has raised me so also will he raise you. Do not despair. In your hour of sin raise your eyes to the skies and you will be again and again saved.'

Resolutely the minister put the thoughts of the woman in the bed out of his mind and began to be something like a lover in the presence of his wife. One evening when they drove out together he turned the horse out of Buckeye Street and in the darkness on Gospel Hill, above Waterworks Pond, put his arm about Sarah Hartman's waist. When he had eaten breakfast in the morning and was ready to retire to his study at the back of his house he went around the table and kissed his wife on the cheek. When thoughts of Kate Swift came into his head, he smiled and raised his eyes to the skies. 'Intercede for me, Master,' he muttered, 'keep me in the narrow path intent on Thy work.'

And now began the real struggle in the soul of the brown-bearded minister. By chance he discovered that Kate Swift was in the habit of lying in her bed in the evenings and reading a book. A lamp stood on a table by the side of the bed and the light streamed down upon her white shoulders and bare throat. On the evening when he made the discovery the minister sat at the desk in the study from nine until after eleven and when her light was put out stumbled out of the church to spend two more hours walking and praying in the streets. He did not want to kiss the shoulders and the throat of Kate Swift and had not allowed his mind to dwell on such thoughts. He did not know what he wanted. 'I am God's child and he must save me from myself,' he cried, in the darkness under the trees as he wandered in the streets. By a tree he stood and looked at the sky that was covered with hurrying clouds. He began to talk to God intimately and closely. 'Please, Father, do not forget me. Give me power to go tomorrow and repair the hole in the window. Lift my eyes again to the skies. Stay with me, Thy servant, in his hour of need.'

Up and down through the silent streets walked the minister and for days and weeks his soul was troubled. He could not understand the temptation that had come to him nor could he fathom the reason for its coming. In a way he began to blame God, saying to himself that he had tried to keep his feet in the true path and had not run about seeking sin. 'Through my days as a young man and all through my life here I have gone quietly about my work,' he declared. 'Why now should I be tempted? What have I done that this burden should be laid on me?'

Three times during the early fall and winter of that year Curtis Hartman crept out of his house to the room in the bell tower to sit in the darkness looking at the figure of Kate Swift lying in her bed and later went to walk and pray in the streets. He could not understand himself. For weeks he would go along scarcely thinking of the schoolteacher and telling himself that he had conquered the carnal desire to look at her body. And then something would happen. As he sat in the study of his own house, hard at work on a sermon, he would become nervous and begin to walk up and down the room. 'I will go out into the streets,' he told himself and even as he let himself in at the church door he persistently denied to himself the cause of his being there. 'I will not repair the hole in the window and I will train myself to come here at night and sit in the presence of this woman without raising my eyes. I will not be defeated in this thing. The Lord has devised this temptation as a test of my soul and I will grope my way out of darkness into the light of righteousness.'

One night in January when it was bitter cold and snow lay deep on the streets of Winesburg, Curtis Hartman paid his last visit to the room in the bell tower of the church. It was past nine o'clock when he left his own house and he set out so hurriedly that he forgot to put on his overshoes. In Main Street no one was abroad but Hop Higgins the night watchman and in the whole town no one was awake but the watchman and young George Willard, who sat in the office of the *Winesburg Eagle* trying to write a story. Along the street to the church went the minister, plowing through the drifts and thinking that this time he would utterly give way to sin. 'I want to look at the woman and to think of kissing her shoulders and I am going to let myself think what I choose,' he declared bitterly and tears came into his eyes. He began to think that he would get out of the ministry and try some other way of life. 'I shall go to some city and get into business,' he declared. 'If my nature is such that I cannot resist sin, I shall give myself over to sin. At least I shall not be a hypocrite, preaching the word of God with my mind thinking of the shoulders and neck of a woman who does not belong to me.'

It was cold in the room of the bell tower of the church on that January night and almost as soon as he came into the room Curtis Hartman knew that if he stayed he would be ill. His feet were wet from tramping in the snow and there was no fire. In the room in the house next door Kate Swift had not yet appeared. With grim determination the man sat down to wait. Sitting in the chair and gripping the edge of the desk on which lay the Bible he stared into the darkness thinking the blackest thoughts of his life. He thought of his wife and for the moment almost hated her. 'She has always been ashamed of passion and has cheated me,' he thought. 'Man has a right to expect living passion and beauty in a woman. He has no right to forget that he is an animal and in me there is something that is Greek. I will throw off the woman of my bosom and seek other women. I will besiege this schoolteacher. I will fly in the face of all men and if I am a creature of carnal lusts I will live then for my lusts.'

The distracted man trembled from head to foot, partly from cold, partly from the struggle in which he was engaged. Hours passed and a fever assailed his body. His throat began to hurt and his teeth chattered. His feet on the study floor felt like two cakes of ice. Still he would not give up. 'I will see this woman and will think the thoughts I have never dared to think,' he told himself, gripping the edge of the desk and waiting.

Curtis Hartman came near dying from the effects of that night of waiting in the church, and also he found in the thing that happened what he took to be the way of life for him. On other evenings when he had waited he had not been able to see, through the little hole in the glass, any part of the schoolteacher's room except that occupied by her bed. In the darkness he had waited until the woman suddenly appeared sitting in the bed in her white night-robe. When the light was turned up she propped herself up among the pillows and read a book. Sometimes she smoked one of the cigarettes. Only her bare shoulders and throat were visible.

On the January night, after he had come near dying with cold and after his mind had two or three times actually slipped away into an odd land of fantasy so that he had by an exercise of will power to force himself back into consciousness, Kate Swift appeared. In the room next door a lamp was lighted and the waiting man stared into an empty bed. Then upon the bed before his eyes a naked woman threw herself. Lying face downward she wept and beat with her fists upon the pillow. With a final outburst of weeping she half arose, and in the presence of the man who had waited to look and to think thoughts the woman of sin began to pray. In the lamplight her figure, slim and strong, looked like the figure of the boy in the presence of the Christ on the leaded window.

Curtis Hartman never remembered how he got out of the church. With a cry he arose, dragging the heavy desk along the floor. The Bible fell, making a great clatter in the silence. When the light in the house next door went out he stumbled down the stairway and into the street. Along the street he went and ran in at the door of the *Winesburg Eagle*. To George Willard, who was tramping up and down in the office undergoing a struggle of his own, he began to talk half incoherently. 'The ways of God are beyond human understanding,' he cried, running in quickly and closing the door. He began to advance upon the young man, his eyes glowing and his voice ringing with fervor. 'I have found the light,' he cried. 'After ten years in this town, God has manifested himself to me in the body of a woman.' His voice dropped and he began to whisper. 'I did not understand,' he said. 'What I took to be a trial of my soul was only a preparation for a new and more beautiful fervor of the spirit. God has appeared to me in the person of Kate Swift, the schoolteacher, kneeling naked on a bed. Do you know Kate Swift? Although she may not be aware of it, she is an instrument of God, bearing the message of truth.'

Reverend Curtis Hartman turned and ran out of the office. At the door he stopped, and after looking up and down the deserted street, turned again to George Willard. 'I am delivered. Have no fear.' He held up a bleeding fist for the young man to see. 'I smashed the glass of the window,' he cried. 'Now it will have to be wholly replaced. The strength of God was in me and I broke it with my fist.'

Green Tea

Sheridan Le Fanu

PROLOGUE

Martin Hesselius, the German Physician

Though carefully educated in medicine and surgery, I have never practised either. The study of each continues, nevertheless, to interest me
profoundly. Neither idleness nor caprice caused my secession from the
honourable calling which I had just entered. The cause was a very trifling
scratch inflicted by a dissecting knife. This trifle cost me the loss of two
fingers, amputated promptly, and the more painful loss of my health, for
I have never been quite well since, and have seldom been twelve months
together in the same place.

In my wanderings I became acquainted with Dr Martin Hesselius, a
wanderer like myself, like me a physician, and like me an enthusiast in
his profession. Unlike me in this, that his wanderings were voluntary,
and he a man, if not of fortune, as we estimate fortune in England, at
least in what our forefathers used to term 'easy circumstances'. He was
an old man when I first saw him; nearly five-and-thirty years my senior.

In Dr Martin Hesselius, I found my master. His knowledge was immense, his grasp of a case was an intuition. He was the very man to
inspire a young enthusiast, like me, with awe and delight. My admiration
has stood the test of time and survived the separation of death. I am sure
it was well founded.

For nearly twenty years I acted as his medical secretary. His immense collection of papers he has left in my care, to be arranged, indexed and bound. His treatment of some of these cases is curious. He writes in two distinct characters. He describes what he saw and heard as an intelligent layman might, and when in this style of narrative he had seen the patient either through his own hall-door, to the light of day, or through the gates of darkness to the caverns of the dead, he returns upon the narrative, and in the terms of his art, and with all the force and originality of genius, proceeds to the work of analysis, diagnosis and illustration.

Here and there a case strikes me as of a kind to amuse or horrify a lay reader with an interest quite different from the peculiar one which it may possess for an expert. With slight modifications, chiefly of language, and of course a change of names, I copy the following. The narrator is Dr Martin Hesselius. I found it among the voluminous notes of cases which he made during a tour of England about sixty-four years ago.

It is related in a series of letters to his friend Professor Van Loo of Leyden. The professor was not a physician, but a chemist, and a man who read history and metaphysics and medicine, and had, in his day, written a play.

The narrative is therefore, if somewhat less valuable as a medical record, necessarily written in a manner more likely to interest an unlearned reader.

These letters, from a memorandum attached, appear to have been returned on the death of the professor, in 1819, to Dr Hesselius. They are written, some in English, some in French, but the greater part in German. I am a faithful, though I am conscious, by no means a graceful translator, and although here and there, I omit some passages, and shorten others and disguise names, I have interpolated nothing.

CHAPTER I

Dr Hesselius Relates How He Met the Reverend Mr Jennings

The Reverend Mr Jennings is tall and thin. He is middle-aged, and dresses with a natty, old-fashioned, high-church precision. He is naturally a little stately, but not at all stiff. His features, without being handsome, are well-formed, and their expression extremely kind but also shy.

I met him one evening at Lady Mary Heyduke's. The modesty and benevolence of his countenance are extremely preposessing.

We were but a small party, and he joined agreeably enough in the conversation. He seems to enjoy listening very much more than contributing to the talk; but what he says is always to the purpose and well said. He is a great favourite of Lady Mary's, who it seems, consults him upon many things, and thinks him the most happy and blessed person on earth. Little knows she about him.

The Reverend Mr Jennings is a bachelor, and has, they say, sixty thousand pounds in the funds. He is a charitable man. He is most anxious to be actively employed in his sacred profession, and yet though always tolerably well elsewhere, when he goes down to his vicarage in Warwickshire, to engage in the actual duties of his sacred calling, his health soon fails him, and in a very strange way. So says Lady Mary.

There is no doubt that Mr Jennings's health does break down in, generally, a sudden and mysterious way, sometimes in the very act of officiating in his old and pretty church at Kenlis. It may be his heart, it may be his brain. But so it has happened three or four times, or oftener, that after proceeding a certain way in the service, he has on a sudden stopped short, and after a silence, apparently quite unable to resume, he has fallen into solitary, inaudible prayer, his hands and eyes uplifted, and then pale as death, and in the agitation of a strange shame and horror, descended trembling, and got into the vestry-room, leaving his congregation, without explanation, to themselves. This occurred when his curate was absent. When he goes down to Kenlis, now, he always takes care to provide a clergyman to share his duty, and to supply his place on the instant should he become thus suddenly incapacitated.

When Mr Jennings breaks down quite, and beats a retreat from the vicarage, and returns to London, where, in a dark street off Piccadilly, he inhabits a very narrow house, Lady Mary says that he is always perfectly well. I have my own opinion about that. There are degrees of course. We shall see.

Mr Jennings is a perfectly gentleman-like man. People, however, remark something odd. There is an impression a little ambiguous. One thing which certainly contributes to it, people I think don't remember, or, perhaps, distinctly remark. But I did, almost immediately. Mr Jennings has a way of looking sidelong upon the carpet, as if his eye followed the movements of something there. This, of course, is not always. It occurs only now and then. But often enough to give a certain oddity, as I have said, to his manner, and in this glance travelling along the floor there is something both shy and anxious.

A medical philosopher, as you are good enough to call me, elaborating theories by the aid of cases sought out by himself, and by him watched and scrutinized with more time at command, and consequently infinitely more minuteness than the ordinary practitioner can afford, falls insensibly into habits of observation, which accompany him everywhere, and are exercised, as some people would say, impertinently, upon every subject that presents itself with the least likelihood of rewarding enquiry.

There was a promise of this kind in the slight, timid, kindly, but reserved gentleman, whom I met for the first time at this agreeable little evening gathering. I observed, of course, more than I here set down; but I reserve all that borders on the technical for a strictly scientific paper.

I may remark, that when I here speak of medical science, I do so, as I hope some day to see it more generally understood, in a much more comprehensive sense than its generally material treatment would warrant. I believe the entire natural world is but the ultimate expression of that spiritual world from which, and in which alone, it has its life. I believe that the essential man is a spirit, that the spirit is an organized substance, but as different in point of material from what we ordinarily understand by matter, as light or electricity is; that the material body is, in the most literal sense, a vesture, and death consequently no interruption of the living man's existence, but simply his extrication from the natural body – a process which commences at the moment of what we term death; and the completion of which, at furthest a few days later, is the resurrection 'in power'.

The person who weighs the consequences of these positions will probably see their practical bearing upon medical science. This is, however, by no means the proper place for displaying the proofs and discussing the consequences of this too generally unrecognized state of facts.

In pursuance of my habit, I was covertly observing Mr Jennings, with all my caution – I think he perceived it – and I saw plainly that he was as cautiously observing me. Lady Mary happening to address me by my name, as Dr Hesselius, I saw that he glanced at me more sharply, and then became thoughtful for a few minutes.

After this, as I conversed with a gentleman at the other end of the room, I saw him look at me more steadily, and with an interest which I thought I understood. I then saw him take an opportunity of chatting with Lady Mary, and was, as one always is, perfectly aware of being the subject of a distant enquiry and answer.

This tall clergyman approached me by-and-by: and in a little time we had got into conversation. When two people, who like reading, and know books and places, having travelled, wish to converse, it is very strange if they can't find topics. It was not accident that brought him near me, and led him into conversation. He knew German, and had read my *Essays on Metaphysical Medicine* which suggest more than they actually say.

This courteous man, gentle, shy, plainly a man of thought and reading, who moving and talking among us, was not altogether of us, and whom I already suspected of leading a life whose transactions and alarms were carefully concealed, with an impenetrable reserve from, not only the world, but his best-beloved friends – was cautiously weighing in his own mind the idea of taking a certain step with regard to me.

I penetrated his thoughts without his being aware of it, and was careful to say nothing which could betray to his sensitive vigilance my suspicions respecting his position, or my surmises about his plans respecting myself.

We chatted upon indifferent subjects for a time; but at last he said:

'I was very much interested by some papers of yours, Dr Hesselius, upon what you term Metaphysical Medicine – I read them in German, ten or twelve years ago – have they been translated?'

'No, I'm sure they have not – I should have heard. They would have asked my leave, I think.'

'I asked the publishers here, a few months ago, to get the book for me in the original German; but they tell me it is out of print.'

'So it is, and has been for some years; but it flatters me as an author to find that you have not forgotten my little book, although', I added, laughing, 'ten or twelve years is a considerable time to have managed without it; but I suppose you have been turning the subject over again in your mind, or something has happened lately to revive your interest in it.'

At this remark, accompanied by a glance of enquiry, a sudden embarrassment disturbed Mr Jennings, analogous to that which makes a young lady blush and look foolish. He dropped his eyes, and folded his hands together uneasily, and looked oddly, and you would have said, guiltily for a moment.

I helped him out of his awkwardness in the best way, by appearing not to observe it, and going straight on, I said: 'Those revivals of interest in a subject happen to me often; one book suggests another, and often sends me back a wild-goose chase over an interval of twenty years. But if you still care to possess a copy, I shall be only too happy to provide you; I have still got two or three by me – and if you allow me to present one I shall be very much honoured.'

'You are very good indeed,' he said, quite at his ease again, in a moment: 'I almost despaired – I don't know how to thank you.'

'Pray don't say a word; the thing is really so little worth that I am only ashamed of having offered it, and if you thank me any more I shall throw it into the fire in a fit of modesty.'

Mr Jennings laughed. He enquired where I was staying in London, and after a little more conversation on a variety of subjects, he took his departure.

CHAPTER II

The Doctor Questions Lady Mary, and She Answers

'I like your vicar so much, Lady Mary,' said I, so soon as he was gone. 'He has read, travelled, and thought, and having also suffered, he ought to be an accomplished companion.'

'So he is, and, better still, he is a really good man,' said she. 'His advice is invaluable about my schools, and all my little undertakings at Dawlbridge, and he's so painstaking, he takes so much trouble – you have no idea – wherever he thinks he can be of use: he's so good-natured and so sensible.'

'It is pleasant to hear so good an account of his neighbourly virtues. I can only testify to his being an agreeable and gentle companion, and in addition to what you have told me, I think I can tell you two or three things about him,' said I.

'Really!'

'Yes, to begin with, he's unmarried.'

'Yes, that's right – go on.'

'He has been writing, that is he *was*, but for two or three years perhaps, he has not gone on with his work, and the book was upon some rather abstract subject – perhaps theology.'

'Well, he was writing a book, as you say; I'm not quite sure what it was about, but only that it was nothing that I cared for, very likely you are right, and he certainly did stop – yes.'

'And although he only drank a little coffee here tonight, he likes tea, at least, did like it, extravagantly.'

'Yes, that's *quite* true.'

'He drank green tea, a good deal, didn't he?' I pursued.

'Well, that's very odd! Green tea was a subject on which we used almost to quarrel.'

'But he has quite given that up,' said I.

'So he has.'

'And, now, one more fact. His mother or his father, did you know them?'

'Yes, both; his father is only ten years dead, and their place is near Dawlbridge. We knew them very well,' she answered.

'Well, either his mother or his father – I should rather think his father, saw a ghost,' said I.

'Well, you really are a conjurer, Dr Hesselius.'

'Conjurer or no, haven't I said right?' I answered merrily.

'You certainly have, and it *was* his father: he was a silent, whimsical man, and he used to bore my father about his dreams, and at last he told him a story about a ghost he had seen and talked with, and a very odd story it was. I remember it particularly, because I was so afraid of him. This story was long before he died – when I was quite a child – and his ways were so silent and moping, and he used to drop in, sometimes, in the dusk, when I was alone in the drawing-room, and I used to fancy there were ghosts about him.'

I smiled and nodded.

'And now having established my character as a conjurer I think I must say goodnight,' said I.

'But how *did* you find it out?'

'By the planets of course, as the gipsies do,' I answered, and so, gaily, we said good-night.

Next morning I sent the little book he had been enquiring after, and a note to Mr Jennings, and on returning late that evening, I found that he had called, at my lodgings, and left his card. He asked whether I was at home, and asked at what hour he would be most likely to find me.

Does he intend opening his case, and consulting me 'professionally', as they say? I hope so. I have already conceived a theory about him. It is supported by Lady Mary's answers to my parting questions. I should like much to ascertain from his own lips. But what can I do consistently with good breeding to invite a confession? Nothing. I rather think he meditates one. At all events, my dear Van L., I shan't make myself difficult of access; I mean to return his visit tomorrow. It will be only civil in return for his politeness, to ask to see him. Perhaps something may come of it. Whether much, little, or nothing, my dear Van L., you shall hear.

CHAPTER III

Dr Hesselius Picks Up Something in Latin Books

Well, I have called at Blank Street.

On enquiring at the door, the servant told me that Mr Jennings was engaged very particularly with a gentleman, a clergyman from Kenlis, his parish in the country. Intending to reserve my privilege and to call again, I merely intimated that I should try another time, and had turned to go, when the servant begged my pardon, and asked me, looking at me a little more attentively than well-bred persons of his order usually do, whether I was Dr Hesselius; and, on learning that I was, he said, 'Perhaps then, sir, you would allow me to mention it to Mr Jennings, for I am sure he wishes to see you.'

The servant returned in a moment, with a message from Mr Jennings, asking me to go into his study, which was in effect his back drawing-room, promising to be with me in a very few minutes.

This was really a study – almost a library. The room was lofty, with two tall slender windows, and rich dark curtains. It was much larger than I had expected, and stored with books on every side, from the floor to the ceiling. The upper carpet – for to my tread it felt that there were two or three – was a Turkey carpet. My steps fell noiselessly. The book-cases standing out, placed the windows, particularly narrow ones, in deep recesses. The effect of the room was, although extremely comfortable, and even luxurious, decidedly gloomy, and aided by the silence, almost oppressive. Perhaps, however, I ought to have allowed something for association. My mind had connected peculiar ideas with Mr Jennings. I stepped into this perfectly silent room, of a very silent house, with a peculiar foreboding; and its darkness, and solemn clothing of books, for except where two narrow looking-glasses were set in the wall, they were everywhere, helped this sombre feeling.

While awaiting Mr Jennings's arrival, I amused myself by looking into some of the books with which his shelves were laden. Not among these, but immediately under them, with their backs upward, on the floor, I lighted upon a complete set of Swedenborg's *Arcana Caelestia*, in the original Latin, a very fine folio set, bound in the natty livery which theology affects, pure vellum, namely, gold letters, and carmine edges. There were paper markers in several of these volumes. I raised and placed them, one after the other, upon the table, and opening where these papers were placed, I read in the solemn Latin phraseology, a series of sentences indicated by a pencilled line at the margin. Of these I copy here a few, translating them into English.

'When man's interior sight is opened, which is that of his spirit, then there appear the things of another life, which cannot possibly be made visible to the bodily sight.'

'By the internal sight it has been granted me to see things that are in the other life, more clearly than I see those that are in the world. From these considerations, it is evident that external vision exists from interior vision, and this from a vision still more interior, and so on.'

'There are with every man at least two evil spirits.'

'With wicked genii there is also a fluent speech, but harsh and grating. There is also among them a speech which is not fluent, wherein the dissent of the thoughts is perceived as something secretly creeping along within it.'

'The evil spirits associated with man are, indeed, from the hells, but when with man they are not then in hell, but are taken out thence. The place where they then are is in the midst between heaven and hell, and is called the world of spirits – when the evil spirits who are with man, are in that world, they are not in any infernal torment, but in every thought and affection of the man, and so, in all that the man himself enjoys. But when they are remitted into their hell, they return to the former state.'

'If evil spirits could perceive that they were associated with man, and yet that they were spirits separate from him, and if they could flow in into the things of his body, they would attempt by a thousand means to destroy him; for they hate man with a deadly hatred.'

'Knowing, therefore, that I was a man in the body, they were continually striving to destroy me, not as to the body only, but especially
as to the soul; for to destroy any man or spirit is the very delight of the
life of all who are in hell; but I have been continually protected by the
Lord. Hence it appears how dangerous it is for man to be in a living
consort with spirits, unless he be in the good of faith.'

'Nothing is more carefully guarded from the knowledge of associate
spirits than their being thus conjoint with a man, for if they knew it
they would speak to him, with the intention to destroy him.'

'The delight of hell is to do evil to man, and to hasten his eternal ruin.'

A long note, written with a very sharp and fine pencil, in Mr Jennings's
neat hand, at the foot of the page, caught my eye. Expecting his criticism
upon the text, I read a word or two, and stopped, for it was something quite
different, and began with these words, *Deus misereatur mei* – 'May God
compassionate me.' Thus warned of its private nature, I averted my eyes,
and shut the book, replacing all the volumes as I had found them, except
one which interested me, and in which, as men studious and solitary in
their habits will do, I grew so absorbed as to take no cognizance of the
outer world, nor to remember where I was.

I was reading some pages which refer to 'representatives' and 'cor-
respondents', in the technical language of Swedenborg, and had arrived
at a passage, the substance of which is, that evil spirits, when seen by
other eyes than those of their infernal associates, present themselves,
by 'correspondence', in the shape of the beast (*fera*) which represents
their particular lust and life, in aspect direful and atrocious. This is a
long passage, and particularizes a number of those bestial forms.

CHAPTER IV

Four Eyes Were Reading the Passage

I was running the head of my pencil-case along the line as I read
it, and something caused me to raise my eyes.

Directly before me was one of the mirrors I have mentioned, in which
I saw reflected the tall shape of my friend Mr Jennings leaning over my
shoulder, and reading the page at which I was busy, and with a face so

dark and wild that I should hardly have known him.

I turned and rose. He stood erect also, and with an effort laughed a little, saying:

'I came in and asked you how you did, but without succeeding in awaking you from your book; so I could not restrain my curiosity, and very impertinently, I'm afraid, peeped over your shoulder. This is not your first time of looking into those pages. You have looked into Swedenborg, no doubt, long ago?'

'O dear, yes! I owe Swedenborg a great deal; you will discover traces of him in the little book on Metaphysical Medicine, which you were so good as to remember.'

Although my friend affected a gaiety of manner, there was a slight flush in his face, and I could perceive that he was inwardly much perturbed.

'I'm scarcely yet qualified, I know so little of Swedenborg. I've only had them a fortnight,' he answered, 'and I think they are rather likely to make a solitary man nervous – that is, judging from the very little I have read – I don't say that they have made me so,' he laughed; 'and I'm so very much obliged for the book. I hope you got my note?'

I made all proper acknowledgements and modest disclaimers.

'I never read a book that I go with, so entirely, as that of yours,' he continued. 'I saw at once there is more in it than is quite unfolded. Do you know Dr Harley?' he asked, rather abruptly.

(In passing, the editor remarks that the physician here named was one of the most eminent who had ever practised in England.)

I did, having had letters to him, and had experienced from him great courtesy and considerable assistance during my visit to England.

'I think that man one of the very greatest fools I ever met in my life,' said Mr Jennings.

This was the first time I had ever heard him say a sharp thing of anybody, and such a term applied to so high a name a little startled me.

'Really! and in what way?' I asked.

'In his profession,' he answered.

I smiled.

'I mean this,' he said: 'he seems to me, one half, blind – I mean one half of all he looks at is dark – preternaturally bright and vivid all the rest; and the worst of it is, it seems *wilful*. I can't get him – I mean he won't – I've had some experience of him as a physician, but I look on him as, in that sense, no better than a paralytic mind, an intellect half dead, I'll tell you – I know I shall some time – all about it,' he said, with a little agitation. 'You stay some months longer in England. If I should be out of town during your stay for a little time, would you allow me to trouble you with a letter?'

'I should be only too happy,' I assured him.

'Very good of you. I am so utterly dissatisfied with Harley.'

'A little leaning to the materialistic school,' I said.

'A *mere* materialist,' he corrected me; 'you can't think how that sort of thing worries one who knows better. You won't tell anyone – any of my friends you know – that I am hippish; now, for instance, no one knows – not even Lady Mary – that I have seen Dr Harley, or any other doctor. So pray don't mention it; and, if I should have any threatening of an attack, you'll kindly let me write, or, should I be in town, have a talk with you.'

I was full of conjecture, and unconsciously I found I had fixed my eyes gravely on him, for he lowered his for a moment, and he said:

'I see you think I might as well tell you now, or else you are forming a conjecture; but you may as well give it up. If you were guessing all the rest of your life, you will never hit on it.'

He shook his head smiling, and over that wintry sunshine a black cloud suddenly came down, and he drew his breath in, through his teeth as men do in pain.

'Sorry, of course, to learn that you apprehend occasion to consult any of us; but, command me when and how you like, and I need not assure you that your confidence is sacred.'

He then talked of quite other things, and in a comparatively cheerful way and after a little time, I took my leave.

CHAPTER V

Dr Hesselius is Summoned to Richmond

We parted cheerfully, but he was not cheerful, nor was I. There are certain expressions of that powerful organ of spirit – the human face – which, although I have seen them often, and possess a doctor's nerve, yet disturb me profoundly. One look of Mr Jennings haunted me. It had seized my imagination with so dismal a power that I changed my plans for the evening, and went to the opera, feeling that I wanted a change of ideas.

I heard nothing of or from him for two or three days, when a note in his hand reached me. It was cheerful, and full of hope. He said that he had been for some little time so much better – quite well, in fact – that he was going to make a little experiment, and run down for a month or so to his parish, to try whether a little work might not quite set him up. There was in it a fervent religious expression of gratitude for his restoration, as he now almost hoped he might call it.

A day or two later I saw Lady Mary, who repeated what his note had announced, and told me that he was actually in Warwickshire, having resumed his clerical duties at Kenlis; and she added, 'I begin to think that he is really perfectly well, and that there never was anything the matter, more than nerves and fancy; we are all nervous, but I fancy there is nothing like a little hard work for that kind of weakness, and he has made up his mind to try it. I should not be surprised if he did not come back for a year.'

Notwithstanding all this confidence, only two days later I had this note, dated from his house off Piccadilly:

'Dear Sir. – I have returned disappointed. If I should feel at all able to see you, I shall write to ask you kindly to call. At present I am too low, and, in fact, simply unable to say all I wish to say. Pray don't mention my name to my friends. I can see no one. By-and-by, please God, you shall hear from me. I mean to take a run into Shropshire, where some of my people are. God bless you! May we, on my return, meet more happily than I can now write.'

About a week after this I saw Lady Mary at her own house, the last person, she said, left in town, and just on the wing for Brighton, for the London season was quite over. She told me that she had heard from Mr Jennings's niece, Martha, in Shropshire. There was nothing to be gathered from her letter, more than that he was low and nervous. In those words, of which healthy people think so lightly, what a world of suffering is sometimes hidden!

Nearly five weeks passed without any further news of Mr Jennings. At the end of that time I received a note from him. He wrote:

'I have been in the country, and have had change of air, change of scene, change of faces, change of everything and in everything – but *myself*. I have made up my mind, so far as the most irresolute creature on each can do it, to tell my case fully to you. If your engagements will permit, pray come to me today, tomorrow, or the next day; but, pray defer as little as possible. You know not how much I need help. I have a quiet house at Richmond, where I now am. Perhaps you can manage to come to dinner, or to luncheon, or even to tea. You shall have no trouble in finding me out. The servant at Blank Street, who takes this note, will have a carriage at your door at any hour you please; and I am always to be found. You will say that I ought not to be alone. I have tried everything. Come and see.'

I called up the servant, and decided on going out the same evening, which accordingly I did.

He would have been much better in a lodging-house, or hotel, I thought, as I drove up through a short double row of sombre elms to a very old-fashioned brick house, darkened by the foliage of these trees, which over-topped, and nearly surrounded it. It was a perverse choice, for nothing could be imagined more triste and silent. The house, I found, belonged to him. He had stayed for a day or two in town, and finding it for some cause insupportable, had come out here, probably because being furnished and his own, he was relieved of the thought and delay of selection, by coming here.

The sun had already set, and the red reflected light of the western sky illuminated the scene with the peculiar effect with which we are all familiar. The hall seemed very dark, but, getting to the back drawing-room, whose windows command the west, I was again in the same dusky light.

I sat down, looking out upon the richly wooded landscape that glowed in the grand and the melancholy light which was every moment fading. The corners of the room were already dark; all was growing dim, and the gloom was insensibly toning my mind, already prepared for what was sinister. I was waiting alone for his arrival, which soon took place. The door communicating with the front room opened, and the tall figure of Mr Jennings, faintly seen in the ruddy twilight, came, with quiet stealthy steps, into the room.

We shook hands, and, taking a chair to the window, where there was still light enough to enable us to see each other's faces, he sat down beside me, and, placing his hand upon my arm, with scarcely word of preface began his narrative.

CHAPTER VI

How Mr Jennings Met His Companion

The faint glow of the west, the pomp of the then lonely woods of Richmond, were before us, behind and about us the darkening room, and on the stony face of the sufferer – for the character of his face, though still gentle and sweet, was changed – rested that dim, odd glow which seems to descend and produce, where it touches, lights, sudden though faint, which are lost, almost without gradation, in darkness. The silence, too, was utter, not a distant wheel, or bark, or whistle from without; and within the depressing stillness of an invalid bachelor's house.

I guessed well the nature, though not even vaguely the particulars of the revelations I was about to receive, from the fixed face of suffering that so oddly flushed stood out, like a portrait of Schalken's, before its background of darkness.

'It began,' he said, 'on the 15th of October, three years and eleven weeks ago, and two days – I keep very accurate count, for every day is torment. If I leave anywhere a chasm in my narrative tell me.

'About four years ago I began a work, which had cost me very much thought and reading. It was upon the religious metaphysics of the ancients.'

'I know,' said I; 'the actual religion of educated and thinking paganism, quite apart from symbolic worship? A wide and very interesting field.'

'Yes; but not good for the mind – the Christian mind, I mean. Paganism is all bound together in essential unity, and, with evil sympathy, their religion involves their art, and both their manners, and the subject is a degrading fascination and the nemesis sure. God forgive me!'

'I wrote a great deal; I wrote late at night. I was always thinking on the subject, walking about, wherever I was, everywhere. It thoroughly infected me. You are to remember that all the material ideas connected with it were more or less of the beautiful, the subject itself delightfully interesting, and I, then, without a care.'

He sighed heavily.

'I believe that everyone who sets about writing in earnest does his work, as a friend of mine phrased it, *on* something – tea, or coffee, or tobacco. I suppose there is a material waste that must be hourly supplied in such occupations, or that we should grow too abstracted, and the mind, as it were, pass out of the body, unless it were reminded often of the connection by actual sensation. At all events, I felt the want, and I supplied it. Tea was my companion – at first the ordinary black tea, made in the usual way, not too strong: but I drank a good deal, and increased its strength as I went on. I never experienced an uncomfortable symptom from it. I began to take a little green tea. I found the effect pleasanter, it cleared and intensified the power of thought so. I had come to take it frequently, but not stronger than one might take it for pleasure. I wrote a great deal out here, it was so quiet, and in this room. I used to sit up very late, and it became a habit with me to sip my tea – green tea – every now and then as my work proceeded. I had a little kettle on my table, that swung over a lamp, and made tea two or three times between eleven o'clock and two or three in the morning, my hours of going to bed. I used to go into town every day. I was not a monk, and, although I spent an hour or two in a library, hunting up authorities and looking out lights upon my theme, I was in no morbid state as far as I can judge. I met my friends pretty much as usual, and enjoyed their society, and, on the whole, existence had never been, I think, so pleasant before.

'I had met with a man who had some odd old books, German editions in medieval Latin, and I was only too happy to be permitted access to them. This obliging person's books were in the City, a very out-of-the-way part of it. I had rather out-stayed my intended hour, and, on coming out, seeing no cab near, I was tempted to get into the omnibus which used to drive past this house. It was darker than this by the time the 'bus had reached an old house, you may have remarked, with four poplars at each side of the door, and there the last passenger but myself got out. We drove along rather faster. It was twilight now. I leaned back in my corner next the door ruminating pleasantly.

'The interior of the omnibus was nearly dark. I had observed in the corner opposite to me at the other side, and at the end next the horses, two small circular reflections, as it seemed to me of a reddish light. They were about two inches apart, and about the size of those small brass buttons that yachting men used to put upon their jackets. I began to speculate, as listless men will, upon this trifle, as it seemed. From what centre did that faint but deep red light come, and from what – glass beads, buttons, toy decorations – was it reflected? We were lumbering along gently, having nearly a mile still to go. I had not solved the puzzle, and it became in another minute more odd, for these two luminous points, with a sudden jerk, descended nearer the floor, keeping still their relative distance and horizontal position, and then, as suddenly, they rose to the level of the seat on which I was sitting, and I saw them no more.

'My curiosity was now really excited, and, before I had time to think, I saw again these two dull lamps, again together near the floor; again they disappeared, and again in their old corner I saw them.

'So, keeping my eyes upon them, I edged quietly up my own side, towards the end at which I still saw these tiny discs of red.

'There was very little light in the 'bus. It was nearly dark. I leaned forward to aid my endeavour to discover what these little circles really were. They shifted their position a little as I did so. I began now to perceive an outline of something black, and I soon saw with tolerable distinctness the outline of a small black monkey, pushing its face forward in mimicry to meet mine; those were its eyes, and I now dimly saw its teeth grinning at me.

'I drew back, not knowing whether it might not meditate a spring. I fancied that one of the passengers had forgot this ugly pet, and wishing to ascertain something of its temper, though not caring to trust my fingers to it, I poked my umbrella softly towards it. It remained immovable – up to it – *through* it! For through it, and back and forward, it passed, without the slightest resistance.

'I can't, in the least, convey to you the kind of horror that I felt. When I had ascertained that the thing was an illusion, as I then supposed, there came a misgiving about myself and a terror that fascinated me in impotence to remove my gaze from the eyes of the brute for some moments. As I looked, it made a little skip back, quite into the corner, and I, in a panic, found myself at the door, having put my head out, drawing deep breaths of the outer air, and staring at the lights and trees we were passing, too glad to reassure myself of reality.

'I stopped the 'bus and got out. I perceived the man look oddly at me as I paid him. I daresay there was something unusual in my looks and manner, for I had never felt so strangely before.'

CHAPTER VII

The Journey: First Stage

'When the omnibus drove on, and I was alone upon the road, I looked carefully round to ascertain whether the monkey had followed me. To my indescribable relief I saw it nowhere. I can't describe easily what a shock I had received, and my sense of genuine gratitude on finding myself, as I supposed, quite rid of it.

'I had got out a little before we reached this house, two or three hundred steps. A brick wall runs along the footpath, and inside the wall is a hedge of yew or some dark evergreen of that kind, and within that again the row of fine trees which you may have remarked as you came.

'This brick wall is about as high as my shoulder, and happening to raise my eyes I saw the monkey, with that stooping gait, on all fours, walking or creeping, close beside me on top of the wall. I stopped looking at it with a feeling of loathing and horror. As I stopped so did it. It sat up on the wall with its long hands on its knees looking at me. There was not light enough to see it much more than in outline, nor was it dark enough to bring the peculiar light of its eyes into stronger relief. I still saw, however, that red foggy light plainly enough. It did not show its teeth, nor exhibit any sign of irritation, but seemed jaded and sulky, and was observing me steadily.

'I drew back into the middle of the road. It was an unconscious recoil, and there I stood, still looking at it. It did not move.

'With an instinctive determination to try something – anything, I turned about and walked briskly towards town with a skance look, all the time, watching the movements of the beast. It crept swiftly along the wall, at exactly my pace.

'Where the wall ends, near the turn of the road, it came down and with a wiry spring or two brought itself close to my feet, and continued to keep up with me, as I quickened my pace. It was at my left side, so close to my leg that I felt every moment as if I should tread upon it.

'The road was quite deserted and silent, and it was darker every moment. I stopped dismayed and bewildered, turning as I did so, the other way – I mean, towards this house, away from which I had been walking. When I stood still, the monkey drew back to a distance of, I suppose, about five or six yards, and remained stationary, watching me.

'I had been more agitated than I have said. I had read, of course, as everyone has, something about "special illusions", as you physicians term the phenomena of such cases. I considered my situation, and looked my misfortune in the face.

These affections, I had read, are sometimes transitory and sometimes obstinate. I had read of cases in which the appearance, at first harmless, had, step by step, degenerated into something direful and insupportable, and ended by wearing its victim out. Still, as I stood there, but for my bestial companion, quite alone, I tried to comfort myself by repeating again and again the assurance, "the thing is purely disease, a well-known physical affection, as distinctly as small-pox or neuralgia. Doctors are all agreed on that, philosophy demonstrates it. I must not be a fool. I've been sitting up too late, and I daresay my digestion is quite wrong, and with God's help, I shall be all right, and this is but a symptom of nervous dyspepsia." Did I believe all this? Not one word of it, no more than any other miserable being ever did who is once seized and riveted in this satanic captivity. Against my convictions, I might say my knowledge, I was simply bullying myself into a false courage.

'I now walked homeward. I had only a few hundred yards to go. I had forced myself into a sort of resignation, but I had not got over the sickening shock and the flurry of the first certainty of my misfortune.

'I made up my mind to pass the night at home. The brute moved close beside me, and I fancied there was the sort of anxious drawing towards the house, which one sees in tired horses or dogs, sometimes, as they come towards home.

'I was afraid to go into town, I was afraid of anyone's seeing and recognizing me. I was conscious of an irrepressible agitation in my manner. Also, I was afraid of any violent change in my habits, such as going to a place of amusement, or walking from home in order to fatigue myself. At the hall door it waited till I mounted the steps, and when the door was opened entered with me.

'I drank no tea that night. I got cigars and some brandy-and-water. My idea was that I should act upon my material system, and by living for a while in sensation apart from thought, send myself forcibly, as it were, into a new groove. I came up here to this drawing-room. I sat just here. The monkey then got upon a small table that then stood *there*. It looked dazed and languid. An irrepressible uneasiness as to its movements kept my eyes always upon it. Its eyes were half closed, but I could see them glow. It was looking steadily at me. In all situations, at all hours, it is awake and looking at me. That never changes.

'I shall not continue in detail my narrative of this particular night. I shall describe, rather, the phenomena of the first year, which never varied, essentially. I shall describe the monkey as it appeared in daylight. In the dark, as you shall presently hear, there are peculiarities. It is a small monkey, perfectly black. It had only one peculiarity – a character of malignity – unfathomable malignity. During the first year it looked sullen and sick. But this character of intense malice and vigilance was always underlying that surly languor. During all that time it acted as if on a plan of giving me as little trouble as was consistent with watching me. Its eyes were never off me. I have never lost sight of it, except in my sleep, light or dark, day or night, since it came here, excepting when it withdraws for some weeks at a time, unaccountably.

'In total dark it is visible as in daylight. I do not mean merely its eyes. It is *all* visible distinctly in a halo that resembles a glow of red embers, and which accompanies it in all its movements.

'When it leaves me for a time, it is always at night, in the dark, and in the same way. It grows at first uneasy, and then furious, and then advances towards me, grinning and shaking, its paws clenched, and, at the same time, there comes the appearance of fire in the grate. I never have any fire. I can't sleep in the room where there is any, and it draws nearer and nearer to the chimney, quivering, it seems, with rage, and when its fury rises to the highest pitch, it springs into the grate, and up the chimney, and I see it no more.

'When first this happened I thought I was released. I was a new man. A day passed – a night – and no return, and a blessed week – a week – another week. I was always on my knees, Dr Hesselius, always, thanking God and praying. A whole month passed of liberty, but on a sudden, it was with me again.'

CHAPTER VIII

The Second Stage

'It was with me, and the malice which before was torpid under a sullen exterior, was now active. It was perfectly unchanged in every other respect. This new energy was apparent in its activity and its looks, and soon in other ways.'

'For a time, you will understand, the change was shown only in an increased vivacity, and an air of menace, as if it was always brooding over some atrocious plan. Its eyes, as before, were never off me.'

'Is it here now?' I asked.

'No,' he replied, 'it has been absent exactly a fortnight and a day – fifteen days. It has sometimes been away so long as nearly two months, once for three. Its absence always exceeds a fortnight, although it may be out by a single day. Fifteen days having past since I saw it last, it may return now at any moment.'

'Is its return,' I asked, 'accompanied by any peculiar manifestation?'

'Nothing – no,' he said. 'It is simply with me again. On lifting my eyes from a book, or turning my head, I see it, as usual, looking at me, and then it remains, as before, for its appointed time. I have never told so much and so minutely before to anyone.'

I perceived that he was agitated, and looking like death, and he repeatedly applied his handkerchief to his forehead; I suggested that he might be tired, and told him that I would call, with pleasure, in the morning, but he said:

'No, if you don't mind hearing it all now. I have got so far, and I should prefer making one effort of it. When I spoke to Dr Harley, I had nothing like so much to tell. You are a philosophic physician. You give spirit its proper rank. If this thing is real –'

He paused, looking at me with agitated enquiry.

'We can discuss it by-and-by, and very fully. I will give you all I think,' I answered, after an interval.

'Well – very well. If it is anything real, I say, it is prevailing, little by little, and drawing me more interiorly into hell. Optic nerves, he talked of. Ah! well – there are other nerves of communication. May God Almighty help me! You shall hear.'

'Its power of action, I tell you, had increased. Its malice became, in a way aggressive. About two years ago, some questions that were pending between me and the bishop having been settled, I went down to my parish in Warwickshire, anxious to find occupation in my profession. I was not prepared for what happened, although I have since thought I might have apprehended something like it. The reason of my saying so, is this –'

He was beginning to speak with a great deal more effort and reluctance, and sighed often, and seemed at times nearly overcome. But at this time his manner was not agitated. It was more like that of a sinking patient, who has given himself up.

'Yes, but I will first tell you about Kenlis, my parish.

'It was with me when I left this place for Dawlbridge. It was my silent travelling companion, and it remained with me at the vicarage. When I entered on the discharge of my duties, another change took place. The thing exhibited an atrocious determination to thwart me. It was with me in the church – in the reading-desk – in the pulpit – within the communion rails. At last, it reached this extremity, that while I was reading to the congregation, it would spring upon the open book and squat there, so that I was unable to see the page. This happened more than once.

'I left Dawlbridge for a time. I placed myself in Dr Harley's hands. I did everything he told me. He gave my case a great deal of thought. It interested him, I think. He seemed successful. For nearly three months I was perfectly free from a return. I began to think I was safe. With his full assent I returned to Dawlbridge.

'I travelled in a chaise. I was in good spirits. I was more – I was happy and grateful. I was returning, as I thought delivered from a dreadful hallucination, to the scene of duties which I longed to enter upon. It was a beautiful sunny evening, everything looked serene and cheerful, and I was delighted. I remember looking out of the window to see the spire of my church at Kenlis among the trees, at the point where one has the earliest view of it. It is exactly where the little stream that bounds the parish passes under the road by a culvert, and where it emerges at the road-side, a stone with an old inscription is placed. As we passed this point, I drew my head in and sat down, and in the corner of the chaise was the monkey.

'For a moment I felt faint, and then quite wild with despair and horror. I called to the driver, and got out, and sat down at the road-side, and prayed to God silently for mercy. A despairing resignation supervened. My companion was with me as I re-entered the vicarage. The same persecution followed. After a short struggle I submitted, and soon I left the place.

'I told you', he said, 'that the beast had before this become in certain ways aggressive. I will explain a little. It seemed to be actuated by intense and increasing fury, whenever I said my prayers, or even meditated prayer. It amounted at last to a dreadful interruption. You will ask, how could a silent immaterial phantom effect that? It was thus, whenever I meditated praying; it was always before me, and nearer and nearer.'

'It used to spring on a table, on the back of a chair, on the chimney-piece, and slowly to swing itself from side to side, looking at me all the time. There is in its motion an indefinable power to dissipate thought, and to contract one's attention to that monotony, till the ideas shrink, as it were, to a point, and at last to nothing – and unless I had started up, and shook off the catalepsy I have felt as if my mind were on the point of losing itself. There are other ways,' he sighed heavily; 'thus, for instance, while I pray with my eyes closed, it comes closer and closer, and I see it. I know it is not to be accounted for physically, but I do actually see it, though my lids are closed, and so it rocks my mind, as it were, and overpowers me, and I am obliged to rise from my knees. If you had ever yourself known this, you would be acquainted with desperation.'

CHAPTER IX

The Third Stage

'I see, Dr Hesselius, that you don't lose one word of my statement. I need not ask you to listen specially to what I am now going to tell you. They talk of the optic nerves, and of spectral illusions, as if the organ of sight was the only point assailable by the influences that have fastened upon me – I know better. For two years in my direful case that limitation prevailed. But as food is taken in softly at the lips, and then brought under the teeth, as the tip of the little finger caught in a mill crank will draw in the hand, and the arm, and the whole body, so the miserable mortal who has been once caught firmly by the end of the finest fibre of his nerve, is drawn in and in, by the enormous machinery of hell, until he is as I am. Yes, Doctor, as *I* am, for while I talk to you, and implore relief, I feel that my prayer is for the impossible, and my pleading with the inexorable.'

I endeavoured to calm his visibly increasing agitation, and told him that he must not despair.

While we talked the night had overtaken us. The filmy moonlight was wide over the scene which the window commanded, and I said:

'Perhaps you would prefer having candles. This light, you know, is odd. I should wish you, as much as possible, under your usual conditions while I make my diagnosis, shall I call it – otherwise I don't care.'

'All lights are the same to me,' he said: 'except when I read or write, I care not if night were perpetual. I am going to tell you what happened about a year ago. The thing began to speak to me.'

'Speak! How do you mean – speak as a man does, do you mean?'

'Yes; speak in words and consecutive sentences, with a perfect coherence and articulation; but there is a peculiarity. It is not like the tone of a human voice. It is not by my ears it reaches me – it comes like a singing through my head.

'This faculty, the power of speaking to me, will be my undoing. It won't let me pray, it interrupts me with dreadful blasphemies. I dare not go on, I could not. Oh! Doctor, can the skill, and thought, and prayers of man avail me nothing!'

'You must promise me, my dear sir, not to trouble yourself with unnecessarily exciting thoughts; confine yourself strictly to the narrative of *facts*; and recollect, above all, that even if the thing that infests you be as you seem to suppose, a reality with an actual independent life and will, yet it can have no power to hurt you, unless it be given from above: its access to your senses depends mainly upon your physical condition – this is, under God, your comfort and reliance: we are all alike environed. It is only that in your case, the *"paries"*, the veil of the flesh, the screen, is a little out of repair, and sights and sounds are transmitted. We must enter on a new course, sir – be encouraged. I'll give tonight to the careful consideration of the whole case.'

'You are very good, sir; you think it worth trying, you don't give me quite up; but, sir, you don't know, it is gaining such an influence over me: it orders me about, it is such a tyrant, and I'm growing so helpless. May God deliver me!'

'It orders you about – of course you mean by speech?'

'Yes, yes; it is always urging me to crimes, to injure others, or myself. You see, Doctor, the situation is urgent, it is indeed. When I was in Shropshire, a few weeks ago' (Mr Jennings was speaking rapidly and trembling now, holding my arm with one hand, and looking in my face), 'I went out one day with a party of friends for a walk: my persecutor, I tell you, was with me at the time. I lagged behind the rest: the country near the Dee, you know, is beautiful. Our path happened to lie near a coal mine, and at the verge of the wood is a perpendicular shaft, they say, a hundred and fifty feet deep. My niece had remained behind with me – she knows, of course, nothing of the nature of my sufferings. She knew, however, that I had been ill, and was low, and she remained to prevent my being quite alone. As we loitered slowly on together the brute that accompanied me was urging me to throw myself down the shaft. I tell you now – oh, sir, think of it! – the one consideration that saved me from that hideous death was the fear lest the shock of witnessing the occurrence should be too much for the poor girl. I asked her to go on and take her walk with her friends, saying that I could go no further. She made excuses, and the more I urged her the firmer she became. She looked doubtful and frightened. I suppose there was something in my looks or manner that alarmed her; but she would not go, and that literally saved me. You had no idea, sir, that a living man could be made so abject a slave of Satan,' he said, with a ghastly groan and a shudder.

There was a pause here, and I said, 'You *were* preserved nevertheless. It was the act of God. You are in his hands and in the power of no other being: be therefore confident for the future.'

CHAPTER X

Home

I made him have candles lighted, and saw the room looking cheery and inhabited before I left him. I told him that he must regard his illness strictly as one dependent on physical, though *subtle* physical, causes. I told him that he had evidence of God's care and love in the deliverance which he had just described, and that I had perceived with pain that he seemed to regard its peculiar features as indicating that he had been delivered over to spiritual reprobation. Than such a conclusion nothing could be, I insisted, less warranted; and not only so, but more contrary to facts, as disclosed in his mysterious deliverance from that murderous influence during his Shropshire excursion. First, his niece had been retained by his side without his intending to keep her near him; and, secondly, there had been infused into his mind an irresistible repugnance to execute the dreadful suggestion in her presence.

As I reasoned this point with him, Mr Jennings wept. He seemed comforted. One promise I exacted, which was that should the monkey at any time return, I should be sent for immediately; and, repeating my assurance that I would give neither time nor thought to any other subject until I had thoroughly investigated his case, and that tomorrow he should hear the result, I took my leave.

Before getting into the carriage I told the servant that his master was far from well, and that he should make a point of frequently looking into his room.

My own arrangements I made with a view to being quite secure from interruption.

I merely called at my lodgings, and with a travelling-desk and carpet-bag, set off in a hackney-carriage for an inn about two miles out of town, called The Horns, a very quiet and comfortable house, with good thick walls. And there I resolved, without the possibility of intrusion or distraction, to devote some hours of the night, in my comfortable sitting-room, to Mr Jennings's case, and so much of the morning as it might require.

(There occurs here a careful note of Dr Hesselius's opinion upon the case and of the habits, dietary, and medicines which he prescribed. It is curious – some persons would say mystical. But on the whole I doubt whether it would sufficiently interest a reader of the kind I am likely to meet with, to warrant its being here reprinted. The whole letter was plainly written at the inn where he had hid himself for the occasion. The next letter is dated from his town lodgings.)

...I left town for the inn where I slept last night at half-past nine, and did not arrive at my room in town until one o'clock this afternoon. I found a letter in Mr Jennings's hand upon my table. It had not come by post, and, on enquiry, I learned that Mr Jennings's servant had brought it, and on learning that I was not to return until today, and that no one could tell him my address, he seemed very uncomfortable, and said that his orders from his master were that he was not to return without an answer.

I opened the letter, and read:

'Dear Dr Hesselius. It is here. You had not been an hour gone when it returned. It is speaking. It knows all that has happened. It knows everything – it knows you and is frantic and atrocious. It reviles. I send you this. It knows every word I have written – I write. This I promised, and I therefore write, but I fear very confused, very incoherently. I am so interrupted, disturbed.

'Ever yours, sincerely, yours

'Robert Lynder Jennings.'

'When did this come?' I asked.

'About eleven last night: the man was here again, and has been here three times today. The last time is about an hour since.'

Thus answered, and with the notes I had made upon his case in my pockets, I was in a few minutes driving towards Richmond, to see Mr Jennings.

I by no means, as you perceive, despaired of Mr Jennings's case. He had himself remembered and applied, though quite in a mistaken way, the principle which I lay down in my *Metaphysical Medicine*, and which governs all such cases. I was about to apply it in earnest. I was profoundly interested, and very anxious to see and examine him while the 'enemy' was actually present.

I drove up to the sombre house, and ran up the steps, and knocked. The door, in a little time, was opened by a tall woman in black silk. She looked ill, and as if she had been crying. She curtseyed, and heard my question, but she did not answer. She turned her face away, extending her hand towards two men who were coming downstairs; and thus having, as it were, tacitly made me over to them, she passed through a side-door hastily and shut it.

The man who was nearest the hall, I at once accosted, but being now close to him, I was shocked to see that both his hands were covered with blood.

I drew back a little, and the man passing downstairs merely said in a low tone, 'Here's the servant, sir.'

The servant had stopped on the stairs, confounded and dumb at seeing me. He was rubbing his hands in a handkerchief, and it was steeped in blood.

'Jones, what is it, what has happened?' I asked, while a sickening suspicion overpowered me.

The man asked me to come up to the lobby. I was beside him in a moment, and frowning and pallid, with contracted eyes, he told me the horror which I already half-guessed.

His master had made away with himself.

I went upstairs with him to the room – what I saw there I won't tell you. He had cut his throat with his razor. It was a frightful gash.

The two men had laid him on the bed and composed his limbs. It had happened, as the immense pool of blood on the floor declared, at some distance between the bed and the window. There was carpet round his bed, and a carpet under his dressing-table, but none on the rest of the floor, for the man said he did not like a carpet in his bedroom. In this sombre, and now terrible room, one of the great elms that darkened the house was slowly moving the shadow of one of its great boughs upon this dreadful floor.

I beckoned to the servant and we went downstairs together. I turned off the hall into an old-fashioned panelled room, and there standing, I heard all the servant had to tell. It was not a great deal.

'I concluded, sir, from your words, and looks, sir, as you left last night, that you thought my master seriously ill. I thought it might be that you were afraid of a fit, or something. So I attended very close to your directions. He sat up late, till past three o'clock. He was not writing or reading. He was talking a great deal to himself, but that was nothing unusual. At about that hour I assisted him to undress, and left him in his slippers and dressing-gown. I went back softly in about half an hour. He was in his bed, quite undressed, and a pair of candles lighted on the table beside his bed. He was leaning on his elbow and looking out at the other side of the bed when I came in. I asked him if he wanted anything, and he said no.

'I don't know whether it was what you said to me, sir, or something a little unusual about him, but I was uneasy, uncommon uneasy about him last night.

'In another half hour, or it might be a little more, I went up again. I did not hear him talking as before. I opened the door a little. The candles were both out, which was not usual. I had a bedroom candle, and I let the light in, a little bit, looking softly round. I saw him sitting in that chair beside the dressing-table with his clothes on again. He turned round and looked at me. I thought it strange he should get up and dress, and put out the candles to sit in the dark, that way. But I only asked him again if I could do anything for him. He said, no, rather sharp, I thought. I asked if I might light the candles, and he said, "Do as you like, Jones." So I lighted them, and I lingered about the room, and he said, "Tell me truth, Jones, why did you come again – you did not hear anyone cursing?" "No, sir," I said, wondering what he could mean.

' "No," said he, after me, "of course, no"; and I said to him, "Wouldn't it be well, sir, you went to bed? It's just five o'clock"; and he said nothing but, "Very likely; good-night, Jones." So I went, sir, but in less than an hour I came again. The door was fast, and he heard me, and called as I thought from the bed to know what I wanted, and he desired me not to disturb him again. I lay down and slept for a little. It must have been between six and seven when I went up again. The door was still fast, and he made no answer, so I did not like to disturb him, and thinking he was asleep, I left him till nine. It was his custom to ring when he wished me to come, and I had no particular hour for calling him. I tapped very gently, and getting no answer, I stayed away a good while, supposing he was getting some rest then. It was not till eleven o'clock I grew really uncomfortable about him – for at the latest he was never, that I could remember, later than half-past ten. I got no answer. I knocked and called, and still no answer. So not being able to force the door, I called Thomas from the stables, and together we forced it, and found him in the shocking way you saw.'

Jones had no more to tell. Poor Mr Jennings was very gentle, and very kind. All his people were fond of him. I could see that the servant was very much moved.

So, dejected and agitated, I passed from that terrible house, and its dark canopy of elms, and I hope I shall never see it more. While I write to you I feel like a man who has but half waked from a frightful and monotonous dream. My memory rejects the picture with incredulity and horror. Yet I know it is true. It is the story of the process of a poison, a poison which excites the reciprocal action of spirit and nerve, and paralyses the tissue that separates those cognate functions of the senses, the external and the interior. Thus we find strange bedfellows, and the mortal and immortal prematurely make acquaintance.

CONCLUSION

A Word for Those Who Suffer

My dear Van L—, you have suffered from an affection similar to that which I have just described. You twice complained of a return of it.

Who, under God, cured you? Your humble servant, Martin Hesselius. Let me rather adopt the more emphasized piety of a certain good old

French surgeon of three hundred years ago: 'I treated, and God cured you.'

Come, my friend, you are not to be hippish. Let me tell you a fact.

I have met with, and treated, as my book shows, fifty-seven cases of this kind of vision, which I term indifferently 'sublimated', 'precocious', and 'interior'.

There is another class of affections which are truly termed – though commonly confounded with those which I describe – spectral illusions. These latter I look upon as being no less simply curable than a cold in the head or a trifling dyspepsia.

It is those which rank in the first category that test our promptitude of thought. Fifty-seven such cases have I encountered, neither more nor less. And in how many of these have I failed? In no one single instance.

There is no one affliction of mortality more easily and certainly reducible, with a little patience, and a rational confidence in the physician. With these simple conditions, I look upon the cure as absolutely certain.

You are to remember that I had not even commenced to treat Mr Jennings's case. I have not any doubt that I should have cured him perfectly in eighteen months, or possibly it might have extended to two years. Some cases are very rapidly curable, others extremely tedious. Every intelligent physician who will give thought and diligence to the task, will effect a cure.

You know my tract on *The Cardinal Functions of the Brain*. I there, by the evidence of innumerable facts, prove, as I think, the high probability of a circulation arterial and venous in its mechanism, through the nerves. Of this system, thus considered, the brain is the heart. The fluid, which is propagated hence through one class of nerves, returns in an altered state through another, and the nature of that fluid is spiritual, though not immaterial, any more than, as I before remarked, light or electricity are so.

By various abuses, among which the habitual use of such agents as green tea is one, this fluid may be affected as to its equality, but it is more frequently disturbed as to equilibrium. This fluid being that which we have in common with spirits, a congestion found upon the masses of brain or nerve, connected with the interior sense, forms a surface unduly exposed, on which disembodied spirits may operate: communication is thus more or less effectually established. Between this brain circulation and the heart circulation there is an intimate sympathy. The seat, or rather the instrument of exterior vision, is the eye. The seat of interior vision is the nervous tissue and brain, immediately about and above the eyebrow. You remember how effectually I dissipated your pictures by the simple application of iced eau-de-cologne. Few cases, however, can be treated exactly alike with anything like rapid success. Cold acts powerfully as a repellant of the nervous fluid. Long enough continued it will even produce that permanent insensibility which we call numbness, and a little longer, muscular as well as sensational paralysis.

I have not, I repeat, the slightest doubt that I should have first dimmed and ultimately sealed that inner eye which Mr Jennings had inadvertently opened. The same senses are opened in delirium tremens, and entirely shut up again when the over-action of the cerebral heart, and the prodigious nervous congestions that attend it, are terminated by a decided change in the state of the body. It is by acting steadily upon the body, by a simple process, that this result is produced – and inevitably produced – I have never yet failed.

Poor Mr Jennings made away with himself. But that catastrophe was the result of a totally different malady, which, as it were, projected itself upon that disease which was established. His case was in the distinctive manner a complication, and the complaint under which he really succumbed, was hereditary suicidal mania. Poor Mr Jennings I cannot call a patient of mine, for I had not even begun to treat his case, and he had not yet given me, I am convinced, his full and unreserved confidence. If the patient do not array himself on the side of the disease, his cure is certain.

Grey Dolphin

The Reverend R. H. Barham

'He won't – won't he? Then bring me my boots!' said the Baron.

Consternation was at its height in the castle of Shurland – a caitiff had dared to disobey the Baron! and – the Baron had called for his boots!

A thunderbolt in the great hall had been a *bagatelle* to it.

A few days before, a notable miracle had been wrought in the neighbourhood; and in those times miracles were not so common as they are now; no royal balloons, no steam, no railroads – while the few Saints who took the trouble to walk with their heads under their arms, or to pull the Devil by the nose – scarcely appeared above once in a century; so the affair made the greater sensation.

The clock had done striking twelve, and the Clerk of Chatham was untrussing his points preparatory to seeking his truckle-bed; a half-emptied tankard of mild ale stood at his elbow, the roasted crab yet floating on its surface. Midnight had surprised the worthy functionary while occupied in discussing it, and with his task yet unaccomplished. He meditated a mighty draft; one hand was fumbling with his tags, while the other was extended in the act of grasping the jorum, when a knock on the portal, solemn and sonorous, arrested his fingers. It was repeated thrice ere Emmanuel Saddleton had presence of mind sufficient to enquire who sought admission at that untimeous hour.

'Open! open! good Clerk of St Bridget's,' said a female voice, small, yet distinct and sweet – an excellent thing in woman.

The Clerk arose, crossed to the doorway, and undid the latchet.

On the threshold stood a lady of surpassing beauty: her robes were rich, and large, and full; and a diadem sparkling with gems that shed a halo around, crowned her brow: she beckoned the Clerk as he stood in astonishment before her.

'Emmanuel!' said the lady; and her tones sounded like those of a silver flute. 'Emmanuel Saddleton, truss up your points, and follow me!'

The worthy Clerk stared aghast at the vision; the purple robe, the cymar, the coronet – above all, the smile; no, there was no mistaking her: it was the blessed St Bridget herself!

And what could have brought the sainted lady out of her warm shrine at such a time of night? and on such a night? for it was as dark as pitch, and, metaphorically speaking, 'rained cats and dogs'.

Emmanuel could not speak, so he looked the question.

'No matter for that,' said the Saint, answering to his thought. 'No matter for that, Emmanuel Saddleton; only follow me, and you'll see!'

The Clerk turned a wistful eye at the corner cupboard.

'Oh! never mind the lantern, Emmanuel: you'll not want it, but you may bring a mattock and a shovel.' As he spoke, the beautiful apparition held up her delicate hand. From the tip of each of her long taper fingers issued a lambent flame of such surpassing brilliancy as would have plunged a whole gas company into despair – it was a 'Hand of Glory', such a one as tradition tells us yet burns in Rochester Castle every St Mark's Eve. Many are the daring individuals who have watched in Gundulph's Tower, hoping to find it, and the treasure it guards – but none of them ever did.

'This way, Emmanuel!' and a flame of peculiar radiance streamed from her little finger as it pointed to the pathway leading to the church-yard.

Saddleton shouldered his tools, and followed in silence.

The cemetery of St Bridget's was some half-mile distant from the Clerk's domicile, and adjoined a chapel dedicated to that illustrious lady, who, after leading but a so-so life, had died in the odour of sanctity. Emmanuel Saddleton was fat and scant of breath, the mattock was heavy, and the Saint walked too fast for him: he paused to take second wind at the end of the first furlong.

'Emmanuel,' said the holy lady good-humouredly, for she heard him puffing; 'rest awhile, Emmanuel, and I'll tell you what I want with you.'

Her auditor wiped his brow with the back of his hand, and looked all attention and obedience.

'Emmanuel,' continued she, 'what did you and Father Fothergill, and the rest of you, mean yesterday by burying that drowned man so close to me? He died in mortal sin, Emmanuel; no shrift, no unction, no absolution; why, he might as well have been excommunicated. He plagues me with his grinning, and I can't have any peace in my shrine. You must howk him up again, Emmanuel!'

'To be sure, madam – my lady – that is, your holiness,' stammered Saddleton, trembling at the thought of the task assigned him. 'To be sure, your ladyship; only – that is –'

'Emmanuel,' said the Saint, 'you'll do my bidding; or it would be better you had!' and her eye changed from a dove's eye to that of a hawk, and a flash came from it as bright as the one from her little finger. The Clerk shook in his shoes; and, again dashing the cold perspiration from his brow, followed the footsteps of his mysterious guide.

The next morning all Chatham was in an uproar. The Clerk of St Bridget's had found himself at home at daybreak, seated in his own arm-chair, the fire out, and – the tankard of ale out too! Who had drunk it? – where had he been? – how had he got home? – all was mystery! – he remembered 'a mass of things, but nothing distinctly'; all was fog and fantasy. What he could clearly recollect was, that he had dug up the Grinning Sailor, and that the Saint had helped to throw him into the river again. All was thenceforth wonderment and devotion. Masses were sung, tapers were kindled, bells were tolled; the monks of St Romuald had a solemn procession, the abbot at their head, the sacristan at their tail, and the holy breeches of St Thomas à Becket in the centre; Father Fothergill brewed a XXX puncheon of holy water. The Rood of Gillingham was deserted; the chapel of Rainham forsaken; everyone who had a soul to be saved, flocked with his offering to St Bridget's shrine, and Emmanuel Saddleton gathered more fees from the promiscuous piety of that one week than he had pocketed during the twelve preceding months.

Meanwhile the corpse of the ejected reprobate oscillated like a pendulum between Sheerness and Gillingham Reach. Now borne by the Medway into the Western Swale, now carried by the refluent tide back to the vicinity of its old quarters, it seemed as though the River God and Neptune were amusing themselves with a game of subaqueous battledore, and had chosen this unfortunate carcass as a marine shuttlecock.

For some time the alternation was kept up with great spirit, till Boreas, interfering in the shape of a stiffish 'Nor'-wester', drifted the bone (and flesh) of contention ashore on the Shurland domain, where it lay in all the majesty of mud. It was soon discovered by the retainers, and dragged from its oozy bed, grinning worse than ever. Tidings of the godsend were of course carried instantly to the castle; for the Baron was a very great man; and if a dun cow had flown across his property unannounced by the warder, the Baron would have kicked him, the said warder, from the topmost battlement into the bottommost ditch – a descent of peril, and one which 'Ludwig the Leaper', or the illustrious Trenck himself, might well have shrunk from encountering.

'An't please your lordship –' said Peter Periwinkle.

'No, villain! it does not please me!' roared the Baron.

His lordship was deeply engaged with a peck of Faversham oysters – he doted on shellfish, hated interruption at meals, and had not yet despatched more than twenty dozen of the 'natives'.

'There's a body, my lord, washed ashore in the lower creek,' said the seneschal.

The Baron was going to throw the shells at his head; but paused in the act, and said with much dignity –

'Turn out the fellow's pockets!'

But the defunct had before been subjected to the double scrutiny of Father Fothergill and the Clerk of St Bridget's. It was ill gleaning after such hands; there was not a single maravedi.

We have already said that Sir Robert de Shurland, Lord of the Isle of Sheppey, and of many a fair manor on the mainland, was a man of worship. He had rights of free-warren, saccage and sockage, cuisage and jambage, fosse and fork, infang theofe and outfang theofe; and all waifs and strays belonged to him in fee simple.

'Turn out his pockets!' said the knight.

'An't please you, my lord, I must say as how they was turned out afore, and the devil a rap's left.'

'Then bury the blackguard!'

'Please your lordship, he has been buried once.'

'Then bury him again, and be –!' The Baron bestowed a benediction.

The seneschal bowed low as he left the room, and the Baron went on with his oysters.

Scarcely ten dozen more had vanished when Periwinkle reappeared.

'An't please you, my lord, Father Fothergill says as how that it's the Grinning Sailor, and he won't bury him anyhow.'

'Oh! he won't – won't he?' said the Baron. Can it be wondered at that he called for his boots?'

Sir Robert de Shurland, Lord of Shurland and Minster, Baron of Sheppey *in comitatu* Kent, was, as has been before hinted, a very great man. He was also a very little man; that is, he was relatively great, and relatively little – or physically little, and metaphorically great – like Sir Sidney Smith and the late Mr Buonaparte. To the frame of a dwarf he united the soul of a giant, and the valour of a gamecock. Then, for so small a man, his strength was prodigious; his fist would fell an ox, and his kick! – oh! his kick was tremendous, and, when he had his boots on would – to use an expression of his own, which he had picked up in the holy wars – would 'send a man from Jericho to June'. He was bull-necked and bandy-legged; his chest was broad and deep, his head large and uncommonly thick, his eyes a little bloodshot, and his nose *retroussé* with a remarkably red tip. Strictly speaking, the Baron could not be called handsome; but his *tout ensemble* was singularly impressive: and when he called for his boots, everybody trembled and dreaded the worst.

'Periwinkle,' said the Baron, as he encased his better leg, 'let the grave be twenty feet deep!'

'Your lordship's command is law.'

'And, Periwinkle' – Sir Robert stamped his left heel into its receptacle – 'and, Periwinkle, see that it be wide enough to hold not exceeding two!'

'Ye – ye – yes, my lord.'

'And, Periwinkle – tell Father Fothergill I would fain speak with his Reverence.'

'Ye – ye – yes, my lord.'

The Baron's beard was peaked; and his moustaches, stiff and stumpy, projected horizontally like those of a tom cat; he twirled the one, he stroked the other, he drew the buckle of his surcingle a thought tighter, and strode down the great staircase three steps at a stride.

The vassals were assembled in the great hall of Shurland Castle; every cheek was pale, every tongue was mute: expectation and perplexity were visible on every brow. What would his lordship do? Were the recusant anybody else, gyves to the heels and hemp to the throat were but too good for him: but it was Father Fothergill who had said 'I won't'; and though the Baron was a very great man, the Pope was a greater, and the Pope was Father Fothergill's great friend – some people said he was his uncle.

Father Fothergill was busy in the refectory trying conclusions with a venison pasty, when he received the summons of his patron to attend him in the chapel cemetery. Of course he lost no time in obeying it, for obedience was the general rule in Shurland Castle. If anybody ever said 'I won't', it was the exception; and, like all other exceptions, only proved the rule the stronger. The Father was a friar of the Augustine persuasion; a brotherhood which, having been planted in Kent some few centuries earlier, had taken very kindly to the soil, and overspread the county much as hops did some few centuries later. He was plump and portly, a little thick-winded, especially after dinner, stood five feet four in his sandals, and weighed hard upon eighteen stone. He was, moreover, a personage of singular piety; and the iron girdle, which, he said, he wore under his cassock to mortify withal, might have been well mistaken for the tyre of a cartwheel. When he arrived, Sir Robert was pacing up and down by the side of a newly-opened grave.

'*Benedicite!* fair son' (the Baron was as brown as a cigar). '*Benedicite!*' said the Chaplain.

The Baron was too angry to stand upon compliment.

'Bury me that grinning caitiff there!' quoth he, pointing to the defunct.

'It may not be, fair son,' said the friar; 'he hath perished without absolution.'

'Bury the body!' roared Sir Robert.

'Water and earth alike reject him,' returned the Chaplain; 'holy St Bridget herself –'

'Bridget me no Bridgets! – do me thine office quickly, Sir Shaveling! or, by the Piper that played before Moses –' The oath was a fearful one; and whenever the Baron swore to do mischief, he was never known to perjure himself. He was playing with the hilt of his sword. 'Do me thine office, I say. Give him his passport to heaven.'

'He is already gone to hell!' stammered the Friar.

'Then do you go after him!' thundered the Lord of Shurland.

His sword half leaped from its scabbard. No! – the trenchant blade, that had cut Suleiman Ben Malek Ben Buckskin from helmet to chine, disdained to daub itself with the cerebellum of a miserable monk – it leaped back again – and as the Chaplain, scared at its flash, turned him in terror, the Baron gave him a kick! – one kick! – it was but one! – but such a one! Despite its obesity, up flew his holy body in an angle of forty-five degrees; then having reached its highest point of elevation, sunk headlong into the open grave that yawned to receive it. If the reverend gentleman had possessed such a thing as a neck, he had infallibly broken it! as he did not, he only dislocated his vertebrae – but that did quite as well. He was as dead as ditch-water!

'In with the other rascal!' said the Baron – and he was obeyed; for there he stood in his boots. Mattock and shovel made short work of it; twenty feet of super-incumbent mould pressed down alike the saint and the sinner. 'Now sing a requiem who list!' said the Baron, and his lordship went back to his oysters.

The vassals at Castle Shurland were astounded, or, as the seneschal Hugh better expressed it, 'perfectly conglomerated', by this event. What! murder a monk in the odour of sanctity – and on consecrated ground too! They trembled for the health of the Baron's soul. To the unsophisticated many it seemed that matters could not have been much worse had he shot a bishop's coach-horse – all looked for some signal judgement. The melancholy catastrophe of their neighbours at Canterbury was yet rife in their memories: not two centuries had elapsed since those miserable sinners had cut off the tail of the blessed St Thomas's mule. The tail of the mule, it was well known, had been forthwith affixed to that of the mayor; and rumour said it had since been hereditary in the corporation. The least that could be expected was, that Sir Robert should have a friar tacked on to his for the term of his natural life! Some bolder spirits there were, 'tis true, who viewed the matter in various lights, according to their different temperaments and dispositions; for perfect unanimity existed not even in the good old times. The verderer, roistering Hob Roebuck, swore roundly, 'Twere as good a deed as eat to kick down the chapel as well as the monk.' Hob had stood there in a white sheet for kissing Giles Miller's daughter. On the other hand, Simpkin Agnew, the bell-ringer, doubted if the devil's cellar, which runs under the bottomless abyss, were quite deep enough for the delinquent, and speculated on the probability of a hole being dug in it for his especial accommodation. The philosophers and economists thought, with Saunders M'Bullock, the Baron's bagpiper, that a 'feckless monk more or less was nae great subject for a clamjamphry', especially as 'the supply considerably exceeded the demand'. While Malthouse, the tapster, was arguing to Dame Martin that a murder now and then was a seasonable check to population, without which the Isle of Sheppey would in time be devoured, like a mouldy cheese, by inhabitants of its own producing. Meanwhile, the Baron ate his oysters and thought no more of the matter.

But this tranquillity of his lordship was not to last. A couple of Saints had been seriously offended; and we have all of us read at school that celestial minds are by no means insensible to the provocations of anger. There were those who expected that St Bridget would come in person, and have the friar up again, as she did the sailor; but perhaps her ladyship did not care to trust herself within the walls of Shurland Castle. To say the truth, it was scarcely a decent house for a female saint to be seen in. The Baron's gallantries, since he became a widower, had been but too notorious; and her own reputation was a little blown upon in the earlier days of her earthly pilgrimage: then things were so apt to be misrepresented – in short, she would leave the whole affair to St Austin, who, being a gentleman, could interfere with propriety, avenge her affront as well as his own, and leave no loop-hole for scandal. St Austin himself seems to have had his scruples, though of their precise nature it would be difficult to determine, for it were idle to suppose him at all afraid of the Baron's boots. Be this as it may, the mode which he adopted was at once prudent and efficacious. As an ecclesiastic, he could not well call the Baron out – had his boots been out of the question; so he resolved to have recourse to the law. Instead of Shurland Castle, therefore, he repaired forthwith to his own magnificent monastery, situate just without the walls of Canterbury, and presented himself in a vision to its abbot. No one who has ever visited that ancient city can fail to recollect the splendid gateway which terminates the vista of St Paul's Street, and stands there yet in all its pristine beauty. The tiny train of miniature artillery which now adorns its battlements is, it is true, an ornament of a later date: and is said to have been added some centuries after by a learned but jealous proprietor, for the purpose of shooting any wiser man than himself, who might chance to come that way. Tradition is silent as to any discharge having taken place, nor can the oldest inhabitant of modern days recollect any such occurrence. Here it was, in a handsome chamber, immediately over the lofty archway, that the Superior of the monastery lay buried in a brief slumber, snatched from his accustomed vigils. His mitre – for he was a mitred Abbot, and had a seat in Parliament – rested on a table beside him; near it stood a silver flagon of Gascony wine, ready, no doubt, for the pious uses of the morrow. Fasting and watching had made him more than usually somnolent, than which nothing could have been better for the purpose of the Saint, who now appeared to him radiant in all the colours of the rainbow.

'Anselm!' said the beatific vision. 'Anselm! are you not a pretty fellow to lie snoring there when your brethren are being knocked at head, and Mother Church herself is menaced? It is a sin and a shame, Anselm!'

'What's the matter? Who are you?' cried the Abbot, rubbing his eyes, which the celestial splendour of his visitor had set a-winking. 'Ave Maria. St Austin himself! Speak, *Beatissime*! what would you with the humblest of your votaries?'

'Anselm!' said the Saint, 'a brother of our order whose soul Heaven assoilzie! hath been foully murdered. He hath been ignominiously kicked to the death, Anselm; and there he lieth cheek-by-jowl with a wretched carcass, which our Sister Bridget has turned out of her cemetery for unseemly grinning. Arouse thee, Anselm!'

'Ay, so please you, *Sanctissime*!' said the Abbot. 'I will order forthwith that thirty masses be said, thirty *Paters*, and thirty *Aves*.'

'Thirty fools' heads!' interrupted his patron, who was a little peppery.

'I will send for bell, book, and candle –'

'Send for an inkhorn, Anselm. Write me now a letter to his Holiness the Pope in good round terms, and another to the Coroner, and another to the Sheriff, and seize me the never-enough-to-be-anathematized villain who hath done this deed! Hang him as high as Haman, Anselm! – up with him! – down with his dwelling-place root and branch, hearth-stone and roof-tree – down with it all, and sow the site with salt and sawdust!'

St Austin, it will be perceived, was a radical reformer.

'Marry will I,' quoth the Abbot, warming with the Saint's eloquence; 'ay, marry will I, and that *instanter*. But there is one thing you have forgotten, most Beatified – the name of the culprit.'

'Robert de Shurland.'

'The Lord of Sheppey! Bless me!' said the Abbot, crossing himself; 'won't that be rather inconvenient? Sir Robert is a bold baron, and a powerful; blows will come and go, and crowns will be cracked, and –'

'What is that to you, since yours will not be of the number?'

'Very true, *Beatissime*! – I will don me with speed, and do your bidding.'

'Do so, Anselm! – fail not to hang the Baron, burn his castle, confiscate his estate, and buy me two large wax candles for my own particular shrine out of your share of the property.'

With this solemn injunction the vision began to fade.

'One thing more!' cried the Abbot, grasping his rosary.

'What is that?' asked the Saint.

'*O Beate Augustine, ora pro nobis!*'

'Of course I shall,' said St Austin. *'Pax vobiscum!'* – and Abbot Anselm was left alone.

Within an hour all Canterbury was in commotion. A friar had been murdered – two friars – ten – twenty; a whole convent had been assaulted, sacked, burned – all the monks had been killed, and all the nuns had been kissed! Murder! fire! sacrilege! Never was city in such an uproar. From St George's Gate to St Dunstan's suburb, from the Donjon to the borough of Staplegate, it was noise and hubbub. 'Where was it?' – 'When was it?' – 'How was it?' The Mayor caught up his chain, the Aldermen donned their furred gowns, the Town Clerk put on his spectacles. 'Who was he?' – 'What was he?' – 'Where was he?' – 'He should be hanged – he should be burned – he should be broiled – he should be fried – he should be scraped to death with red-hot oyster-shells!' – 'Who was he?' – 'What was his name?'

The Abbot's Apparitor drew forth his roll and read aloud: – 'Sir Robert de Shurland, Knight banneret, Baron of Shurland and Minster, and Lord of Sheppey.'

The Mayor put his chain in his pocket, the Aldermen took off their gowns, the Town Clerk put his pen behind his ear. It was a county business altogether: the Sheriff had better call out the *posse comitatus*.

While saints and sinners were thus leaguing against him, the Baron de Shurland was quietly eating his breakfast. He had passed a tranquil night, undisturbed by dreams of cowl or capuchin; nor was his appetite more affected than his conscience. On the contrary, he sat rather longer over his meal than usual: luncheon-time came, and he was ready as ever for his oysters: but scarcely had Dame Martin opened his first half-dozen when the warder's horn was heard from the barbican.

'Who the devil's that?' said Sir Robert. 'I'm not at home, Periwinkle. I hate to be disturbed at meals, and I won't be at home to anybody.'

'An't please your lordship,' answered the Seneschal, 'Paul Prior hath given notice that there is a body –'

'Another body!' roared the Baron. 'Am I to be everlastingly plagued with bodies? No time allowed me to swallow a morsel. Throw it into the moat!'

'So please you, my lord, it is a body of horse – and – and Paul says there is a still larger body of foot behind it; and he thinks, my lord – that is, he does not know, but he thinks – and we all think, my lord, that they are coming to – to besiege the castle!'

'Besiege the castle! Who? What? What for?'

'Paul says, my lord, that he can see the banner of St Austin, and the bleeding heart of Hamo de Crevecœur, the Abbot's chief vassal; and there is John de Northwood, the sheriff, with his red cross engrailed; and Hever, and Leybourne, and Heaven knows how many more; and they are all coming on as fast as ever they can.'

'Periwinkle,' said the Baron, 'up with the drawbridge: down with the portcullis; bring me a cup of canary, and my nightcap. I won't be bothered with them. I shall go to bed.'

'To bed, my lord?' cried Periwinkle, with a look that seemed to say, 'He's crazy!'

At this moment the shrill tones of a trumpet were heard to sound thrice from the champaign. It was the signal for parley: the Baron changed his mind; instead of going to bed, he went to the ramparts.

'Well, rapscallions! and what now?' said the Baron.

A herald, two pursuivants, and a trumpeter, occupied the foreground of the scene; behind them, some three hundred paces off, upon a rising ground, was drawn up in battle-array the main body of the ecclesiastical forces.

'Hear you, Robert de Shurland, Knight, Baron of Shurland and Minster, and Lord of Sheppey, and know all men, by these presents, that I do hereby attach you, the said Robert, of murder and sacrilege, now, or of late, done and committed by you, the said Robert, contrary to the peace of our Sovereign Lord the King, his crown and dignity: and I do hereby require and charge you, the said Robert, to forthwith surrender and give up your own proper person, together with the castle of Shurland aforesaid, in order that the same may be duly dealt with according to law. And here standeth John de Northwood, Esquire, good man and true, sheriff of this his Majesty's most loyal county of Kent, to enforce the same, if need be, with his *posse comitatus* –'

'His what?' said the Baron.

'His *posse comitatus*, and –'

'Go to Bath!' said the Baron.

A defiance so contemptuous roused the ire of the adverse commanders. A volley of missiles rattled about the Baron's ears. Nightcaps avail little against contusions. He left the walls and retired to the great hall.

'Let them pelt away,' quoth the Baron: 'there are no windows to break, and they can't get in.' So he took his afternoon nap, and the siege went on.

Towards evening his lordship awoke, and grew tired of the din. Guy Pearson, too, had got a black eye from a brickbat, and the assailants were clambering over the outer wall. So the Baron called for his Sunday hauberk of Milan steel, and his great two-handed sword with the terrible name – it was the fashion in feudal times to give names to swords: King Arthur's was christened Excalibur; the Baron called his Tickletoby, and whenever he took it in hand it was no joke.

'Up with the portcullis! down with the bridge!' said Sir Robert; and out he sallied, followed by the *élite* of his retainers. Then there was a pretty-to-do. Heads flew one way – arms and legs another; round went Tickletoby; and, wherever it alighted, down came horse and man: the Baron excelled himself that day. All that he had done in Palestine faded in the comparison; he had fought for fun there, but now it was for life and lands. Away went John de Northwood; away went William of Hever, and Roger of Leybourne. Hamo de Crevecœur, with the church vassals and the banner of St Austin, had been gone some time. The siege was raised, and the Lord of Sheppey was left alone in his glory.

But, brave as the Baron undoubtedly was, and total as had been the defeat of his enemies, it cannot be supposed that *La Stoccata* would be allowed to carry it away thus. It has before been hinted that Abbot Anselm had written to the Pope, and Boniface the Eighth piqued himself on his punctuality as a correspondent in all matters connected with Church discipline. He sent back an answer by return of post; and by it all Christian people were strictly enjoined to aid in exterminating the offender, on pain of the greater excommunication in this world, and a million of years of purgatory in the next. But then, again, Boniface the Eighth was rather at a discount in England just then. He had affronted Longshanks, as the royal lieges had nicknamed their monarch; and Longshanks had been rather sharp upon the clergy in consequence. If the Baron de Shurland could but get the King's pardon for what, in his cooler moments, he admitted to be a peccadillo, he might sniff at the Pope, and bid him 'do his devilmost'.

Fortune, who, as the poet says, delights to favour the bold, stood his friend on this occasion. Edward had been for some time collecting a large force on the coast of Kent, to carry on his French wars for the recovery of Guienne; he was expected shortly to review it in person; but, then, the troops lay principally in cantonments about the mouth of the Thames, and His Majesty was to come down by water. What was to be done? – the royal barge was in sight, and John de Northwood and Hamo de Crevecœur had broken up all the boats to boil their camp-kettles. A truly great mind is never without resources.

'Bring me my boots!' said the Baron.

They brought him his boots, and his dapple-grey steed along with them. Such a courser! all blood and bone, short-backed, broad-chested, and – but that he was a little ewe-necked – faultless in form and figure. The Baron sprang upon his back, and dashed at once into the river.

The barge which carried Edward Longshanks and his fortunes had by this time nearly reached the Nore; the stream was broad and the current strong, but Sir Robert and his steed were almost as broad, and a great deal stronger. After breasting the tide gallantly for a couple of miles, the knight was near enough to hail the steersman.

'What have we got here? said the King. 'It's a mermaid,' said one. 'It's a grampus,' said another. 'It's the devil,' said a third. But they were all wrong; it was only Robert de Shurland. 'Grammercy,' said the King, 'that fellow was never born to be drowned!'

It has been said before that the Baron had fought in the Holy Wars; in fact, he had accompanied Longshanks, when only heir-apparent, in his expedition twenty-five years before, although his name is unaccountably omitted by Sir Harris Nicolas in his list of crusaders. He had been present at Acre when Admirand of Joppa stabbed the prince with a poisoned dagger, and had lent Princess Eleanor his own toothbrush after she had sucked out the venom from the wound. He had slain certain Saracens, contented himself with his own plunder, and never dunned the commissariat for arrears of pay. Of course he ranked high in Edward's good graces, and had received the honour of knighthood at his hands on the field of battle.

In one so circumstanced it cannot be supposed that such a trifle as the killing of a frowsy friar would be much resented, even had he not taken so bold a measure to obtain his pardon. His petition was granted, of course, as soon as asked; and so it would have been had the indictment drawn up by the Canterbury town-clerk, viz., 'That he, the said Robert de Shurland, etc., had then and there, with several, to wit, one thousand, pairs of boots, given sundry, to wit, two thousand kicks, and therewith and thereby killed divers, to wit, ten thousand, Austin Friars,' been true to the letter.

Thrice did the gallant grey circumnavigate the barge, while Robert de Winchelsey, the chancellor and archbishop to boot, was making out, albeit with great reluctance, the royal pardon. The interval was sufficiently long to enable his Majesty, who, gracious as he was, had always an eye to business, just to hint that the gratitude he felt towards the Baron was not unmixed with a lively sense of services to come; and that, if life were now spared him, common decency must oblige him to make himself useful. Before the archbishop, who had scalded his fingers with the wax in affixing the great seal, had time to take them out of his mouth, all was settled, and the Baron de Shurland had pledged himself to be forthwith in readiness, *cum suis*, to accompany his liege lord to Guienne.

With the royal pardon secured in his vest, boldly did his lordship turn again to the shore; and as boldly did his courser oppose his breadth of chest to the stream. It was a work of no common difficulty or danger; a steed of less 'mettle and bone' had long since sunk in the effort; as it was, the Baron's boots were full of water, and Grey Dolphin's chamfrain more than once dipped beneath the wave. The convulsive snorts of the noble animal showed his distress; each instant they became more loud and frequent; when his hoof touched the strand, and 'the horse and his rider' stood once again in safety on the shore.

Rapidly dismounting, the Baron was loosening the girths of his demi-pique, to give the panting animal breath, when he was aware of as ugly an old woman as he had ever clapped eyes upon, peeping at him under the horse's belly.

'Make much of your steed, Robert Shurland! Make much of your steed!' cried the hag, shaking at him her long and bony finger. 'Groom to the hide, and corn to the manger! He has saved your life, Robert Shurland, for the nonce; but he shall yet be the means of your losing it for all that!'

The Baron started: 'What's that you say, you old faggot?' He ran round by his horse's tail; the woman was gone!

The Baron paused; his great soul was not to be shaken by trifles; he looked around him, and solemnly ejaculated the word 'Humbug!' then, slinging the bridle across his arm, walked slowly on in the direction of the castle.

The appearance, and still more, the disappearance of the crone, had, however, made an impression; every step he took he became more thoughtful. ' 'Twould be deuced provoking, though, if he *should* break my neck after all.' He turned and gazed at Dolphin with the scrutinizing eye of a veterinary surgeon. 'I'll be shot if he is not groggy!' said the Baron.

With his lordship, like another great commander, 'Once to be in doubt, was once to be resolved': it would never do to go to the wars on a rickety prad. He dropped the rein, drew forth Tickletoby, and, as the enfranchised Dolphin, good easy horse, stretched out his ewe-neck to the herbage, struck off his head at a single blow. 'There, you lying old beldame!' said the Baron; 'now take him away to the knacker's.'

Three years were come and gone. King Edward's French wars were over; both parties having fought till they came to a standstill, shook hands, and the quarrel, as usual, was patched up by a royal marriage. This happy event gave his Majesty leisure to turn his attention to Scotland, where things, through the intervention of William Wallace, were looking rather queerish. As his reconciliation with Philip now allowed of his fighting the Scotch in peace and quietness, the monarch lost no time in marching his long legs across the border, and the short ones of the Baron followed him, of course. At Falkirk, Tickletoby was in great request; and in the year following, we find a contemporary poet hinting at his master's prowess under the walls of Caerlaverock –

> Ovec eus fu achiminez
> Li beau Robert de Shurland
> Ki haut seoit sur le cheval
> Ne sembloit home ke someille

A quatrain which Mr Simpkinson translates,

> With them was marching
> The good Robert de Shurland,
> Who, when seated on horseback,
> Does not resemble a man asleep!

So thoroughly awake, indeed, does he seem to have proved himself, that the bard subsequently exclaims in an ecstasy of admiration,

> Si ie estote une pucelette
> Je il doutie ceur et cors
> Tant est du Ju bons if recors.

> If I were a young maiden,
> I would give my heart and person,
> So great is his fame!

Fortunately the poet was a tough old monk of Exeter; since such a present to a nobleman, now in his grand climacteric, would hardly have been worth the carriage. With the reduction of this stronghold of the Maxwells seem to have concluded the Baron's military services; as on the very first day of the fourteenth century we find him once more landed on his native shore, and marching, with such of his retainers as the wars had left him, towards the hospital shelter of Shurland Castle. It was then, upon that very beach, some hundred yards distant from high-water mark, that his eye fell upon something like an ugly old woman in a red cloak. She was seated on what seemed to be a large stone, in an interesting attitude, with her elbows resting upon her knees, and her chin upon her thumbs. The Baron started: the remembrance of his interview with a similar personage in the same place, some three years since, flashed upon his recollection. He rushed towards the spot, but the form was gone – nothing remained but the seat it had appeared to occupy. This, on examination, turned out to be no stone, but the whitened skull of a dead horse! A tender remembrance of the deceased Grey Dolphin shot a momentary pang into the Baron's bosom: he drew the back of his hand across his face; the thought of the hag's prediction in an instant rose, and banished all softer emotions. In utter contempt of his own weakness, yet with a tremor that deprived his redoubtable kick of half its wonted force, he spurned the relic with his foot. One word alone issued from his lips, elucidatory of what was passing in his mind – it long remained imprinted on the memory of his faithful followers – that word was 'Gammon!' The skull bounded across the beach till it reached the very margin of the stream – one instant more and it would be engulfed for ever. At that moment a loud 'Ha! ha! ha!' was distinctly heard by the whole train to issue from its bleached and toothless jaws: it sank beneath the flood in a horse-laugh.

Meanwhile Sir Robert de Shurland felt an odd sort of sensation in his right foot. His boots had suffered in the wars. Great pains had been taken for their preservation. They had been 'soled' and 'heeled' more than once – had they been 'goloshed' their owner might have defied Fate! Well has it been said that 'there is no such thing as a trifle'. A nobleman's life depended upon a question of ninepence.

The Baron marched on; the uneasiness in his foot increased. He plucked off his boot – a horse's tooth was sticking in his great toe!

The result may be anticipated. Lame as he was, his lordship, with characteristic decision, would hobble on to Shurland; his walk increased the inflammation; a flagon of *aqua vitæ* did not mend matters. He was in a high fever; he took to his bed. Next morning the toe presented the appearance of a Bedfordshire carrot; by dinner-time it had deepened to beetroot; and when Bargrave, the leech, at last sliced it off, the gangrene was too confirmed to admit of remedy. Dame Martin thought it high time to send for Miss Margaret, who, ever since her mother's death, had been living with her maternal aunt, the abbess, in the Ursuline convent at Greenwich. The young lady came, and with her came one Master Ingoldsby, her cousin-german by the mother's side; but the Baron was too far gone in the dead-thraw to recognize either. He died as he lived, unconquered and unconquerable. His last words were – 'Tell the old hag she may go to –' Whither remains a secret. He expired without fully articulating the place of her destination.

But who and what *was* the crone who prophesied the catastrophe? Ay, 'that is the mystery of this wonderful history'. – Some say it was Dame Fothergill, the late confessor's mamma; others, St Bridget herself; others thought it was nobody at all, but only a phantom conjured up by conscience. As we do not know, we decline giving an opinion.

And what became of the Clerk of Chatham? Mr Simpkinson avers that he lived to a good old age, and was at last hanged by Jack Cade, with his inkhorn about his neck, for 'setting boys copies'. In support of this he adduces his name 'Emmanuel', and refers to the historian Shakespeare. Mr Peters, on the contrary, considers this to be what he calls one of Mr Simpkinson's 'Anacreonisms', inasmuch as, at the introduction of Mr Cade's reform measure, the Clerk, if alive, would have been hard upon two hundred years old. The probability is that the unfortunate alluded to was his great-grandson.

Margaret Shurland in due course became Margaret Ingoldsby: her portrait still hangs in the gallery at Tappington. The features are handsome, but shrewish, betraying, as it were, a touch of the old Baron's temperament; but we never could learn that she actually kicked her husband. She brought him a very pretty fortune in chains, owches, and Saracen ear-rings; the barony, being a male fief, reverted to the Crown.

In the abbey-church at Minster may yet be seen the tomb of a recumbent warrior, clad in the chain-mail of the thirteenth century. His hands are clasped in prayer; his legs, crossed in that position so prized by Templars in ancient, and tailors in modern days, bespeak him a soldier of the faith in Palestine. Close behind his dexter calf lies sculptured in bold relief a horse's head: and a respectable elderly lady, as she shows the monument, fails not to read her auditors a fine moral lesson on the sin of ingratitude, or to claim a sympathizing tear to the memory of poor 'Grey Dolphin'!

The Olive Grove

Guy de Maupassant

The small Provençal port of Garandou is situated at the head of the Bay of Pisca, which lies between Marseilles and Toulon.

Catching sight of the Abbé Vilbois's boat on its way home from the fishing grounds, the men at the village came down to the shore to lend a hand in beaching it. The abbé was alone in the boat, and he handled his oars with the skill of a born sailor and with an energy surprising in a man of fifty-eight. His sleeves were turned up over his muscular forearms; the top buttons of his cassock were undone and the skirts tucked up between his knees. His three-cornered hat lay beside him on the thwart, and his head was protected from the sun's rays by a cork bell-helmet with a white cover. He looked like one of those priests of tropic climes, stout fellows, not without eccentricity, who suggest a capacity for adventure rather than for priestly functions.

From time to time he stopped to cast a glance over his shoulder and make sure of his landing-place. Then, resuming his oars, he rowed with strong rhythmic strokes, to show these southern lubbers yet again how men of the North handle their sculls.

Under the compulsion of his vigorous strokes, the boat reached the shore and glided on its keel up the sloping sand, as though bent upon reaching the top of the beach. When it came to a stop the five men who had been watching the boat's approach came down with obvious pleasure to give their priest a friendly greeting.

'Well, your reverence, what luck?' one of them asked in a strong Provençal accent.

The Abbé Vilbois shipped his oars, removed his cork helmet, put on his three-cornered hat, turned down his sleeves, and buttoned up his cassock. With this attention to the proprieties he resumed his pastoral dignity.

'Not too bad. Three bass, two muraenas, and some *girelles*.'

The fat bass, the flat-headed, repulsive, snake-like muraenas, the *girelles* with their stripes of violet and orange-gold, lay in the bottom of the boat, and the five fishermen came nearer and bending over the gunwale, inspected the catch with the air of experts.

'I'll take them up to your cottage, your reverence,' one of them volunteered.

'Thank you, my man.'

The priest shook hands all round and set off homewards, with one of the fishermen following him. The others stayed behind and busied themselves about the boat.

The abbé walked with long, slow strides. Energy and dignity characterized his bearing. He was still heated from his exertions at the oars, and whenever he passed under the shade of the olive trees, he removed his hat, so as to allow the evening air, which was tempered by a slight breeze from the open sea, to play upon his head, upon his stiff, close-cropped, white hair, and upon the square-set countenance, which suggested the soldier rather than the priest. Presently he came in sight of the village, which was situated on rising ground in the midst of a wide, flat valley-bottom, sloping towards the sea.

It was a July evening. The declining sun had almost reached the serrated crest of the distant hills. The dazzling rays fell upon the white road, which was thick with dust. The priest's shadow, prolonged by the sloping beams, fell diagonally across the path. His three-cornered hat, magnified to an inordinate size, cast on the adjoining fields a huge black blot which danced now on the tree trunks, now on the ground, now in and out amongst the olives.

In summer these southern roads have a mantle of dust, as fine as flour. Disturbed by the abbé's feet, it rose like a cloud of smoke about his cassock, and covered the skirts with a grey layer, gradually increasing in density. He was cooler now. Thrusting his hands into his pockets he walked on, with the strong, steady gait of a mountaineer ascending a slope. His calm eyes scanned the village, his own village, where he had been for twenty years parish priest. He had chosen it himself, and had obtained the charge of it as a special favour. In it he proposed to end his days. Its cottages lay on the slope of the hill, in the form of a great pyramid, the apex formed by the church with its two square, ill-matched towers of brown stone, their ancient outlines suggesting the defences of a stronghold rather than the belfries of a sacred edifice.

The abbé was pleased with his catch. In the eyes of his parishioners, it constituted yet another small triumph on the part of one whose special claim to their respect lay in the fact that he had probably, despite his age, the finest muscular development of any man in that countryside. He could snip a flower-stalk with a pistol bullet; he practised feats of swordsmanship with his neighbour the tobacconist who was an old master-at-arms; and he was the finest swimmer along that coast. These innocent vanities were now his greatest pleasures in life.

There had been a time when he was a well-known figure in the social world. But the Baron de Vilbois, that mirror of elegance, had in his thirty-second year taken Holy Orders, in consequence of an unhappy love affair.

The ancient family of Picardy, royalist and Catholic, from which he sprang, had for many centuries sent its scions to the army, the magistrature, or the priesthood. His earliest impulse, at the prompting of his mother, was to take Holy Orders, but reconsidering this on his father's advice, he decided instead to go to Paris, study law, and thereafter find some serious employment about the courts. While he was still engaged in his studies, his father succumbed to pneumonia contracted while shooting in the marshes, and his mother, who was overwhelmed by grief at his loss, died shortly afterwards. Having thus suddenly inherited a substantial fortune, he renounced his project of making a career for himself and surrendered to the charms of a life of idle opulence.

He was attractive and intelligent, but his mind was bounded by certain fixed beliefs, traditions, and principles which, like his muscles, he had inherited from ancestral squires of Picardy. He created a good impression, was well received in serious circles, and enjoyed life like a popular young man of sound principles and ample means.

Then came the unexpected. At the house of a friend he met on several occasions a young actress, who, while still in her novitiate at the Conservatoire, had made a startlingly successful first appearance at the Odéon. The Baron de Vilbois fell in love with her with the violence and headlong passion of a man whose natural temperament leaves him at the mercy of his ideals. This sudden passion was conceived when he saw her steeped in the glamour of the romantic role in which she had, on the day of her début, scored so notable a triumph.

She was pretty, but had an ingrained perversity of character. Her face wore an innocent and childlike expression, which he called her angel look. She succeeded in reducing him to abject slavery. She transformed him into one of those ecstatic madmen, whom the glance of a woman's eyes, the flutter of her skirts, can thrust into the fiery furnace of inextinguishable passion. He made her leave the stage. She came to live with him, and for four years he loved her with ever-increasing ardour. In spite of his noble birth and the aristocratic traditions of his race, he would eventually have made her his wife, had he not one day discovered that she had for long been deceiving him with the friend who had first brought them together.

This revelation was the more grievous from the fact that she was expecting to become a mother, and he was only awaiting the birth of the child as a deciding factor in his intention to marry her. He had come upon some letters in a drawer, and confronting her with these proofs, he reproached her for her faithlessness, her treachery, her shamelessness, with all the brutality of his semi-barbaric nature.

She was, however, a true child of the Paris streets, as impudent as she was immodest. Convinced of the sureness of her hold both on the baron and his rival, and endued moreover with the hardihood of these women of the lower class, who in sheer effrontery perch themselves on the top of the barricades, she defied him and flung back his insults. When he lifted his hand to strike her, she paraded her figure before him.

He checked himself. Pale with the thought that the polluted flesh, the vile body, of so foul a creature enshrined his child, he hurled himself at her, intending to destroy the pair of them, to annihilate in a single blow his twofold shame. Overwhelmed with terror she gave herself up for lost. Felled by a blow of his fist, she saw his heel ready to crush her and the budding life within her, and as she stretched out her hands to ward off his fury, she cried out:

'Don't kill me. The child is not yours. It is his.'

He started back, in such a state of stupefaction and consternation that, like that menacing heel, his wrath was stayed.

'You ... you ... What's that you say?' he stammered.

She had caught the threat of murder, not only in his eyes, but in his terrifying gestures. Crazed with fear she repeated:

'It is not yours. It is his.'

Utterly bewildered, he muttered between clenched teeth:

'The child?'

'Yes.'

'Liar!'

Again he raised his foot to stamp on her. She had struggled to her knees, and was trying to move back out of his reach, but all the time she kept stammering:

'I tell you it is his. If it was yours, shouldn't I have had it long ago?'

This argument struck home with all the force of truth. In one of those lightning flashes of thought, which combine every process of reasoning with illuminating lucidity and are at once precise, irrefutable, conclusive, and irresistible, he was possessed by the conviction that he was not the father of that wretched unborn brat. In a moment his fury abated. Tranquil, calm, almost appeased, he renounced his intention of destroying this wanton creature.

In quieter tones he said:

'Get up. Off with you. Never let me see you again.'

Utterly defeated, she docilely removed herself, and he never saw her again. He too departed. He made his way southwards, to the land of sunshine, and finally came to a halt at a village situated on a knoll in a broad valley, by the shores of the Mediterranean. He found, facing the sea, an inn which attracted him, and taking a room there, he went no farther. Here he remained for eighteen months in complete isolation. Sunk in mortification and despair, he was forever haunted by devastating memories of the woman who had betrayed him; he recalled her charm, her fascination, her mysterious witchery, and he never ceased yearning for her presence and for her caresses.

As he wandered among the Provençal valleys, where the sun's rays filtered down through the grey-green olive leaves, his tortured brain was racked by these obsessions. This melancholy solitude had, however, the effect of bringing back to him the pious predilections of his youth. Very gently, with their ardour a little sobered, they stole back into his heart. Religion, which had once appealed to him as a shelter against the unknown perils of life, he now viewed as a refuge from its tortures and deceptions. He had never lost his habit of prayer, and in his desolation he clung to it. He would often go at twilight and kneel in the darkening church where the lamp, the sacred guardian of the sanctuary, the symbol of the Divine Presence, shed its solitary ray from the recesses of the choir. To his God he confided his anguish, to Him he told his troubles, asking of Him pity, succour, protection, consolation. The increasing fervour wherewith he repeated his daily orisons, was evidence of the growing depth of the emotion which prompted them. Bruised and corroded by his passion for a woman, his heart still remained tender, impressionable, eager for love. Constant in prayer, living a hermit's life, and growing ever more assiduous in the practice of piety, he surrendered himself to the secret communion which unites devout souls to the Saviour, who comforts the wretched and draws them to Him. The mystic love of God entered into him, and his baser affections were subdued. His thoughts turned again to the projects of his early youth, when he had dreamed of giving his virgin heart to the Church. He now decided to offer upon the altar his broken life. He accordingly took Holy Orders.

Family interest procured for him the appointment of parish priest to the Provençal village in which chance had cast him up. He consecrated the greater part of his wealth to charitable works, only retaining sufficient to enable him to be of practical assistance to the poor of his parish during the remainder of his life. Thus he found a refuge in a tranquil existence of pious observances and of devotion to his fellow-creatures.

His views were narrow, but he was a good priest, although in his manner of guiding his flock there was more of the soldier than the pastor. The forest of life is full of by-ways which lead us astray. Erring humanity wanders blindfold in a labyrinth of instincts, preferences, and desires. He drove, rather than led, his people into the right path. But in his new sphere he still retained many of his former tastes. Violent exercise appealed to him as strongly as ever. He enjoyed the nobler forms of sport and the practice of arms. But he shrank from all women with the instinctive fear of a child when confronted with some danger which it cannot understand.

II

The fisherman who followed the abbé had the true southerner's irresistible desire to talk. But the abbé kept his flock in good order, and the man was afraid to begin. At last, however, he ventured a remark.

'You are quite comfortable in your little shanty, your reverence, I hope?'

This cottage of the abbé's was one of those tiny buildings in which people from Provençal towns and villages take up their quarters in the summer for the sake of the country air. His official residence was built up against the walls of the church, right in the centre of the parish, and was uncomfortably small. He had accordingly rented this cottage in a field at five minutes' distance from the parsonage. Even in summer he did not occupy it regularly, but spent a few days there from time to time, in order to immerse himself in the peace of the country and also to practise pistol-shooting.

'Yes, my friend,' he replied to the fisherman, 'I'm quite comfortable here.'

The little, pink-washed cottage came into view. It stood in an unwalled field, which had been planted with olive trees, and it looked as if it had sprung up like a Provençal mushroom. The branches and leaves of the olive trees cast a dappled pattern of striped and criss-crossed shadows upon the walls of the house. Outside the door his buxom housekeeper was laying a small table with methodical slowness, making a journey into the house for each separate article she placed upon it – the cloth, the plate, the napkin, the tumbler, and the hunk of bread. She wore the little Arlesian bonnet, a cone of black silk or velvet trimmed with a white mushroom-shaped ornament. When the abbé arrived within earshot, he called out to her. She looked round and recognized her master.

'Oh, it's you, your reverence, is it?'

'Yes. I've brought home a fine catch. You must set to work and fry a bass for me. Cook it in butter, just butter, you understand.'

The servant came nearer and with the eye of a connoisseur examined the fish which the boatman was carrying.

'There is a chicken and rice all ready for you,' she said.

'Never mind. Fish don't improve with keeping. I'll indulge in a little orgy for once. I don't often do it. And after all it isn't a mortal sin.'

The woman picked out the bass from the rest of the fish. As she turned away with it, she said:

'There has been a man asking for you. He came three times.'

'A man? What sort of man?' the abbé asked with indifference.

'Well, his looks were no recommendation.'

'A beggar?'

'I dare say. He might be that. To me he had more the look of a *maoufatan*.'

The Abbé Vilbois laughed when he heard this Provençal word, signifying malefactor or vagabond. He knew that Marguerite, who was a timorous soul, could never live in the cottage without imagining all the time, and especially at night, that they were going to be murdered.

The abbé dismissed the sailor with a few coppers, and then, having preserved the dainty habits of his unregenerate days, he went to wash his face and hands.

Marguerite was in the kitchen scraping the bass from tail to head with a knife, and the scales, slightly tinged with blood, came away like tiny, silver sequins.

'There he is again,' she called out.

The abbé turned towards the road, and to be sure there was the man, slowly approaching the house. Even from a distance his clothes seemed to be in a dreadful condition.

'Upon my soul,' reflected the abbé, 'Marguerite is right. He has all the appearance of a *maoufatan.*'

While awaiting the stranger, he continued to smile at the recollection of his handmaiden's terror.

The unknown man approached with his hands in his pockets. He strolled leisurely along, and kept his eyes fixed on the priest. He was young, and had a fair, curling beard, and his hair waved under the brim of a soft felt hat which was so dirty and battered that the original colour and shape were undiscernible. He wore a long brown overcoat; the bottoms of his trouser legs were frayed, and he had on his feet a pair of rope-soled canvas shoes which gave him the furtive, disquieting gait of a prowling thief. Arrived within a few paces of the abbé, he raised his hat with a touch of the theatrical, and revealed a face which, though branded with the marks of debauchery, was not ill-favoured. The crown of his head was bald, which in a man, whose age certainly did not exceed twenty-five, was a sign either of an enfeebled constitution or of precocious vice.

The priest, too, took off his hat. He was intuitively aware that this person was neither the ordinary vagabond or out-of-work, nor the habitual offender, who drifts from prison to prison, and can lay his tongue to naught save the mysterious jargon of the jail-bird.

'Good evening, monsieur,' said the stranger.

The abbé replied with a simple 'Good evening', not wishing to use the word *monsieur* to this dubious-looking tatterdemalion. The priest and the young man looked each other up and down, and under the vagabond's scrutiny the Abbé Vilbois experienced a sensation of discomfort. He felt as if he were confronted with some mysterious hostility, and he was seized by one of those curious presentiments which send a thrill of apprehension through the human frame.

At last the vagabond broke the silence.

'Well, do you remember me?'

'Remember you?' replied the abbé in great astonishment. 'Certainly not. I don't know you at all.'

'Ah, you don't know me at all. Just take another look at me.'

'It's no use my looking at you. I've never set eyes on you before.'

'That is true,' the other assented in ironic tones. 'But I am going to show you someone whom you will have no difficulty in recognizing.'

He put on his hat and unbuttoned his overcoat, revealing his bare chest. A red belt was fastened round his lean waist and served to keep his trousers in position. Out of his pocket he took an envelope, mottled with every possible variety of stain, one of those preposterous envelopes, treasured by wandering outcasts in the lining of their clothes, and containing documents, genuine or forged, stolen or honestly come by, which are to their owners precious guarantees of personal liberty against the patrolling gendarme. From it he drew forth a photograph of the old-fashioned cabinet size. It was yellow and faded, having been carried for many a day in contact with the defiling warmth of his body. He raised the photograph to the level of his face and then said:

'What about this one?'

The abbé came two steps nearer. He turned pale with consternation, for the portrait was his own. It had been taken for the woman whom he had loved long ago. He was too bewildered to reply, and the vagabond pressed his question.

'Do you recognize it?'

'I do,' faltered the priest.

'Who is it?'

'It is myself.'

'It is really you?'

'Undoubtedly.'

'Well then, look at me and at your likeness. Look at the two of us side by side.'

The miserable abbé had already realized that these two faces, the one in the photograph and the mocking countenance beside it, were as like as two brothers. Still he did not understand.

'Tell me what you want of me,' he stammered.

In venomous tones, the stranger replied:

'What do I want of you? What I want is that you should first of all acknowledge me.'

'Acknowledge you? But who are you?'

'Who am I? Ask any passer-by, ask your servant, ask the mayor of this place. Show him this photograph, and I tell you he will laugh. Ah! you don't want to admit that I am your son, my reverend papa?'

The elder man raised his arms to heaven with the gesture of a biblical patriarch in despair.

'It is not true,' he groaned.

The young man came up close to him, so that they stood face to face.

'Oh, indeed, not true, isn't it? None of your lies, my friend. Understand that.'

The expression on his face was menacing. His fists were clenched. His voice rang out with such conviction that the abbé, as he yielded ground before him, wondered whether it was himself or the stranger who was mistaken. But again he asserted:

'I never had a child.'

'Or a mistress either, I suppose,' the other retorted.

With courage and dignity the abbé replied in three words:

'A mistress, yes.'

'And when you sent her away was she not about to become a mother?'

At these words the ancient anger, which he had smothered twenty-five years before, blazed up again. It had never been fully extinguished; through the years it had lain in the depths of the lover's heart, where he had walled it up, building over it a crypt of faith, of resignation, of renunciation. But in one moment the flames broke through. Beside himself he cried out:

'I turned her away because she was unfaithful to me. The child was of another man's begetting. Had it not been so I should have killed her, and you along with her.'

The young man was taken aback by the abbé's vehemence. It was his turn to be surprised, and his reply was couched in more subdued tones.

'Who told you that you were not the child's father?'

'She, she herself, as she defied me.'

The vagabond did not dispute this statement. He merely remarked, with the casual air of a ruffian who is giving his verdict on a case:

'Well, it was mamma's mistake. She was bluffing you, that's all.'

His outburst of rage having subsided, the abbé became more master of himself.

'Who told you that you were my son?' he questioned him.

'My mother. On her deathbed. If you want more evidence look at this.'

Again he held out the photograph. The abbé took it and slowly, minutely, compared his old likeness with the face of this unknown tramp. His heart was brimming over with anguish. But he could doubt no longer. The man who stood before him was in very truth his son.

His soul was wrung with agony, with inexpressible emotion that tortured him, like remorse for a sin committed long ago. With the help of his actual knowledge and his own conjectures he recalled the brutal scene of that separation. It was to save her life, which was threatened by the man whose pride she had outraged, that the deceitful and perfidious woman had hurled this lie at him. The lie had done its work. And a child, his child, had been born, and had grown up into this squalid tramp, who stank of vice, as a he-goat stinks of animalism.

'Will you take a turn with me,' said the abbé, 'so as to get the matter a little clearer?'

'Why certainly,' sneered the other. 'That's the very thing I have come for.'

They walked side by side through the olive grove. The sun had set, and the sudden chill that comes with twilight to these Mediterranean shores, descended on the countryside like a cold invisible shroud. The abbé shivered. Raising his eyes suddenly, as he was wont to do while officiating at divine service, he saw all around and above him, quivering between him and the heavens, the grey-green foliage of the sacred tree, whose tenuous shadow had screened the greatest of all agonies, Christ's one and only manifestation of weakness.

A brief, despairing prayer gushed from him, not in spoken words, but framed with that inner voice which does not pass the lips, the voice wherewith the believer implores his Savour to succour him.

'Then your mother is dead?' he asked, turning to his son.

When he said these words his heart was wrung with yet another pang. He felt that strange, physical agony of a man who cannot forget, a cruel reminder of the torture he had once undergone. Or, now that she was dead, was it not rather a thrill of that brief, intoxicating youthful bliss, of which no trace remained in his heart, save the scar of an ancient wound?

'Yes, my mother is dead,' replied the young man.

'Was it long ago?'

'Three years.'

A fresh suspicion flashed across the priest's mind.

'Why didn't you come to see me sooner?' he asked.

The young man hesitated a moment before replying.

'I hadn't a chance. There were ... h'm ... obstacles. But will you pardon me if I postpone my confidences for a little. I shall make them as detailed as you please. But in the meantime I must tell you I have had nothing to eat since yesterday morning.'

The abbé was smitten by a sudden shock of compassion. He stretched out his hands and said:

'My poor boy!'

The young man's slender trembling fingers were clasped by the strong hands held out to him. He replied, with the air of cynical mockery which was habitual with him:

'That's all right. I reckon we'll come to an understanding after all.'

The abbé turned towards the house.

'Let us go in to dinner,' he said, and he suddenly thought, with an instinctive thrill of strange, confused pleasure, of the fine fish he had so opportunely caught, and of Marguerite's chicken and rice. The two dishes would make a splendid meal for the wretched youth.

Marguerite had by this time become uneasy and was inclined to be peevish. She was waiting in front of the door.

'Marguerite,' the abbé called out, 'take the table into the dining-room and lay covers for two. As quickly as possible, please.'

Such was Marguerite's consternation at the idea of her master dining in the company of such an unmistakable ruffian that she stood paralysed; so the abbé set to work himself, and began to remove the knives and forks into the room, which occupied the entire ground-floor of the house. Five minutes later he and the vagabond were seated opposite each other, with a tureen of steaming cabbage-soup between them.

III

The broth was ladled out, and the visitor set to without delay. He plied his spoon busily and swallowed down his soup with avidity. But the abbé had no appetite. He slowly sipped the savoury liquid, but left the bread in his plate untouched.

'What name do you go by?' he suddenly asked.

The other laughed. The process of satisfying his hunger had raised his spirits.

'Paternity unknown,' he said. 'So the only family name I have is that of my mother, which doubtless you have not forgotten. I have, however, two Christian names which, I may venture to say, do not suit me at all: Philippe-Auguste.'

The abbé had a feeling of constriction in his throat. Turning pale he asked:

'Why did they give you those names?'

The vagabond shrugged his shoulders.

'You ought to be able to guess. When my mother left you she wanted to make your rival believe that he was my father. He did believe it, until I was fifteen or thereabouts. At that age I began to have a suspicious likeness to you. So the dirty dog denied paternity. Still, there I was, with his two names. If I had only had the luck not to resemble anyone in particular, or if I had merely been the son of some third scallywag, who had kept out of the way, I should now be calling myself the Vicomte Philippe-Auguste de Pravallon, whose relationship had been somewhat tardily recognized by his father, the count of the same name. I have baptized myself since then, however, and call myself "No-luck-at-all." '

How did you find out all these facts?'

'Because they conducted their controversies in my presence. Plain-speaking it was, I can tell you. Ah! that's the sort of thing that teaches you what life is.'

Much as the abbé had suffered during the preceding half-hour, the feelings that now swept over him had fresh poignancy, an enhanced power to torture him. He felt as if he were choking, with an oppression that would become stronger and stronger until it killed him. It arose not so much from the bare facts to which he was listening, as from the way in which they were recounted; from something in the face of the dissolute wretch who narrated them, which imbued them with disgusting significance. Between him and this creature, who was his son, he began to realize that there lay a trench brimming with moral filth, with a foulness that is mortal poison to a healthy mind. And that was his son! And yet he could hardly believe it. He must have all the proofs, every possible proof. He must learn all, he must listen, understand, and endure each pang. Again he thought of the olive-trees that surrounded his little house. And again the prayer came to his lips:

'O God in heaven, succour me.'

Philippe-Auguste had finished his plate of soup.

'Is that all there is to eat?' he asked.

The kitchen was built on to the house, and Marguerite could not hear the abbé when he called. He used to summon her with a few strokes upon a Chinese gong which hung just behind his chair. He took the leather-covered gong-stick and struck the round disc of metal two or three times. The sound, feeble at first, grew louder and harsher till the tones rang out sharp, shrill, ear-piercing, with the plaintive clang of bronze.

Marguerite answered the summons. Her face was rigid with disapproval. She cast furtive glances at the *maoufatan*, as though, with the instinct of a faithful hound, she had some presentiment of the tragedy that hung over her master. She brought in the dish with the grilled bass, which diffused a fragrant odour of melted butter.

The abbé divided the fish lengthways with a spoon and offered the back fillet to the son of his youth.

'I have just caught this fish myself,' he declared, with a touch of pride, which emerged through his distress.

Marguerite had remained in the room.

'Fetch some wine. The best wine. The white wine of Cap Corse,' the abbé ordered.

She made a gesture which almost threatened disobedience, and he had to repeat his order in a severe tone.

'Come now. Fetch the wine. Two bottles.'

When he had the rare pleasure of offering wine to a guest, he always indulged in a bottle himself. Radiant with expectation, Philippe-Auguste murmured:

'First-rate! It's a long time since I had a meal like this.'

Marguerite came back in a couple of minutes, but to the abbé, who was now consumed, as by the flames of hell, by a necessity to know the whole truth, the time of her absence seemed as long as two eternities.

After the bottles were uncorked, Marguerite lingered on in the room with her eyes fixed upon the stranger.

'You may go,' said the abbé.

She pretended not to hear him.

'I asked you to leave us,' the abbé said peremptorily, and at that she took herself off.

Philippe-Auguste devoured the fish with voracious rapidity. His father, watching him, observed with increasing amazement and chagrin how deeply the face, which was so like his own, was branded with the marks of degradation. He himself could not eat the morsels of fish which he put into his mouth and continued to masticate. His throat felt constricted; he could not swallow. A thousand questions thronged into his mind, and he kept searching for the one which would elicit the answer he was most eager to provoke. Finally, in a low tone, he asked:

'Of what did she die?'

'Consumption.'

'Was she ill for long?'

'About eighteen months.'

'What brought it on?'

'They couldn't say.'

A silence fell on them and the abbé continued to reflect. His ignorance weighed on his mind. There was so much that he was now eager to hear. He knew nothing of what had happened to her since the day when, after he had been within an ace of killing her, he had sent her away. It was true that for many years he had lost all desire to learn. He had resolutely cast her and his days of happiness into the gulf of oblivion. But, now, at the news of her death, he was seized with a desire to know all, a desire fraught with the jealousy, almost with the ardour, of a lover.

'She was not alone at the time?'

'No. She was still living with him.'

'With him? With Pravallon?' the abbé asked, with a start.

'Why, yes.'

So the same woman, who had betrayed and deceived him, had lived for over thirty years with his rival. The next question came involuntarily to his trembling lips.

'Were they happy together?'

Philippe-Auguste replied, with a sneering laugh:

'Well, yes. They had their ups and downs. They would have got on all right if I hadn't been there. I was always the fly in the ointment.'

'Why so?'

'I've told you that already. Till I was about fifteen he thought I was his son. But the old boy was no fool. He noticed the resemblance of his own accord, without help from anybody, and then there was a to-do. I used to listen at the keyhole. He accused my mother of having let him down, and she said: "Well, was it my fault? You knew very well that I was the other man's mistress at the time you took me on." The other man was you.'

'Ah! then they used to speak of me sometimes?'

'Yes, but they never mentioned your name in my presence except at the end, right at the end, during the last few days, when my mother felt she was going. And even then they didn't trust each other.'

'And you ... you learned pretty early that your mother's position was irregular?'

'What do you think? I'm no greenhorn. For that matter, I never was one. As soon as a man begins to know a bit of the world, he gets the hang of a situation like that.'

Philippe-Auguste was helping himself freely to the wine. His eyes were lit up and he was yielding to the rapid intoxication that overtakes a half-starving man. The abbé noticed this, but did nothing to check him. He reflected that drunkenness sapped a man's self-control and induced him to talk more freely. He accordingly refilled the young man's glass.

Marguerite brought in the chicken and rice, and placed it on the table. Then she fixed her gaze anew upon her master's disreputable guest.

'He's drunk, your reverence. Only look at him,' she said indignantly.

'Kindly leave us alone,' replied the abbé. 'And go away.'

She slammed the door as she went out.

The abbé turned to his guest.

'Tell me what your mother used to say about me.'

'Oh, just the sort of thing they always say when they leave a man in the lurch. She said you weren't easy to get on with, and you got on her nerves, and you would have made her life very difficult with your queer notions.'

'Did she often say that?'

'Yes. Sometimes she wrapped it up so that I shouldn't understand it, but I could always guess.'

'How did the two of them treat you?'

'Very well, at first. Very badly, afterwards. As soon as my mother saw that I was queering her pitch she bundled me out.'

'How did she manage that?'

'How? Oh, quite easily. I went a bit on the loose when I was sixteen or so, and the dirty sweeps stuck me into a reformatory, to get rid of me.'

He put his elbows on the table, rested his cheeks on his hands, and, his brain being turned with the wine, he suddenly yielded to that irresistible impulse which drives a drunken man to indulge in fantastic boasts. He smiled. And in his smile there was an attractiveness, a feminine grace, and at the same time, an element of perversity, which the abbé recognized. Not only did he recognize it, but he again felt the charm of it, hateful yet insidious, which had formerly conquered and destroyed him. At that moment it was the likeness to his mother that was noticeable. The resemblance did not lie in the actual features, but in that expression, so captivating, so insincere, in the seductiveness of that treacherous smile, which parted his lips, merely that they might give vent to all the vileness that lay behind them. Philippe-Auguste pursued his narrative.

'Ah! It was a queer life I led after I left the reformatory! Any great novelist would pay me well to tell him all about it. I assure you, the elder Dumas with his *Monte Cristo* never imagined anything weirder than the things that happened to me.'

He fell into a silence. His face wore the portentous gravity of the meditative drunkard. Then he began to speak again, with deliberation.

'If you want a boy to turn out well, you should never send him to a reformatory, whatever he has done. He learns things there. I picked up a notion or two myself, but they didn't work. I was racketing about one evening with three pals. We were all a bit sprung. It was about nine o'clock on the main road, near the Folac ferry. I came across a carriage with all the occupants sound asleep. They consisted of the driver and his family, people from Martinon who had been dining in town. I took the horse by the reins, led him up on to the ferryman's barge, and then I pushed the barge off into deep water. The driver of the carriage, disturbed by the noise I made, woke up, and suspecting nothing, whipped up his horse. Off goes the horse, and down goes the carriage into the river. Every soul was drowned. My pals gave me away. They were willing enough to laugh while they saw me performing my little joke. Of course, it never occurred to any of us that the thing would turn out so badly. Just for the fun of it, we thought we would give those people a ducking. On my honour I didn't deserve to be punished for it. However, I did worse things later on, and took my revenge that way. But they are hardly worth the trouble of telling you. I'll just tell you one of my exploits, the latest, because I'm sure you'll be delighted with it. I avenged you, my dear papa!'

The abbé could not eat another morsel. He merely gazed at his son with horrified eyes.

Philippe-Auguste was about to resume his narrative, when his father interrupted him, and asked him to wait one moment. He turned and struck the strident Chinese gong, and Marguerite entered immediately. He issued his orders to her in so harsh a tone that she cowered before him in terrified obedience.

'Bring in the lamp and the rest of the food. After that, don't come in again, unless I strike the gong.'

She went out, and presently returned carrying a white porcelain lamp with a green shade. Then she brought in a large piece of cheese and some fruit, set them on the table, and retired.

'Now,' said the abbé in resolute tones, 'I am ready. Go on.'

Philippe-Auguste calmly helped himself to the dessert and to another glass of wine. The second bottle was nearly finished, although the abbé had hardly touched it. The young man's speech was thick and heavy with the food and wine he had consumed. He stammered as he told his story.

'Well, this was my latest ... pretty hot stuff ... I had come back home, and I stayed on in the house because those two were afraid of me ... yes ... afraid ... Ah, people had better not play the fool with me ... I don't care what I do when I get my back up ... You know ... they were living together and yet not together. He had two houses, a senator's house and another for his mistress. But he spent most of his time with my mother because he was no longer able to do without her. Oh, my mother was a cunning one, and clever. She was the one to keep a hold on a man. She had that fellow in her power, body and soul, and she held on to him to the last day of her life. What fools men are! Well, I was at home and I got the whip-hand over them by making them afraid of me. I tell you, I'm a nailer at wriggling out of trouble when it has got to be done, and if it comes to dodges and tricks, or force either, I'm afraid of nobody. My mother fell ill and he put her into a fine house near Meulan. It stood in the middle of a park as big as a forest. That lasted about eighteen months, as I told you. Then we saw that the end was near. Pravallon used to come from Paris every day to see her, and his grief was genuine. It really was. One morning they had been talking for about an hour and I was wondering what they could be jabbering about for such a long time, when they called me in, and my mother said to me:

' "I am going to die very soon and there is a secret I wish to tell you, although the count thinks I oughtn't to." She always called him the count when she referred to him. "Your father is still alive, and I am going to tell you his name."

'I had asked her times out of number to tell me this ... times out of number ... the name of my father ... times out of number ... and she had always refused. I believe one day I boxed her ears to make her speak, but even that was no good. In order to get rid of me, she declared that you had died a pauper, that you were a nobody, a casual error of her young days, a girlish blunder. She reeled it all off so plausibly that I believed every word about your death.

' "Your father's name", she said.

'Pravallon was sitting there in an arm-chair and he called out just like this, three times:

' "You are wrong, you are wrong, you are wrong, Rosette."

'My mother sat up in bed. I can see her still, with her flushed cheeks and bright eyes. In spite of everything she was very fond of me, and she said:

' "Then you must do something for him, Philippe."

'She used to call him Philippe and me Auguste.

'He began to shout like a madman.

' "For that blackguard? For that worthless wretch, for that jail-bird, for that ..."

'He found as many names for me as if he had spent all his life thinking them out.

'I was getting a bit annoyed, but my mother made me keep quiet. She said to him:

' "You want him to die of hunger. You know that I have nothing to give him."

'Not in the least perturbed, he replied:

' "Rosette, for thirty years I have given you thirty-five thousand francs a year. That makes more than a million francs. Thanks to me you have lived the life of a woman of wealth, you have been cherished, and I venture to maintain, happy. I owe nothing to this wretch who has spoiled our last years together, and from me he shall have not a farthing. It is useless your insisting. Tell him his father's name if you wish. I disapprove, but I wash my hands of him.'

'Then my mother turned to me. I was just thinking to myself: "That's all right. Now I shall discover my real father. If he has money, I'm saved."

'My mother continued:

' "Your father, the Baron de Vilbois, passes now under the name and title of the Abbé Vilbois, parish priest of Garandou, near Toulon. He was my lover and I left him and came to the count."

'Then she told me the whole story. She omitted, however, to let me know that she had fooled you over her child's paternity. Women are women, you know. They can't ever tell the whole truth.'

He sniggered cynically, hardly aware of the vileness of his own utterances. He drank some more wine, and then, with the same expression of amusement on his face, went on with his story.

'My mother died two days . . . two days later. He and I both followed her coffin to the cemetery. Funny, wasn't it? He and I. And the three servants. That was all. He wept like a cow. We were standing side by side. Anyone would have taken us for father and son. Then we went back to the house. We two, alone. I was thinking to myself that I would have to clear out. I had just fifty francs. Not another farthing. What possible way was there for me to be revenged on him? He touched me on the arm and said:

' "I want to speak to you."

'I followed him into his office-room. He seated himself at his table and then, spluttering through his tears he told me that he didn't mean to be as hard on me as he had said to my mother. He begged me not to make myself a nuisance to you. But that – that lies between you and me. He offered me a banknote of a thousand . . . a thousand francs. What use was a thousand-franc note to a man like me? I noticed that he had a whole heap of them in his drawer. When I caught sight of those banknotes I felt like sticking a knife into him. I stretched out my hand to take the note he was offering me, but instead of accepting his alms I jumped on top of him, I threw him down on the floor, and squeezed his throat till his eyes nearly popped out of his head. I didn't loosen my grip until he was nearly done. Then I gagged him, tied him up firmly, stripped his clothes off him, and then turned him over on his face. Ha ha ha! I avenged you properly.'

Philippe-Auguste choked with mirth till he coughed. His upper lip was curled with cruel gaiety, and again the Abbé Vilbois recognized the smile he had known so well in bygone years, the smile of the woman who had lured him to destruction.

'And after that?'

'After that – ha ha ha! – there was a great fire in the chimney-place. It was December, very cold; that's what killed my mother. It was a big coal fire. I took the poker and made it red-hot, and then I branded him all over the back with crosses, eight or ten of them, I don't remember how many, and then I turned him over again and branded his belly. Wasn't that a good joke, papa? That's how they used to brand the convicts in old times. He squirmed like an eel, but he couldn't say a word. I had him well gagged. Then I took the banknotes, twelve of them; and that made thirteen, counting my own; an unlucky number for me. Then I cleared out, after telling the servants they were not to disturb their master until dinner-time because he was asleep. Considering that he was a senator I was convinced that he would keep his mouth shut for fear of the scandal. But I made a mistake there. I was arrested four days later in a Paris restaurant, and I got three years' imprisonment. That is the reason why I couldn't come sooner to look you up.'

He took another drink. Stuttering so badly that he could hardly bring out his words, he said:

'Now then ... Papa ... my reverend papa ... what a joke to have a parish priest for a papa! Ha ha! You'll have to be nice to me, very nice to little me, because I'm rather unusual ... and I served him out ... I did ... quite handsomely ... that old boy ...'

The Abbé Vilbois now felt himself roused by this loathsome creature to the same fury that had maddened him when confronted by the woman who had betrayed him. In the name of God, he had given absolution for many sins, for shocking secrets, which had been whispered to him in the mystery of the confessional. But now in his own person, he had neither pity nor pardon. He no longer invoked that God of mercy, helpfulness, and compassion, for he realized that the protection of neither God nor man will avail to save, on this earth below, those who are the victims of such dread mischances. All the ardour of his passionate heart, all the rage of his fiery temper, which he had restrained in virtue of his holy office, burst forth into irresistible revolt against this wretch who was his son; against the resemblance he bore not only to his father, but to his mother, to that unworthy mother who had conceived him after her own nature: against the fatality which riveted this scoundrel to his parent as the cannon-ball riveted to the ankle of the galley-slave. Roused by this shock from the dreamy piety and tranquillity of five-and-twenty years, he faced the situation and foresaw the future with sudden lucidity. He realized that he must use the strong hand with this ruffian, and terrify him at the first onset. His jaws were clenched in fury. Forgetting that the man was drunk, he said:

'Now that you have told me all, you can listen to me. You will leave this village tomorrow morning. You will go to a place which I shall indicate to you, and you will not leave that place without my orders. I shall make you an allowance which will be enough for you to live on. It will be small. I am a poor man myself now. If you disobey my orders on any single occasion, I shall stop my remittances, and you will have to deal with me personally.'

Stupefied with drink as he was, Philippe-Auguste understood the threat. The criminal in him suddenly rose to the surface. Venomously, between hiccups, he spat out these words:

'Ah, papa ... mustn't do that ... papa is a parish priest ... I've got you ... under my thumb ... you'll sing small, like the rest of them.'

The abbé started. He felt in his old, but still herculean muscles, an invincible impulse to seize this monster, to bend him like a twig, and show him that he must give way. He seized the table, and shook it, and hurled his words right into the vagabond's face:

'Have a care. I warn you. Have a care. I'm afraid of no man ...'

The drunken man lost his balance and rocked from side to side in his chair. Realizing that he was on the point of falling, and that he was in the abbé's power, he stretched forth his hand towards a knife which lay on the table-cloth. The gleam of murder in his eyes was unmistakable. The Abbé Vilbois saw the movement and pushed the table with such force that his son fell over backwards and lay at full length on the floor. The lamp upset, and the room was in darkness. There was a jingling of wine-glasses, and for a few seconds the clear bell-like notes vibrated through the room. Then came a rustling sound as of some soft body crawling along the paved floor. And after that, silence.

With the breaking of the lamp darkness had descended upon them, so sudden and unexpected and profound, that both men were aghast as at some terrifying accident. The drunkard, cowering against the wall, never stirred. The abbé remained seated in his chair. The deep night in which he was plunged had the effect of subduing his anger. The veil of blackness that had fallen upon him immobilized his raging impulses. And gradually other thoughts took possession of him, thoughts as dark and gloomy as the enveloping obscurity.

Silence. Silence as impenetrable as the silence of a walled-in tomb. A silence of death. No sound came from without; not so much as the rolling of a distant carriage-wheel, or the barking of a dog; not even the whispering passage of the wind through the olive branches or along the walls.

This silence lasted for a long, long time, perhaps an hour. Then suddenly the gong rang out. Once only it sounded, smitten by a hard, sharp, vigorous stroke. On the top of that came the crash of a fall, and of the upsetting of a chair.

Marguerite, who had been all the time on the alert, came running in from the kitchen, but when she opened the dining-room door she started back in terror from the impenetrable darkness. A trembling seized her, her heart beat fast, and in fear-stricken tones she gasped:

'Master, where are you? Speak.'

There was no reply. Nothing stirred in the room.

'Good Heavens,' she thought. 'What have they been doing? What has happened?'

She had not the courage either to advance into the room or to go back to the kitchen for a light. Her limbs shook under her; she would have given the world to be able to escape, to run away, to scream. But all she could do was to keep on saying:

'Master, where are you? Speak. It is Marguerite.'

Then, despite her fears, a sudden and instinctive desire to come to the help of her master surged up within her. She was inspired with that panic-stricken courage which sometimes comes to women in such moments, and renders them capable of heroic actions. Running to her kitchen, she came back with a lamp. She stopped on the threshold of the dining-room and looked in. The first thing she saw was the stranger lying at full length on the floor, close to the wall. He was sleeping, or feigning sleep. Next she noticed the overturned lamp. And last of all, under the table, she saw the feet and legs of the abbé, in their black shoes and stockings. He had seemingly struck the gong with his head and had then collapsed on to his back on the floor.

She was trembling in every limb.

'Good God!' she said again and again. 'Good God! What has happened?'

Timidly and slowly she went forward into the room. Her feet slipped on something slimy and she nearly came down. She stooped and examined the red flagstones. All about her feet she saw a crimson fluid, which trickled in the direction of the door. It was blood.

She hurled away the lamp so that she might see no more. Beside herself with horror, she fled from the house, out into the open country, and made for the village. In her blind flight she kept running into the trunks of the olive-trees. She screamed as she ran, and her eyes were fixed on the distant lights of the village. Her shrieks pierced the darkness like the sinister cry of the screech-owl, and she went on shouting:

'*Le maoufatan, le maoufatan, le maoufatan!*'

When she reached the outlying houses of the hamlet the frightened villagers ran out and gathered round her, but she had completely lost her head and could not answer their questions. She was still struggling with overwhelming terror. But they gathered that some disaster had occurred in the abbé's house among the olives, and the men snatched up weapons and ran to the help of their priest.

The abbé's pink-washed cottage in the olive orchard was invisible in the dark and silent night. When the solitary lamp which lighted its one window had been extinguished, like the closing of an eye, the house was plunged in shadow, lost in the darkness, undiscoverable by anyone save a native of the country. Presently the lanterns, which were carried close to the ground, could be seen approaching the house, across the plantation of olives. The long yellow streaks of light shot over the parched grass. Under the distortion of these rays the gnarled trunks of the olives took on the semblance of monsters, of a hell-brood of serpents, interlaced and writhing. In the farthest flashes of light there suddenly rose out of the darkness a phantom shape, which presently revealed itself as the low right-angled wall of the pink-washed house, its colour showing up in the glow of the lanterns. These were carried by peasants, who formed an escort to the two gendarmes, armed with revolvers, to the rural policeman and the mayor. Marguerite was with them, but had to be supported on either side, being on the verge of collapse. There was a momentary recoil before the dark and terrifying cavern beyond the doorway. But the sergeant seized a lantern and entered the house, while the others followed him.

Marguerite's story was true. The blood, now coagulated, spread like a carpet on the floor. It had reached as far as Philippe-Auguste; his legs and one of his hands were crimson with it.

Father and son slept.

The abbé's throat was cut. Philippe-Auguste was plunged in drunken sleep, but his father's sleep was the slumber of eternity. The two gendarmes threw themselves upon the son and clasped the handcuffs round his wrists before he had time to wake up. When he came to himself he rubbed his eyes. He was still in the stupor of intoxication. At the sight of the abbé's corpse he seemed frightened and bewildered.

'Why did he not make his escape?' the mayor asked.

'He was too drunk,' the sergeant replied.

Everyone present agreed with him. It would never have occurred to any of them that the Abbé Vilbois might perhaps have died by his own hand.

The Black Monk

Anton Chekhov

Andrey Vassilitch Kovrin, who held a master's degree at the University, had exhausted himself, and had upset his nerves. He did not send for a doctor, but casually, over a bottle of wine, he spoke to a friend who was a doctor, and the latter advised him to spend the spring and summer in the country. Very opportunely a long letter came from Tanya Pesotsky, who asked him to come and stay with them at Borissovka. And he made up his mind that he really must go.

To begin with – that was in April – he went to his own home, Kovrinka, and there spent three weeks in solitude; then, as soon as the roads were in good condition, he set off, driving in a carriage, to visit Pesotsky, his former guardian, who had brought him up, and was a horticulturist well known all over Russia. The distance from Kovrinka to Borissovka was reckoned only a little over fifty miles. To drive along a soft road in May in a comfortable carriage with springs was a real pleasure.

Pesotsky had an immense house with columns and lions, off which the stucco was peeling, and with a footman in swallow-tails at the entrance. The old park, laid out in the English style, gloomy and severe, stretched for almost three-quarters of a mile to the river, and there ended in a steep, precipitous clay bank, where pines grew with bare roots that looked like shaggy paws; the water shone below with an unfriendly gleam, and the peewits flew up with a plaintive cry, and there one always felt that one must sit down and write a ballad. But near the house itself, in the court-yard and orchard, which together with the nurseries covered ninety acres, it was all life and gaiety even in bad weather. Such marvellous roses, lilies, camellias; such tulips of all possible shades, from glistening white to sooty black – such a wealth of flowers, in fact, Kovrin had never seen anywhere as at Pesotsky's. It was only the beginning of spring, and the real glory of the flower-beds was still hidden away in the hot-houses. But even the flowers along the avenues, and here and there in the flower-beds, were enough to make one feel, as one walked about the garden, as though one were in a realm of tender colours, especially in the early morning when the dew was glistening on every petal.

What was the decorative part of the garden, and what Pesotsky con-temptuously spoke of as rubbish, had at one time in his childhood given Kovrin an impression of fairyland.

Every sort of caprice, of elaborate monstrosity and mockery at Nature was here. There were espaliers of fruit-trees, a pear-tree in the shape of a pyramidal poplar; spherical oaks and lime-trees, an apple-tree in the shape of an umbrella, plum trees trained into arches, crests, candelabra, and even into the number 1862 – the year when Pesotsky first took up horticulture. One came across, too, lovely, graceful trees with strong, straight stems like palms, and it was only by looking intently that one could recognize these trees as gooseberries or currants. But what made the garden most cheerful and gave it a lively air, was the continual coming and going in it, from early morning till evening; people with wheelbarrows, shovels, and watering-cans swarmed round the trees and bushes, in the avenues and the flower-beds, like ants ...

Kovrin arrived at Pesotsky's at ten o'clock in the evening. He found Tanya and her father, Yegor Semyonitch, in great anxiety. The clear starlight sky and the thermometer foretold a frost towards morning, and meanwhile Ivan Karlovitch, the gardener, had gone to the town, and they had no one to rely upon. At supper they talked of nothing but the morning frost, and it was settled that Tanya should not go to bed, and between twelve and one should walk through the garden, and see that everything was done properly, and Yegor Semyonitch should get up at three o'clock or even earlier.

Kovrin sat with Tanya all the evening, and after midnight went out with her into the garden. It was cold. There was a strong smell of burning already in the garden. In the big orchard, which was called the commercial garden, and which brought Yegor Semyonitch several thousand clear profit, a thick, black, acrid smoke was creeping over the ground and, curling round the trees, was saving those thousands from the frost. Here the trees were arranged as on a chessboard, in straight and regular rows like ranks of soldiers, and this severe pedantic regularity, and the fact that all the trees were of the same size, and had tops and trunks all exactly alike, made them look monotonous and even dreary. Kovrin and Tanya walked along the rows where fires of dung, straw, and all sorts of refuse were smouldering, and from time to time they were met by labourers who wandered in the smoke like shadows. The only trees in flower were the cherries, plums, and certain sorts of apples, but the whole garden was plunged in smoke, and it was only near the nurseries that Kovrin could breathe freely.

'Even as a child I used to sneeze from the smoke here,' he said, shrugging his shoulders, 'but to this day I don't understand how smoke can keep off frost.'

'Smoke takes the place of clouds when there are none . . .' answered Tanya.

'And what do you want clouds for?'

'In overcast and cloudy weather there is no frost.'

'You don't say so.'

He laughed and took her arm. Her broad very earnest face, chilled with the frost, with her delicate black eyebrows, the turned-up collar of her coat, which prevented her moving her head freely, and the whole of her thin, graceful figure, with her skirts tucked up on account of the dew, touched him.

'Good heavens! she is grown up,' he said. 'When I went away from here last, five years ago, you were still a child. You were such a thin, long-legged creature, with your hair hanging on your shoulders; you used to wear short frocks, and I used to tease you, calling you a heron . . . What time does!'

'Yes, five years!' sighed Tanya. 'Much water has flowed since then. Tell me, Andryusha, honestly,' she began eagerly, looking him in the face: 'do you feel strange with us now? But why do I ask you? You are a man, you live your own interesting life, you are somebody . . . To grow apart is so natural! But however that may be, Andryusha, I want you to think of us as your people. We have a right to that.'

'I do, Tanya.'

'On your word of honour?'

'Yes, on my word of honour.'

'You were surprised this evening that we have so many of your photographs. You know my father adores you. Sometimes it seems to me that he loves you more than he does me. He is proud of you. You are a clever, extraordinary man, you have made a brilliant career for yourself, and he is persuaded that you have turned out like this because he brought you up. I don't try to prevent him from thinking so. Let him.'

Dawn was already beginning, and that was especially perceptible from the distinctness with which the coils of smoke and the tops of the trees began to stand out in the air.

'It's time we were asleep, though,' said Tanya, 'and it's cold, too.' She took his arm. 'Thank you for coming, Andryusha. We have only uninteresting acquaintances, and not many of them. We have only the garden, the garden, the garden, and nothing else. Standards, half-standards,' she laughed. 'Aports, Reinettes, Borovinkas, budded stocks, grafted stocks . . . All, all our life has gone into the garden. I never even dream of anything but apples and pears. Of course, it is very nice and useful, but sometimes one longs for something else for variety. I remember that when you used to come to us for the summer holidays, or simply a visit, it always seemed to be fresher and brighter in the house, as though the covers had been taken off the lustres and the furniture. I was only a little girl then, but yet I understood it.'

She talked a long while and with great feeling. For some reason the idea came into his head that in the course of the summer he might grow fond of this little, weak, talkative creature, might be carried away and fall in love; in their position it was so possible and natural! This thought touched and amused him; he bent down to her sweet, preoccupied face and hummed softly:

> 'Onyegin, I won't conceal it;
> I madly love Tatiana . . .'

By the time they reached the house, Yegor Semyonitch had got up. Kovrin did not feel sleepy; he talked to the old man and went to the garden with him. Yegor Semyonitch was a tall, broad-shouldered, corpulent man, and he suffered from asthma, yet he walked so fast that it was hard work to hurry after him. He had an extremely preoccupied air; he was always hurrying somewhere, with an expression that suggested that if he were one minute late all would be ruined!

'Here is a business, brother ...' he began, standing still to take breath. 'On the surface of the ground, as you see, is frost; but if you raise the thermometer on a stick fourteen feet above the ground, there it is warm ... Why is that?'

'I really don't know,' said Kovrin, and he laughed.

'H'm! ... One can't know everything, of course ... However large the intellect may be, you can't find room for everything in it. I suppose you still go in chiefly for philosophy?'

'Yes, I lecture in psychology; I am working at philosophy in general.'

'And it does not bore you?'

'On the contrary, it's all I live for.'

'Well, God bless you!' said Yegor Semyonitch, meditatively stroking his grey whiskers. 'God bless you! I am delighted about you ... delighted, my boy ...'

But suddenly he listened, and, with a terrible face, ran off and quickly disappeared behind the trees in a cloud of smoke.

'Who tied this horse to an apple-tree?' Kovrin heard his despairing, heart-rending cry. 'Who is the low scoundrel who has dared to tie this horse to an apple-tree? My God, my God! They have ruined everything; they have spoilt everything; they have done everything filthy, horrible, and abominable. The orchard's done for, the orchard's ruined. My God!'

When he came back to Kovrin, his face looked exhausted and mortified.

'What is one to do with these accursed people?' he said in a tearful voice, flinging up his hands. 'Styopka was carting dung at night, and tied the horse to an apple-tree! He twisted the reins round it, the rascal, as tightly as he could, so that the bark is rubbed off in three places. What do you think of that! I spoke to him and he stands like a post and only blinks his eyes. Hanging is too good for him.'

Growing calmer, he embraced Kovrin and kissed him on the cheek.

'Well, God bless you! God bless you! ...' he muttered. 'I am very glad you have come. Unutterably glad ... Thank you.'

Then, with the same rapid step and preoccupied face, he made the round of the whole garden, and showed his former ward all his greenhouses and hot-houses, his covered-in garden, and two apiaries which he called the marvel of our century.

While they were walking the sun rose, flooding the garden with brilliant light. It grew warm. Foreseeing a long, bright, cheerful day, Kovrin recollected that it was only the beginning of May, and that he had before him a whole summer as bright, cheerful, and long; and suddenly there stirred in his bosom a joyous, youthful feeling, such as he used to experience in his childhood, running about in that garden. And he hugged the old man and kissed him affectionately. Both of them, feeling touched, went indoors and drank tea out of old-fashioned china cups, with cream and satisfying krendels made with milk and eggs; and these trifles reminded Kovrin again of his childhood and boyhood. The delightful present was blended with the impressions of the past that stirred within him; there was a tightness at his heart, yet he was happy.

He waited till Tanya was awake and had coffee with her, went for a walk, then went to his room and sat down to work. He read attentively, making notes, and from time to time raised his eyes to look out at the open windows or at the fresh, still dewy flowers in the vases on the table; and again he dropped his eyes to his book, and it seemed to him as though every vein in his body was quivering and fluttering with pleasure.

II

In the country he led just as nervous and restless a life as in town. He read and wrote a great deal, he studied Italian, and when he was out for a walk, thought with pleasure that he would soon sit down to work again. He slept so little that everyone wondered at him; if he accidentally dozed for half an hour in the daytime, he would lie awake all night, and, after a sleepless night, would feel cheerful and vigorous as though nothing had happened.

He talked a great deal, drank wine, and smoked expensive cigars. Very often, almost every day, young ladies of neighbouring families would come to the Pesotskys', and would sing and play the piano with Tanya; sometimes a young neighbour who was a good violinist would come, too. Kovrin listened with eagerness to the music and singing, and was exhausted by it, and this showed itself by his eyes closing and his head falling to one side.

One day he was sitting on the balcony after evening tea, reading. At the same time, in the drawing-room, Tanya taking soprano, one of the young ladies a contralto, and the young man with his violin, were practising a well-known serenade of Braga's. Kovrin listened to the words – they were Russian – and could not understand their meaning. At last, leaving his book and listening attentively, he understood: a maiden, full of sick fancies, heard one night in her garden mysterious sounds, so strange and lovely that she was obliged to recognize them as a holy harmony which is unintelligible to us mortals, and so flies back to heaven. Kovrin's eyes began to close. He got up, and in exhaustion walked up and down the drawing-room, and then the dining-room. When the singing was over he took Tanya's arm, and with her went out on to the balcony.

'I have been all day thinking of a legend,' he said. 'I don't remember whether I have read it somewhere or heard it, but it is a strange and almost grotesque legend. To begin with, it is somewhat obscure. A thousand years ago a monk, dressed in black, wandered about the desert, somewhere in Syria or Arabia... Some miles from where he was, some fisherman saw another black monk, who was moving slowly over the surface of a lake. This second monk was a mirage. Now forget all the laws of optics, which the legend does not recognize, and listen to the rest. From that mirage there was cast another mirage, then from that other a third, so that the image of the black monk began to be repeated endlessly from one layer of the atmosphere to another. So that he was seen at one time in Africa, at another in Spain, then in Italy, then in the Far North... Then he passed out of the atmosphere of the earth, and now he is wandering all over the universe, still never coming into conditions in which he might disappear. Possibly he may be seen now in Mars or in some star of the Southern Cross. But, my dear, the real point on which the whole legend hangs lies in the fact that, exactly a thousand years from the day when the monk walked in the desert, the mirage will return to the atmosphere of the earth again and will appear to men. And it seems that the thousand years is almost up... According to the legend, we may look out for the black monk today or tomorrow.'

'A queer mirage,' said Tanya, who did not like the legend.

'But the most wonderful part of it all,' laughed Kovrin, 'is that I simply cannot recall where I got this legend from. Have I read it somewhere? Have I heard it? Or perhaps I dreamed of the black monk. I swear I don't remember. But the legend interests me. I have been thinking about it all day.'

Letting Tanya go back to her visitors, he went out of the house, and, lost in meditation, walked by the flower-beds. The sun was already setting. The flowers, having just been watered, gave forth a damp, irritating fragrance. Indoors they began singing again, and in the distance the violin had the effect of a human voice. Kovrin, racking his brains to remember where he had read or heard the legend, turned slowly towards the park, and unconsciously went as far as the river. By a little path that ran along the steep bank, between the bare roots, he went down to the water, disturbed the peewits there and frightened two ducks. The last rays of the setting sun still threw light here and there on the gloomy pines, but it was quite dark on the surface of the river. Kovrin crossed to the other side by the narrow bridge. Before him lay a wide field covered with young rye not yet in blossom. There was no living habitation, no living soul in the distance, and it seemed as though the little path, if one went along it, would take one to the unknown, mysterious place where the sun had just gone down, and where the evening glow was flaming in immensity and splendour.

'How open, how free, how still it is here!' thought Kovrin, walking along the path. 'And it feels as though all the world were watching me, hiding and waiting for me to understand it . . .'

But then waves began running across the rye, and a light evening breeze softly touched his uncovered head. A minute later there was another gust of wind, but stronger – the rye began rustling, and he heard behind him the hollow murmur of the pines. Kovrin stood still in amazement. From the horizon there rose up to the sky, like a whirlwind or a waterspout, a tall black column. Its outline was indistinct, but from the first instant it could be seen that it was not standing still, but moving with fearful rapidity, moving straight towards Kovrin, and the nearer it came the smaller and the more distinct it was. Kovrin moved aside into the rye to make way for it, and only just had time to do so.

A monk, dressed in black, with a grey head and black eyebrows, his arms crossed over his breast, floated by him . . . His bare feet did not touch the earth. After he had floated twenty feet beyond him, he looked round at Kovrin, and nodded to him with a friendly but sly smile. But what a pale, fearfully pale, thin face! Beginning to grow larger again, he flew across the river, collided noiselessly with the clay bank and pines, and passing through them, vanished like smoke.

'Why, you see,' muttered Kovrin, 'there must be truth in the legend.'

Without trying to explain to himself the strange apparition, glad that he had succeeded in seeing so near and so distinctly, not only the monk's black garments, but even his face and eyes, agreeably excited, he went back to the house.

In the park and in the garden people were moving about quietly, in the house they were playing – so he alone had seen the monk. He had an intense desire to tell Tanya and Yegor Semyonitch, but he reflected that they would certainly think his words the ravings of delirium, and that would frighten them; he had better say nothing.

He laughed aloud, sang, and danced the mazurka; he was in high spirits, and all of them, the visitors and Tanya, thought he had a peculiar look, radiant and inspired, and that he was very interesting.

III

After supper, when the visitors had gone, he went to his room and lay down on the sofa: he wanted to think about the monk. But a minute later Tanya came in.

'Here, Andryusha; read father's articles,' she said, giving him a bundle of pamphlets and proofs. 'They are splendid articles. He writes capitally.'

'Capitally, indeed!' said Yegor Semyonitch, following her and smiling constrainedly; he was ashamed. 'Don't listen to her, please; don't read them! Though, if you want to go to sleep, read them by all means; they are a fine soporific.'

'I think they are splendid articles,' said Tanya, with deep conviction. 'You read them, Andryusha, and persuade father to write oftener. He could write a complete manual of horticulture.'

Yegor Semyonitch gave a forced laugh, blushed, and began uttering the phrases usually made use of by an embarrassed author. At last he began to give way.

'In that case, begin with Gaucher's article and these Russian articles,' he muttered, turning over the pamphlets with a trembling hand, 'or else you won't understand. Before you read my objections, you must know what I am objecting to. But it's all nonsense . . . tiresome stuff. Besides, I believe it's bedtime.'

Tanya went away. Yegor Semyonitch sat down on the sofa by Kovrin and heaved a deep sigh.

'Yes, my boy . . .' he began after a pause. 'That's how it is, my dear lecturer. Here I write articles, and take part in exhibitions, and receive medals . . . Pesotsky, they say, has apples the size of a head, and Pesotsky, they say, has made his fortune with his garden. In short, "Kotcheby is rich and glorious." But one asks oneself: what is it all for? The garden is certainly fine, a model. It's not really a garden, but a regular institution, which is of the greatest public importance because it marks, so to say, a new era in Russian agriculture and Russian industry. But, what's it for? What's the object of it?'

'The fact speaks for itself.'

'I do not mean in that sense. I meant to ask: what will happen to the garden when I die? In the condition in which you see it now, it would not be maintained for one month without me. The whole secret of success lies not in its being a big garden or a great number of labourers being employed in it, but in the fact that I love the work. Do you understand? I love it perhaps more than myself. Look at me; I do everything myself. I work from morning to night: I do all the grafting myself, the pruning myself, the planting myself. I do it all myself: when anyone helps me I am jealous and irritable till I am rude. The whole secret lies in loving it – that is, in the sharp eye of the master; yes, and in the master's hands, and in the feeling that makes one, when one goes anywhere for an hour's visit, sit, ill at ease, with one's heart far away, afraid that something may have happened in the garden. But when I die, who will look after it? Who will work? The gardener? The labourers? Yes? But I tell you, my dear fellow, the worst enemy in the garden is not a hare, not a cockchafer, and not the frost, but any outside person.'

'And Tanya?' asked Kovrin, laughing. 'She can't be more harmful than a hare? She loves the work and understands it.'

'Yes, she loves it and understands it. If after my death the garden goes to her and she is the mistress, of course nothing better could be wished. But if, which God forbid, she should marry,' Yegor Semyonitch whispered, and looked with a frightened look at Kovrin, 'that's just it. If she marries and children come, she will have no time to think about the garden. What I fear most is: she will marry some fine gentleman, and he will be greedy, and he will let the garden to people who will run it for profit, and everything will go to the devil the very first year! In our work females are the scourge of God!'

Yegor Semyonitch sighed and paused for a while.

'Perhaps it is egoism, but I tell you frankly: I don't want Tanya to get married. I am afraid of it! There is one young dandy comes to see us, bringing his violin and scraping on it; I know Tanya will not marry him. I know it quite well; but I can't bear to see him! Altogether, my boy, I am very queer. I know that.'

Yegor Semyonitch got up and walked about the room in excitement, and it was evident that he wanted to say something very important, but could not bring himself to it.

'I am very fond of you, and so I am going to speak to you openly,' he decided at last, thrusting his hands into his pockets. 'I deal plainly with certain delicate questions, and say exactly what I think, and I cannot endure so-called hidden thoughts. I will speak plainly: you are the only man to whom I should not be afraid to marry my daughter. You are a clever man with a good heart, and would not let my beloved work go to ruin; and the chief reason is that I love you as a son, and I am proud of you. If Tanya and you could get up a romance somehow, then – well! I should be very glad and even happy. I tell you this plainly, without mincing matters, like an honest man.'

Kovrin laughed. Yegor Semyonitch opened the door to go out, and stood in the doorway.

'If Tanya and you had a son, I would make a horticulturist of him,' he said, after a moment's thought. 'However, this is idle dreaming. Good-night.'

Left alone, Kovrin settled himself more comfortably on the sofa and took up the articles. The title of one was 'On Intercropping'; of another, 'A Few Words on the Remarks of Monsieur Z. Concerning the Trenching of the Soil for a New Garden'; a third, 'Additional Matter concerning Grafting with a Dormant Bud'; and they were all of the same sort. But what a restless, jerky tone! What nervous, almost hysterical passion! Here was an article, one would have thought, with most peaceable and impersonal contents: the subject of it was the Russian Antonovsky Apple. But Yegor Semyonitch began it with '*Audiatur altera pars*', and finished it with '*Sapienti sat*'; and between these two quotations a perfect torrent of venomous phrases directed 'at the learned ignorance of our recognized horticultural authorities, who observe Nature from the height of their university chairs', or at Monsieur Gaucher, 'whose success has been the work of the vulgar and the dilettanti'. And then followed an inappropriate, affected, and insincere regret that peasants who stole fruit and broke the branches could not nowadays be flogged.

'It is beautiful, charming, healthy work, but even in this there is strife and passion,' thought Kovrin. 'I suppose that everywhere and in all careers men of ideas are nervous, and marked by exaggerated sensitiveness. Most likely it must be so.'

He thought of Tanya, who was so pleased with Yegor Semyonitch's articles. Small, pale, and so thin that her shoulder-blades stuck out, her eyes, wide and open, dark and intelligent, had an intent gaze, as though looking for something. She walked like her father with a little hurried step. She talked a great deal and was fond of arguing, accompanying every phrase, however insignificant, with expressive mimicry and gesticulation. No doubt she was nervous in the extreme.

Kovrin went on reading the articles, but he understood nothing of them, and flung them aside. The same pleasant excitement with which he had earlier in the evening danced the mazurka and listened to the music was now mastering him again and rousing a multitude of thoughts. He got up and began walking about the room, thinking about the black monk. It occurred to him that if this strange, supernatural monk had appeared to him only, that meant that he was ill and had reached the point of having hallucinations. This reflection frightened him, but not for long.

'But I am all right, and I am doing no harm to anyone; so there is no harm in my hallucinations,' he thought; and he felt happy again.

He sat down on the sofa and clasped his hands round his head. Restraining the unaccountable joy which filled his whole being, he then paced up and down again, and sat down to his work. But the thought that he read in the book did not satisfy him. He wanted something gigantic, unfathomable, stupendous. Towards morning he undressed and reluctantly went to bed: he ought to sleep.

When he heard the footsteps of Yegor Semyonitch going out into the garden, Kovrin rang the bell and asked the footman to bring him some wine. He drank several glasses of Lafitte, then wrapped himself up, head and all; his consciousness grew clouded and he fell asleep.

IV

Yegor Semyonitch and Tanya often quarrelled and said nasty things to each other.

They quarrelled about something that morning. Tanya burst out crying and went to her room. She would not come down to dinner nor to tea. At first Yegor Semyonitch went about looking sulky and dignified, as though to give everyone to understand that for him the claims of justice and good order were more important than anything else in the world; but he could not keep it up for long, and soon sank into depression. He walked about the park dejectedly, continually sighing: 'Oh, my God! My God!' and at dinner did not eat a morsel. At last, guilty and conscience-stricken, he knocked at the locked door and called timidly:

'Tanya! Tanya!'

And from behind the door came a faint voice, weak with crying but still determined:

'Leave me alone, if you please.'

The depression of the master and mistress was reflected in the whole household, even in the labourers working in the garden. Kovrin was absorbed in his interesting work, but at last he, too, felt dreary and uncomfortable. To dissipate the general ill-humour in some way, he made up his mind to intervene, and towards evening he knocked at Tanya's door. He was admitted.

'Fie, fie, for shame!' he began playfully, looking with surprise at Tanya's tear-stained, woebegone face, flushed in patches with crying. 'Is it really so serious? Fie, fie!'

'But if you knew how he tortures me!' she said, and floods of scalding tears streamed from her big eyes. 'He torments me to death,' she went on, wringing her hands. 'I said nothing to him . . . nothing . . . I only said that there was no need to keep . . . too many labourers . . . if we could hire them by the day when we wanted them. You know . . . you know the labourers have been doing nothing for a whole week . . . I . . . I . . . only said that, and he shouted and . . . said . . . a lot of horrible insulting things to me. What for?'

'There, there,' said Kovrin, smoothing her hair. 'You've quarrelled with each other, you've cried, and that's enough. You must not be angry for long – that's wrong . . . all the more as he loves you beyond everything.'

'He has . . . has spoiled my whole life,' Tanya went on, sobbing. 'I hear nothing but abuse and . . . insults. He thinks I am of no use in the house. Well! He is right. I shall go away tomorrow; I shall become a telegraph clerk . . . I don't care . . .'

'Come, come, come . . . You mustn't cry, Tanya. You mustn't, dear . . . You are both hot-tempered and irritable, and you are both to blame. Come along; I will reconcile you.'

Kovrin talked affectionately and persuasively, while she went on crying, twitching her shoulders and wringing her hands, as though some terrible misfortune had really befallen her. He felt all the sorrier for her because her grief was not a serious one, yet she suffered extremely. What trivialities were enough to make this little creature miserable for a whole day, perhaps for her whole life! Comforting Tanya, Kovrin thought that, apart from this girl and her father, he might hunt the world over and would not find people who would love him as one of themselves, as one of their kindred. If it had not been for those two he might very likely, having lost his father and mother in early childhood, never to the day of his death have known what was meant by genuine affection and that naïve, uncritical love which is only lavished on very close blood relations; and he felt that the nerves of this weeping, shaking girl responded to his half-sick, overstrained nerves like iron to a magnet. He never could have loved a healthy, strong, rosy-cheeked woman, but pale, weak, unhappy Tanya attracted him.

And he liked stroking her hair and her shoulders, pressing her hand and wiping away her tears... At last she left off crying. She went on for a long time complaining of her father and her hard, insufferable life in that house, entreating Kovrin to put himself in her place; then she began, little by little, smiling, and sighing that God had given her such a bad temper. At last, laughing aloud, she called herself a fool, and ran out of the room.

When a little later Kovrin went into the garden, Yegor Semyonitch and Tanya were walking side by side along an avenue as though nothing had happened, and both were eating rye bread with salt on it, as both were hungry.

V

Glad that he had been so successful in the part of peacemaker, Kovrin went into the park. Sitting on a garden seat, thinking, he heard the rattle of a carriage and a feminine laugh – visitors were arriving. When the shades of evening began falling on the garden, the sounds of the violin and singing voices reached him indistinctly, and that reminded him of the black monk. Where, in what land or on what planet, was that optical absurdity moving now?

Hardly had he recalled the legend and pictured in his imagination the dark apparition he had seen in the rye-field, when, from behind a pine-tree exactly opposite, there came out noiselessly, without the slightest rustle, a man of medium height with uncovered grey head, all in black, and barefooted like a beggar, and his black eyebrows stood out conspicuously on his pale, deathlike face. Nodding his head graciously, this beggar or pilgrim came noiselessly to the seat and sat down, and

Kovrin recognized him as the black monk.

For a minute they looked at one another, Kovrin with amazement, and the monk with friendliness, and, just as before, a little slyness, as though he were thinking something to himself.

'But you are a mirage,' said Kovrin. 'Why are you here and sitting still? That does not fit in with the legend.'

'That does not matter,' the monk answered in a low voice, not immediately turning his face towards him. 'The legend, the mirage, and I are all the products of your excited imagination. I am a phantom.'

'Then you don't exist?' said Kovrin.

'You can think as you like,' said the monk, with a faint smile. 'I exist in your imagination, and your imagination is part of nature, so I exist in nature.'

'You have a very old, wise, and extremely expressive face, as though you really had lived more than a thousand years,' said Kovrin. 'I did not know that my imagination was capable of creating such phenomena. But why do you look at me with such enthusiasm? Do you like me?'

'Yes, you are one of those few who are justly called the chosen of God. You do the service of eternal truth. Your thoughts, your designs, the marvellous studies you are engaged in, and all your life, bear the Divine, the heavenly stamp, seeing that they are consecrated to the rational and the beautiful – that is, to what is eternal.'

'You said "eternal truth" ... But is eternal truth of use to man and within his reach, if there is no eternal life?'

'There is eternal life,' said the monk.

'Do you believe in the immortality of man?'

'Yes, of course. A grand, brilliant future is in store for you men. And the more there are like you on earth, the sooner will this future be realized. Without you who serve the higher principle and live in full understanding and freedom, mankind would be of little account; developing in a natural way, it would have to wait a long time for the end of its earthly history. You will lead it some thousands of years earlier into the kingdom of eternal truth – and therein lies your supreme service. You are the incarnation of the blessing of God, which rests upon men.'

'And what is the object of eternal life?' asked Kovrin.

'As of all life – enjoyment. True enjoyment lies in knowledge, and eternal life provides innumerable and inexhaustible sources of knowledge, and in that sense it has been said: "In My Father's house there are many mansions." '

'If only you knew how pleasant it is to hear you!' said Kovrin, rubbing his hands with satisfaction.

'I am very glad.'

'But I know that when you go away I shall be worried by the question of your reality. You are a phantom, an hallucination. So I am mentally deranged, not normal?'

'What if you are? Why trouble yourself? You are ill because you have overworked and exhausted yourself, and that means that you have sacrificed your health to the idea, and the time is near at hand when you will give up life itself to it. What could be better? That is the goal towards which all divinely endowed, noble natures strive.'

'If I know I am mentally affected, can I trust myself?'

'And are you sure that the men of genius, whom all men trust, did not see phantoms, too? The learned say now that genius is allied to madness. My friend, healthy and normal people are only the common herd. Reflections upon the neurasthenia of the age, nervous exhaustion and degeneracy, etcetera, can only seriously agitate those who place the object of life in the present – that is, the common herd.'

'The Romans used to say: *Mens sana in corpore sano*.'

'Not everything the Greeks and the Romans said is true. Exaltation, enthusiasm, ecstasy – all that distinguishes prophets, poets, martyrs for the idea, from the common folk – is repellent to the animal side of man – that is, his physical health. I repeat, if you want to be healthy and normal, go to the common herd.'

'Strange that you repeat what often comes into my mind,' said Kovrin. 'It is as though you had seen and overheard my secret thoughts. But don't let us talk about me. What do you mean by "eternal truth"?'

The monk did not answer. Kovrin looked at him and could not distinguish his face. His features grew blurred and misty. Then the monk's head and arms disappeared; his body seemed merged into the seat and the evening twilight, and he vanished altogether.

'The hallucination is over,' said Kovrin; and he laughed. 'It's a pity.'

He went back to the house, light-hearted and happy. The little the monk had said to him had flattered, not his vanity, but his whole soul, his whole being. To be one of the chosen, to serve eternal truth, to stand in the ranks of those who could make mankind worthy of the kingdom of God some thousands of years sooner – that is, to free men from some thousands of years of unnecessary struggle, sin, and suffering; to sacrifice to the idea everything – youth, strength, health; to be ready to die for the common weal – what an exalted, what a happy lot! He recalled his past – pure, chaste, laborious; he remembered what he had learned himself and what he had taught to others, and decided that there was no exaggeration in the monk's words.

Tanya came to meet him in the park: she was by now wearing a different dress.

'Are you here?' she said. 'And we have been looking and looking for you . . . But what is the matter with you?' she asked in wonder, glancing at his radiant, ecstatic face and eyes full of tears. 'How strange you are, Andryusha!'

'I am pleased, Tanya,' said Kovrin, laying his hand on her shoulders. 'I am more than pleased: I am happy. Tanya, darling Tanya, you are an extraordinary, nice creature. Dear Tanya, I am so glad, I am so glad!'

He kissed both her hands ardently, and went on:

'I have just passed through an exalted, wonderful, unearthly moment. But I can't tell you all about it or you would call me mad and not believe me. Let us talk of you. Dear, delightful Tanya! I love you, and am used to loving you. To have you near me, to meet you a dozen times a day, has become a necessity of my existence: I don't know how I shall get on without you when I go back home.'

'Oh,' laughed Tanya, 'you will forget about us in two days. We are humble people and you are a great man.'

'No; let us talk in earnest!' he said. 'I shall take you with me, Tanya. Yes? Will you come with me? Will you be mine?'

'Come,' said Tanya, and tried to laugh again, but the laugh would not come, and patches of colour came into her face.

She began breathing quickly and walked very quickly, but not to the house, but further into the park.

'I was not thinking of it . . . I was not thinking of it,' she said, wringing her hands in despair.

And Kovrin followed her and went on talking, with the same radiant, enthusiastic face:

'I want a love that will dominate me altogether; and that love only you, Tanya, can give me. I am happy! I am happy!'

She was overwhelmed, and huddling and shrinking together, seemed ten years older all at once, while he thought her beautiful and expressed his rapture aloud:

'How lovely she is!'

VI

Learning from Kovrin that not only a romance had been got up, but that there would even be a wedding, Yegor Semyonitch spent a long time in pacing from one corner of the room to the other, trying to conceal his agitation. His hands began trembling, his neck swelled and turned purple, he ordered his racing droshky and drove off somewhere. Tanya, seeing how he lashed the horse, and seeing how he pulled his cap over his ears, understood what he was feeling, shut herself up in her room, and cried the whole day.

In the hot-houses the peaches and plums were already ripe; the packing and sending off of these tender and fragile goods to Moscow took a great deal of care, work, and trouble. Owing to the fact that the summer was very hot and dry, it was necessary to water every tree, and a great deal of time and labour was spent on doing it. Numbers of caterpillars made their appearance, which, to Kovrin's disgust, the labourers and even Yegor Semyonitch and Tanya squashed with their fingers. In spite of all that, they had already to book autumn orders for fruit and trees, and to carry on a great deal of correspondence. And at the very busiest time, when no one seemed to have a free moment, the work of the fields carried off more than half their labourers from the garden. Yegor Semyonitch, sunburnt, exhausted, ill-humoured, galloped from the fields to the garden and back again; cried that he was being torn to pieces, and that he should put a bullet through his brains.

Then came the fuss and worry of the trousseau, to which the Pesotskys attached a good deal of importance. Everyone's head was in a whirl from the snipping of the scissors, the rattle of the sewing-machine, the smell of hot irons, and the caprices of the dressmaker, a huffy and nervous lady. And, as ill-luck would have it, visitors came every day, who had to be entertained, fed, and even put up for the night. But all this hard labour passed unnoticed as though in a fog. Tanya felt that love and happiness had taken her unawares, though she had, since she was fourteen, for some reason been convinced that Kovrin would marry her and no one else. She was bewildered, could not grasp it, could not believe herself . . . At one minute such joy would swoop down upon her that she longed to fly away to the clouds and there pray to God, at another moment she would remember that in August she would have to part from her home and leave her father; or, goodness knows why, the idea would occur to her that she was worthless – insignificant and unworthy of a great man like Kovrin – and she would go to her room, lock herself in, and cry bitterly for several hours. When there were visitors, she would suddenly fancy that Kovrin looked extraordinarily handsome, and that all the women were in love with him and envying her, and her soul was filled with pride and rapture, as though she had vanquished the whole world; but he had only to smile politely at any young lady for her to be trembling with jealousy, to retreat to her room – and tears again. These new sensations mastered her completely; she helped her father mechanically, without noticing peaches, caterpillars or labourers, or how rapidly the time was passing.

It was almost the same with Yegor Semyonitch. He worked from morning till night, was always in a hurry, was irritable, and flew into rages, but all of this was in a sort of spellbound dream. It seemed as though there were two men in him: one was the real Yegor Semyonitch, who was moved to indignation, and clutched his head in despair when he heard of some irregularity from Ivan Karlovitch the gardener; and another – not the real one – who seemed as though he were half drunk, would interrupt a business conversation at half a word, touch the gardener on the shoulder, and begin muttering:

'Say what you like, there is a great deal in blood. His mother was a wonderful woman, most high-minded and intelligent. It was a pleasure to look at her good, candid, pure face; it was like the face of an angel. She drew splendidly, wrote verses, spoke five foreign languages, sang... Poor thing! she died of consumption. The Kingdom of Heaven be hers.'

The unreal Yegor Semyonitch sighed, and after a pause went on:

'When he was a boy and growing up in my house, he had the same angelic face, good and candid. The way he looks and talks and moves is as soft and elegant as his mother's. And his intellect! We were always struck with his intelligence. To be sure, it's not for nothing he's a Master of Arts! It's not for nothing! And wait a bit, Ivan Karlovitch, what will he be in ten years' time? He will be far above us!'

But at this point the real Yegor Semyonitch, suddenly coming to himself, would make a terrible face, would clutch his head and cry:

'The devils! They have spoilt everything! They have ruined everything! They have spoilt everything! The garden's done for, the garden's ruined!'

Kovrin, meanwhile, worked with the same ardour as before, and did not notice the general commotion. Love only added fuel to the flames. After every talk with Tanya he went to his room, happy and triumphant, took up his book or his manuscript with the same passion with which he had just kissed Tanya and told her of his love. What the black monk had told him of the chosen of God, of eternal truth, of the brilliant future of mankind and so on, gave peculiar and extraordinary significance to his work, and filled his soul with pride and the consciousness of his own exalted consequence. Once or twice a week, in the park or in the house, he met the black monk and had long conversations with him, but this did not alarm him, but, on the contrary, delighted him, as he was now firmly persuaded that such apparitions only visited the elect few who rise up above their fellows and devote themselves to the service of the idea.

One day the monk appeared at dinner-time and sat in the dining-room window. Kovrin was delighted, and very adroitly began a conversation with Yegor Semyonitch and Tanya of what might be of interest to the monk; the black-robed visitor listened and nodded his head graciously, and Yegor Semyonitch and Tanya listened, too, and smiled gaily without suspecting that Kovrin was not talking to them but to his hallucination.

Imperceptibly the fast of the Assumption was approaching, and soon after came the wedding, which, at Yegor Semyonitch's urgent desire, was celebrated with 'a flourish' – that is, with senseless festivities that lasted for two whole days and nights. Three thousand roubles' worth of food and drink was consumed, but the music of the wretched hired band, the noisy toasts, the scurrying to and fro of the footmen, the uproar and crowding, prevented them from appreciating the taste of the expensive wines and wonderful delicacies ordered from Moscow.

VII

One long winter night Kovrin was lying in bed, reading a French novel. Poor Tanya, who had headaches in the evenings from living in town, to which she was not accustomed, had been asleep a long while, and, from time to time, articulated some incoherent phrase in her restless dreams.

It struck three o'clock. Kovrin put out the light and lay down to sleep, lay for a long time with his eyes closed, but could not get to sleep because, as he fancied, the room was very hot and Tanya talked in her sleep. At half-past four he lighted the candle again, and this time he saw the black monk sitting in an arm-chair near the bed.

'Good-morning,' said the monk, and after a brief pause he asked: 'What are you thinking of now?'

'Of fame,' answered Kovrin. 'In the French novel I have just been reading, there is a description of a young *savant*, who does silly things and pines away through worrying about fame. I can't understand such anxiety.'

'Because you are wise. Your attitude towards fame is one of indifference, as towards a toy which no longer interests you.'

'Yes, that is true.'

'Renown does not allure you now. What is there flattering, amusing, or edifying in their carving your name on a tombstone, then time rubbing off the inscription together with the gilding? Moreover, happily there are too many of you for the weak memory of mankind to be able to retain your names.'

'Of course,' assented Kovrin. 'Besides, why should they be remembered? But let us talk of something else. Of happiness, for instance. What is happiness?'

When the clock struck five, he was sitting on the bed, dangling his feet to the carpet, talking to the monk:

'In ancient times a happy man grew at last frightened of his happiness – it was so great! – and to propitiate the gods he brought as a sacrifice his favourite ring. Do you know, I, too, like Polykrates, begin to be uneasy of my happiness. It seems strange to me that from morning to night I feel nothing but joy; it fills my whole being and smothers all other feelings. I don't know what sadness, grief, or boredom is. Here I am not asleep; I suffer from sleeplessness, but I am not dull. I say it in earnest; I begin to feel perplexed.'

'But why?' the monk asked in wonder. 'Is joy a supernatural feeling? Ought it not to be the normal state of man? The more highly a man is developed on the intellectual and moral side, the more independent he is, the more pleasure life gives him. Socrates, Diogenes, and Marcus Aurelius, were joyful, not sorrowful. And the Apostle tells us: "Rejoice continually"; "Rejoice and be glad." '

'But will the gods be suddenly wrathful?' Kovrin jested; and he laughed. 'If they take from me comfort and make me go cold and hungry, it won't be very much to my taste.'

Meanwhile Tanya woke up, and looked with amazement and horror at her husband. He was talking, addressing the arm-chair, laughing and gesticulating; his eyes were gleaming, and there was something strange in his laugh.

'Andryusha, whom are you talking to?' she asked, clutching the hand he stretched out to the monk. 'Andryusha! Whom?'

'Oh! Whom?' said Kovrin in confusion. 'Why, to him ... He is sitting here,' he said, pointing to the black monk.

'There is no one here ... no one! Andryusha, you are ill!'

Tanya put her arm round her husband and held him tight, as though protecting him from the apparition, and put her hand over his eyes.

'You are ill!' she sobbed, trembling all over. 'Forgive me, my precious, my dear one, but I have noticed for a long time that your mind is clouded in some way ... You are mentally ill, Andryusha ...'

Her trembling infected him, too. He glanced once more at the arm-chair, which was now empty, felt a sudden weakness in his arms and legs, was frightened, and began dressing.

'It's nothing, Tanya; it's nothing,' he muttered, shivering. 'I really am not quite well ... it's time to admit that.'

'I have noticed it for a long time ... and father has noticed it,' she said, trying to suppress her sobs. 'You talk to yourself, smile somehow strangely ... and can't sleep. Oh, my God, my God, save us!' she said in terror. 'But don't be frightened, Andryusha; for God's sake don't be frightened ...'

She began dressing, too. Only now, looking at her, Kovrin realized the danger of his position – realized the meaning of the black monk and his conversations with him. It was clear to him now that he was mad.

Neither of them knew why they dressed and went into the dining-room: she in front and he following her. There they found Yegor Semyonitch standing in his dressing-gown and with a candle in his hand. He was staying with them, and had been awakened by Tanya's sobs.

'Don't be frightened, Andryusha,' Tanya was saying, shivering as though in a fever; 'don't be frightened ... Father, it will all pass over ... it will all pass over ...'

Kovrin was too much agitated to speak. He wanted to say to his father-in-law in a playful tone: 'Congratulate me; it appears I have gone out of my mind'; but he could only move his lips and smile bitterly.

At nine o'clock in the morning they put on his jacket and fur coat, wrapped him up in a shawl, and took him in a carriage to a doctor.

VIII

Summer had come again, and the doctor advised their going into the country. Kovrin had recovered; he had left off seeing the black monk, and he had only to get up his strength. Staying at his father-in-law's, he drank a great deal of milk, worked for only two hours out of the twenty-four, and neither smoked nor drank wine.

On the evening before Elijah's Day they had an evening service in the house. When the deacon was handing the priest the censer the immense old room smelt like a graveyard, and Kovrin felt bored. He went out into the garden. Without noticing the gorgeous flowers, he walked about the garden, sat down on a seat, then strolled about the park; reaching the river, he went down and then stood lost in thought, looking at the water. The sullen pines with their shaggy roots, which had seen him a year before so young, so joyful and confident, were not whispering now, but standing mute and motionless, as though they did not recognize him. And, indeed, his head was closely cropped, his beautiful long hair was gone, his step was lagging, his face was fuller and paler than last summer.

He crossed by the footbridge to the other side. Where the year before there had been rye the oats stood, reaped, and lay in rows. The sun had set and there was a broad stretch of glowing red on the horizon, a sign of windy weather next day. It was still. Looking in the direction from which the year before the black monk had first appeared, Kovrin stood for twenty minutes, till the evening glow had begun to fade ...

When, listless and dissatisfied, he returned home the service was over. Yegor Semyonitch and Tanya were sitting on the steps of the verandah, drinking tea. They were talking of something, but, seeing Kovrin, ceased at once, and he concluded from their faces that their talk had been about him.

'I believe it is time for you to have your milk,' Tanya said to her husband.

'No, it is not time yet ... he said, sitting down on the bottom step. 'Drink it yourself; I don't want it.'

Tanya exchanged a troubled glance with her father, and said in a guilty voice:

'You notice yourself that milk does you good.'

'Yes, a great deal of good!' Kovrin laughed. 'I congratulate you: I have gained a pound in weight since Friday.' He pressed his head tightly in his hands and said miserably: 'Why, why have you cured me? Preparations of bromide, idleness, hot baths, supervision, cowardly consternation at every mouthful, at every step – all this will reduce me at last to idiocy. I went out of my mind, I had megalomania; but then I was cheerful, confident, and even happy; I was interesting and original. Now I have become more sensible and stolid, but I am just like everyone else: I am – mediocrity; I am weary of life ... Oh, how cruelly you have treated me!... I saw hallucinations, but what harm did that do to anyone? I ask, what harm did that do anyone?'

'Goodness knows what you are saying!' sighed Yegor Semyonitch. 'It's positively wearisome to listen to it.'

'Then don't listen.'

The presence of other people, especially Yegor Semyonitch, irritated Kovrin now; he answered him drily, coldly, and even rudely, never looked at him but with irony and hatred, while Yegor Semyonitch was overcome with confusion and cleared his throat guiltily, though he was not conscious of any fault in himself. At a loss to understand why their charming and affectionate relations had changed so abruptly, Tanya huddled up to her father and looked anxiously in his face; she wanted to understand and could not understand, and all that was clear to her was that their relations were growing worse and worse every day, that of late her father had begun to look much older, and her husband had grown irritable, capricious, quarrelsome and uninteresting. She could not laugh or sing; at dinner she ate nothing; did not sleep for nights together, expecting something awful, and was so worn out that on one occasion she lay in a dead faint from dinner-time till evening. During the service she thought her father was crying, and now while the three of them were sitting together on the terrace she made an effort not to think of it.

'How fortunate Buddha, Mahomed, and Shakespeare were that their kind relations and doctors did not cure them of their ecstasy and their inspiration,' said Kovrin. 'If Mahomed had taken bromide for his nerves, had worked only two hours out of the twenty-four, and had drunk milk, that remarkable man would have left no more trace after him than his dog. Doctors and kind relations will succeed in stupefying mankind, in making mediocrity pass for genius and in bringing civilization to ruin. If only you knew,' Kovrin said with annoyance, 'how grateful I am to you.'

He felt intense irritation, and to avoid saying too much, he got up quickly and went into the house. It was still, and the fragrance of the tobacco plant and the marvel of Peru floated in at the open window. The moonlight lay in green patches on the floor and on the piano in the big dark dining-room. Kovrin remembered the raptures of the previous summer when there had been the same scent of the marvel of Peru and the moon had shone in at the window. To bring back the mood of last year he went quickly to his study, lighted a strong cigar, and told the footman to bring him some wine. But the cigar left a bitter and disgusting taste in his mouth, and the wine had not the same flavour as it had the year before. And so great is the effect of giving up a habit, the cigar and the two gulps of wine made him giddy, and brought on palpitations of the heart, so that he was obliged to take bromide.

Before going to bed, Tanya said to him:

'Father adores you. You are cross with him about something, and it is killing him. Look at him; he is ageing, not from day to day, but from hour to hour. I entreat you, Andryusha, for God's sake, for the sake of your dead father, for the sake of my peace of mind, be affectionate to him.'

'I can't, I don't want to.'

'But why?' asked Tanya, beginning to tremble all over. 'Explain why.'

'Because he is antipathetic to me, that's all,' said Kovrin carelessly; and he shrugged his shoulders. 'But we won't talk about him: he is your father.'

'I can't understand, I can't,' said Tanya, pressing her hands to her temples and staring at a fixed point. 'Something incomprehensible, awful, is going on in the house. You have changed, grown unlike yourself... You, clever, extraordinary man as you are, are irritated over trifles, meddle in paltry nonsense... Such trivial things excite you, that sometimes one is simply amazed and can't believe that it is you. Come, come, don't be angry, don't be angry,' she went on, kissing his hands, frightened of her own words. 'You are clever, kind, noble. You will be just to father. He is so good.'

'He is not good; he is just good-natured. Burlesque old uncles like your father, with well-fed, good-natured faces, extraordinarily hospitable and queer, at one time used to touch me and amuse me in novels and in farces and in life; now I dislike them. They are egoists to the marrow of their bones. What disgusts me most of all is their being so well-fed, and that purely bovine, purely hoggish optimism of a full stomach.'

Tanya sat down on the bed and laid her head on the pillow.

'This is torture,' she said, and from her voice it was evident that she was utterly exhausted, and that it was hard for her to speak. 'Not one moment of peace since the winter... Why, it's awful! My God! I am wretched.'

'Oh, of course, I am Herod, and you and your father are the innocents. Of course.'

His face seemed to Tanya ugly and unpleasant. Hatred and an ironical expression did not suit him. And, indeed, she had noticed before that there was something lacking in his face, as though ever since his hair had been cut his face had changed, too. She wanted to say something wounding to him, but immediately she caught herself in this antagonistic feeling, she was frightened and went out of the bedroom.

IX

Kovrin received a professorship at the University. The inaugural address was fixed for the second of December, and a notice to that effect was hung up in the corridor at the University. But on the day appointed he informed the students' inspector, by telegram, that he was prevented by illness from giving the lecture.

He had hæmorrhage from the throat. He was often spitting blood, but it happened two or three times a month that there was a considerable loss of blood, and then he grew extremely weak and sank into a drowsy condition. This illness did not particularly frighten him, as he knew that his mother had lived for ten years or longer suffering from the same disease, and the doctors assured him that there was no danger, and had only advised him to avoid excitement, to lead a regular life, and to speak as little as possible.

In January again his lecture did not take place owing to the same reason, and in February it was too late to begin the course. It had to be postponed to the following year.

By now he was living not with Tanya, but with another woman, who was two years older than he was, and who looked after him as though he were a baby. He was in a calm and tranquil state of mind; he readily gave in to her, and when Varvara Nikolaevna – that was the name of his friend – decided to take him to the Crimea, he agreed, though he had a presentiment that no good would come of the trip.

They reached Sevastopol in the evening and stopped at an hotel to rest and go on the next day to Yalta. They were both exhausted by the journey. Varvara Nikolaevna had some tea, went to bed and was soon asleep. But Kovrin did not go to bed. An hour before starting for the station, he had received a letter from Tanya, and had not brought himself to open it, and now it was lying in his coat pocket, and the thought of it excited him disagreeably. At the bottom of his heart he genuinely considered now that his marriage to Tanya had been a mistake. He was glad that their separation was final, and the thought of that woman who in the end had turned into a living relic, still walking about though everything seemed dead in her except her big, staring, intelligent eyes – the thought of her roused in him nothing but pity and disgust with himself. The handwriting on the envelope reminded him how cruel and unjust he had been two years before, how he had worked off his anger at his spiritual emptiness, his boredom, his loneliness, and his dissatisfaction with life by revenging himself on people in no way to blame. He remembered, also, how he had torn up his dissertation and all the articles he had written during his illness, and how he had thrown them out of the window, and the bits of paper had fluttered in the wind and caught on the trees and flowers. In every line of them he saw strange, utterly groundless pretension, shallow defiance, arrogance, megalomania; and they made him feel as though he were reading a description of his vices. But when the last manuscript had been torn up and sent flying out of the window, he felt, for some reason, suddenly bitter and angry; he went to his wife and said a great many unpleasant things to her. My God, how he had tormented her! One day, wanting to cause her pain, he told her that her father had played a very unattractive part in their romance, that he had asked him to marry her. Yegor Semyonitch accidentally overheard this, ran into the room, and, in his despair, could not utter a word, could only stamp and make a strange, bellowing sound as though he had lost the power of speech, and Tanya, looking at her father, had uttered a heart-rending shriek and had fallen into a swoon. It was hideous.

All this came back into his memory as he looked at the familiar writing. Kovrin went out on to the balcony; it was still warm weather and there was a smell of the sea. The wonderful bay reflected the moonshine and the lights, and was of a colour for which it was difficult to find a name. It was a soft and tender blending of dark blue and green; in places the water was like blue vitriol, and in places it seemed as though the moonlight were liquefied and filling the bay instead of water. And what harmony of colours, what an atmosphere of peace, calm, and sublimity!

In the lower storey under the balcony the windows were probably open, for women's voices and laughter could be heard distinctly. Apparently there was an evening party.

Kovrin made an effort, tore open the envelope, and, going back into his room, read:

'My father is just dead. I owe that to you, for you have killed him. Our garden is being ruined; strangers are managing it already – that is, the very thing is happening that poor father dreaded. That, too, I owe to you. I hate you with my whole soul, and I hope you may soon perish. Oh, how wretched I am! Insufferable anguish is burning my soul ... My curses on you. I took you for an extraordinary man, a genius; I loved you, and you have turned out a madman ...'

Kovrin could read no more, he tore up the letter and threw it away. He was overcome by an uneasiness that was akin to terror. Varvara Nikolaevna was asleep behind the screen, and he could hear her breathing. From the lower storey came the sounds of laughter and women's voices, but he felt as though in the whole hotel there were no living soul but him. Because Tanya, unhappy, broken by sorrow, had cursed him in her letter and hoped for his perdition, he felt eerie and kept glancing hurriedly at the door, as though he were afraid that the uncomprehended force which two years before had wrought such havoc in his life and in the life of those near him might come into the room and master him once more.

He knew by experience that when his nerves were out of hand the best thing for him to do was to work. He must sit down to the table and force himself, at all costs, to concentrate his mind on some one thought. He took from his red portfolio a manuscript containing a sketch of a small work in the nature of a compilation, which he had planned in case he should find it dull in the Crimea without work. He sat down to the table and began working at this plan, and it seemed to him that his calm, peaceful, indifferent mood was coming back. The manuscript with the sketch even led him to meditation on the vanity of the world. He thought how much life exacts for the worthless or very commonplace blessings it can give a man. For instance, to gain, before forty, a university chair, to be an ordinary professor, to expound ordinary and second-hand thoughts in dull, heavy, insipid language – in fact, to gain the position of a mediocre learned man, he, Kovrin, had had to study for fifteen years, to work day and night, to endure a terrible mental illness, to experience an unhappy marriage, and to do a great number of stupid and unjust things which it would have been pleasant not to remember. Kovrin recognized clearly, now, that he was a mediocrity, and readily resigned himself to it, as he considered that every man ought to be satisfied with what he is.

The plan of the volume would have soothed him completely, but the torn letter showed white on the floor and prevented him from concentrating his attention. He got up from the table, picked up the pieces of the letter and threw them out of the window, but there was a light wind blowing from the sea, and the bits of paper were scattered on the window-sill. Again he was overcome by uneasiness akin to terror, and he felt as though in the whole hotel there were no living soul but himself ... He went out on the balcony. The bay, like a living thing, looked at him with its multitude of light blue, dark blue, turquoise and fiery eyes, and seemed beckoning to him. And it really was hot and oppressive, and it would not have been amiss to have a bathe.

Suddenly in the lower storey under the balcony a violin began playing, and two soft feminine voices began singing. It was something familiar. The song was about a maiden, full of sick fancies, who heard one night in her garden mysterious sounds, so strange and lovely that she was obliged to recognize them as a holy harmony which is unintelligible to us mortals, and so flies back to heaven ... Kovrin caught his breath and there was a pang of sadness at his heart, and a thrill of the sweet, exquisite delight he had so long forgotten began to stir in his breast.

A tall black column, like a whirlwind or a waterspout, appeared on the further side of the bay. It moved with fearful rapidity across the bay, towards the hotel, growing smaller and darker as it came, and Kovrin only just had time to get out of the way to let it pass ... The monk with bare grey head, black eyebrows, barefoot, his arms crossed over his breast, floated by him, and stood still in the middle of the room.

'Why did you not believe me?' he asked reproachfully, looking affectionately at Kovrin. 'If you had believed me then, that you were a genius, you would not have spent these two years so gloomily and so wretchedly.'

Kovrin already believed that he was one of God's chosen and a genius; he vividly recalled his conversations with the monk in the past and tried to speak, but the blood flowed from his throat on to his breast, and not knowing what he was doing, he passed his hands over his breast, and his cuffs were soaked with blood. He tried to call Varvara Nikolaevna, who was asleep behind the screen, he made an effort and said:

'Tanya!'

He fell on the floor, and propping himself on his arms, called again:

'Tanya!'

He called Tanya, called to the great garden with the gorgeous flowers sprinkled with dew, called to the park, the pines with their shaggy roots, the rye-field, his marvellous learning, his youth, courage, joy – called to life, which was so lovely. He saw on the floor near his face a great pool of blood, and was too weak to utter a word, but an unspeakable, infinite happiness flooded his whole being. Below, under the balcony, they were playing the serenade, and the black monk whispered to him that he was a genius, and that he was dying only because his frail human body had lost its balance and could no longer serve as the mortal garb of genius.

When Varvara Nikolaevna woke up and came out from behind the screen, Kovrin was dead, and a blissful smile was set upon his face.

A Fisher of Men

John Galsworthy

Long ago it is, now, that I used to see him issue from the rectory, followed by his dogs, an Irish and a fox-terrier. He would cross to the churchyard, and, at the gate, stand looking over the Cornish upland of his cure of souls, towards the sea, distant nearly a mile. About his black thin figure there was one bright spot, a little gold cross, dangling on his vest. His eyes at such moments were like the eyes of fishermen watching from the cliffs for pilchards to come by; but as this fisher of men marked the grey roofs covered with yellow lichen where his human fishes dwelt, red stains would come into his meagre cheeks. His lips would move, and he would turn abruptly in at the gate over which was written; 'This is the Gate of Heaven.'

A certain green spot within that churchyard was kept clear of gravestones, which thickly covered all the rest of the ground. He never – I believe – failed to look at it, and think: 'I will keep that corner free. I will not be buried amongst men, who refuse their God!'

For this was his misfortune, which, like a creeping fate, had come on him year by year throughout his twenty years of rectorship. It had eaten into his heart, as is the way with troubles which a man cannot understand. In plain words, his catch of souls had dwindled season by season till, from three hundred when he was first presented to the living, it barely numbered forty. Sunday after Sunday he had conducted his three services. Twice a week from the old pulpit, scanning through the church twilight that ever scantier flock of faces, he had in his dry, spasmodic voice

– whose harsh tones, no doubt, were music to himself – pronounced this conduct blessed, and that accursed, in accordance with his creed. Week after week he had told us all the sinfulness of not attending God's House, of not observing the Lord's Day. He had respected every proper ritual and ceremony; never refusing baptism even to the illegitimate, nor burial to any but such as took their own lives; joining in marriage with a certain exceptional alacrity those whose conduct had caused scandal in the village. His face had been set, too, against irreverence; no one, I remember, might come to his church in flannel trousers.

Yet his flock had slowly diminished! Living, unmarried, in the neglected rectory, with his dogs, an old housekeeper, and a canary, he seemed to have no interests, such as shooting, or fishing, to take him away from his parish duties; he asked nothing better than to enter the houses and lives of his parishioners; and as he passed their doors – spare, black, and clean-shaven – he could often be seen to stop, make, as it were, a minatory gesture, and walk on with his hungry eyes fixed straight before him. Year by year, to encourage them, he printed privately and distributed documents containing phrases such as these: 'It were better for him that a mill-stone were hanged about his neck, and he were cast into the sea.' 'But the fearful and unbelieving shall have their part in the lake which burneth with fire and brimstone.' When he wrote them, his eyes – I fancy – flared, as though watching such penalties in process of infliction. Had not his parishioners in justice merited those fates?

If, in his walks, he came across a truant, some fisherman or farmer, he would always stop, with his eyes fastened on the culprit's face:

'You don't come to church now; how's that?'

Like true Cornishmen, hoping to avoid unpleasantness, they would offer some polite excuse: They didn't knaw ezactly, zur – the missus 'ad been ailin'; there was always somethin' – like – that! This temporizing with the devil never failed to make the rector's eyes blaze, or to elicit from him a short dry laugh: 'You don't know what you're saying, man! You must be mad to think you can save your soul that way! This is a Christian country!'

Yet never after one of these encounters did he see the face of that parishioner in his church again. 'Let un wait!' they would murmur, 'tidden likely we'm gwine to his church t'be spoke to like dogs!'

But, indeed, had they been dogs, the rector would not have spoken to them like that. To dogs his conduct was invariably gentle. He might be seen sometimes beside a field of standing corn, where the heads of his two terriers could be marked spasmodically emerging above the golden stalks, as they hunted a covey of partridges or brood of young pheasants which they had scented. His harsh voice could be heard calling them: 'Jim, Jim! Pat, Pat! To heel, you rascals!' But when they came out, their tongues lolling ecstatically, he only stooped and shook his finger at them, and they would lick his hand, or rub themselves against his trousers, confident that he would never strike them. With every animal, with every bird and insect he was like this, so gentle that they trusted him completely. He could often be surprised sitting on a high slate stile, or standing in a dip of the wide road between banks of gorse and bramble, with his head, in its wide hat, rather to one side, while a bullfinch or hedge-sparrow on a branch, not three feet off, would be telling him its little tale. Before going for a walk he would sweep his field-glass over the pale-gold landscape of cornfield, scorched pasturage and sand-dune, to see if any horse seemed needing water, or sheep were lying on its back. He was an avowed enemy, too, of traps, and gins, and whenever he met with one, took pains to ensure its catching nothing. Such consistent tenderness to dumb animals was perhaps due to a desire to take their side against farmers who would not come to church; but more, I think, to the feeling that the poor things had no souls, that they were here today and gone tomorrow – they could not be saved and must be treated with compassion, unlike those men with immortal spirits entrusted by God specially to his care, for whose wanton disobedience no punishment, perhaps, could be too harsh. It was as if, by endowing him with her authority over other men, the Church had divided him into two.

For the view he took of life was very simple, undisturbed by any sense of irony, unspoiled by curiosity, or desire to link effect with cause, or, indeed, to admit the necessity of cause at all. At some fixed date God had made the earth of matter; this matter He had divided into the inanimate and the animate, unconnected with each other; animate matter He had again divided into men, and animals; in men He had placed souls, making them in His own image. Men again He had divided into the Church and other men; and for the government and improvement of these other men, God had passed Himself into His Church. That Church again had passed herself into her ministers. Thus, on the Church's minister – placed by Providence beyond the fear of being in the wrong – there had been enjoined the bounden duty of instructing, ruling, and saving at all costs the souls of men.

This was why, I think, when he encountered in the simple folk committed to his charge a strange dumb democratic spirit, a wayward feeling that the universe was indivisible, that power had not devolved, but had evolved, that things were relative, not absolute, and so forth – expressed in their simple way, he had experienced from the first a gnawing irritation which, like a worm, seemed to have cankered his heart. Gradually one had seen this canker stealing out into his face and body, into his eyes and voice, into the very gestures of his lean arms and hands. His whole form gave the impression of a dark tree withered and eaten by some desiccating wind, like the stiff oaks of his Cornish upland, gnarled and riven by the Atlantic gales.

Night and day in the worn old rectory, with its red conservatory, he must have brooded over the wrong done him by his people, in depriving him of his just due, the power to save their souls. It was as though an officer, gagged and bound at the head of his company, should have been forced to watch them manoeuvring without him. He was like a schoolmaster tied to his desk amongst the pandemonium of his scholars. His failure was a fact strange and intolerable to him, inexplicable, tragic – a fact mured up in the mystery which each man's blindness to the nature of his own spirit wraps round his relations with his fellow beings. He could not doubt that, bereaved by their own wilful conduct of his ministrations, of the Church in fact, and, through the Church, of God, his parishioners were given up to damnation. If they were thus given up to damnation, he, their proper pastor – their rightful leader, the symbol of the Church, that is of God – was but a barren, withered thing. This thought he could not bear. Unable to see himself as others saw him, he searched to find excuses for them. He found none; for he knew that he had preached no narrow doctrines cursed with the bigotry which he recognized in the Romish or Nonconformist faiths. The doctrines and dogmas he was appointed to administer were of the due and necessary breadth, no more, no less. He was scrupulous, even against his own personal feeling, to observe the letter of the encyclicals. Thus, nothing in the matter of his teaching could account for the gradual defection of his flock. Nor in the manner of it could he detect anything that seemed to himself unjustified. Yet, as the tide ebbed from the base of the grey cliffs, so, without haste, with deadly certainty, the tide ebbed from his church. What could he, then, believe but that his parishioners meant to be personally offensive to himself?

In the school-house, at the post office, on the green, at choir practice, or on the way to service, wherever he met them, one could see that he was perpetually detecting small slights or incivilities. He had come, I think, almost to imagine that these people, who never came to church, fixed the hours of their births and deaths and marriages maliciously, that they might mock at the inconvenience caused to one who neither could, nor would, refuse to do his duty. It was blasphemy they were committing. In avoiding God's church, yet requiring such services of His minister, they were making God their servant.

One could find him any evening in his study, his chin resting on his hand, the oil-lamp flaring slightly, his dogs curled up beside him, and the cloth cover drawn over the cage of his canary so that the little creature should not suffer from the light. Almost the first words he spoke would show how ceaselessly he brooded. 'Nothing,' he would say, 'ever prospers in this village; I've started this and that! Look at the football club, look at the Bible class – all no good! With people such as these, wanting in all reverence, humility, and love of discipline! You have not had the dealings with them that I have!'

In truth his dealings with them had become notorious throughout the district. A petition, privately subscribed, and presented to the Bishop for his removal, had, of course, met with failure. A rector could not be removed from his living for any reason – it had been purchased for him by his father. Nor could his position as minister be interfered with on any such excuse as that of the mere personal dislike of his parishioners – as well, indeed, seek by petition to remove the Church herself. The knowledge of his unassailable position found expression among his parishioners in dogged looks, and the words: 'Well, we don't trouble!'

It was in the twentieth year of his rectorship that a slight collision with the parish council drew from him this letter: 'It is my duty to record my intention to attend no more meetings, for I cannot, as a Christian, continue to meet those who obstinately refuse to come to church.'

It was then late September, and the harvest festival had been appointed for the following Sunday. The week passed, but the farmers had provided no offerings for the decoration of the church; the fishermen, too, accustomed by an old tradition in that parish to supply some purchased fruit in lieu of their shining fishes, sent nothing. The boycott had obviously been preconcerted.

But when the rector stepped that Sunday into the pulpit the church was fuller than it had been for many years. Men and women who had long ceased to attend had come, possessed evidently by an itch to see how 'th' old man' would take it. The eyes of the farmers and fishermen, hardened by the elements, had in them a grim humorous curiosity, such as one may remark in the eyes of a ring of men round some poor wretch, whom, moved by a crude sense of justice, they have baited into the loss of dignity. Their faces, with hardly an exception, seemed to say: 'Sir, we were given neither hand nor voice in the choosing of you. From the first day you showed us the cloven hoof. We have never wanted you. If we must have you, let us at all events get some sport out of you!'

The rector's white figure rising from the dark pulpit received without movement the shafts of all our glances; his own deep-set hungering eyes were fixed on the Bible in his hand. He gave out his text: 'The kindly fruits of the earth, in due season –'

His voice – strangely smooth and low that morning, I remember – began discoursing of the beneficence and kindliness of God, who had allowed the earth to provide men year by year with food, according to their needs. It was as though the mellow sentiment of that season of fruition had fallen on his exiled spirit. But presently he paused, and, leaning forward, looked man by man, woman by woman, at us all. Those eyes now had in them the peculiar flare which we knew so well. His voice rose again: 'And how have you met this benefaction, my brethren, how have you shown your gratitude to God, embodied in His Church and in me, her appointed representative? Do you think, then, that God will let you insult Him with impunity? Do you think in your foolish pride that God will suffer you unpunished to place this conspired slight on Him? If you imagine this, you are woefully mistaken. I know the depths of your rebellious hearts; I read them like this Book. You seek, you have always sought, to set my authority at defiance – a wayward and disobedient generation. But let me tell you: God, who has set His Holy Church over you, is a just and strong God; as a kind master chastises his dogs for their own good, so will He chastise you. You have sought to drive me out from among you' – and from his pale twisting lips, through the hush, there came a sound like a laugh – 'to drive the Church, to drive God Himself, away! You could not have made a grosser error. Do you think that we, in solemn charge of your salvation, are to be moved by such puerile rebellion? Not so! God has appointed us – to God alone we are accountable. Not if every man and woman in the parish, aye, and every child, deserted this church, would I recoil one step from my duty, or resign my charge! As well imagine, forsooth, that your great Church is some poor man-elected leader, subject to your whims, and to be deposed as the fancy takes you! Do you conceive the nature of the Church and of my office to be so mean and petty that I am to feed you with the food you wish me to feed you with, to lead you into such fields as you dictate? No! my brethren, you have not that power! Is the shepherd elected by the sheep? Listen, then, to the truth, or to your peril be it! The Church is a rock set up by God amongst the shifting sands of life. It comes from Heaven, not from this miserable earth. Its mission is to command, yours to obey. If the last man in this Christian country proved a rebel and a traitor, the Church and her ministers would stand immovable, as I stand here, firm in my sacred resolve to save your souls. Go down on your knees, and beg God to forgive you for the wanton insult you have offered Him! . . . Hymn 266: "Lead, kindly Light, amid the encircling gloom!" '

Through the grey aisles, where so great a silence reigned, the notes of the organ rose. The first verse of that hymn was sung only by the choir and a few women's voices; then one by one the men joined in. Our voices swelled into a shout louder than we had ever heard in the little church before – a mutinous, harsh, roaring sound, as though, in the words of that gentle hymn, each one of this grim congregation were pouring out all the resentment in his heart. The roar emerging through the open door must have startled the passing tourists, and the geese in the neighbouring farmyard. It ended with a groan like the long-drawn sob of a wave sucking back.

In the village all the next week little except this sermon was discussed. Farmers and fishermen are men of the world. The conditions of their lives, which are guarded only by their own unremitting efforts, which are backed by no authority save their own courage in the long struggle with land and sea, gives them a certain deep philosophy. Amongst the fishermen there was one white-bearded old fellow who even seemed to see a deep significance in the rector's sermon. 'Mun putts hissel' above us, like the Czar o' Roossia,' he said, ' 'tes the sperrit o' the thing that's wrong. Talk o' lovin' kindness, there's none 'bout the Church, 'sfar's I can see, 'tes all: "Du this, or ye'll be blasted!" This man – he's a regular chip o' the old block!' He spoke, indeed, as though the rector's attitude towards them were a symbol of the Church's attitude to men. Among the farmers such analogies were veiled by the expression of simpler thoughts:

'Yu med tak' a 'arse to the watter, yu can't mak' un drink!'

'Whu wants mun, savin' our souls! Let mun save's own!'

'We'm not gude enough to listen to his prachin', I rackon!'

It was before a congregation consisting of his clerk, two tourists, three old women, one of them stone deaf, and four little girls, that the unfortunate man stood next Sunday morning.

Late that same wild and windy afternoon a jeering rumour spread down in the village: 'Th' old man's up to Tresellyn 'Igh Cliff, talkin' to the watters!'

A crowd soon gathered, eager for the least sensation that should break monotony. Beyond the combe, above the grey roofs of the fishing village, Tressellyn High Cliff rises abruptly. At the top, on the very edge, the tiny black shape of a man could be seen standing with his arms raised above his head. Now he kneeled, then stood motionless for many minutes with hands outstretched; while behind him the white and brown specks of his two terriers were visible, couched among the short grass. Suddenly he could be seen gesticulating wildly, and the speck shapes of the dogs leaping up, and cowering again as if terrified at their master's conduct.

For two hours this fantastic show was witnessed by the villagers with gloating gravity. The general verdict was: 'Th' old man's carryin' on praaperly.' But very gradually the sight of that tiny black figure appealing to his God – the God of his Church militant which lived by domination – roused the superstition of men who themselves were living in primitive conflict with the elements. They could not but appreciate what was so in keeping with the vengeful spirit of a fighting race. One could see that they even began to be afraid. Then a great burst of rain, sweeping from the sea, smothered all sight of him.

Early next morning the news spread that the rector had been found in his armchair, the two dogs at his feet, and the canary perched on his dead hand. His clothes were unchanged and wet, as if he had sunk into that chair, and passed away, from sheer exhaustion. The body of 'the poor unfortunate gentleman' – the old housekeeper told me – was huddled and shrunk together; his chin rested on the little gold cross dangling on his vest.

They buried him in that green spot, apart from his parishioners, which he had selected for his grave, placing on the tombstone these words:

> HIC JACET
>
> P— W—
>
> PASTOR ECCLESIÆ BRITANNICÆ
>
> 'GOD IS LOVE'

Brother John's Bequest

Arthur Gray

On a certain morning in the summer of the year 1510 John Eccleston, Doctor in Divinity and Master of Jesus College in Cambridge, stood at the door of his lodge looking into the cloister court. There was a faint odour of extinguished candles in the air, and a bell automatically clanked in unison with its bearer's step. It was carried by a young acolyte, who lagged in the rear of a small band of white-robed figures who were just disappearing from sight at the corner of the passage leading to the entrance court. They were the five Fellows of the newly constituted College.

As they disappeared, the Master, with much deliberation, spat into the cloister walk.

To spit behind a man's back might be accounted a mark of disgust, contempt, malice – at least of disapproval. Such were not the feelings of Dr Eccleston.

It is a fact known all over the world, Christian and heathen, that visitants from the unseen realm cannot endure to be spat at. The Master's action was prophylactic. For supernatural visitings of the transitory, curable kind the rites of the Church are, no doubt, efficacious. In inveterate cases it is well to leave no remedy untried.

With bell, book and candle the Master and Fellows had just completed a lustration of the lodge. The bell had clanked in the Founder's Chamber and in the Master's oratory. The Master's bedchamber had been well soused with holy water. The candle had explored dark places in cupboards and under the stairs. If It was there before it was almost inconceivable that It remained there now. But one cannot be too careful.

Two days previously a funeral had taken place in the College. It was a shabby affair. The deceased, John Baldwin, late a brother of the dissolved Hospital of St John, was put away in an obscure part of the College churchyard – now the Master's garden – behind some elder bushes which grew in the corner bounded by the street and the 'chimney'. The mourners were the grave-digger, the sexton and the parson of All Saints' Church. Though Brother John had died in a college chamber, the Society of Jesus marked its reprobation of his manner of living by absenting themselves from his obsequies.

Brother John had been a disappointment: uncharitable persons might say he was a fraud. He had got into the College by false pretences. In life he had disgraced it by his excesses, and, when he was dead, he had perpetrated a mean practical joke on the Society. It is not well for a man in religious orders to joke when he is dead.

How did it come that Brother John Baldwin, late Granger of the Augustinian Hospital of Saint John, died in Jesus College?

The Hospital of Saint John was dissolved in the year 1510, to make room for the new college designed by the Lady Margaret. Bishops of Ely for three centuries and more had been its patrons and visitors, and dissolute James Stanley, bishop in 1510, fought stoutly for its maintenance. But circumstances were too strong for the bishop. The ancient Hospital was hopelessly bankrupt. The buildings were ruinous: there was not a doit in the treasury chest: the household goods were pawned to creditors in the town. The Master, William Tomlyn, had disappeared, none knew whither, and only two brethren were left in the place. One of them was John Baldwin: the other was the Infirmarer, a certain Bartholomew Aspelon.

On the eve of the dissolution, Bishop Stanley wrote a letter to the Master and Fellows of the other Cambridge society of which he was a visitor, namely Jesus College. He commended to their charitable care Brother John Baldwin, an aged man of godly conversation who was disposed to bestow his worldly goods for the comfort and sustenance of the Master and Fellows in consideration of their maintenance of him in College during the remaining years of his earthly pilgrimage. It was a not uncommon practice in those days for monasteries and colleges to accept as inmates persons, clerical or lay, who wished to withdraw from the world and were willing, either during life or by testamentary arrangements, to guarantee their hosts against pecuniary loss.

Report said that, though the Hospital was penniless, Brother John in his private circumstances was well-to-do and even affluent. It did not befit the Master and Fellows to enquire how he had come by his wealth. They were wretchedly poor, and the bishop's certificate of character was all that could be desired. They thanked the bishop for his prudent care for their interests and covenanted to give the religious man a domicile in the College with allowance for victuals, barber, laundress, wine, wax and all other things necessary for celebrating Divine service, as to any Fellow of the College. Brother John promptly transferred himself to his new quarters which were in a room called 'the loft', on the top floor above the Founder's Chamber in the Master's lodge.

The Master and Fellows were disappointed in Brother John's luggage. It consisted simply of two brass-bound boxes, heavy but unquestionably small, even for a man of religion. An encouraging feature about them was that they bore the monogram of Saint John's Hospital. Brother John and his former co-mate of the Hospital, Bartholomew Aspelon, constantly affirmed that the missing Master, William Tomlyn, had decamped with the contents of the Hospital treasury. But the Society of Jesus hoped that they were not telling the truth. Brother John kept the two boxes under his bed. They were always carefully locked, but Brother John threw out vague hints that their contents were destined for a princely benefaction to his hospitable entertainers.

In other respects Brother John's equipment was not such as would betoken a man of wealth. Rather it savoured of monastical austerity. His only suit of clothing was ancient, and even greasy. It was never changed, night or day. Brother John was apparently under a religious obligation to abstain from washing.

As a man of godly conversation Brother John was unfortunate in his personal appearance. It was presumably a stroke of paralysis which had drawn up one side of his face and correspondingly depressed the other. His mouth was a diagonal compromise with the rest of his features. One eye was closed, and the other was bleared and watery. His nose was red, but the rest of his face was of a parchment colour.

Brother John was an elderly person, and continued ill-health unfortunately confined him to his chamber, above the Master's. He expressed a deep regret that he could not share the society of the Fellows in the Hall at their meals of oatmeal porridge, salt fish, and thin ale. His distressing ailments necessitated a sustaining diet of capons and oysters, supplied to him in his chamber by the College. He was equally debarred from attending services in the Chapel, but the wine with which the Society had covenanted to supply him was punctually consumed at the private offices which he performed in his chamber. A suitable pecuniary compensation was made to him on the ground that his domestic arrangements rendered the services of the College laundress unnecessary.

Bartholomew Aspelon, who lodged in an alehouse in the town, was the constant and affectionate attendant at Brother John's sick bed: for, indeed, he seldom got out of it. From a neighbouring tavern he brought to him abundant supplies of the ypocras and malmsey wine which were requisite for the maintenance of the invalid's failing strength. Brother Bartholomew was an individual of a merry countenance and gifted with cheerful song. In the sick room the Fellows would often hear him trolling a drinking catch, to which the invalid joined a quavering note. So constant and familiar was the lay that John Bale, one of the Fellows, remembered it thirty years afterwards, and put it in the mouth of a roystering monk whom he introduced as one of the characters in his play, *King Johan*. The words ran thus:

> Wassayle, wassayle, out of the mylke payle,
> Wassayle, wassayle, as whyte as my nayle,
> Wassayle, wassayle, in snow, frost and hayle,
> Wassayle, wassayle, with partriche and rayle,
> Wassayle, wassayle, that much doth avayle,
> Wassayle, wassayle, that never wyll fayle.

The invasion of the college silences by this unusual concert was marked by the Fellows with growing disapproval: and they were not comforted when they discovered that the new robe which they had contracted to supply to their guest had been pledged to the host of the Sarazin's Head in part payment of an account rendered. But they possessed their souls in patience as they noted that the health of their venerable guest was declining with obvious rapidity. With some insistence they pointed out to the Master the desirability of having a prompt and clear understanding about Brother John's testamentary dispositions. Dr Eccleston was entirely of the Fellows' mind in the matter.

One evening in June, some three months after Brother John had begun his residence in the College, it seemed to Dr Eccleston that the time had come to sound him about his intentions. The patient was very low, and Brother Bartholomew was much depressed. With inkhorn and pen the Master went upstairs to the sick man's chamber. Nuncupatory wills were in those days accepted as legal obligations, and the Master was minded that he would not leave Brother John until he had obtained, from his dictation, a statement of his intentions as to the disposal of his goods.

Obviously Brother John's mind was wandering when the Master entered the room, for he greeted his arrival with a snatch of the old scurvy tune,

> Wassayle, wassayle, that never wyll fayle,

and feebly added, 'Art there, bully Bartholomew? Bear me thy hand to the bottle, for I am dry.'

'Brother John, Brother John,' said the Master, 'bestir thee, and think of thy state. It is time for thee to consider of thy world's gear and how thou wilt bestow it according to thy promise to our poor company, for their tendance of thee.'

Brother John raised himself in his bed and opened his serviceable eye. Something like a grin puckered up his sloping mouth. 'Art thou of that counsel, goodman Doctor?' said he: 'then have with thee. I were a knave if I did not thank you for your kindness, and, trust me, ye shall not be the losers for your pains. Take quill and write. I will dictate my will in two fillings of thy pen. Write': and the Master wrote.

To the Master and Fellows of Jesus College I give and bequeath that chest that lieth beneath my bed and is marked with a great letter A, and all that is in it. To Brother Bartholomew Aspelon, late of the Hospital of Saint John, in like manner I bequeath that other chest that is marked B.

'Is that all?' asked the Master.

'Gogswouns, it is all I have,' said Brother John. 'Yet stay, good Master. Nothing for nothing is a safe text. Thou shalt write it as a condition, on pain of forfeiting my bequest, that ye shall bury me in the aisle of your church, immediately before the High Altar: that ye shall keep my obit, or anniversary, with *placebo* and *dirige* and mass of requiem; and that once each week a Fellow that is a priest shall pray and sing for the soul of John Baldwin, the benefactor of the College. Is it rehearsed, master doctor?'

'It is written,' said the Master.

'*Ite, missa est,*' said the invalid, 'and fetch me a stoup of small ale, good Master.'

A few days later John Baldwin made his unimproving, unregretted end. Brother Bartholomew carried off his portion of the legacy. The other chest was deposited on the table in the Founder's Chamber and opened by the Master before the assembled Fellows.

It contained half a dozen bricks, a fair quantity of straw and shavings, and nothing else – nothing except a small scrap of torn and dirty paper at the bottom of the box. With one voice the Master and Fellows decreed that their unworthy guest should be buried in the least respectable portion of the churchyard. Which thing was done, as I have already mentioned.

Of course the dirty paper under the straw was scrutinized by the Master and Fellows. But it was of no importance. It looked like a deed or a will, in which the deceased, in return for nursing in sickness, proposed to give some unspecified property to his disreputable friend, Aspelon, and apparently stipulated that he should be buried in the choir of the Hospital chapel. But it was not witnessed: it had obviously been torn up, and all that was left of it was the part on the scribe's right hand. It ran thus:

> *ego Johannes Baldewyn nuper frat*
> *rigiam do lego et confirmo domino*
> *u pro mea in egritudine relevaci*
> *domino Bartolomeo Aspelon confrat*
> *ne quod habeat uter prior invener*
> *am in tumulo sepultus subter quen*
> *parte chori in sacello Hospitalis*
> *theshede*

The last word, if rightly read, was unintelligible.

But the College had by no means done with Brother John. On the evening after his burial, as the Master and Fellows were leaving the Chapel, their steps were suddenly arrested as they heard the familiar Wassail stave raised in a thin tuneless voice. It came from the open window of the deceased brother, and unquestionably the voice was not Aspelon's. In consternation they listened till it died ineffectually away in an attempted chorus strain. After brief deliberation they resolved to visit the 'loft' in a body – Master, Fellows, 'disciples' and servants – and see what this thing might mean. They found the place as blank and silent as it remained when the deceased had been taken out to his burial. But before they reached the stair-foot in their descent the thin piping strain fell on their ears again, and this time none were bold enough to go back. After that, at all times of night and day, the interminable ditty was fitfully renewed, and panic held the College. At night the 'disciples' huddled in one room, and the Fellows lay two in a bed.

Unfortunately for Dr Eccleston, he was condemned to the solitude of the lodge, deserted even by his *famulus*, the sizar who attended him. He sat up all night and studied works of divinity, in the hope that theology, if it did not put the songster to rout, would at least distract his own thoughts from the devilish roundelay in the garret above his head. On the second night he began to congratulate himself on the success of his experiment, for the singer relapsed into silence. In his exhaustion he might have slept, but that the door of his study had a gusty habit of flying open unexpectedly and closing with a bang. He had actually begun to drowse over his folio when a sharp pressure on his right shoulder aroused him. Hastily turning his head he saw the papery countenance of the dead brother gazing at him with all the affection that one eye could testify, the chin planted on the Master's shoulder, and the mouth slewed into a simulation of innocent mirth. Dr Eccleston read no more divinity that night.

Early next morning a College meeting was summoned by the Master. It was resolved by the unanimous voice of the Society that Brother John's remains should be exhumed and re-interred in the middle of the chancel aisle, in accordance with the stipulation of the deceased: and there was no delay in carrying the resolution into effect. The Master also insisted that the whole Society should help in the purgation of his lodge and the loft above it, in accordance with the ritual of the Church in that case applying: and this too was incontinently done, as I have already described. The consideration of the performance of the rest of the contract entered into by the Master with the late brother was deferred until it should be ascertained how far the deceased was satisfied with the measures already adopted.

Whether John Baldwin acquiesced in this somewhat lame execution of his wishes, or whether his perturbed spirit was laid to rest by the rites of exorcism it is impossible to say. It is quite certain that he troubled the College no more.

But in the afternoon following his re-interment an incident happened which possibly had some connection with the placation of his shade. Bartholomew Aspelon had not attended Brother John's funeral in the churchyard. In truth, he was filled with a moral resentment at his late friend's lack of feeling and good taste which was only equalled by that of the Society of Jesus: and the motive was the same. On opening the treasure chest bequeathed to him he had found it filled with bricks and straw, just like the other. If the Fellows were indignant Bartholomew was more so: for, from private sources of information which he possessed as a member of the dissolved Hospital, he was assured that Brother John had prospered in its service to the extent of £200, at the least, and he was profoundly convinced that the whole sum had gone into the treasury of Jesus College. Under the straw he had found a morsel of paper, which was, indeed, too fragmentary to give any connected clue to its drift, but which, nevertheless, rather plainly indicated on the part of the deceased an intention of bequeathing to the College a certain treasure, the where-abouts of which, owing to the imperfection of the document, were not stated. He was confirmed in his interpretation of the manuscript by the honourable interment given to Brother John's remains in the Chapel.

Filled with resentment at the ingratitude of the patient whom he had so tenderly nursed and at the duplicity of the 'dons' who had robbed him of the reward of his devoted service, Bartholomew sought the Master's lodge. He used no language of studied courtesy in representing to Dr Eccleston the nature of his grievance: and the Master, whose temper was severely tried by want of sleep and the disagreeable nature of the interment ceremony in which he had just unwillingly participated, replied with equal vehemence.

'Ye are robbers all,' cried Bartholomew: 'you cheated him in his weakness into signing his property away from the friend who smoothed his pillow in his dying hours.'

'Thou naughty knave,' retorted the Master, 'talk not to me of bricks and straw. It was gold that was contained in thy box, and the devil knows by what scurvy arts thou didst cozen us of our promised reward. His own paper convicts thee of the fraudulent attempt to get him to will his goods to thee. See what he left in the bottom of our box.' And the Master threw the scrap above-transcribed upon the table. 'Take it and never let me see thy rogue's face again.'

Brother Bartholomew leaped in his skin as he grabbed the document. He made no ceremony of leave-taking, but bolted down the stairs. When he got into the cloister outside he took from his pouch a dingy scrap of paper, which was the fellow of that which the Master had thrown to him. What he read on it was this:

Sciant omnes presentes et futuri quod
er Hospitalis Divi Johannis apud Canteb
doctori Ecclyston et sociis Collegii Jes
one equaliter inter se dividendum aut
ri meo in antedicto Hospitali ea racio
it totum thesaurum meum ita ut extat cl
dam lapidem iacentem in septentrionali
eiusdem cuius istud signum extat a dea

Then brother Bartholomew put the two pieces together, and it was
thus that he translated the continuous lines:

Know all men present and to come that | I, John Baldwin, late a broth
er of the Hospital of Saint John at Camb | ridge, give, grant and
bequeath to
     master
doctor Eccleston and the fellows of the College of Jes | u for
my relief during
     sick
ness, equally to be divided among them, or | to master Bartholomew
     Aspelon, a brother
of mine in the aforesaid Hospital, provid | ed that he shall have it
who is
     first fin
der, all my treasure as it now lies pri | vily buried in a tomb under a
cert
ain stone lying on the northern side | of the choir in the chapel of the
     Hospital
aforesaid, of which this is the sign, a dea | th's head.

Of what further pertains to Brother John Baldwin and his bequest I
have no more to say than that his name is not included in the Form for
the Commemoration of Benefactors of Jesus College. Also that for twenty
years after the events here recorded a cheerful individual, in a lay habit,
might be seen, seated of custom on the ale-bench at the Sarazin's Head.
He drank of the best, paid in cash and never lacked for money. He could
tell a good tale and he sang a good song. His Wassail song was always
in request at the Sarazin's Head.